SACRED HEARTS

Also by Sarah Dunant

Novels

IN THE COMPANY OF THE COURTESAN

THE BIRTH OF VENUS

MAPPING THE EDGE

TRANSGRESSIONS

UNDER MY SKIN

FATLANDS

BIRTH MARKS

SNOW STORMS IN A HOT CLIMATE

Non-fiction

THE WAR OF THE WORDS: THE POLITICAL
CORRECTNESS DEBATE (*editor*)

THE AGE OF ANXIETY (*co-editor with Roy Porter*)

SACRED HEARTS

SARAH DUNANT

virago

VIRAGO

First published in Great Britain in 2009 by Virago Press

Copyright © Sarah Dunant

A CIP catalogue record for this book
is available from the British Library.

ISBN 978-1-84408-331-2

Typeset in Perpetua by M Rules
Printed and bound in Great Britain by
Clays Ltd, St Ives plc

Papers used by Virago Press are natural, renewable and ·
recyclable products sourced from well-managed forests and certified
in accordance with the rules of the Forest Stewardship Council.

Mixed Sources
Product group from well-managed
forests and other controlled sources
www.fsc.org Cert no. SGS-COC-004081
© 1996 Forest Stewardship Council
FSC

Virago Press
An imprint of
Little, Brown Book Group
100 Victoria Embankment
London EC4Y 0DY

An Hachette UK Company
www.hachette.co.uk

www.virago.co.uk

HISTORICAL NOTE

By the second half of the sixteenth century, the price of wedding dowries had risen so sharply within Catholic Europe that most noble families could not afford to marry off more than one daughter. The remaining young women were dispatched – for a much lesser price – into convents. Historians estimate that in the great towns and city states of Italy, up to half of all noble women became nuns.

Not all of them went willingly . . .

This story takes place in the northern Italian city of Ferrara, in 1570 in the Convent of Santa Caterina . . .

DAILY ORDER OF OFFICES IN A SIXTEENTH-CENTURY BENEDICTINE CONVENT

(Exact times will alter according to the hours of sunset and sunrise)

Lauds	Daybreak	
Prime	The first hour of the day	6.00 a.m.
	Refreshment	
Terce	The third hour of the day	9.00 a.m.
	Work hours	
Sext	The sixth hour of the day	Noon
	Main meal of the day	
Nones	The ninth hour of the day	3.00 p.m.
	Work hours	
Vespers	Before sunset	5.00 p.m.
	Smaller meal	
Compline	Before retiring	7.30 p.m.
Matins		2.00 a.m.

PART ONE

The Convent of Santa Caterina, Ferrara, 1570

ONE

Before the screaming starts, the night silence of the convent is alive with its own particular sounds.

In a downstairs cell, Suora Ysbeta's lap dog, swaddled like a baby in satin cloth, is hunting in its dreams, muzzled grunts and growls marking the pleasure of each rabbit cornered. Ysbeta herself is also busy with the chase, her silver tray doubling as a mirror, her right hand poised as she closes a pair of bone tweezers over a stubborn white hair on her chin. She pulls sharply, the sting and the satisfaction of the release in the same short 'aahaa' of breath.

Across the courtyard two young women, plump and soft-cheeked as children, lie together on a single pallet, entwined like kindling twigs, their faces so close that they seem almost to be exchanging breaths, the one inhaling as the other lets go. In. Out. In. Out. There is a slight sweetness to the air. Angelica perhaps. Or sweet mint, as if they have both eaten the same sugared cake or drunk from the same spiced wine cup. Whatever it is they have imbibed it has left them both sleeping soundly, their contentment a low hum of pleasure in the room.

Suora Benedicta, meanwhile, can barely contain herself, there is so much music inside her head. Tonight it is a setting of the

Gradual for the feast of the Epiphany, the different voices like coloured tapestry threads weaving in and over each other. Sometimes they move so fast that she can barely chalk them down, this forest of white notes on her slate blackboard. There are nights when she doesn't seem to sleep at all, or when the voices are so insistent she is sure she must be singing out loud with them. Still, no-one admonishes her next day, nor wakes her if she slips into a sudden nap in the refectory. Her compositions bring honour and benefactors to the convent and so her eccentricities are overlooked.

In contrast, young Suora Perseveranza is in thrall to the music of suffering. A single tallow candle spits shadows across her cell. Her shift is so thin that she can feel the winter damp as she leans back against the stone wall. She pulls the cloth up over her calves and thighs, then more carefully across her stomach, letting out a series of fluttering moans as the material sticks and catches on the open wounds underneath. She stops, breathing fast once or twice to still herself, then tugs harder where she meets resistance, until the half-formed skin tears and lifts off with the cloth. The candlelight reveals a leather belt nipped around her waist, a series of short nails on the inside, a few so deeply embedded into the flesh beneath that all that can be seen are the crusted, swollen wounds where the leather and the skin have fused together. Slowly, deliberately, she presses on one of the studs. Her hand jumps back involuntarily, a cry bursting out of her, but there is an exhilaration to the sound, a challenge to herself as her fingers go back again.

She keeps her gaze fixed on the wall ahead, where the guttering light picks out a carved wooden crucifix; Christ, young, alive, his muscles running through the grain as his body strains forward against the nails, his face etched with sorrow. She stares at him, her own body trembling, tears wet on her cheeks, her eyes bright. Wood, iron, leather, flesh. Her world is contained in this moment. She is within His suffering. He is within hers. She is not alone. Pain has become pleasure. She presses the stud again and her breath comes out in a long satisfying growl, almost an animal sound, consumed and consuming.

In the next-door cell, Suora Umiliana's fingers pause briefly over her chattering rosary beads. The sound of the young sister's devotion is like the taste of honey in her mouth. When she was younger she too had sought out God through open wounds but now as novice mistress it is her duty to put others' spiritual well-being before her own. She bows her head and returns to her beads.

In her cell above the infirmary, Suora Zuana, Santa Caterina's dispensary mistress, is busy with her own kind of prayer. She sits bent over Brunfels' great book of herbs, her forehead creased in concentration. Next to her is a recently finished sketch of a geranium plant, the leaves of which have proved effective at staunching cuts and flesh wounds – one of the younger nuns has started passing clots of blood and she is searching for a compound to stop a wound she cannot see.

Perseveranza's moans echo along the upper cloister corridor. Last summer, when the heat brought the beginnings of infection to the wounds and those who sat next to the young nun in chapel complained about the smell, the abbess had sent her to the dispensary for treatment. Zuana had washed and dressed the angry lesions as best she could and given her ointment to reduce the swelling. There is nothing else she can do. While it is possible that Perseveranza might eventually poison herself with some deeper infection, she is healthy enough otherwise and from what Zuana knows of the way the body works she doesn't think this will happen. The world is full of stories of men and women who live with such mutilations for years; and while Perseveranza might talk fondly enough of death, it's clear that she gains too much joy from her suffering to want to end it prematurely.

Zuana herself doesn't share this passion for self-mortification. Before she came to the convent she had lived for many years as the only child of a professor of medicine. His very reason for being alive had been to explore the power of nature to heal the body and she cannot remember a moment in her life when she didn't share his fervour. She would have made a fine doctor or teacher like him, had such a thing been possible. As it is, she is fortunate that after his death his name and his estate were good enough to buy her a cell in the convent of Santa Caterina, where so many noble women of Ferrara find space to pursue their own ways to live inside God's protection.

Still, any convent, however well adjusted, trembles a little when it takes in one who really does not want to be there.

Zuana looks up from her table. The sobbing coming from the recently arrived novice's cell has now become too loud to be ignored. What had started as ordinary tears has grown into angry howls. As dispensary mistress it is Zuana's job, should things become difficult, to settle any newcomer by means of a sleeping potion. She turns over the hourglass. The draught is already mixed and ready in the dispensary. The only question is how long she should wait.

It is a delicate business, judging the depth of a novice's distress. Once the feasting is over, the family have left and the great doors are bolted against the world, a certain level of upset is only natural and even the most devout of young women can suffer a rush of panic when faced with the solitude and silence of the closed cell.

Those with relatives inside are the easiest to settle. Most of them have cut their teeth on convent cakes and biscuits, been so pampered and fussed over through years of visiting that the cloister is already a second home to them. If — as it might — the day itself unleashes a flurry of exhausted tears, there is always an aunt, sister or cousin on hand to cajole or comfort them.

For others, who might have harboured dreams of a more flesh-and-blood bridegroom or left a favourite brother or doting mother, the tears are as much mourning the past as fear of the future. The sisters in charge treat them gently as they clamber out of dresses and petticoats, shivering from nerves rather than cold, their naked arms raised high in the air in readiness for the shift. But all the care in the world cannot disguise the loss of freedom and though some might later substitute silk for serge (such fashionable transgressions are ignored rather than allowed), that first night girls with soft skin and no proclivity for penance can be driven mad by the itch and the scratch. These tears have an edge of self-pity to them and it is better that they cry them now, for they can become a slow poison if left to fester.

Eventually the storm blows itself out and the convent returns to sleep. The watch sister will patrol the corridors, keeping tally of the hour until Matins, two hours after midnight, at which point she will pass through the great cloister in the dark, knocking on each door in turn but missing out that of the latest arrival. It is a custom of Santa Caterina that the newcomer spends her first night undisturbed, so the next day will find her refreshed and better prepared to enter her new life.

Tonight, however, no-one will do much sleeping.

In the bottom of the hourglass the hill of sand is almost complete, the wailing is grown so violent that Zuana feels it in her stomach as well as her head: as if a wayward troop of devils had forced its way inside the girl's cell and was even now winding her intestines on to a spit. In their dormitory the young boarders will be waking in terror. The hours between Compline and Matins mark the longest sleep of the night and any disturbance now will make the convent bleary-eyed and foul-tempered tomorrow. In between the screams Zuana registers a cracked voice rising up in tuneless song from the infirmary. Night fevers can conjure up all manner of visions among the ill, not all of them holy, and it will not help to have the crazed and the sickly joining in the chorus.

Zuana leaves her cell swiftly, not bothering to take a candle, her feet knowing the way better than her eyes. She moves down the stairs into the cloister and as she enters the great courtyard she is held for a second, as she often is, by its sheer beauty. From the first moment she stood here, sixteen years ago, with the walls around threatening to crush her, it has offered a space for peace and dreams. By day the air is so still it seems as if time itself has stopped, while in the dark you can almost hear the rush of angels' wings behind you. Not tonight, though. Tonight the stone well in the middle looms up like a grey ship in a sea of black, the sound of the girl's sobbing a wild wind echoing around it. It reminds her of the story her father used to tell of the time he sailed to the East Indies to collect plant specimens and how they found a merchant boat abandoned in steamy waters, the only sign of life the screeching of a starving parrot left on board. 'Just imagine, carissima. If only we could have understood that bird's language, what secrets might it have revealed?'

Unlike him, Zuana has never seen the ocean and the only siren voices she knows are those of soaring sopranos in chapel or wailing women in the night. Or the yelping of noisy dogs – like the one now yapping in Suora Ysbeta's cell, a small, matted ball of hair and bad smells with teeth sharp enough to bite through its night muzzle and join in the drama. Yes, it is time for the sleeping draught.

The air in the infirmary is thick with tallow candle smoke and the rosemary fumigant that she keeps burning constantly to counteract the stench of illness. She passes the young choir sister crippled by her bleeding insides, her body curled in over itself, eyes tight shut in a way that speaks of prayer rather than sleep. In the remaining beds the other sisters are as old as they are ill, their lungs filled with winter damp so they bubble and rasp as they breathe. Most of them are deaf to anything but the voices of angels, though not above competing as to whose choir is the sweetest.

'Oh, sweet Jesus! It is coming. Save us all.'

While Suora Clementia's ears are still sharp enough to make out the pad of a cat's paw, her mind is so clouded that she might read it as the footfall of the devil's messenger or the first sign of the second coming.

'Huuushhh.'

'Hear the screaming. Hear the screaming!' The old woman is bolt upright in the last bed, her arms flapping as if to beat off some invisible attack. 'The graves are opening. We will all be consumed.'

Zuana catches her hands and pulls them down on to the sheets, holding them still while she waits for the nun to register her presence. In the Great Silence which runs from Compline until daybreak the ill and the mad will be forgiven for breaking the rule but others risk grave penance for any squandered speech.

'Sshsssh.'

Across the courtyard another howl rises up, followed by a crash and a splintering of wood. She pushes the old nun gently back down towards the bed, settling her as best she can. The tang of fresh urine lifts off the sheet. It can wait until morning. The servant sisters will be gentler if they have had some sleep.

Taking the night light, she moves swiftly into the dispensary, which lies behind a door at the far end of the infirmary. In front of her a wall of pots, vials and bottles dances in rhythm to the flickering flame. She knows each and every one of them; this room is her home, more familiar to her even than her cell. She takes a glass vial from a drawer and, after a second's hesitation, reaches for a bottle from the second shelf, uncorks it and adds some further drops of syrup. Any novice who breaks furniture as well as silence will need a stronger soporific.

Back in the main cloisters Zuana notes a ribbon of light now glowing under the door of the abbess's outer chamber. Madonna Chiara will be up and dressed, sitting at her carved walnut table, head erect, prayer book open under the silver crucifix, a cloak around her shoulders, no doubt, to keep out the night draughts. She will not interfere – not unless for some reason Zuana's intervention fails. They have an understanding on such matters.

Zuana moves quickly down the corridor, stopping briefly outside Suora Magdalena's door. She is the oldest nun in the convent, so old that there is no-one left alive who knows her age. Her decrepitude should have had her in the infirmary long ago, but her will and her piety are so fused that she will accept no comfort but prayer. She talks to no-one and never leaves her cell. Of all the souls inside Santa Caterina, God must surely be most eager for hers. Yet still He keeps her at arm's length. There are times when Zuana passes her cell at night when she might swear she can hear her lips moving through the wood, each word inching her closer to Paradise.

'*But God is good and his mercy endureth for ever. Be thankful to Him and bless his name.*' The words of the psalm flow into Zuana's head without her bidding as she moves along the corridor.

The new girl is in the double cell in the corner. Some might argue that it was an unfortunate choice. Less than a month before, the sweet-voiced Suora Tommasa had been singing the latest madrigals in here, verses slipped in by a sister who had learned them at court, until some malignant growth had erupted in her brain and she had keeled over into a fit from which she never woke. They had barely cleaned the vomit off the walls by the time the new entrant had been approved. Zuana wonders now if perhaps they didn't clean hard enough. Over the years she has come to suspect that convent cells hold on to their past longer than other places. Certainly, she wouldn't be the first young novice to feel ecstasy or malignancy pulsing off the walls around her.

The sobs grow louder as she trips the outer latch and pushes open the door. For a second she has an image of a child in an endless tantrum, flailing across the bed or crouched, cornered like an animal, but instead her candle throws up a figure flat against the wall, shift sweat-sucked to her skin, hair plastered around her face. When glimpsed through the grille in church the girl had seemed too delicate for such a voice but she is more substantial in the flesh, every sob fuelled by a great lungful of air. The one she is reaching for now stops in her throat. What does she see in front of her? A jailer or a saviour? Zuana can still feel the terror of those first days; the way in which each and every nun looked the same. When had she started to spot the differences under the cloth? How strange that she can no longer remember something she thought she would never forget.

'Benedictus,' she says quietly, the word denoting her intention to break the Great Silence. In her head she hears the abbess's voice adding the absolution, 'Deo gracias.' Within her penance it will be recognised that she is about convent duty.

'God be with you, Serafina.' She lifts the candle higher so that the girl might see there is no malice in her eyes.

'Aaaaagh!' The held breath explodes in a wind of fury. 'I am not Serafina. That's not my name.'

The words reach Zuana as flecks of saliva on her face.

'You will feel better when you have had some sleep.'

'Ha! Ha . . . I will feel better when I'm dead.'

How old is this one? Fifteen? Maybe sixteen? Young enough to have a life to look forward to. Old enough to know when it is being cut short. What had the abbess told them when they had voted her in? That hers was a noble family from Milan with important business connections to Ferrara, eager to show loyalty to the city by giving their daughter to one of its greatest convents: a pure child bred on God's love, with a voice like that of a nightingale. Sadly no-one had seen fit to mention the howling of a werewolf.

'Maybe I am dead already. Buried in this . . . this stinking tomb.' She kicks furiously at the ground, sending a ball of horse-hair spinning along the floor.

Zuana lifts the candle higher and registers the debris of the room: the bed tipped over on its side, the mattress and bolster ripped open, stuffing strewn everywhere. The chaos is impressive in its way.

The girl rubs the back of her hand roughly across her nose to stop the stream of tears and mucus. 'You don't understand.' And now there is a furious pleading in the voice. 'I should not be here. I am put in against my will.'

Zuana sees her, kneeling in a whirlpool of velvet before the altar, head bowed while the priest guides her through the litany of assent.

'What about the vows you spoke in chapel,' she says gently.

'Words. I said words, that's all. They came from my mouth, not my heart.'

Ah. Now it is clearer. The phrase is as well known as any

litany. Words from the mouth, not from the heart: the official language of coercion. In the right court, before a sympathetic judge, this is the defence a wife might use to try to get a desperate marriage annulled, or a novice before her bishop to have her vows dissolved. But they were a long way from any court here and it would help neither the girl nor the convent to be awake all night debating the problem.

'Then you must tell the abbess. She is a wise woman and will guide you.'

'So where is she now?'

Zuana smiles. 'Like the rest of us she is trying to sleep.'

'You think I am stupid?' And the voice rises again. 'She does not care about me. I'm only another dowry to her. Oh, I have no doubt my father paid very generously to keep me hidden.'

Each word that breaks the Great Silence is as painful to the Lord as it should be to the nun who utters it, but kindness and charity are also virtues within these walls; and anyway, Zuana is committed now. 'Even the greatest dowries come with souls,' she says gently. 'You will come to understand that soon enough.'

'No! Agh!' And the girl flings her head against the wall, hard enough for them both to hear the thud. 'No, no, no.'

But now when the tears come they are of despair as much as fury or pain, as if she knows the battle is already half lost and all she can do is mourn it. There are some sisters in Santa Caterina, women of great faith and compassion, who believe that this is the moment when Christ first truly enters into the young woman's soul, His great love sowing seeds of hope and obedience in the soil of desperation. Zuana's harvest had taken longer and over the years she has come to understand that the only true comfort that can be offered is the one that you yourself feel. While it is not something she is proud of, at moments such as this it is impossible to pretend otherwise.

'Listen to me,' she says quietly, moving closer now. 'I cannot open the gates for you. But I can, if you let me, make tonight easier. Which in its way will help you with tomorrow, I promise you.'

And the girl is listening now. She can feel it. Her body has started to tremble and her eyes dart everywhere. What is going through her head? Escape? The cell is not locked and there is no-one to stop her flight. If she wanted she could easily push past her out of the door, across the cloisters, down the corridor towards the gatehouse – only to find that when she got there it was not the gatekeeper who held the night keys to the main door, but the abbess herself. Or out into the gardens, through the orchards until eventually she reaches the outer walls – except that they are so smooth and high that scaling them would be like trying to climb a sheet of ice. All this, of course, is common knowledge to those living within. Indeed for some the real terror only starts to bite when they imagine standing in the world outside.

'No. No . . .' But it is more a moan than a protest. She covers her face with her hands and slides slowly down the wall, her back scraping against the stone, until she is crouching, curled over, crushed with the sorrow.

Zuana kneels on the floor beside her.

She jerks away from her. 'Get away from me. I don't want your prayers.'

'That's just as well,' Zuana says lightly, sweeping away the horsehair to find a safe spot to rest the candle. 'Since our Lord is surely temporarily deaf by now.' She smiles so the girl will know the words are meant kindly. Close to, in the candlelight, she has a lovely enough face, though a little swollen and pockmarked now with rage. Zuana can think of half a dozen giggling young novices who would happily help nurse her back to beauty again.

She takes the vial out from under her robe and uncorks it.

'Stop crying.' Her voice is firm now. 'This panic that you feel will pass. And it will do nothing for you or your cause if you keep the convent awake all night. Do you understand me?'

Their eyes connect over the vial.

'Here.'

'What is it?'

'Something to make you rest.'

'What?' She doesn't touch it. 'I still won't sleep.'

'If you drink this you will, I promise. The ingredients are those they give to criminals on the cart to the gallows so their drowsiness will blunt the torment long enough for the worst to be carried out. For those suffering less it brings a faster and sweeter relief.'

'The gallows . . .' She laughs bitterly. 'Then you must be my executioner.'

I am the jailer then, Zuana thinks. So be it. How much energy it takes to fuel rebellion. And how hard it is when you are the only one . . . She holds the vial out further, as one might offer a titbit to a wild animal that could bolt at any moment.

Slowly, slowly the girl's fingers reach out to take it. 'It will not make me give in.'

Now Zuana cannot help but smile. If she knew how to make a draught that could do that every convent in the country would want her for their infirmary. 'You don't need to worry. My job is to tend your body, not your soul.'

The girl's eyes lock on to Zuana's as she swallows. The taste is strong and makes her choke, her throat raw already from the yelling. If that talk of a nightingale was not another lie, she will need a soothing syrup to coax her singing voice back out of her.

She finishes the draught and puts her head back against the wall. The tears keep flowing, but with less noise. Zuana watches carefully, the healer in her now alert to the progress of the drug.

'*Hear my prayer, O Lord, and let my crying come unto Thee.*'

When was the last time she had to use this level of dosage? Two, no, three years ago, on a girl with an equally fat dowry but a hidden history of fitting. Her first-night panic had unleashed such a violent seizure that it had taken three sisters to hold her down. Had the family been more powerful the convent might have been forced to keep her, for though epilepsy is one of the few recognised causes for the annulment of vows, that, like many things, depends on levels of influence. As it was, Madonna Chiara had successfully negotiated her return, along with a portion of her dowry somewhat reduced for their trouble. Such was the diplomatic acumen of Santa Caterina's current abbess — though what she might do with this recalcitrant young spirit was yet to be seen.

'*Hide not Thy face from me in the day of my distress.*'

The voice inside Zuana's head grows into a whisper.

'*Through the noise of my groaning my bones will scarce cleave to my flesh.*'

When she thinks back on it later, she cannot remember what makes her pick this particular psalm, though once started, the words are apposite enough.

'*I am like a pelican in the wilderness. Like an owl of the desert. I watch and I am as a sparrow that sitteth alone on the house top.*'

'It's not working.' The girl shakes herself upright, flailing, angry again.

'Yes, yes, it is. Stop fighting and just breathe. *I have eaten ashes as if it were bread and mingled drink with weeping.*'

The novice gives a little cry, then slumps back down again.

'*For Thou hast set me up and cast me down. My days fade away like shadows and I am withered like grass.*'

She groans and closes her eyes.

It won't be long now. Zuana moves closer so that she can support her when she starts to slide. The girl pulls her arms tight around her knees, then after a while drops her head down on to them. It is a gesture of tiredness as much as defeat.

'*But Thee, O God, endureth for ever: and Thy remembrance throughout all generations.*'

Outside, the night silence renews itself, moving out through the cloisters, across the courtyard, nosing its way under the door frames. The convent lets out the breath it has been holding and slides towards sleep. The girl's body starts to lean towards Zuana's.

'*So will He regard the prayers of the humble destitute and He will not despise their call.*'

It is over: the rebellion is ended. In that moment Zuana registers a certain sadness mixed in with the relief, as if the words of the psalm might not after all be enough to guarantee comfort. She chides herself for the unworthiness of the thought. Her job is not to question, but to settle.

And it is happening. The girl will be unconscious soon enough. Zuana glances round the cell.

At the entrance to the second chamber is a heavy chest. With cunning packing a nun might carry half a world within it. Certainly she would have her own linen; those whose dowries buy double cells sleep on satin sheets and goose-feather pillows. The bed frame can be turned upright without help but even with the remains of the mattress in place she will need thicker covers. Her body, no longer heated by the force of her distress, will grow clammy and what has started as outrage might turn into fever.

'*For He maketh the storm to cease so that the waters thereof are still.*'

She moves her gently back against the wall and goes over to

the chest. The lid releases a wave of beeswax and camphor. A set of silver candlesticks lies across a bed of fabrics, a velvet cloak and linen shifts next to a wooden Christ-child doll. Further down there is a rug, thick Persian weave, and next to it a handsome Book of Hours, the cover elaborately embossed, newly commissioned no doubt for her entrance. She can think of a few sisters who will find themselves wrestling with the sin of envy when they see this in chapel. As she picks it up it falls open on to a lavishly illustrated text of the Magnificat: intricate figures and animals entwined in swirling tendrils of gold leaf, shimmering in the candlelight. And tucked inside, like a page marker, some sheets of paper covered in handwriting. Had they been read and passed as acceptable? Or had the inspecting gate sister perhaps missed them in among such riches? It would not be the first time.

'What are you doing?' She is alert again now, head jerking up despite the pull of the drug. 'Those are mine.'

Mine. It is a word she will have to learn to use less in the coming months. The girl's panic answers her question. Not prayers, evidently. Poems perhaps? Even letters from a loved one . . . As precious as any prayer . . . The light is too dim to make out any words. It is better that way. What she cannot read she cannot be expected to condemn.

She thinks of her own chest, and how the books inside it saved her life all those years ago. What if someone had seen fit to confiscate them? She would have needed more than a sleeping draught to dull the pain.

'You have a rich life in here.' She shuts the book and slips it back into the chest. 'And you are lucky to have these rooms,' she says, pulling out a piece of heavy velvet cloth. 'The sister before you here kept court some evenings between dinner and Compline. Served wine and biscuits and played music, sang court madrigals even.' She moves the bed upright and hauls the remains of the mattress back on to the frame.

'From the outside the walls are forbidding, I know. But once you get used to it, life in here need not be the desert you fear it to be.'

'Iss yourjob to tend mabody, no my soul.' Though she is still propped against the wall her eyes are half closed now and her words fall away into one another. While the spirit may be unwilling, the flesh at least is now weak.

'*And they are glad because they are at rest and He bringeth them to a heaven wherein they would be.*'

Zuana lays the coverlet carefully over the open mattress so she will not have the worst of the horsehair sticking into her skin. When she is finished the girl's eyes are closed again.

She pulls her up by the armpits, putting one of the girl's arms over her own shoulder and supporting her around the waist so she can steady her as they move. Her body is as plump as a partridge and heavy now with the drug. The remains of a perfumed oil she must have used that morning are mixed in with the sourness of her sweat. She feels her breath on her cheek, tangy from the poppy syrup. Ah – along with the club-footed and the squinty-eyed, Our Lord takes the most lovely of young women into his care to keep them from the defilement of the world beyond. She herself had never been so desirable. Not that such things had mattered to her, anyway.

'I amno . . . sleep,' she slurs defiantly as she falls on to the bed.

'Husssh.' She wraps the coverlet over her, tucking it tight underneath like a swaddling cloth. '*Give thanks unto God, for he is good and his mercy endureth for ever.*'

But there is no-one listening to her any more.

She manoeuvres the girl's body on to her side so that her face is tilted to the mattress, as experience has taught her. Her father once treated a violent patient who – unbeknownst to him – had preceded the draught with an excess of wine. Halfway through the night he had retched up some of it and almost drowned in his own vomit as he lay unconscious on his back. Trial and observation. The true path to learning.

'See how the marvels of nature work, Faustina? How a medicament, which taken alone can be fatal, becomes a healer if you understand how it moves with and complements other substances?'

His voice, as always, is ready at the edges of her mind, waiting for the moment when the prayers end and there is space for her own thoughts.

There was a time, at the beginning – she can no longer remember quite how long it went on – when his closeness was almost unbearable because it reminded her so powerfully of everything she could no longer have. But the idea of being without him had been even worse and eventually the grief had softened, so that his presence had become benign; a living teacher as much as a dead father. Of course she knows it is its own transgression for a nun to live in her past rather than her convent present but his companionship has become so normal that she doesn't bother to take it to confession any more. There is a limit to the penance one can do for a sin that one cannot – will not – give up.

Watching over the sleeping young woman now, she invites him in again.

'You must be sure to note the extra dose in your records. I know – I know – a few drops may seem a little but they can be a lot. Ah, what a harmony there is in measurement, child. Authority and empiricism, trial and observation: the combination of ancient knowledge in our new world. Of course, we can't do as the Greeks did and test out our remedies on criminals. If that were possible we might have rediscovered the secret of theriac by now and our dominion over all poisons would be secure. Imagine that! Still, we have already found much that was lost. And when you are unsure or when there is no patient on whom to test new compounds or balances then you can always try them on yourself. Though with potions that deaden the senses you should take every precaution and mark the moments constantly before you fall asleep, so that in this way you will have a close enough approximation when you wake up.'

She smiles. It was fine enough advice for all those university students who had queued for hours in the fog of a Ferrarese winter to gain entrance to his lectures and dissections. Over the years she had even met a few of them; his army of eager young scholars/physicians dedicated to prising the secrets out of God's wondrous universe. And she too had grown fat on his wisdom alongside them, though, of course, she could never show it in public. While his acolytes went on to courts and universities, taking their knowledge with them, she was tenured into another form of God's service, one where the pursuit of knowledge was second to acts of devotion, eight times a day, seven days a week, until death would them part. No wonder it had hurt so much at the beginning. There was precious little space for experiment within these walls. No time for a nun to become her own patient here.

Still, having worked her way to the office of dispensary sister, she does now as he would have done: harvests her plants, distils their juices and notes down their influences. While the steps may be small, she moves forward. It is more than she would have been allowed without him outside.

She puts a hand on the girl's pulse: steady, if a little slow. How long will she sleep? It is late already. They will never wake her in time for Lauds, perhaps not even for Prime and Terce, though if they do rouse her she will have no appetite for resistance. Whatever the power of her will, for a while at least it will be tempered by physical compliance. The girl won't thank her for it, but Zuana more than most knows that it is a gift of sorts. If true acceptance comes only from God, nevertheless there is a kind of comfort to be gained from the passing of time; hour upon hour, day upon day, time falling like thick flakes of snow, the next laid upon the last, again and again, until what has been is gradually covered over, its original shape and colour hidden under the blanket of what is now.

Eventually the Matins bell rings out from the chapel. She hears the watch sister's footfalls on the flagstones as she makes her way through the cloisters. The knocks on the doors are sharp tonight. Habit (how apt that they should wear on their bodies what they have also to wear on their souls) will have some of them up and moving before they even know they are awake. But there will be others who have only just found sleep and will want to stay within it. In such circumstances the watch sister will be allowed to enter and shake the sleeper once by the shoulder. The ones who don't rise then will be confessing their misdemeanour before the abbess in chapter later.

The cell doors start to open, followed by the shuffling of feet as the nuns gather and move after the watch sister, a procession of black shadows moving through the gloom, candles flickering like fireflies in the darkness. As they pass the novice's door someone stifles a yawn.

Zuana waits. While the abbess knows of her night wanderings, it is important that she should disturb the routine of the convent as little as possible. The door to the chapel groans open on heavy hinges then closes again after the procession has passed through. Further snarls of wood mark out a first, then a second latecomer. The sound of chanting is already seeping under the door frame as she leaves the cell and crosses into the darkness. In front of her she notices a small figure with a slight limp moving out into the courtyard from the upstairs cloister. This is a night wandering that wants to keep itself hidden. She lets the image slide from her mind. There has been enough emotion spent tonight. No point in making more trouble.

She waits until the chapel door is closed again, then enters quickly, head bowed, moving between the choir stalls to where the great crucifix hangs down in front of the grille that divides the nuns from the outer public church. She prostrates herself before it, registering the momentary shock of cold stone through her robes, before slipping into her place at the end of the second row of the choir stalls. She is without her breviary – the book left sitting on the table in her cell. While she knows the lessons and the psalms by heart its absence is still a misdemeanour. The abbess's eye passes quickly over her. Zuana opens her mouth and begins to sing.

The convent is not at its best tonight. Winter has scoured a number of throats and the chanting is disturbed by ragged bouts of coughing and sniffing. At night the church is fiercely cold and across the choir stalls the dozen or so novices are struggling. With their fat cheeks and downy skin they look too young to be up both so late and so early. When they are tired, Zuana has noticed, some of them rub their eyes with their fists like small children. The convent's indefatigable novice mistress, Suora Umiliana, is of the opinion that each new batch is worse than the last, more selfish and more prone to the vanities of life. The truth is probably more complex, since Umiliana herself is also changing, growing more fervent and demanding with the years, while they at least remain young. Either way, Zuana feels sympathy for them. Girls of their age are greedy for sleep and

Matins, slicing its way through the middle of the night, is the harshest of all the convent offices.

Yet its brutality is also its great sweetness, for its very meaning is to coax and draw up the soul through the body's resistance, and when one is pulled from sleep there can be less distraction from the noise and chatter of the mind. Zuana knows sisters who, as they age, grow to love this service above all others, to feed off it like nectar: for once you have disciplined yourself to transcend tiredness the wonder of being in His presence while the rest of the world is asleep is a rare gift; a form of privilege without pride, feasting without gluttony.

A few can become so close to God during such moments that they have been known to see angels hovering above them or in one case the figure of Christ lifting his arms off the great wooden crucifix and stretching out towards them. Such tremors of the soul happen more at Matins than at any other devotion, which is helpful for the young ones, as the occasional drama of palpitations or even fainting keeps them open to the possibility of ecstasy. Even Zuana herself, who has never been prone to visions, has felt moments of wonder: the way in which the night silence seems to make the voices more melodious, or how their breaths make the candles flare in the darkness, causing the most solid statues to melt and send dancing liquid shadows on to the walls.

There is little chance of such marvels tonight. Old Suora Agnesina sits febrile with devotion, head cocked to one side, vigilant as ever for the divine note inside the human chorus, but in the back stalls Suora Ysbeta is already asleep, making much the same wheezing sounds as her rancid little dog, and for the rest it is an achievement just to keep their minds on the text.

To counter her weariness Zuana pulls herself upright until

her shoulders connect with the back of the seat. In most choir stalls, nuns rest their backs against plain wood, polished by years of cloth rubbing against it. But Santa Caterina is different. For here the seats are decorated by the wonder of intarsia: hundreds of cuts of different coloured woods, inlaid and glued together to create scenes and pictures. The stalls were a gift from one of the convent's benefactresses during the reign of the great Borso d'Este over a century before and the story is that it took a father and son over twenty years to complete them. Now, as the sisters of Santa Caterina pray to God, each and every spine rests against a different image of their beloved city: streets, rooftops, chimney pots and spires, recognisable even down to the slivers of cherry or chestnut wood that mark out the edges of the wharves and the dark walnut veins that make the River Po. In this way, though they live separated from the city of their birth, their beloved Ferrara is kept alive for them.

When Zuana's mind suffers badly from distraction, as it does tonight, she uses these little jewels of perspective as a way of connecting back to God's devotion. She imagines the voices floating upwards, a cloud of sound rising high into the nave, up and through the chapel roof into the air outside, then moving like a long plume of smoke out into that same city; twisting and turning around warehouses and palazzos, passing along the side of the cathedral, hovering over the dank moat surrounding the d'Este Palace, poking its way through the windows and releasing mellifluous echoes around the great chambers, before slipping out and returning down to the edge of the river itself, from where it rises up towards the night stars and the heavens behind.

And the beauty and clarity of that thought makes her tiredness fall away, so that she too feels herself lifting free and growing towards something greater, even if the transcendence does not manifest itself in the beating of angels' wings or the warmth of Christ's arms around her in the night.

In the cell across the courtyard, the angry novice moves heavily in her sleep, full of the wonder and madness of drugged dreams.

TWO

'How quickly was she calmed?'

'After the draught, soon enough. She was sleeping deeply when I left.'

'Very deeply indeed. I could not wake her for Prime or Terce.' Suora Umiliana's tone is sharp. 'I feared that God might have taken her to Him in the night.'

'It was my duty to settle her. In my experience when a body is warm and breathing it is easy enough to tell life from death.'

'Oh, I don't doubt your medicinal skills, Suora Zuana. But I am concerned for her soul . . . and it is impossible to bring God's comfort to a young woman who can barely sit up, let alone kneel.'

'Sisters, sisters, we are all weary and it does no good to anyone to find fault with each other. Suora Zuana – you are to be thanked for calming her. The convent needed its rest. And Suora Umiliana, as novice mistress you have, as always, done all that could be asked of you. This novice is given to us as a challenge. And we must do what we can for her.'

The two nuns bow their heads in obedience to their abbess's voice. It is early afternoon and they are gathered in her outer

27

chamber. The room is heated by a wood fire but outside its immediate orbit the air remains bitterly cold. The abbess herself sits with a rabbit-fur cape around her shoulders, leather shoes, newly tooled, peeking out from under spread robes. She is forty-three years of age but looks younger. Recently, Zuana has noticed, a few wispy curls have been allowed to escape from under her wimple and her face is softened by them. While there are those who might suspect such attention to worldly detail as vanity, Zuana sees it more as a reflection of how fastidious she is with everything; from the painted finish on the gesso religious figures that the convent produces for sale, to the pastoral care of her flock. Besides, God and fashion sit more easily together than those outside might imagine, and the sisters of Santa Caterina absorb the latest styles with the same appetite with which their choir voices explore the latest complexities of polyphony. In this way, while they may be cloistered, they are still true daughters of their fashionable, musical city.

'So. Let us consider the young soul we are dealing with. Your thoughts first, Suora Zuana. How did you find her?'

'Angry.'

'Yes, well, that much we could all hear. What else?'

'Afraid. Sad. Outraged. There was a lot of spirit.'

'Though little of it directed towards our Saviour, I would assume.'

'No. I think it safe to say she does not enter with a vocation.'

'Ah, always the diplomat with words, Zuana.' She laughs and one of the curls dances on her forehead. It is not surprising that she is admired by the young as well as the old, since her style combines elements of the benign elder sister along with those of the strict mother. 'Did she have anything to say on the matter?'

'She told me that the vows came from her mouth but not her heart.'

'I see.' The abbess pauses. 'Those were the actual words she used?'

'Yes.'

At Zuana's side, Suora Umiliana sighs heavily, as if this is a burden she is already shouldering. 'I feared as much during the ceremony. She was opening her mouth but I could barely hear any words.'

'Well, if she had been coerced then she gave no indication of it when I met her with her father. Had she been beaten, do you think, Zuana?'

Zuana feels the body again, soft and heavy in her arms. There had been no sign of wounds, or none that the girl herself seemed aware of. 'I . . . I am not sure, but I think not.'

'Suora Umiliana. What of your impressions?'

The novice mistress clasps her hands together, as if asking for help before she speaks. In contrast to the abbess, she is a well-padded woman whose wimple is fixed so tight that it seems to have impacted into her features, squashing them ever more closely together, her squirrel-fat cheeks and her mouth small and puckered, with a covering of wispy white hairs across her upper lip and chin. She must have been young once but Zuana cannot remember a time when she looked any different. While she is a ferocious shepherd of her novice flock, few go through her hands without gaining some sense of Christ's majesty, and the older sisters who go to her looking for spiritual respite report that beneath her crumpled exterior she has a soul as smooth as an unpacked bolt of silk. There are times when Zuana has felt something akin to envy for the simplicity of her certainty, though in such a close community it does not do to dwell on what one does not have.

'I agree with Suora Zuana. There is a great storm in her. When we undressed her after the ceremony her face was set like a black mask. I would not be surprised if her education has been directed more towards vanity than spirit.'

'If that is so it will come as a surprise to her family,' the abbess, says, fielding the implied rebuke to her judgement gently. 'They have an excellent name in Milan. One of the best.'

'Also she didn't sing – or even open her mouth – at Compline.'

'Perhaps she is unfamiliar with the texts,' Zuana says softly. 'Not everybody knows them when they arrive.'

'Even those with no voice are able to read the words aloud,' Umiliana says tartly, in what may or may not be a reference to Zuana, who everyone knows arrived tone deaf and ignorant of everything but her remedies. 'We were told that her singing was a marvel. Suora Benedicta has been beside herself waiting for her to arrive.'

'Indeed she has.' The abbess smiles. 'Though she is no stranger to such a . . . heightened state, glory be to God. And she holds the welfare of the convent dear to her. The wedding of the Duke's sister already brings noble audiences into our church and it would be a fine thing if this new young songbird could find her voice in time for the Feast of Agnes and Carnival. Which I am sure she will.' Her voice is now as deliberately soothing as the novice mistress's is agitated. 'We have come through such heavy seas before. It was barely two summers ago that young Carità spent her first weeks soaked in tears. And look at her now: the most eager seamstress in the convent.'

Umiliana frowns and her face collapses further into itself. In her eyes noble weddings bring only distraction and Suora Carità's sense of vocation with her embroidery needle is as much about fashion as the solace of prayer. This is not, however, the time to mention such things.

'Madonna abbess? If I might suggest . . .?' And she keeps her eyes to the ground, so that unless the abbess sees fit to interrupt her she will go on anyway. 'I would like to separate her from the rest of the novices for a while. That way she will have time to contemplate her rebellion and her intransigence will not infect others.'

'Thank you for that thought, Suora Umiliana.' The abbess's smile is immediate and full. 'I am confident, however, that under your tutelage such a thing would not happen. And isolation at this stage might agitate rather than calm her.' She pauses. Zuana drops her eyes. She has witnessed it before, this quiet battle of authority between the two women. 'Indeed I think perhaps we should leave any further instruction until she has recovered from the effects of Suora Zuana's draught.'

Zuana feels Umiliana stiffen, though her expression remains impassive. Within the rule of St Benedict the first degree of humility is obedience without delay. 'As you wish, Madonna Chiara.'

'I think at this stage nothing of what happened last night need go any further than these walls. With all the dictates and instructions from the last meetings of the Council at Trent our dear Bishop has far more important things on his plate than a rebellious novice. Perhaps you might make that clear to any novices who have family visiting, Suora Umiliana.'

The novice mistress bows her head, then hesitates, waiting for a sign from Zuana that the two nuns will leave the room together.

'Oh – and Suora Zuana, would you stay for a moment longer? I have dispensary business to discuss with you.'

Zuana keeps her head down until the door closes. When she looks up the abbess is rearranging her skirts and drawing her cape further round her. 'Are you cold? You could come closer to the fire.'

Zuana shakes her head. Lack of sleep is beginning to overcome her and she needs the chill to keep her mind alert.

'Perhaps you should tell me about the draught.'

'It is possible that I put too much poppy syrup in it.' She remembers her father's words. 'A few extra drops is a little, but it can be a lot.'

'Well, do not blame yourself too fiercely. She was making an awful din and I doubt even Suora Umiliana's prayers could have quietened her on their own.'

'I did say psalms while the draught was taking effect.'

'You did? Which ones?'

'*And they cry unto God in their trouble: who delivereth them out of their distress. . .*'

'*. . . For He maketh the storm to cease: so that the waves thereof are still: and He bringeth them to the haven.*' Her voice joins in, melodious and soft. 'One hundred and seven. A great solace and very apt. Are you sure you are not cold? Did you rest?'

'A few hours before Prime. Enough.'

The abbess looks at her for a while. 'So. It seems we have a problem. Do you think we are looking at greensickness?'

Zuana frowns. It is a slippery illness, greensickness, since although it arrives with the onset of menstruation, many of its symptoms – rage, despair, excessive exhilaration – come naturally to young women and pass without any treatment at all. 'No. I believe she is just angry and frightened.'

'Is there anything else I should know?'

'Only that she thinks her dowry was a bribe to get us to accept her.'

'Oh! There is hardly a dowry that isn't a bribe these days, whoever the husband. She would need to be a simpleton not to know that. Still, she is right about its size. The city agent says the rent on the commercial properties alone will bring in an extra hundred ducats a year – which makes it a substantial sum indeed.'

Substantial enough to make the vote in chapter unanimous when the abbess had announced it. Honour, breeding, a fat dowry and a superior choir voice. What reason could there have been for refusing her? Did it matter that much if she needed a little coaxing? Hadn't most of them? While it might damage their sense of charity to admit it, there was a certain satisfaction to be had from watching others pass through the same flame.

Zuana waits. The silence grows. With Umiliana gone they are comfortable in each other's presence, these two brides of Christ. They have known each other for many years and have more in common than at first glance it might appear. Though one was born to the veil with all the appetite for politics and gossip that convent life entailed, and the other unwillingly inducted, they both have a leaning to the life of the mind as much as the spirit and an enjoyment of the challenges that come with it. It was a bond forged early, when a newly appointed assistant novice mistress had befriended an angry, grieving novice and helped her through the tempests of convent entrance.

Since Suora Chiara's elevation, the strength of their connection has loosened, as it must, given the shift in their relative status. No abbess who cares for her flock should be seen to show favouritism and as head of her family faction in the convent she has support enough to call on should she need advice. Nevertheless, Zuana suspects there are times when Chiara mourns the freedom she enjoyed before the weight of such responsibility, just as Zuana herself misses the informality, even the companionship, that they once shared. And, whatever the abbess chooses to say now, they both know Zuana's lips will remain closed. With plants and invalids as her closest companions, whom would she tell anyway?

'Her father insisted that she had been bred for the veil.' She clicks her tongue. It is a gesture Zuana recognises well: it comes

33

when she is frustrated with herself. 'He made a most convincing case for Ferrara as a better home for her than Milan. Certainly her voice will be better used here. It seems that Cardinal Borromeo is turning out to be more of a reformer than the Pope himself. From what I hear if he has his way all the nuns of Milan will be singing plain chant with barely a few organ notes for accompaniment.' She laughs. 'Imagine how our city would react to that! Half of our benefactors would desert us immediately. Though I dare say you would find the settings easier to follow,' she adds, almost mischievously.

Zuana smiles. When it comes to the glory of music her reputation for having cloth ears is well known and over the years she has grown used to the teasing. 'I still don't understand. Was her father hiding the truth? Was she really expecting marriage and not the veil?'

'If she was, then I have heard nothing about it.' The abbess gives a sharp sigh. While her information is extensive in Church matters, Milan is a long way away when it comes to domestic gossip and clearly she is worried that she might have missed something. 'There is another daughter, younger. To marry them both he would need a fortune. Eight hundred is a fine dowry for a nun but it wouldn't buy much on the Milan marriage market. What? You look surprised.'

'No. I . . . I was . . . thinking how much my father's estate paid.'

'Ah, well, that was a long time ago and you came cheaply,' the abbess says bluntly, but with good humour. '"Good family over bad fortune", I think was the phrase.' And she smiles broadly now. 'Though I recall you had reservations enough when you first arrived.'

Reservations . . . It is a cunning thing, convent language, full of words that smother as they try to smooth. Zuana, bred on the precision of her father's use of words, has never adapted well to it. 'Yes. A few.'

No doubt they are both thinking of the same moment: a great trunk deposited outside the main convent gate, so packed with a famous father's books that the servant sisters could not carry it inside without help from the city porters, who, in turn, were not allowed to cross further than the entrance. And by its side his one and only child, a young woman, her face disfigured with grief, refusing point blank to take a step further without it. Such was the impasse that a small crowd had gathered to watch. The drama had been ended only by the intervention of the energetic, newly appointed assistant novice mistress, one Suora Chiara, who suggested that they push the trunk half in and half out of the gatehouse and then unload the heaviest books into wheelbar-rows brought from the gardens.

It had been nobody's fault directly. The truth was that there had been no time to arrange anything. Her father was barely cold in his grave, yet his house was cleared and she, as part of his estate, was being walled up for her own protection. What other option was there? A single woman living on her own in a house with no immediate family to absorb her? Impossible. Marriage? Which man in his right mind would take on a twenty-three-year-old virgin with a dowry of forbidden knowledge and hands stinking of the distillery? Even had there been one willing, she would have refused him. No. This young woman wanted what she could not have: her old life back, the freedom of her father's house, the satisfaction of their work and the pleasure of his com-pany and knowledge.

'How long do you think it will take for the maggots and the worms to regenerate my body, Faustina? I would very much like to know that. It is the greatest pity I did not train you as a gravedigger. You could have eavesdropped on the process for me.'

Sixteen years next All Saint's Day; surely his body would have given birth to a commonwealth of worms by now.

'Still, you are well settled now.'

She says it as a statement rather than a question. The fire cracks open a log in the grate, and the wood spits a shower of fireworks into the air.

'In fact . . .' The abbess pauses. ' . . . there might be some who would almost envy you – would see in your way of life things that were not so easy in the world beyond the walls.'

They have not referred to this for a while, the two of them: how when the wind of Church reform blew into Ferrara, it had brought trouble even to those within the university; instances of men, scholars who sat at her father's table or taught alongside him, who had been forced to make choices between certain books and the purity of their faith. Zuana has often wondered how he would have dealt with it; the myriad of ways in which he would have convinced them, for in his world there was nothing in nature that was not part of God's divinity and vice versa, and he had never done anything to offend or deny either. As it was, he had been saved the ordeal. A rich life and a timely death. They might all wish for as much for their tombstones.

'You are right, Madonna Chiara, I am as fortunate as I am content.' She pauses. The civic atmosphere is milder now. Nevertheless the chest under her bed remains heavier in response to the stories told, and there are some books which she consults only while others are asleep. 'And as diligent.' What is not known about cannot be taken away – nor cause distress to those whose job it might be to prohibit them.

'I am pleased to hear it.' The abbess smiles, sitting more upright and smoothing her skirts. It is another gesture that Zuana has come to recognise: the abbess drawing attention to her own authority. 'So: how was the rest of the convent last night?' Even her voice is changed. Whatever closeness there has been between them is now ended. 'Suora Clementia was in good voice, I heard.'

'She . . . she is eager for our Lord's coming and seems convinced that it will happen during the hours of darkness.'

'So I gather. Last week the night-watch sister says she found her roaming the second cloisters singing psalms. Perhaps we would do better to restrain her further during the night.'

'I fear that would make it worse. If you allow it I will keep a closer watch on her.'

'Just as long as you do not interfere with the watch sister. I have better things to do than adjudicate territorial squabbles.'

'Also . . . I stopped by Suora Magdalena's cell.' Since they are back to convent business, Zuana has her own flock to take care of. 'I think that given her condition she would be more comfortable in the infirmary now.'

'Your charity is exemplary. However, as you know, Suora Magdalena made her views clear some time ago. She has no wish to be moved and it is our duty to respect that.' Her tone is a little sterner now. 'Anything else I should be informed of?'

Zuana sees again the novice's sheaf of papers tucked fast into the breviary: also the limping figure emerging from a cell that is not her own. She hesitates. The line between gossip and necessary information has never come easily to her.

'I broke the rule of silence and squandered words,' she says, deciding on her own confession rather than those of others.

'More than was necessary for the bringing of comfort?'

'I – perhaps a few.'

'Then it is just as well that you were about God's business.' The abbess, if she has registered the hesitation, says nothing about it.

'I also came to chapel without my breviary.'

37

'Did you?' And her surprise sounds convincing enough, though it had been clear to them both that she had noted it at the time. There is a pause. 'Anything more?'

Zuana hesitates. 'Only the usual things.'

'You still spend as much time talking with your father as you do with God?'

Though her tone is gentler, Zuana registers the question almost as an intrusion. When they were sisters together rather than abbess and choir nun such confessions had come more easily. 'Maybe a little less. He . . . he helps me with my work.'

The abbess gives a sigh, as if deciding what or how much more to say. 'Of course it is your duty to honour him as any child would a parent, indeed more so since he was both your mother and your father. But it is also your duty to honour the Lord in front of and above all others. Forget your people and your father's house. Remember the vow you took? For He is the font of all life on this earth and the next and it is only through Him that you will find a true and lasting place in the mercy of His infinite love.'

For the first time the silence between them has an edge within it. Zuana finds it strange how she speaks like this sometimes. While it is an abbess's business to care for her flock, there is something in her manner these days, as though God's counsel were a quality that she now received first-hand through the grace of her position, naturally, effortlessly, like a young plant rising up towards the sun. While everyone accepts that her elevation to abbess was more about the influence of her family than the state of her soul, recently even her opponents have been heard to speak of a growing humility. Knowing her as well as she does, Zuana has assumed it is politics, the need to appeal to the whole convent and not simply those who naturally agree with her. But there are moments now when even she is not sure.

'You must live more in the present and less in the past, Zuana. It is for your own good. It will make you a better – more contented – nun and bring you closer to God. Which is what we must all strive for.'

'I shall work on myself and take my faults to Father Romero,' Zuana says, dropping her eyes to hide her irritation.

'Ah, yes, Father Romero. Well, I . . . I am sure he will be able to guide you,' the abbess says coolly.

The fact is they both know that Father Romero could not guide a mouse out of a goblet of wine. With the storms of heretic propaganda about lascivious priests and nuns poisoning the air, in recent years such confessors have become almost fashionable: cautious bishops recruiting the most elderly into convent service, men in such advanced stages of decrepitude that they are oblivious not only to their own desires but also to any that might seep out from cloistered women, some of whom might appreciate, even seek out, a little male attention.

Father Romero avoids any such temptation by being asleep most of the time. In fact it is a current joke among the novices that when he is not propped up in the confessional box, he spends his life upside down in the church rafters, such is his resemblance to a shrunken bat.

'I believe he is at his best in the early morning,' the abbess adds quietly. It seems the joke has reached her ears, too.

Zuana bows her head. 'Then I will make sure that is when I go. Thank you, Madonna abbess.'

The audience is ended. She is halfway to the door when Chiara calls her back. She turns.

'You did the convent a fine service last night. Your remedies are their own kind of prayer. I am sure Our Lord understands that better than I.' She pauses as if she is unsure of what she is going to say. 'Oh, and speaking of remedies . . . I have an order from our Bishop for lozenges and ointments. The festivities around the wedding have taken their toll on his voice and his digestion. Can we dispatch him some within the next few weeks?'

'I . . . I am not sure.' Zuana shakes her head. 'The convent is drowning in winter phlegm and the melancholy of black bile. To do so I would need to put his care above those in my own.'

'And if you could be excused a few of the daily offices over the coming weeks?'

Zuana appears to consider the offer. While it takes a particularly rebellious nun to cross her abbess on spiritual decisions, it is accepted that each convent officer has her own sphere of expertise and must defend her territory when she sees fit. In reality such negotiations are part of the responsibility of command on both sides. How else would a good abbess hone the skills of arbitration required to keep a community of almost a hundred women living together in peace and harmony? Over her four years Madonna Chiara has developed considerable talent in this area.

'If that were the case then yes, I think it could be done.'

'Very well. Take the time you need, but leave word of when you will not be in chapel so it will not be noted as a fault. I wonder, do you think *she* could help you in this?'

'Who?'

'Our troublesome novice,' she says, ignoring Zuana's deliberate slowness.

'I . . . I have no need of help. It would take me much longer to instruct someone than to do it myself.'

'Nevertheless, she must be put to work in some way, and you and she have already established some connection.' The abbess hesitates, as if this is an idea that has just come to her and is only being thought through as she speaks. 'Once I have seen her I shall send her to you. You may show her around the convent and then find her something useful to do in the dispensary. She is a bright enough young woman and may even find some pleasure in the instruction.' And now there is a ghost of smile on her lips. 'Or you in the giving of it.'

Zuana thinks briefly of the drawings on her desk and the notes needed on the varying strengths of the draughts, not to mention her coveted solitude which allows her father's voice as her hidden companion. The Lord giveth and the Lord taketh away. She bows her head. 'This is my penance?'

'Not at all. No. This is a gift rather than a penance. For both of you. For penance you will forgo dinner tonight and eat scraps from the table. There, I think that completes the matter.'

They hold each other's eyes for a moment and then the abbess turns to the brushing of her gown again.

THREE

Oh sweet, sweet Jesus . . . is this how it will be? Day after day after day, is this how it will be? Because if it is, then surely she will die of it. There has not been a second when she has not been prodded by or spied upon by somebody – starting from the moment they had shaken her awake that morning, and she had felt so sick and dizzy that she could barely focus, her head filled with tumbling nightmares, and she had opened her eyes on to this fat, bearded woman's face, thrusting itself into hers, telling her to thank the Lord for bringing her safely through the night, and glory be to Him for this, her first day in Santa Caterina.

And as soon as she heard those words she was back again: the same prison hole, only dark now, straw and debris everywhere, and another mad black-and-white magpie in front of her, but this one with a voice like a velvet cloak, trying to get her to drink something from a poison vial. She knew she shouldn't have taken it. That it was giving in and that it would not – could not – help. Her kindness – for she was kinder than the rest – had made her want to howl and scream and howl again until the very pillars in the cloister had started to shake and the whole place had come smashing down around them. Only by then she was so tired, and suddenly she couldn't cry any more. So much sorrow, so many tears had come out of her these past few weeks that her very insides were hollowed out and there was no more left. She had almost been grateful when the drink had made her quiet. It was as if everything around her was going on behind a gauze curtain. Even the stone walls were no longer hard any more, and when the magpie had opened up her dowry chest, waves of scarlet and gold light seemed to flow over and out of it.

And the woman had been so gentle: she had sat and talked to her, had picked her up and held her – yes, she had done that; she had held her – so that she had felt the warmth of another body seeping through the robes and it had reminded her of . . . and then she had wanted to cry all over again, only she was really too muddled and too tired.

After that there had been nothing, then too much of every-thing, an avalanche of awesome, awful, dreams, so vivid that they were more real than life itself, ending in one when she was half buried in a lake of liquid stone so that every time she opened her mouth to sing, molten rock poured in. She was so frightened that she started to scream, only then the stone poured in even faster until she couldn't breathe.

That was when she had been shaken awake by the squashed-faced crone who propped her up while she kept spitting and babbling about God's grace. And though it was morning and she was no longer drowning, she was still in a cell in the convent of Santa Caterina in the city of Ferrara, while everyone she loved was far away, leaving her to the un-tender mercies of an army of gargoyles, all so stuffed with piety that they can no longer remember what it is like to be living, breathing women.

Of course she cannot say that to them. Nor show it, or even think it. Because they are cunning, these pious, pecking birds. Oh yes, already they are trying to get inside her thoughts. Not all of them. Not the fat, warty servant one who dressed her this morning – so angry and clumsy that her face now hurts from the tightness of the ugly head scarf she had strapped and pinned around her. But the others: the hairy-faced novice mistress and the abbess – oh, especially the abbess, she with the girlish curls and the kind-but-not-so-kind manner. Inside all her understanding words about how hard it was to be so young and lovely and plucked from the world (and what would she know about it?), or how Our Dear Lord himself did not expect her to find it easy, but that in His Loving Mercy He would guide them all to help her . . . inside all that caressing had been a constant stream of questions: 'How old is your sister?' 'Is there promise of marriage for her?' 'When did you start your menses?' 'How often did you have confession?' 'Did you both have singing and dancing lessons?'

Of course she hadn't told her anything. In some ways she didn't even mind the poking: it meant her mad behaviour the night before must have had some impact, since the abbess was clearly worrying that she might have been sold a fake. In fact it had made her feel better to say nothing. Or if she did speak, just to hold to the same phrase that she had used with the dispensary magpie, though her voice came out scratched from all the howling the night before: 'The words came from my mouth, not my heart.'

It had made the abbess angry, her refusal to talk. Not that she showed it, or not directly. Instead she had put on a pious face and emphasised how the Bishop was such an important, busy man and the shame of scandal, the ruin of the family . . . After a while she had stopped listening, had started singing songs silently inside her head instead, until the abbess became impatient and finished the interview abruptly. And while all the concentrating on not concentrating had made her head ache, she had felt pleased with herself. Because she had been within this stinking prison a whole twenty-four hours and it had not dented her resolve one bit.

Now, as she walks across the cloisters – how cold the stone is all around her, truly like the inside of a crypt – alone with her thoughts for the first time that day, on her way to meet last night's magpie, she promises herself that she will not be so scared or mad any more, but instead will use her wits as much as her fear. Yet even as she thinks it she feels a great rush of fire inside her, such a combustion of fury and panic that she wonders if it might consume her before it ever reaches the world outside.

No, no, she cannot stay. She cannot. A whole year before anyone will even listen to her! Three hundred and sixty-four more days of poking and prodding and dead time full of endless prayer. Even if she could hold to her resolve it would kill her. No – she has to get out. Though such a thing might bring down a storm of scandal on her father's house, she will do it. Well, he is not so blameless. He had lied to her, locked her up, betrayed her. In such a case a father is no longer a father, and she is no longer his daughter. Only now, the flame of panic flares up again and she feels sick to her stomach and has to stop as she walks to spit the bile out of her mouth.

Anyway, *he* will not let her rot in here. No. She knows that. Oh God, she knows that as certainly as she knows the sun will rise tomorrow, except that in this infernal city there is only fog and grey so that no-one might actually see it happening. No, he will not forget her. In some way or other he will find her, just as he said he would. Until then she will make herself ready and bide her time, and whatever happens she will not let the fire inside get the better of her.

FOUR

Though Zuana is bound by the rule of obedience, it is the memory of the distress of her own first days that determines her patience and good humour when the girl comes to her that afternoon.

The after effects of the draught are obvious. Where last night she was all spit and fury, now she is sullen and heavy. Whoever has dressed her this morning has bound her novice head scarf too tight and there is an angry indentation along her forehead and her cheeks where the starched material is biting into soft skin. As the drug subsides she will notice a pain in her head as well as her heart.

Her eyes are so dull that for a moment Zuana is not sure that she recognises her.

'God be with you, novice Serafina.'

'And with you, Suora Jailer.'

Yes, she is remembered. Jailer. The word had been her own, but now in the novice's mouth it is shocking. But then the girl knows that.

'How do you feel today?'

'Like a dog who has been poisoned on bad meat,' she says, her voice raw and scratched.

'Well, it will pass soon enough. Madonna Chiara has asked that I show you something of the convent. Are you well enough to walk? The air might help.'

She shrugs.

'Good. Here.' She hands her a cloak. 'The weather is inhospitable today.'

Outside, a mist drapes the cloisters in grey gauze, sending plumes of smoke out of their mouths as they walk. Zuana has often thought that if fathers must offer their unwilling daughters to God they would do better to pick the warmer months to do the giving. Were it summer now they might stop in the orchard to split open a few bursting pomegranates or dawdle by the fish pond to catch the sun on the scales of the darting carp. But as anyone born and bred in Ferrara knows, the city is famed for its winter fog, which seeps down even to the bone, so that Zuana must keep the walk fast and the circuit short.

From the magnificence of the main cloister they move through a short corridor into another, smaller one. They pass an elderly sister walking quickly with a small procession of young girls, eight or nine years old, following like ducklings in her wake. One of them glances up at the novice, frankly curious, then when she catches Zuana's eye looks down again. Among the boarders of Santa Caterina some are in safe keeping for marriage while others are destined for the veil. It is not, Zuana thinks, always evident which is which. Still, had their latest novice been born in Ferrara, it is likely that as a child she would have learned both her letters and her piety here, which might have saved them all a lot of trouble now.

This second cloister is humbler, older, weeds growing through the courtyard slabs, its brick pillars crumbling in places. Yet there is more sense of life here. Along two sides, dormitories run above the kitchens, bakery and laundry rooms, housing the converse, the servant sisters, with a few cells opposite for those poorer choir nuns who come with less of a dowry. By her side the girl is now interested, Zuana notes with some amusement, her eyes darting everywhere. The smell of roasting meat sauce and boiling cabbage is in the air and there is a clatter of pots and pans. In winter the heat of the work done here can make it almost inviting but come the first hot spell and it turns into an inferno, with the night almost as hot as the day. In the doorway of the bakery a scrawny tortoiseshell cat lies sprawled on her side, half a dozen blind kittens mewling and clambering over each other for her teats. Suora Federica who runs the kitchens considers it an offence against God to put an extra spoonful on any plate yet she is soft as butter when it comes to nursing mothers – or at least those ones who have not taken vows of chastity.

Once through the courtyard, they stop briefly in the herb garden for Zuana to check the plants for frost damage, before passing alongside the kitchen garden, then out behind the slaughter and hanging house and – not so far that the noise of death does not carry – the animal pens.

In the open, with no cover of buildings, the temperature drops rapidly. Zuana sees the girl shiver.

'Why don't we save the rest for another day?'

'No.' The girl shakes her head fiercely. 'No, no, I want to go on.'

'You are not cold?'

'I'm not going back inside,' she says again sharply. 'If I am to be buried alive then I want at least to see the shape of my coffin.'

'In which case pull your shroud closer,' Zuana answers mildly. 'You would not want to expire before the walk has ended.'

To keep the blood warm she quickens the pace. Above them a band of squabbling seagulls chased inland by bad weather wheel and scream before disappearing back into the mist. They cross through the open gardens down to the carp pond; clumps of frozen reed caught upright inside thin floating islands of ice. In the distance to the left a few grey-robed figures digging in the vegetable plots rise out of the mist, then fade away again, like so many lost souls.

'Who are they?' The girl peers into the gloom after them.

'Converse. Servants to the choir nuns. Some of them work the gardens, some the laundry and kitchens. You will have your own assigned to you already to clean your cell and help you dress.'

She brings a hand involuntarily up to her head.

Which one have they given her, Zuana wonders? Augustina or Daniela? Malice or mischief, with a certain cruelty either way.

'How much did their fathers pay to put them here?' the girl mutters, almost to herself.

'Considerably less than yours. You're lucky we are not one of those Poor Clare convents where the sisters rejoice in doing the manual work themselves. Here Our Lord offers us many other ways to serve Him.'

'I am surprised you have to bolt the gates, then. Unless it is to prevent everyone from flocking in.'

The girl scowls, then bends down and grabs a great handful of stones. Zuana watches as she tosses them petulantly at the pond, the fatter ones sinking while a few others skitter and flash against the ice, and she thinks, not for the first time, that once she stops railing, there are ways in which she might fit in well here; for under the guise of humility the cloisters harbour more than their fair share of tart tongues.

They make their way through the orchard, with its army of pruned fruit trees stubby-fisted in the gloom, until they reach the convent wall, sheering up in front of them to meet a leaden sky. The air is a thick grey now, the fog already swallowing up the buildings they have left behind.

'Oh. How big is this place?' The girl's voice is dull with the scale of her incarceration.

'The walls mark out three blocks on each side. It is one of the largest convents in the city.'

So large, in fact, that girls from country families sometimes find solace in the amount of open ground and sky. Others, brought up on stories of court life and city streets, are less comforted, though even they can be surprised at the amount of land a rich convent can carve for itself in the middle of a town. How impressed was Zuana when she first walked here? All she remembers now is how small and ill-stocked the herb garden was, and how half the cuttings that she'd brought with her, wrapped inside her chest, had died in a freak snowstorm that first winter. Winter. Yes, always the most painful time of the novice's first year.

'It takes maybe half an hour to walk the line of the walls all the way round. Of course you can only do that from the inside as the fourth wall is the river. You do not know any of this?'

The girl shrugs. If a prospective novice has not been a boarder it is usual for them to at least visit the place where they are to spend the rest of their lives. But even this she has not done. Would it have made her passage any easier? Certainly the wealthy benefactors who come to see how their money is spent, or to reassure themselves about a daughter's prospective future, are eager to be shown the wonders of it all, for Santa Caterina has a past as rich as its present. One of the first foundations in the city, it had originally been a small house for Benedictine monks on an island in the river, but over the years water fever scythed down so many souls that it fell into disuse, to be rebuilt and refounded only when trading money drained the marshes, rechannelling the river and with it the most deadly of the infections.

Every nun knows the litany of its current success: how, with better drainage and now the use of distilled oils and herbs for fumigants in all the main rooms and corridors (such additions have been Zuana's work, though the rules of modesty would prohibit any singling out for personal praise), the worst of the summer contagions are kept at bay, so that today Santa Caterina sustains a community of almost sixty choir nuns, eight or nine novices, a few young boarders and twenty-five converse, all working so tirelessly together that most years the convent sends out baskets of early figs and pomegranates as gifts to the local bishop and as thanks – and encouragement – to its more generous patrons.

Not that they live on charity. Far from it. The river border- ing the fourth side of the convent is its trade route as well as an extra form of security. Coming upon it from the water, a visitor sees a dock carved out of the outer wall with a locked door, behind which are a set of supply rooms, themselves locked again from the inner side so that all business can take place without the merchants or traders ever having to encounter the nuns directly. From here the convent takes in flour, fresh fish, what- ever meat it does not rear itself, wine, spices, sugar, cloth, threads, inks and paper. Some of the same barges that bring deliveries leave almost full again, with cases of hand-copied breviaries and hour books, embroidered cloths and church robes, medicines, liquors and painted religious figurines. The convent's cellars are packed with good wines for feast days and festivals, and the kitchens produce fresh daily bread spiked with rosemary along with bottles of the earliest pressings of olive oil, as green and fragrant as the pulp it is squeezed from. Add to this income the dowries of the choir nuns, the fees from the board- ers and the rents from a dozen or so properties bequeathed in perpetuity and there are years when Santa Caterina boasts account books to rival a few great estates.

Zuana offers Serafina morsels of this colourful picture as they pass along by the walls and the river storehouse and there are moments when the young woman seems engaged enough even to ask questions. She would like to tell her more, but she knows there is no point.

It is always hard, understanding what is being gained in the moment at which something is also being taken away. For such a young woman to appreciate, for example, the different meanings of incarceration and freedom. How while outside these walls 'free' women will live their whole lives dictated by the decisions of others, yet inside, to a remarkable extent, they govern themselves. How here each and every nun has a voice and a vote (where else in Christendom would you find such a thing?), where they discuss and decide together everything from the menu for the next saint's day to the appointment of a new abbess or choir mistress or a dozen other posts essential to the smooth government of what is, in effect, a business as well as a spiritual refuge.

How in this 'prison' there are no fathers to bully or rage at the expensive uselessness of daughters, no brothers to tease and torment weaker sisters, no rutting, drunken husbands poking constantly at tired or pious wives. Women live longer here: the plague finds it harder to jump the walls, and they are saved from all the scabby, pus-filled diseases that pass from husband to wife. Here no-one's womb drops out of her body from an excess of pregnancies, no-one dies in the sweated agonies of childbirth, nor has to suffer the pain of burying half a dozen of her own children. And if it is the sweetness of cherub flesh that pulls your heart strings, then there are young ones enough to coddle and nurture, either in the girl children sent to learn to read and write or in the new-born and wide-eyed infants who pass through the parlatorio on family visits. Indeed, while angry new novices might laugh at the idea of leaving the gates open to the world, the fact is that for each half-dozen young women who come in howling, there is often an older one, newly widowed or longing to be so, eager for the moment when she might enter of her own accord.

But this is not the time for such special pleading and Zuana keeps her thoughts to herself as she loops their course back towards the main buildings. As they reach the third quarter where the street begins again, there is sudden noise and chatter behind the walls: the rumble of carts on cobbles, snatches of laughter and raised voices, the everyday business of unsequestered life. Beside her Serafina stiffens.

'Where are we? What is on the other side now?'

'Borgo San Bernadino,' Zuana says, orientating herself. At times, when she was young, she had accompanied her father on visits to his patients, and as a result knows – or at least once knew – the city better than most. 'It starts from the river and moves north west towards the market square and the cathedral and the palace.'

The girl looks confused.

'You don't know the great d'Este Palace or the cathedral? Oh, they are marvels of the city. Those and the university, which has a medical school to rival Padua and Bologna in its teaching. The next time you are in chapel with time to spare, run your fingers over the backs of some of the choir stalls. It is all there, fashioned through a thousand little cuts of the wood.'

But the girl is fading now, the cold and the disembodied life behind the walls suddenly pressing down on her.

'Come.' She touches her arm. 'It is time to go back inside.'

They re-enter the main cloisters to the sound of the chapel bell marking out the end of rest time and the beginning of afternoon work. As they move up the corner staircase the opening bars of a lute are joined by a single rising voice, pure as spring water.

The girl's head lifts sharply, like an animal taking in new scent.

'It is a setting for the feast of the Epiphany. You like to sing?' Zuana puts the question casually, then watches as a manufactured scowl comes over her face in response.

'I have no voice any more,' she says hoarsely.

'Then we will all pray for its return – as should you. The convent's choir mistress – who you should know is the abbess's cousin – was taught composition by no less a man than the Duke's father's chapel master and her settings are famous throughout the city. She is eager to meet you. The best voices get to practise when others are working. In fact you will be amazed at the privileges that come from being a songbird here.'

Their route to the music room takes them by way of the scriptorium, where a dozen desks are positioned to catch every last ray of daylight, with a dozen heads bent diligently over them, the silence broken only by the tapping of pens against inkwells and the scratching of nibs across paper. At the podium, Suora Scholastica, her face as large and bright as the full moon, smiles up at them as they stand in the doorway. Zuana nods back. When she is not copying holy words, Scholastica is writing ones of her own, dramatic plays of saints and sinners in rhyming couplets, the best of them produced at Carnival or on special saints' days. Her dedication infuses the atmosphere. There are other work rooms where a certain restlessness is always present, but over the years Zuana has come to notice how those who choose books and manuscripts over other forms of labour are the ones who become most absorbed in their work; for while the task is mostly to copy what already exists, there are great skills to be learned and a slow pleasure to be had in watching an empty page fill. During the first six months when she had been frantic for the garden and her pestle and mortar, even she had sucked some sweetness here, not to mention the mischief of using only medicinal herbs as her border illustrations, drawn accurately enough to signal a cure for all manner of ills, if only the reader knew how to recognise them.

They move further along the upper cloister, past the embroidery room where an intermittent starling chatter slides out from underneath the door. Francesca, the supervising sister here, is lenient with high spirits, believing as she does that laughter is one of God's methods of purifying the heart, and as a result some of the younger nuns congregate here and take advantage of her every which way. While there are those who disapprove, Zuana is more forgiving: in her eyes small transgressions can often prevent bigger ones.

Today though, the starlings can wait. That single voice has now become a dance between many, a shoal of silvered fish slipping in and over one another in a fast-flowing stream, and Serafina's footsteps are moving faster in response. When they reach the music room, Zuana pushes open the door quietly and moves aside to let her in.

Given the colour of the sound, it is almost a shock to find the room so monochrome. In the grey light a nun sits bent over a lute, while others stand grouped in fives and sixes. A few move their heads to the music but most are statue-still. They all hold texts in front of them, but their eyes are constantly pulled towards a small figure in front whose arms flutter up and down, fingers bent as if she were plucking each and every note from her own set of invisible strings in the air. The atmosphere is so charged with concentration that no-one seems to notice them come in. Zuana glances towards Serafina. Though she might later spend a lifetime denying it, there is evident appetite in her now. And wonder.

Even Zuana herself, whose voice has always been more seagull than lark, cannot help but be affected. Every woman in this room is familiar to her: she has treated them all for a host of ailments that raked their throats or splintered their voices, not to mention the hundred other pains and boils and bad humours of the bowels or stomach to which human bodies are prone. With the exception of Suora Benedicta, all of them are remarkably unremarkable outside this room, no better, no worse, no farther from and certainly no closer to God than any other of their convent sisters. Yet here, you only have to close your eyes on their faces (which, in effect, every citizen of Ferrara does when they sit in church and hear only disembodied voices through the altar grille) and such is their sound that you would be tempted to think you were in close proximity to a choir of angels.

In this respect heaven and earth are excellently connected in Ferrara, since the sweeter the voices of its nuns, the closer to Paradise a city begins to feel. And the closer to Paradise, the greater the worldly gratitude its rich citizens send flowing back into the convents that house such angels. Even the least musical of novices learns that fast enough, just as it is common knowledge that there are some convents in Bologna or Siena or Venice that attract so many high-ranking visitors that the best choir voices are excused from Matins in winter to save their throats from the chills of the night air. Of course such overt favouritism can bring resentment and in Santa Caterina the abbess is careful to keep the peace with a semblance of equality. Nevertheless there are all manner of ways to show favour.

The last note brings each voice together, rising, expanding, then falling through a graceful arc towards a silence which, when it finally comes, is as alive as the sound itself. 'Huurgh.' Benedicta lets out a curious throaty sigh. 'There is not enough clarity between the first and second parts on "quia Gloria Domini super te orta est". And Eugenia, the first two "alleluias" are too thin next to Suora Margarita's. And not sustained long enough.'

The door of the room jumps open a little with the wind then catches back on its hinges, giving away their presence. While the tiny figure of Benedicta does not seem to hear it, the nuns, who are used to moving from heaven to earth with almost preternatural speed, are instantly curious. Any newcomer is fodder for gossip, let alone one who comes with the vocal power to disturb a whole convent through a closed door.

'Eugenia, can you mar—'

Finally she registers their presence and turns.

'Suora Benedicta.' Zuana bows her head. 'I have brought the new novice to hear the choir at work.'

'Ah!' And the tiny woman's face lights up. 'Ah, ah, yes, yes. The voice from Milan. Come, come, come. We have been waiting for you.'

But the girl does not move.

'Welcome. Oh, look at you. You are well grown. Your menses have come already, yes? Is your voice settled yet?' She pauses but does not seem to notice too much when she gets no answer. 'You read music? Possibly you were not taught – but you are not to worry – it is not as difficult as they make out. Still, your voice will learn it quicker than your mind. I have scored your part in the Gradual for the upper register but it can be adapted easily enough if you have more depth. It moves like this . . .'

And she opens her mouth on to a tumble of hummed notes, bubbling up faster even than her speech and, to Zuana's ears at least, impossible to follow. Serafina, though, is clearly listening, even if she never lifts her eyes from the ground.

Benedicta stops. 'Will that be too high for you?'

In the silence that follows there is a snigger from somewhere within the choir, audible to everyone but Benedicta.

'What? What is it? Are you not well?'

'I do not sing any more,' she says finally, her voice now more cracked and splintered than Zuana knows it to be.

'But why?' She comes over to her, ignoring Zuana but grabbing hold of the young woman's hands. 'Oh, oh, but you are so cold. You have been outside? No wonder your voice is gone. It is a chill. The wind often steals the best voices. Or a strain perhaps, from your long journey here. You must take care of yourself and do exactly as Suora Zuana tells you. Though she herself has been given only a mediocre instrument, God has compensated her with a prodigious talent to help others.' And she beams benignly at Zuana.

'Eugenia.' She turns back to the choir. 'Come. Sing the part for our new novice, so she can have the notes in her head while her voice is healing.'

In the front row, young Eugenia, who could barely keep her eyes open last night in chapel, is now as chirpy as a newly fledged bird. As she puffs up her feathers to sing, Zuana notices the hint of what is surely a wispy curl peeking out from under her headband, homage no doubt to the abbess's change of style.

'Surge, illuminare, Jerusalem . . .'

The words turn to burnished silver in her mouth. She is young and one of the best voices in the choir, with a healthy appetite for the gossip and drama of convent life. Six months before, she had arrived in Zuana's dispensary nursing a limp from an infected splinter embedded while walking on Christ's crown of thorns to share His Passion. Only it had begun to hurt so much that now she wanted it taken out. A week later she was chasing squirrels through the orchard during free time, her high spirits more infectious and inspiring than her half-hearted attempts at mortification. Zuana has felt a certain fondness towards her ever since.

'. . . alleluia.'

Those that know might say that she holds the last note a little too long, as befits a songbird marking her territory against possible newcomers. In church no doubt it would have a few young bloods constructing their own versions of heaven.

All eyes are now on Serafina. She is standing taut, her face drawn and pale, her skin almost grey, her eyes focused somewhere out in front of her. Slowly she bends over, one arm clutched over her stomach.

As her head comes up again Zuana thinks for a moment she might even be laughing; something about the way she is catching her breath. In the choir someone giggles nervously. Zuana realises too late what is happening.

Serafina opens her mouth and the retching sound that comes out is followed by an arching stream of bile.

FIVE

'Drink it.'

The girl shakes her head.

'It is only water with an infusion of ginger.'

'In which case you drink it.'

Zuana lifts the clay pot and takes a mouthful.

'Ask any of the sisters – my poisons are faster acting than my remedies. If I am still on my feet now you can be sure it is benign.' She takes another gulp, then puts the pot down in front of the girl. 'You can do as you wish but if you want to stop the sickness I suggest you take it.'

As she hopes, the edge of impatience in her voice sparks something in the novice's eyes. She picks it up and drinks, small sips first, then deeper ones. They sit in silence while Zuana makes herself busy clearing away bottles and measuring bowls. When she turns back the girl has more colour in her cheeks.

'Better?'

'What was in it?'

'I told you. Ginger root. It is good for the stomach.'

'I meant last night's poison.'

'Ah . . . nightshade, wolfsbane, crushed poplar leaves, poppy syrup.'

'And what part of that is making me sick now?'

'The poppy, I suspect. It seems to linger in the body longer.'

Serafina is sitting on the window sill in the dispensary. Outside, in the distance a simple plot of land marks the convent cemetery: a history of piety arranged in lines of small, neat wooden crosses. Zuana had chosen to avoid it in her tour and it is best if it remains unnoticed now.

'Did you dream?'

She nods slowly, clearly unsure how much to tell. It is a reticence Zuana remembers well: in the early days, the horror of incarceration could make one suspicious of even the simplest intercessions and kindnesses.

'Nightmares?'

'I was drowning.' The girl's voice is dark with the memory. 'The water was stone, liquid stone. I kept trying to shout but each time I opened my mouth more of it poured in.'

How many stories like this one has Zuana heard? Her father used to keep records of dreams, for he was interested in how the ancients had studied them and what one could learn from them. Those induced by the poppy were often the wildest, as the drug seemed to feed off the anxieties and fears of the person taking it.

'The draught can set off strange visions. But they will be gone soon enough.'

'Unlike me?' the girl says tartly. She takes another sip. 'I won't stay here, you know. The words came from my mouth, not my heart.'

And she is fierce again, head down, determined.

Zuana watches her quietly. Of course they will have discussed it, the two of them together in the abbess's chamber: how any novice forced into a convent against her will can after a year refuse to take her final vows and petition the bishop for her release. What else would they have talked about? Certainly the abbess would have seen it as her duty to emphasise the disgrace of such an action, to explain how, if the convent was unable to soothe the trouble at source, there would be barely a bishop in the Church who would listen to such a protest, let alone a family that would be willing to take her back. So that in the end the only real choice open to the young woman would be to yell herself into crazed silence or, with God's grace, find the wit to turn rebellion into acceptance of what cannot be resisted. Just as so many others have done before her.

'You think I'll change my mind!'

'I have no idea what you will do. Though since my stock of wolfsbane has been damaged by the frost and it works as well with toothache as it does with tantrums, I hope you won't spend too much time screaming in the night.'

'If I did, I wouldn't take your potions. I – ah—' She stops, bringing her hands up over her ears.

'What is it? Are you sick again?'

She shakes her head. 'There is a throbbing behind my eyes.'

'It's the pressure of the head scarf. You can hear your own voice echoing between your ears? You will feel it more acutely when you start to sing. Who dressed you this morning?'

'I . . . I don't know. She had a fat nose and a wart on her chin.'

Ah, malice rather than mischief. 'Augustina. The butcher's daughter. She grew up wringing the necks of chickens and likes to practise her skills elsewhere. You would do better to find someone else to tend your cell.'

'How do I do that?'

'I am sure as soon as your voice returns the choir mistress will organise it for you.'

She watches the scowl, then relents. It is too cruel to leave it like that.

'I could loosen it for you now if you like.'

The girl hesitates. Asking for help is not the same thing as giving in.

'Yes.' There is a pause. 'Please.'

She sits statue-still as Zuana approaches and slips her hands round the back of her head under the material to locate the pins. Close to in the daylight, her skin is creamy now and moist with youth, the mouth cupid-full above a strong jaw and the eyes so deep and dark – black rather than brown – that it is hard to tell the iris from the pupil. No melting Madonna beauty here, but a presence, nevertheless, strong, even striking.

She reaffixes the stiff material more gently. 'Don't worry. You will get used to it fast enough. Soon it will feel more strange to be without it.'

The girl blinks and the line of a fat tear wells up and overflows, because of course that idea is even more unbearable to her. For a moment Zuana wants to tighten her arms around her, whisper into her ear all the ways in which resistance will tear her apart and how quickly wounds can heal when the right remedies and ointments are applied. The strength of her own feeling alarms her and she moves her arms back to her side. It has never been her role, the soothing of souls, and there is no reason to start now. Not least because some things one must learn for oneself.

She moves back to the table and starts pulling out boards and graters. The Bishop's remedies will take more time than they have, even with the dispensation to miss orders, and one day is almost passed. When she turns the girl is standing next to her.

'This is where you work?'

'Here and the distillery, yes.'

'Who works with you?'

'There is a conversa sister who helps with the patients. But in the dispensary I am alone.'

'Is that allowed?'

'Since my voice is as cracked as my fingers, it is accepted that I am better employed on my own than in the choir or the embroidery room.'

It's true enough. Even when she arrived her hands had been more the labourer's than the lady's and over the years they have grown worse, the skin eaten and stained by the processes of gardening and the chemicals of distillation. As for her singing – well, in the hierarchy of convent voices everyone knows she is a minnow swimming next to fat carp. She smiles at the thought. It does not worry her. There are times when she thinks that she might offer up her own kind of music here, for surely each and every ingredient she collects has its own voice, soft, loud, dark, light, each distinct enough when alone, yet capable of making all manner of different sounds and resonances when mixed together.

At last count there were near to ninety glass bottles here. A veritable choir of cures! She has done penance for the pride of such a thought in the past but the image stubbornly remains. Her father would have understood. He was forever in search of the music of nature, handed down through the spheres. Though in church he too could barely hold a note.

'There are so many of them!' The girl is standing staring at the shelves. 'How long did it take you to collect them all?'

'Perhaps it is better you don't know,' Zuana says lightly. But she likes the fact that she is interested.

'And is every one of these a different remedy?'

'Some work alone, yes. They are known as simples. Others need to be mixed together to form compounds.'

'So what is that?' She points up at a bottle with a small, twisted root inside.

'White hellebore.'

'What does it do?'

'It purges the system.'

'Of what?'

'Anything that is inside you. It causes powerful vomiting.'

'Worse than mine?'

'You can lose half your stomach with this if you're not careful.'

'Really! What, do you eat it?'

'Not on its own. There is too much poison in it.'

'So how does it work?'

Curiosity. It is not a characteristic of a recalcitrant novice. But then the inside of an apothecary's shop is not something that would excite any young girl's imagination, except of course for the love potions – and Zuana has had no use for them in her study. 'A way of making well people ill' was how her father saw them, though from things she heard people say about her mother he must have been ill thus once himself, however briefly.

'You put a portion of the root inside an apple or a pear and bake it in hot ashes. When it is cooked you throw away the hellebore and eat the pulp of the fruit instead.'

'How do you know how much to put in?'

'It depends on how heavy or light the person is. Or on the nature of what you are looking to expel.'

'You mean you use a poison to cure a poison?'

'In a way, yes. There are a number of ingredients that change their effect depending on their mixing.'

The girl points to another, further along. 'And this?'

'Verbena leaves.'

'What ills do they cure?'

'When they are fresh their sweat against the skin is good for headaches. When the root is cooked it dulls toothache.'

'And when they are like this?'

'Mixed in sweet wine with St Mary's mint they are good for monthly cramps.' Of which the convent has more than a few, for empty wombs gathered together seem to produce regulated and in many cases singular suffering.

'Ha. I know someone who would have paid a fortune for this.' And there is a touch of venom in her voice. 'Do you have something to dissolve unwanted babies, too?'

'Unwanted babies? In a nunnery?' Zuana laughs.

Of course there are always stories. Nuns as the milking cows for the lust of the Church. Luther's poison had leaked everywhere though a monk who married a nun would have to have constructed gross heresy to save himself – and his apostate wife – from hell. However, even in Santa Caterina you hear things . . . such as the island convent in Venice where the confessor ran it as a house of ill repute with himself as the only client. The whole of the city, it was said, had come out to watch him burn.

'Why? Do you know someone who has need of that as well?'

She scowls. Certainly she would not be the first daughter to find her future prospects altered by a sister's strategic lust. But she is not about to tell Zuana her secrets. Not yet, anyway.

'And the poppy that gave me the foul dreams. Which one is that?'

'It is there. On one of the shelves.'

The girl follows her eye. 'This one? Or this one?' She reaches a hand out.

'No, no. And be careful with that.'

'Why? Is it poison, too?'

'No, it is blood.'

'Blood? Whose?'

'Sister Prudenza's. She has begun to suffer from fits and I am tending her.'

'It doesn't look like blood.'

'That is because it is mixed with crow's egg.'

The girl looks at Zuana as if the devil had just slid from under her skirts. So that Zuana has to smile.

'It is a known remedy. When taken internally in small doses regularly, it can help with the fitting, if the affliction is mild.'

'And if it is serious?'

'Then I wouldn't be able to help her.' And she sees again a young novice, her body like a fish pulled out of water, rigid and thrashing on the slabs of the cell floor.

The girl puts the bottle back on the shelf, as if the very handling of it might contaminate her. 'Are there many you can't help?'

'That depends on what ails them.'

Zuana knows what she is thinking, of course: that she is the one that will never be cured, for her ailment is too grave.

'I wonder that they let you do all this,' she says, looking around.

'What? You think because nuns serve God we should have to die sooner or hurt more?'

'No. I mean . . . well, there is not much praying about it.'

'Oh, but you are wrong . . .' Of course she has heard it before; this blindness to finding God in anything which does not involve praying or suffering. 'This room is full of prayer. Look around you. Everything here, every herb, every juice, every ingredient of every remedy comes from nature and the earth, which along with the heavens has been created by Him for us to worship. Even our capacity to understand it is given by Him.

'*Honour the physician for the need one has of him. For the most High has created him.*' Ecclesiasticus 38 verse 1.'

The girl stares at her, then laughs nervously, as if they have changed places and now she is the solid one to Zuana's madness.

Of course. When she first arrived it was those women who spoke in rivers of scriptures who were the worst company, the sheer intensity of their absorption making her feel even more abandoned. She is easier with them now. Sometimes they even bring her texts about herbs they have found in the scriptures, though they have yet to show her one she did not know before.

'You know a lot. Did you learn it all here?'

'No. My father taught me much of it. The rest I learned from books – or have found out myself.'

'Your father? Was he the one who put you inside?'

'No. Yes.' She pauses. 'When he died there was nowhere else for me to go.'

'And what about you? Did you want to be here?'

'I . . .' She stops. Which is the worse sin: to lie or to encourage despair? 'There was nowhere else for me to go.'

Serafina stares at her. 'How long ago was that?'

'Sixteen years.'

Zuana registers her shocked intake of breath. The pity is palpable. She, of course, never intends to be so old, nor so defeated.

She has turned and is looking out of the window. Upright now, she will be able to see the edge of the graveyard beyond the herb garden wall. Zuana watches as she stands transfixed. Then she turns back.

'*She* says I have to work with you.'

'Madonna Chiara?'

'Yes. She says the Lord brings each of us to him in different ways. And that you are a good and loving nun.'

'Then you must listen to her. She is the abbess and is picked for her humility and learning.'

'Really. Is that why she wears bits of her hair curled like a court lady?'

Once again Zuana admires the nimbleness of her mind. When she stops yearning for what she cannot have, such wit will add texture to the quotidian nature of convent life, which can seem so barren when you first experience it.

'Maybe it is her way of trying to make you feel at home.'

'What? By wearing yesterday's style?' she retorts sourly. 'Anyway, I will never ever feel that way here.'

But the fact is the process has started already. She just doesn't know it yet.

SIX

She pulls the stones out of her pocket. What if none of them is big enough? They had been easy enough to scoop up into her sleeve as she had thrown the handful into the pond but there had been no time to sort out the heavy from the light. She rubs off the dirt and lays them down on one of the sheets of paper taken from her breviary. She does not need to read the words to know what is written there.

> *Who hath not gazed into my Lady's eyes,*
> *nor gathered her sweet glances here on earth;*
> *he knoweth not Love's Hell nor Paradise*
> *who never heard her sighs as light as air,*
> *the gentle music of her speech and mirth.*

She sings quietly, keeping the sound within her own head. Yes, her voice is still there, thank God. If she opened her mouth now they would all hear it. Ha! If she chose she could pierce the very stones of the cell with it. That would bring the choir mistress running fast enough, her mad music gushing out of her as if from a broken water pipe. 'Oh, our great city is filled with music lovers.' Well, let them wait. All of them: nobles and nuns. Hell will freeze before she opens her mouth for them.

On the table the tallow candle splutters and she has to coax it back to life, protecting the flame with her hands. No, no, the stones are too small! She takes the biggest and tries to fold the paper around it. It wraps round four times, but stiffly, and when she throws it up into the air towards the bed the paper is already uncurled and falling off before it lands. Heavier stones (where would she get them?) would help but she would still need something to secure the edges. And even if she finds what she needs – the right stones and the right kind of glue – even if she somehow manages to get out into the gardens and lob it over into the street, how in God's name will she know where to throw it?

When they talked about it – that one snatched, desperate conversation through her bedroom door as it was all coming apart around them – she had imagined a building with windows or a bell tower; at worst a finite run of wall so he would know where to look. But this place is so endless you could walk round the perimeter for a month and still not recognise one bit from the next. What if she mistook the measurements and threw it into the river? Or it landed in some pothole or gutter where it would just rot and get lost? Maybe the gutters were full of them: notes of longing hurled out by women long since bearded and forgotten.

But how else could she respond to him when he came? How could she possibly get any message out? The outside façade has barely more windows than a prison and those that exist are so high that the only thing that can reach them is light – and God knows, there is little enough of that either. At least in the gardens you can see, and breathe. Though it's like taking water into your lungs, the air is so damp. This whole city is thick with perpetual gloom. Urrgh. What had the jailer sister said about all the old monks dying of swamp infection? No wonder. In Milan in winter, even though it could get cold enough to make you cry, you could still look out of the window and see the blue of the sky. But here there is not even real sky, just a swollen ceiling the colour of dead rat fur and heavy as stone.

She can feel the tears smarting at the back of her eyes and makes herself take deep breaths. When they first closed the door on her tonight, she had started howling again, the panic welling up like sudden sickness, but with the drug still curdling her stomach she couldn't keep it going for long. Oh – if she could have found the energy she would have yelled and screamed and smashed her fists against the door all night every night, so that they would all be driven mad by her madness. Only she is scared that if she does they will drug her again and that maybe – who knows – this time there will be blood and crow's egg in it so she might be sent into fits. That slimy abbess had said as much when she had been pretending not to listen to her: how a convent kept awake at night was a bad-tempered place and if the alternative was a novice kept under lock and key too drugged to enjoy any recreation, then sad though it was . . .

Well, she would not give them that satisfaction. Not when there were other ways to make her mark.

For all her cunning she had not planned it – the refusal to sing. She had not really thought about it until the afternoon when they had entered the cloisters and heard the voices practising and the dispensary sister had asked her if she liked to sing. But then the closer they got to the room, the more perfect it had seemed: how if they wanted her for her voice (and God knows they were in need of it if that scrawny nun with her motet was anything to go by – far too much breath and thinness on the high notes), if it was that important to them, then that was exactly what she would deny them. Though they might have her body, they would never have her voice. Which means that they have nothing of her, for it is in her voice where she is most herself. As he — of all the people in her life — had understood.

> *Here she sang sweetly, here she was seated.*
> *Here with her lovely eyes she pierced my heart . . .*
> *My soul bereft that thinks of nothing else,*
> *my ears gone deaf, with nothing left to hear*
> *when her sweet words have vanished from our midst.*

No, she will not sing for them. Of course she will have to talk sometimes, but as long as she makes her voice raw as she did today she can fool most of them. The dispensary sister will be the hardest. She is clever, even has some wit in her, though God knows how she keeps it flowering in this tomb of dried-up old flesh. Sixteen years! Imagine! Locked in that cell for sixteen years with just books and stinking bottles for company. And all that strange poetry about heaven and earth and divine remedies . . .

Still, if you had to work anywhere in this prison, the dispensary would do well enough (better than a lifetime spent blind and hunched with a pen in your hand — most of the magpies in the scriptorium looked dead already from the effort). At least on her shelves there are some wonders to be learned, if you could tell the consistency of blood from poppy syrup. You could put a whole convent to sleep if you knew the right recipe. She sees an image of a line of nuns, sipping deep from the communion wine then keeling over, one by one. The sheer viciousness of the thought makes her smile. The only one who might survive is that young gargoyle with the harelip that runs like a dredged canal from her mouth into her nostrils. She can barely drink at all. Ugh. At dinner she has to bend her head back at an angle to make sure the water in her glass doesn't dribble back down into her bowl.

It makes her sick even to think about it. Maybe her father chose this place deliberately, knowing it to be packed with monstrosities: hunchbacks, idiots who smile when there's nothing to smile about, the one whose right foot follows half an hour after her left, and the most scary one of all – the novice with the poxy face, the scars so angry that she might even have been lovely not so long ago.

The girl from the Dominici family who lived not far from her had suffered the same horror: one Sunday flicking lizard tongues at the boys beneath her veil in church, six weeks later so foul and pitted that her headdress at mass was thick as a winter curtain and everyone who sat near to her said they could hear her sobbing behind it. The story was that she asked to be put into a convent because she could not bear to be among sweet faces any more. For who would possibly want her now? Oh dear God, what if this one still has the disease or if some other kind of pox slides in through the windows here? They would all be dead or maimed within weeks. No. Please, please, Virgin Mother, don't let such a thing happen to her.

> Love opened my left side with his right hand,
> and there within my very heart he planted
> a laurel tree, so green that its rich hue
> exceeds the colour of all emeralds.

She can feel hot tears flowing again. Ha! Outside she registers the footsteps of the watch sister moving into the cloisters on her rounds and she moves swiftly to blow out the candle, so swiftly that the wax from the flame spatters on to her fingers.

She winces from its heat then registers the change as it

coagulates and sticks to her fingers. Hot wax. Like a seal. Of course! A seal. Yes!

As soon as she finds bigger stones she will use the candle to seal the paper around them. At least that way she will be ready when he comes. Because come he will. She is sure of that.

SEVEN

These things Zuana has never seen, nor probably ever will:

> the ocean;
> the great veins underneath the earth where
> precious metals grow;
> the animal known as the lamia;
> a new-born baby;
> the insides of a dead person . . .

Though when it comes to the last she has been closer than most.

Her father was by no means the first to take his knife publicly to a human corpse. By the time he stood up in the lecture hall of Ferrara university, his butcher's apron tied around him, anatomical dissection was already an accepted part of medical education in cities such as Bologna and Padua. (The great Vesalius himself worked for many years in Padua and it was there that he laid the foundations for his book on the fabric of the human body: this is a fact she has known for so long that Zuana cannot remember any more when she was told it first.) But thanks to scholars like

Mancardi and Brasalola, Ferrara had not been far behind and by the time she was old enough to understand the difference between a vein and a muscle a public dissection was taking place under the auspices of the university every other year: an audience of a hundred or more medical students bundled into thick cloaks and hats, packed alongside a few strong-stomached Ferrarese citizens with the curiosity and appetite to look inside themselves.

The event was held either in one of the regular lecture rooms, makeshift stacked seating arranged as best they could to let as many people as possible to see the corpse espaliered on the table, or later, when the press grew too large, in a nearby church specially commandeered for the process. In both cases the spaces were bitterly cold, the tang of preserving alcohol a persistent incense in the air. Dissection was, by necessity, a winter business, with windows and doors kept open so that the bodies remained fresh over the two or three days it took to complete the process (though when it came to work on living dogs and pigs, it meant you could hear their terror and agony halfway round the town).

At moments when convent weather spikes to the bone – as it does now – or a task in the dispensary demands for the same preserving fluid, or some feast day calls for the slaughtering of one of the pigs, their high-pitched squealing echoing through the cloisters, then Zuana is instantly pulled back: imagining herself as a young woman, beside herself with anticipation as she peers down on to the table, her father's voice booming out across the hall as he makes the first incision along the collarbone and down the side to create the skin flap which, when lifted, will expose the breast bone and the lungs and finally the heart underneath.

Alas, it is a dream that never happened. Oh, the sensations were real enough: the smells (her father stank of them when he returned that night), the cold, the hysteria of the penned, waiting animals, which always seemed to know what was to happen to them, and the parallel sense of rising excitement in the streets as the students queued and then finally dispersed after the spectacle. But the rest took place behind closed doors for her. It was not for want of trying. By the age of fourteen she knew enough in theory to recognise most of the organs the knife would have revealed. And by sixteen she was tall and broad enough that with a cap and gown she might even have got lost in the crowd. But her father was adamant. While she might stand next to him in the study measuring and mixing, or help him in the gardens gathering the herbs and roots – even down to the mandrake, which looked like a miniature human body as it was pulled from the earth . . . while together they might trace a man's insides through the study of a hundred woodcuts, when it came to witnessing the actual flesh flayed back to reveal the wonders inside, to understand this divine creation in all its glory as God had made it, that could never be woman's work, even to a mind as big as his.

She had come close to defying him once. Had got as far as hiding a cloak and a hat, left over by different visitors, ready to slip out as soon as he was gone. But he seemed to sense her excitement and chose not to leave the house until the dissection was almost due to begin, so that by the time she could get out, the lecture hall was already exploding with bodies and the queue stretched halfway down the street. Later, when his death had them all running in circles working out what to do with her, she wondered if he had already been beginning to question whether the young woman he had so lovingly filled with his knowledge might not be becoming a liability to herself as much as a treasure to him.

Perhaps he had thought he would live for ever. She certainly had.

Thus her medical experience had been severely circum-
scribed, so that now in order to penetrate the insides of the
human body she must rely on books: muscles, sinews, viscera,
bones and blood, all reduced to flat patterns of black lines on a
white page. Had she kept the volumes of Vesalius' great anatomical work – oh, if only – she might have been able to educate
herself afresh each time she opened its pages, for there was
nowhere his knife and his curiosity had not penetrated. But when
the scavengers descended after her father's death there were a
few key treasures that had walked out of his study before she had
had the time or wit to hide them, and Vesalius' fat volumes had
been the greatest loss. As for the bodies in the flesh, well, though
she might feel swellings or catch glimpses through or under the
habits of the convent women when their pain was great enough
to disturb their modesty, any understanding of a man's body was
to be forever denied to her.

Except, that is, for one.

For she, like every one of her sisters, spends each and every
day in the presence of the most perfect male body: that of God
Himself made flesh.

And in this, although it would, no doubt, shock those in the
church hierarchy to hear it, the convent has been, for Zuana,
its own medical school. Because His body is everywhere: in the
altars and nave of the main church, open to the nuns when it is
closed to the city; in their own chapel behind the altar where
they pray eight times day and night; on the walls of the cloisters
where they walk or in the refectory where they eat or even the
cells they sleep in. Everywhere. And in each and every stage of
life and death: from the rosy plumpness of the holy baby reaching, arms outstretched, from his mother's lap, through the
beauty of a grave young man, broad-shouldered and slim-
hipped under gathered robes, to the brutal, step-by-step

destruction of that same perfect body in its most exquisite state of manhood.

It is its destruction, though, that makes the greatest impact.

Over the years Christ's naked, broken body has become more familiar to Zuana even than her own, for not only is it everywhere, but it is also lovingly, truthfully, anatomically depicted. She had recognised that in the very first days of her confinement: how the men who carved and sculpted the two most powerful crucifixes in Santa Caterina – the great wooden one that hangs above the altar and the stone statue on the wall at the end of the main cloisters – were as informed about the human body as any anatomist, which was only to be expected, since for many years now any painter or sculptor with blood in his veins had made it his business to find his way into charnel houses or even those same lecture theatres that she had been denied, in order to perfect his craft.

In their hands dead material became flesh. The very surface of the wood or stone appeared tender; you could see – feel – how the layers of skin were vulnerable to the sting and sear of the whip. The way the thorns pierced and hooked into the thin flesh of the forehead. The bowing of the spine and shoulders under the burden of carrying the great cross. The force of the blows that sent iron nails smashing through tendon and bone, the knotting and screaming of the sinews as they took the body's hanging weight, and how once punctured, a man might bleed so copiously that, unless staunched, life can seep out through a single vicious opening.

On the crucifix in the chapel, the wound in Christ's side has coagulated, so the edges of the gash lie open like thick scarlet lips with only a single ribbon of blood to be seen. But the figure in the cloisters has a deep, fresh hole that weeps a river of brightest red, cascading down his side and his legs on to the rock into which the cross is fixed. Even in the deepest winter mists, the fiery red stands out against his white skin, so that as they walk many sisters feel their eyes pulled upwards to register the damage before moving on.

Of course not everyone feels or even sees the same thing: this too was a revelation that came early to her. For some, usually the ones who come youngest or live longest, the very habit of such images has made them familiar, ordinary even – Christ's death as a kind of furniture, glimpsed out of the corner of an eye when hurrying, late for office, or marking the usual route from one place to another. For others it is a reason, some might say an excuse, for decoration: the exquisite beauty of Suora Camilla's silver crucified Christ or the ostentation of the abbess's jewelled one.

Then there are the few – Suora Perseveranza is the most active – who in contrast find the experience of His suffering so constantly new and affecting that it makes them yearn to share the agony. Or those so moved by His resignation and loneliness on the cross that they are in danger of being constantly overwhelmed by the pity of it all. Before she had been confined to the infirmary, Suora Clementia could be found at all hours of the day and night huddled over the crucifixion in the cloisters trying to wipe the blood from His feet with a cloth. She had always been consumed by her compassion for Christ (more, it must be said, than she ever showed towards her fellow nuns), but recently she had spent so much of her life weeping that the abbess decided she would do better in with the sick. Zuana herself had been less sure; in many ways she had seemed quite content being sad and too many touched old souls together in the same place can create their own wind of madness. It is true that Clementia cries less now but, separated from familiar surroundings, what was left of her mind has slipped away with her sorrow, hence her distress and occasional night wanderings.

Still, better her than the ones who go around parading His pain like their coat of arms. The worst offender here is Suora Elena, who spends her life telling anyone who will listen how much she suffers. 'Oh, I could not sleep last night because of the great stabbing in my side.' Or limping into chapel wincing and groaning until someone is forced to ask her what is wrong. 'Oh, it pleases God to let a thigh wound fester. I am grateful for it, though it is nothing compared with his suffering,' before limping off, smug in the knowledge that He has marked her out as more special than anyone else – though those with sharp eyes might notice how quickly she recovers her step when she thinks no-one is watching.

Zuana, in contrast, has never felt any of these things.

Her fault – for she understands that is what it is – lies in a different direction: the need to heal Him. So much is she her father's daughter that by the time she became old enough to understand the Passion of Christ her instinct had been to save rather than worship Him. In her first weeks in the convent, when her future had felt like a life sentence, she had kept herself from despair during the endless hours in chapel by studying that great hanging body, detailing the ways in which, had she been called upon, she might have repaired the damage: which poultices and herbs she might have used to staunch the flow of blood, the salves with which she would have treated the whip lashes and the cuts, the ointments she would have rubbed around the jagged flesh to avoid infection. Even, most heretical of all, the draught she might have given him to blunt the pain.

Had her father ever felt the same thing? She wonders

sometimes what he would have made of this world she lives in now. He had not been a total stranger to it. As a doctor at the university with connections to the court he had occasionally been called upon to treat noble nuns, if their condition was dangerous enough and the abbess sanctioned his visit. Perhaps if he had taken her with him, she might have found it easier. As it was, she only heard these stories when he wrote them up in his treatment books. And out of those she remembers just one: the time he came back from a convent on the outskirts of the city where he treated a nun who had done violence to herself – first beating her head against the wall until the blood ran and then, when they confined her to her cell, somehow getting hold of a kitchen knife with which she stabbed herself a dozen times before they prised the weapon away from her. When he arrived she had been tied down and was delirious, her life dripping out through those dozen wounds on to the floor. So much blood had been lost that there was nothing he could do except offer something to help her with the shock and the suffering. But the abbess had refused, convinced that the devil was inside her and that if she was soothed by the potion he might renew his attack. 'When I questioned them, they said no-one had noticed anything amiss with her before that morning,' he had said, shaking his head, though whether from disbelief or pity he did not say.

She thinks about it sometimes, that story: how it could be possible that something so powerful should erupt out of nothing. In her experience a well-run convent is as alert to the distress of its sisters as to an excess of joy, since either can tilt the balance of calm living. And even if it had been the work of the devil (and though she has come across mischief – even occasional malice – in this republic of women, she has yet to make the devil's acquaintance), why had the abbess or the novice mistress seen no signs of it? So she gives thanks to God that when it came to the decision as to where she would spend the rest of her life, it had been Santa Caterina that had taken her in, welcoming her thin voice and her dowry chest as full of remedies as of prayers.

EIGHT

Because she has some understanding of the relationship between exhaustion and acquiescence and because she does not want to resort to further draughts and potions to counter rebellion, Zuana finds herself taking a good deal of care in the planning of how she and the young woman begin their work together.

Over the first few days as the effects of the poppy wear off, so the impact of physical labour takes over: two hours, twice a day, every day excluding Sunday, either out in the cold tending the herb garden or inside cleaning the infirmary and the dispensary; sweeping and mopping floors, scouring pots and bowls, scrubbing down the work benches. The eradication of previous ingredients to avoid the slippage of leftovers into new ones was a part of her father's teaching, but Zuana has dismissed the conversa servant who usually does the heavy manual cleaning and uses only her new assistant instead.

At first the girl's resistance is palpable, her moods as storm-tossed as the weather: one day rage and rolling thunder with much slamming and crashing about, the next a hunched, haunted sadness, her shaking body turned defiantly away over the work-top, silent tears like unstoppable rain. Zuana does nothing to intervene. Better for her to vent her feelings through the scrubbing and scouring. At least that way she will eventually tire herself enough to sleep at night and so, step by step, the process of acceptance might begin.

Though the convent rules allow for speech when necessary during working hours, Zuana makes sure these first days – whatever the emotional weather – pass in silence. Looking back on the memory of her own journey through those early painful weeks, she has come to understand how silence had been part of the balm, albeit so slow and gradual that the physician in her found it hard sometimes to mark its progress. Now she finds herself studying it in another.

When they first enter, the young (particularly the more lively ones or those with less vocation) find it so hard to adapt to the restrictions on speech. The appetite for conversation is deeply embedded in them; it is there as they gather at table or in chapel, close enough to whisper but forbidden in both places to do so. Or in the way they move past one another through the cloisters during the quiet hours, unspoken words spinning out between them like glistening spiders' threads. Watching them during those first weeks, Zuana has often thought that chatter is the hardest abstinence of all, harder to bear in some ways even than chastity – for while there is little temptation in that direction, the promise of careless talk is everywhere all the time.

But with this girl it is different. Certainly there are other novices who are keen to talk to her, to draw her into their circle of gossip. Adrianna, Angelica, Teresa are all as hungry for life as they are for God and the manner of her entrance has made her notable, with all kind of stories in circulation about indiscretions with an older sister's suitor or some mad passion for the dancing master. There is a fashion for nuns' tales in cultivated circles nowadays and a few of the more colourful ones have no doubt slipped in via the smuggler's route of the visitor's parlatorio. Or it could be that they simply make it up, fusing together bits of memory and longing. While Umiliana, in her role as novice mistress, sees only the devil in such gossip, Zuana is less disapproving: youth fades fast enough inside convent walls and there are only so many hours when one can be on one's knees.

Serafina, however, is not interested in their friendship. In fact this incandescently angry young woman hardly speaks to anyone. And when it comes to those eight offices in chapel, well, while her lips move obediently enough to the words in her breviary, no voice comes out of her mouth, though whatever strain her howling might have caused has long since passed, soothed by the dandelion tea that Zuana makes each afternoon and which they drink together before the girl is dispatched to Umiliana for further novice instruction.

Tomorrow, however, will come their first day in earnest on the Bishop's remedies and the rhythm of work will change between them.

They meet that morning in the herb garden straight after early Prime in a knife-sharp wind. The task: the harvesting of figwort root, the freshness of which is vital to the first recipe. The ground is so hard they have to use skewers to penetrate the topsoil, and the bitter weather collides with the girl's morning tiredness so that by the time they come inside she is almost blue, teeth chattering uncontrollably, too frozen even for resistance. The fire under the cauldron comes as a powerful relief, as does the ginger and molasses ball Zuana now gives her to suck, the slow release of warmth radiating through her body. Strictly speaking, such refreshment during work hours is against the rules but they are starting the exacting business of measuring and making today, for which Zuana needs her full attention, if not her goodwill. Equally, the rule of silence within work hours is dependent on the nature of the task in hand and if the girl is to be any help as an assistant then she is going to have to understand as well as obey. It is time to start talking. Particularly since his Holiness's afflictions, while not life-threatening, are a somewhat delicate matter, affecting, as they do, both ends of his body.

The harvested figwort root sit on the table between them, dirty clumps of misshapen flesh-like nodules. Zuana explains the reason for it as simply — and as plainly — as she can.

'Urrech! How revolting.'

For the first words after so much silence, they erupt out of her with almost endearing energy.

'And extremely painful. Those who suffer from it say it is like trying to pass great lumps of itching, burning coal that can never be expelled. It leaves the sufferer in an almost perpetual bad temper.'

'How do you know this?'

'He told me.'

'What? The Bishop told you that he had these . . . these things?'

'Haemorrhoids. Piles. Certainly. The last time he visited he could barely sit down to eat the feast the kitchen had prepared for him and complained about everything. The conversa who cleaned his rooms heard him groaning in the outhouse and the next day there were specks of blood on the sheets. The urine from his chamber pot confirmed the diagnosis.'

She watches the girl's face crinkle in further disgust. The young are always repulsed by the afflictions of their elders. What was it her father used to say? That it took a saint or a doctor to seek pleasure in the suppurating indignities of decay. Still, there is also a macabre fascination to be found in the grotesque.

'And — as you will see — the remedy is apt enough.'

'Urrgh,' she says again, staring down at the figwort. 'They're as revolting as the disease.'

'Exactly.' Zuana laughs. 'That is the secret. You have never heard of signifiers? The power of correspondence? The way certain plants are shaped by God to show us the ailment that they heal?'

The girl shakes her head.

'Oh – it is one of the great wonders of nature. I have books if you want to study it further. This is a perfect example. One warty nodule to cure another. You would be astonished how elegant and simple it is. You grate and boil the roots with pork fat and mushroom until they are all dissolved, then leave the mixture to congeal. The figwort reduces the swelling, the mushroom – smooth and soft – soothes the itching and the pork fat provides the ointment, with lavender added at the last minute to soak up the smells. It works on character as well as constitution. Most doctors believe that if the heretic Luther had found a physician to treat him early enough he would never have needed to rebel against the true Church.'

Though Zuana keeps her countenance sombre as she says this, she is alert to the spark that ignites in those dark, watching eyes. Even were the girl immune to wit (and she already knows she is not), she needs the Bishop to be a man of even temper as much as they all do.

'Here. Be careful how you handle it.' She hands her a clump of root. 'It is extremely bitter to the taste and is not meant to be imbibed. And it must be finely grated, with every bit of it used.'

The girl takes it and turns it over in her hands, then brings it to her nose. Zuana thinks of all the other smells and tastes that she could demonstrate. But it will not do to hurry her.

They set to work side by side. And after a while the silence between them becomes natural rather than imposed. The room throws up its own sounds – the spitting of the boiling water, the chopping, the grating, the scrape of the pestle inside the mortar, the simple rhythms of repetition. The air grows warmer with the fire and the crushed lavender starts to release its scent. If there is another world out there, it seems a long way away. Even for those who might yearn to be in it.

Zuana glances across at her as she works. Her hands against the wood of the worktop are pale and unmarked, smoothed and softened no doubt by night creams and perfumed gloves. If there had been suitors they would surely have enjoyed praising them. But underneath the prettiness the fingers have a deftness to them: given a task that takes some skill – the grater's edge is sharp and does not distinguish between skin and root – she is dextrous and focused, showing a natural aptitude for it. Of course she is still unhappy – how could she not be? But there is less energy at hand now to indulge it. This much Zuana remembers: the way that it is hard to be in constant turmoil when such a level of concentration is called for. How while your mind might stubbornly refuse to quieten during chapel or private prayer, it can sometimes be tricked into stillness through work.

On the work bench Matalius' great illustrated book of plants lies open ('at last, a botanist who draws what he sees instead of just repeating what the ancients tell him' – she can hear her father's voice, caught between praise and envy), alongside his own handwritten book of remedies, the paper crisped and spattered from years of dispensary use. While Zuana knows the process without looking, she makes the girl study each and every step of the texts and then gets her to read them aloud so that she might learn them better. Later, to her surprise, she catches her flipping through the pages further when she thinks she is not being observed.

From the cutting and measuring they move on to the combining of the ingredients. Serafina hands Zuana the grated figwort and watches as she folds it into the boiling pork fat, careful to keep herself out of spitting distance of the pan.

'You say that you told this . . . disease . . . from his urine,' she says after a while.

'Partly, yes.'

'But how do you know just from looking at it?'

Over the years she has noticed that those who fight hardest often have the liveliest minds and are, without realising it, looking for a place to accommodate them. Well, there is a whole world to absorb her here if she will only allow herself to become interested. 'I have a chart. It was my father's – doctors use them. It marks the colours or the smell or the cloudiness of the liquid, so you can distinguish which area of the body is ailing.'

She shudders. 'Ergh. I . . . I can't imagine anything worse – studying an old man's pee.'

'You're right,' Zuana says smiling. 'Making sick people better is a disgusting thing to do. I cannot think why our Lord spent so much time doing it.'

But that afternoon while the mixture is simmering on the fire and Zuana visits the infirmary briefly to check on the condition of her bleeding patient, she comes back to find the young woman deep in one of the books.

The next day, her mood changes again. She arrives with a drawn face and sunken eyes, ill temper issuing from her like a bad smell.

'Did you sleep badly?'

'Ha! How does anyone sleep well when there is no night to sleep in?'

'I know it's hard. It takes time to adjust to such a different rhythm. But you will find that you—'

'Get used to it? What? In the same way I will get used to lumps of fat floating in the soup or the moans that come out from that mad woman who sticks nails into herself every night? Well, thank you, Suora Jailer, your wisdom is almost as comforting as the Bearded Sister's.'

Zuana suppresses a smile. 'I see you have come from instruction with the novice mistress.'

She scowls.

Suora Umiliana's nickname is common knowledge. There is even a debate among the choir nuns as to how many years have gone by since the novice mistress last saw herself in any kind of mirror. To which they might fruitfully add, how many more of them would be like her if the rules against vanity weren't so easily ignored?

Zuana can still remember the time, years ago now, when an old bishop with a new broom set out to ban reflecting surfaces entirely from the convent. It took barely a week for the first silver tray to arrive under a relative's skirts, during which time a number of the nuns had spent their resting hours poised like Narcissus over the surface of the fish pond. The over-zealous confessor that the bishop had recruited didn't last much longer. After six months of confessions where a queue of nuns kept him busy from morning till night with a litany of misdemeanours so trivial as to be unpunishable – except to the ligaments in his knees – he begged to be transferred to another convent. The day before he left they sang specially composed Vespers and slaughtered two chickens for supper. All in his honour, of course.

'It is an interesting question: what, if anything, smooth chins have to do with smooth souls. You might be surprised to find how quickly some women here start to feel a certain prickling under the skin.'

'Ho! You think I'm going to grow a beard as well as every-thing else?'

'Not necessarily. I think God has better things to do with His miracles. As I'm sure you have noticed already, we make room for both kinds here: smooth and hairy. Which means that you will be able to choose.'

The girl stares at her for a moment, as if still teasing out the meaning from under the words. Zuana turns her attention to the work desk, arranging the pots into which they will put the con-gealing liquid from the pans to cool. It is risky, saying such direct things, even indirectly, to a novice. She knows that. But the girl has been given into her care by the abbess and if she is to help her, then it can only be in the way she has helped herself: by telling the truth of how it is, alongside the wonder of how it might be for others.

Once she is back at work the girl's bad temper does not last long. They are halfway through the process of scooping the liquid into the pots when she makes it her business to ask about the next stage of the remedies.

'His Holiness suffers from sore throats. So bad at times that he can barely swallow, let alone preach. We make him lozenges and syrup. Boiled treacle and honey, mixed with cinnamon, ginger and lemon. Plus a few secret ingredients.'

'What are they?'

Zuana pauses.

'If I am to be your assistant I should know. Unless you are worried I'll sell them around town as soon as I get out.' And there is possibly a touch of mischief in her voice now.

'Very well. When the mixture is simmering we shall add angelica, mithridate, penny royal and hyssop. I doubt they mean much to you.'

'Why are they so secret then?'

'Because as long as we are the only apothecary which uses them the Bishop's own physicians must remain faithful to us. A little diplomacy is needed here. The fact is the Bishop suffers from a third ailment — one of which he himself is unaware but that wounds others deeply.'

'What is it?'

'He has venomous breath.'

She snorts. 'Did you tell that from his pee also?'

'You may laugh. But it is a serious affliction in a man who speaks the word of God. It's well known in Ferrara that when the inquisition needed to get the old Duke's French wife, Renata, to take communion as a test to her commitment to the true faith, he was one of the priests they brought in to persuade her, so that in the end she would give in just to stop him talking.'

'Is that true?'

'Why would I risk penance for your amusement? If you want to know more, next time you sit with Suora Apollonia at recreation ask her about when the Bishop came for his first inspection and she was one of the nuns who met him at the gates. She thought she was going to die from the experience.'

She sees it again as she tells it: Apollonia and Ysbeta, staggering their way into the infirmary with hands over their faces, fanning themselves like mad women, making so much noise that the novice mistress of the day finally had to come in to hush them.

The disbelief on Serafina's face gives her sudden pleasure. It is generally accepted that a little gossip can be as vital as prayer to the settling of a recalcitrant novice — well, accepted by everyone but Suora Umiliana, who is so immune to its contagious properties that most of her news is ten years out of date. Alone in her dispensary Zuana has suffered somewhat from the same complaint but she can still dredge up a few titbits when called upon. It has been a surprise to her, these last few days, how much she has enjoyed imparting them. But then she has never had such a vital young mind working alongside her in the dispensary.

'When I was young, my father had a fellow teacher at the university – a brilliant man by all accounts – whose breath was so foul that his students could not stand being in his lectures. When my father examined his mouth he found his gums were half eaten away with yellow pus and rot. Yet in other ways his humours were dry rather than moist. He lived on nothing but meats in sweet sauces and strong wine, so my father put him on a diet of fish and vegetables and water. After three months his gums stopped suppurating completely. But by then they were so shrunken that most of his teeth had fallen out, so the students could barely make out a word he was saying anyway. And thus does brilliance go to the grave unnoticed.'

'And your father . . .' The girl's expression is once again a mixture of horror and fascination. 'I mean . . . he thought it was . . . good to teach you things like this?'

'I . . . I don't know that he thought about it much. At the beginning they were more stories than lessons.' Was that how it started, she wonders? A hunger grown from listening? Or had it been that she had always wanted to learn?

'Well, I was never told such stories ever in my life. And certainly not by my father.' The girl shrugs. 'But if your remedies for bad breath are that good then you should dose the old crone they have put me next to in chapel. Every time she opens her mouth it smells as if something has died in there.'

Ah! The weapon of Maria Lucia. When kindness fails the temptation for punishment takes over.

Zuana skims off the last of the ragged surface of the ointment ready to move the pots on to the outside ledge of the window for the cold to congeal them. It is time to move from gossip to the business in hand.

'I'm afraid I can do nothing for Suora Maria Lucia. Her gums are already rotted beyond my skills. However, there is one thing you could do.' She pauses. 'Start singing. The minute that happens you'll find yourself moved to sweeter air fast enough.'

NINE

She holds her hand steady and tilts the candle a little more to the right over the folded edge of the paper. The thin hot wax dribbles on to it and quickly she presses the two sides together. They stick for a few seconds, then spring open again. The failure makes her want to scream but instead she closes her eyes and tries again. The same thing happens once more, only by now the paper is filthy with the grease stain. The problem is the wax: it is tallow, cheap and runny. The cell already stinks of its smoke, sour and fleshy, like the animal parts it comes from. It makes her eyes water and stuffs up her nose.

At home she and her sister said their prayers to the smell of scented beeswax; two candles in silver candlesticks by the bed, with the satin sheets turned down ready, the clay bed warmer folded in at the bottom. Their knees rested on the thick weave of a rug and when they were finished the maid would brush their hair, a hundred and fifty strokes until it gleamed, warm as a cloak around their shoulders. Yet here when the foul Augustina unpins and pulls off her head scarf her hair hangs in rat tails, abandoned and filthy. She hears that some of the novices pay their conversa to wash it and even brush it dry. But for that she must find herself another conversa and she is not willing to do what is needed to make that happen – in the same way that she will not take the rug from her chest and lay it over the stones, even though the floor would be less unforgiving on her knees, because it would be admitting in some way that this was her home now.

She would dearly like a little comfort, though. Sweet Jesus, she has never been so tired. It is more like being imprisoned within a Greek myth than a convent; one of those stories where the gods' punishment is fashioned as an endless repetition of the same horror. For days on end she has done nothing but the crudest, cruellest manual labour: no rest, just another scrubbing brush on another surface – and then always more. Her limbs throb from all the rubbing and scouring and cleaning and lifting. Some mornings she is so exhausted that all she can do is cry; some nights so numb that there is not even enough energy for tears. Inside the workroom there have been times when the panic and fury has grabbed her by the throat and she has had to clasp her hands together to avoid smashing every bottle off the shelf. But if the magpie Zuana notices, she pretends that she doesn't, just keeping on with what she is doing.

She has come close to refusing outright. 'If you want it scrubbed cleaner, do it yourself.' She even said the words, under her breath though loud enough to be heard. But nothing came in return, only the sound of the other brush moving to and fro across the wood.

Stupid silence. Stupid rules. The only consolation is that at the end of every day before the bell sounds, she – the magpie – makes up this special tea and they stop and drink it together (the nun is clever enough to know that unless she tasted it first she wouldn't touch it either). And it is good – so good – like a river of spices moving warmth and sweetness down into every part of your body until even the worst of the tiredness feels soothed away.

Warmth. Sweetness. Love like the penetration of a sword blade. From scrubbing to praying. 'It is a blade of goodness that will pierce to the very centre of your being, filling you with mercy and grace.' As if the work wasn't bad enough, every day she has to suffer the inquisition of the novice mistress, hairy chin and squashed face, eyes like burning pebbles, trying to prise her open for the entrance of His love. 'Talk to Him. He is waiting for you. You are His child as well as His betrothed bride and He is always listening for your voice. He hears before you speak, feels before you have felt it yourself. Each prayer, each silence, each office that you offer Him brings you closer to comfort, to the great joy of His love and the final wondrous embrace of death.'

Aach . . . the more she talks, the more you can feel your insides squirming. But you cannot not listen. You can be angry, sad, desperate. You can fear her, laugh at her, even hate her, but you cannot not listen to her. Some of them are already turning. She can see it, see them getting teary-eyed with the prospect of so much joy. But when you are tired all the time even the word comfort makes you want to give in; because resisting further seems more than it is possible to bear.

So it has gone on, day after day. There are nights when she has been asleep almost before she lies down. Then, what seems like minutes later, they are hammering on the door to get her up for Matins. She sleepwalks into the chapel, props herself upright against the wood (if there is indeed a whole city at her back then she is far too tired to look for it), and moves her mouth over the words, no understanding, no thought. She might even be asleep. Others are. Yesterday one of the novices fainted – just heaved a great sigh and keeled over. What was it? Had she seen anything? Been pierced by some vision or some sign? That's all they wanted to know. Ha! The poor girl probably just saw a feather bed by the altar or a plate of roasted pork rising up within the candle smoke and the smell of it overwhelmed her. She herself has barely eaten anything for weeks, the food is so foul. Wait until the feast days, they all say. You will taste heaven then. But for now all that there is is fatty meats and watered wine. And cabbage. Sweet Jesus, if she has to eat any more cabbage she will surely start passing green water. Maybe the dispensary magpie would have a remedy for that too. Certainly she would be able to diagnose it. God knows she can diagnose and cure everything else.

Oh, but she is a weird one, this Zuana bird. In some ways the weirdest of them all. Kind and fierce. Sweet and sour. And clever – there are times when she barely understands what she says, it has so many layers to it. She is a law unto herself. She makes a fuss about rules of silence and work and abstinence, then a few days later breaks them all by serving ginger sweets and telling all manner of outrageous stories. All that stuff about beards and souls, heretics and bishop's boils and poisonous breath. Even the novices when they are alone together do not gossip in such a way.

Of course, she is trying to coax her out of rebellion, just like the rest of them. Using stories in the way her father did (oh, he must have been a lunatic to teach his daughter such things), so that you can almost feel your eyes widening with surprise and before you know it you are interested in what comes next. No piercing with swords of love here – just God's great plan through herbs and clumps of filthy roots. No wonder she ended buried in this tomb. Who else would ever have had her?

She tilts the candle again and now the wax moves too fast and the flame almost drowns in its own juice. She steadies her hands. Once it has gone out, it can't be relit until the watch sister comes round at Matins with a taper. Even then you have to be careful. If she sees you have no candle left it will be clear you've been awake later than the appointed hour and you might be liable to penance for disobedience.

Not all those who disobey are found out, though. She's not so tired that she hasn't worked that one out. The last few nights when she's opened her door a crack – the watch sister's rounds are regular enough to be circumvented if you have the concentration to time them – she's been able to make out flickering lights under two or three of the others. One belongs to Suora Zuana, but she has dispensation for working late (though she, too, must be dropping with exhaustion, for during all the days of cleaning she never stopped, either), as does the fat-faced sister from the scriptorium, because it seems she is writing some play or other for Carnival. Suora Apollonia, though, has no such permission. But then to look at her you would think she is at court still, all those lacy collars and silky skirts, not to mention the hours she must spend on her toilette. Really! She has the whitest skin and the most perfectly plucked eyebrows. She must have a source for extra candles, too, since at Matins she always seems to have the same amount left as everyone else. As the supply is controlled by the chief conversa who oversees the storerooms there has to be a black market operating. Again, the trick is which conversa serves you, which means that for now there is nothing she can do. Alongside her brutality, Augustina has proved incorruptible when it comes to bribery. She barely speaks and appears – or pretends – to understand nothing that is said to her.

Well, until she can get herself another servant she must make do with what she has. It could be worse. When she takes the time to curb her panic she can see that. Yes, this place is foul beyond words. But had it been a convent in Milan, the abbess would have known the family, no doubt have heard the gossip and alerted them to the fuss she was causing. Here she was still an ordinary rebel rather than one with the mark of Cain. They have even given her work in the one place where she might learn something useful if she keeps her wits about her. She is lucky that way, for she has always had a good memory. *He* had just to sing a melody once for her to have it. Not that anyone else cared. Certainly not her father. He had only had her voice trained as a complement to her dowry. To go with a pretty face. And a docile temperament. Like her sister. Her sister – ha! – who was so 'shy' that her eyelashes couldn't help but flutter whenever a man who was not her father looked at her.

She gets up and rolls the blanket back against the bottom of the door to block any sign of candlelight. It is almost time for the next watch round. When she returns to the table the candle is spluttering again, the wick curling over into the thin lake of hot wax. She tries to lift it up to save the flame but it spits once, twice, then goes out. She gathers up the drops around the wick, fast to avoid the burn, trying to flick them while still molten on to the paper, but in the dark it is useless. She can feel tears at the back of her eyes as hot and angry as the wax. Self-pity. Self-pity born of tiredness, that is all the tears are, and she will not give in to them. She lies down on the bed and curls the blanket around her. Once the watch has gone by she will get up again.

She has promised herself that in between watches tonight, with or without the candle, she will move out of the cell and time how long it takes her to get as far as the gardens and back, so she can start the routine.

But by the time the sister passes her door she is deeply asleep.

Zuana registers the watch sister's footsteps and looks up from her books, stretching her spine to counteract the ache in her lower back. The candle on the desk is half burned. It is well past the hour of retirement but all this caring for the novice has left her no time for other work, most importantly the condition of young Suora Imbersaga in the infirmary, and she has asked for, and been given, permission to stay up a few hours later. The geranium and willow compound she tried had stemmed the bleeding for a while but that morning the young woman had passed another clot of blood and she has become weaker since. When Zuana had checked on her after Compline her face had been ghostly pale, though her pulse was stable.

The woodcut diagram in front of her shows a view of a body's intestines. The face is blank, with arms and legs crudely drawn, but from the stomach down there are a mass of diagrammatic lines, with arrows coming out of each and every area. As far as she can ascertain, the problem in the young woman's body is coming from inside the womb. In her experience once a woman starts flooding outside of her moon cycle, the problem can quite quickly become grave; it is as if the womb somehow loses the will to stay healthy without children growing in it. But what if it is not that? What if the bleeding comes from some tear or obstruction within her kidneys? It would certainly explain the pain: her father often spoke of stones being expelled through the urethra and how as they passed down from the kidney men would writhe and cry out in an agony worse than any torturer's screws. Yet if that is the answer, then why has the only expulsion here been liquid and not mass?

She closes her books and kneels to say her final prayers. Her knees crack as they reach the ground. She will be forty years old soon – too old to spend her days scrubbing so many floors and worktops, though remembering the last few days and the novice's new-found curiosity, she does not regret it. Before it can start to bring comfort, the discipline of service must first take its toll. In this she and Suora Umiliana would no doubt agree. She thanks God for her health and prays for his help in allowing her to continue her work. She asks him to guard and take care of young sister Imbersaga, in pain in the infirmary, and for all the other nuns, both sick and well within these walls. She prays for the souls of her father and her mother and for all those who continue his work helping and training others, for the benefactors of the convent and all their families; to hold them within His love and guide their journeys through life and, where necessary, to lessen their stay in purgatory. And finally she prays for the journey of the novice, who while still angry and confused seems – with His infinite love and mercy – to be showing signs of a willingness to settle. God be praised.

When she finishes, she gets up and goes quietly to the door, opening it and stepping out into the corridor, from where she will be able to make out any crying or distress from the infirmary below. But everything is still and quiet.

She stands for a moment taking in the atmosphere of the convent asleep around her. Out in the silence, from somewhere on the other side of the walls, comes the sound of a man singing, as he rolls home from a night in some drinking hole, no doubt. It is a fine voice: light, but full, an edge of longing in its rises and cadences. The language of love. The song ends and in the quiet that follows she hears the trill of a night songbird, indignantly protecting its territory from all intruders. As she stands there listening to its bright and insistent voice, her tiredness falls away and a feeling of sudden well-being floods through her: the sense of man and nature interlocking, the order and the beauty, both within God's plan. And she here, now; hearing, receiving it.

Matins tonight will be a cause for special celebration, even if Christ's body does not move for her on the cross. She wonders if she should look in on Suora Magdalena. Letizia, her conversa, has reported that she has been agitated recently, but she is mindful of the abbess's exhortation to keep herself free of the watch sister's jurisdiction and she does not want to meet her on her rounds.

Around her the convent is in total darkness, no tell-tale candle glow from anywhere. Matins will come fast enough now and she should sleep. As she closes her cell door another man's voice lifts up, this one deeper and darker but equally fine, offering up a swooping run of notes, as if in playful competition with the bird. There is always something to show God's wonder. She smiles. It will need a fat rook or a crow to rival this one.

TEN

'I don't see why we can't at least ask.'

'Because it would not be fitting, that is why.'

Half an hour into chapter and the convent factions are happily at each other's throats.

A watery twilight filters in through a row of high-set windows and despite the weather the place is warm from the heat of so many bodies. Gathered together they make a strange tribe: novices to one side, converse to the other and in the middle a great swathe of choir nuns, with the abbess on a raised dais at the end, immaculate in her newly pressed robes. Zuana looks out over the great room. There are times when she feels as much sense of community here as she does in chapel. A stranger coming upon them now might see only a flock of identical black-and-white birds (magpies are the most common joke) but for those with sharp eyes the differences are there as soon as you start to look.

The most obvious are the deformities. Like many cities', Ferrara's marriage market is cruel; it is easier to find a camel going through the eye of a needle than a cripple or a hump-back being serenaded into her wedding bed, and Santa Caterina has its fair share of rejects. Yet as they become familiar, are they really so monstrous? Consider Suora Lucrezia, sitting two rows in front of her. The first impression would shock anyone, since she was born with a gaping cleft where her upper lip should be. But if you could stop gawping long enough to lift your gaze from her malformed mouth to her eyes you would find yourself drowning in pools of deepest lapis lazuli. Then there is Suora Stefana, whose peach-down skin and perfect Cupid mouth might have poets out-versing themselves, if it wasn't for the fact that they would have to negotiate their way round the great question mark of her spine in order to find her assets.

But the ones who twist Zuana's heart are the sisters, Credenza and Affiliata. It appears their love for each other was so great from the start that they could not bear to leave the togetherness of the womb. The elder, Credenza, had to be pulled out first and the new-fangled tongs they used, though they saved her life, left her with such a mangled right leg that she walks like a listing ship. Affiliata, who came five minutes later, might win an army of suitors on the sweetness of her smile alone, except that after a while one senses an unnerving vacuity behind it. Not surprising perhaps since it was her head that the tongs squeezed hardest to get her out. Put together they would make a whole woman and a good wife for some great nobleman. As it is, in lieu of better offers, they are wedded to Christ and each other. As always, they are sitting together now, robes spread generously to hide the fact that their hands are linked.

Zuana finds herself smiling as she looks at them. They do not notice. Like the rest they are busy watching and listening. In the refectory everyone must keep their eyes on their plate and in chapel they must address themselves only to God. But in chapter – oh, in chapter – they may look at and talk with whoever they wish. And the greatest freedom of all is to be able to disagree.

'But why is it not fitting? Everyone wants to hear him and there is still time within our Carnival calendar for such an event.'

'Really, Suora Apollonia? Do you really think Our Lord would approve of such a thing?'

In the front row, Umiliana is in fighting form. With the city still reeling from the d'Este marriage and the climax of Carnival barely six weeks away, she has much to get agitated about, since the possibilities for mischief are considerable. Before long the streets will be packed with revellers and everything, including convent rules, will bend a little to incorporate them. The convent itself will perform a short theatrical piece on the martyrdom of St Caterina, written by their wordsmith copyist Suora Scholastica, in front of a specially invited audience of women benefactors, and there will also be a special concert in the parlatorio for families and friends of both sexes. Meanwhile, some of the city's best known musicians will pass by, or even stand inside the portico of the main gates for the nuns to listen to them.

The talk this year is all of the new singer the Duke has brought back from Mantua, a man with a voice so high and pure that every woman who hears him bursts into hot tears of envy. He has had to lose his manhood to achieve it but according to Suora Apollonia's aunt, herself a regular at the Duke's most intimate soirées, he is happy enough with his state. While such men have been talked of before, this is the first time that one has ever been in the city and such is the excitement that the convent is in debate as to whether, given the curtailed state of his manhood, he might be allowed to visit and give a recitation of his artistry.

'I don't see why not,' Suora Apollonia says, raising her artfully plucked eyebrows in feigned innocence. Still a creature of the court as much as of the cloisters, she can always be relied upon to fight for her – and others' – pleasures. 'I mean since "he" is not even a true "he" any more, as long as he . . . or whatever he is . . . is a good Christian and comes with Suora Standini's family in attendance surely it does not infringe any rules that we are bound by.'

A murmur runs like a breeze through grass. A castrato in the parlatorio? Whatever next? The novices, who attend chapter and can even speak if they have the courage, though they are not yet allowed to vote, can barely contain their enthusiasm at such a level of drama. Zuana locates Serafina in among them. She had started out the meeting with her usual closed expression, but even she is visibly interested now.

'I am against it, Suora Apollonia – as you should be – because our job is to serve God humbly and quietly without worldly distraction, not to be blown off course by each and every scandal or petty novelty.'

Protecting her novice flock from the 'contamination' that she sees seeping like rotten damp through the convent walls has become Suora's Umiliana's life work. Certainly without her chapter would be a more mundane, even boring affair.

'And Carnival is a living source of such temptation, as this convent knows only too well. It is bad enough that in the lead-up to such debauchery we will have to suffer every would-be minstrel of Ferrara parading round the walls serenading chaste women who do not want to hear it.'

'Oh yes, indeed. In fact it has started already.' Where the novice mistress goes, Suora Felicità is never far behind. 'Surely I am not the only one who was kept awake last night with the noise? Two of them, one with a voice as deep as the chapel bell – marching up and down, howling like love-sick puppies. But at least theirs were proper men's voices created by God, not the barber's knife. Our novice mistress is right. Such a "half man" condition is an abomination of nature. Wouldn't you agree, Suora Benedicta?'

'Oh, dear, oh, I simply cannot say, for I have never heard one of them.' Zuana has to drop her eyes now, she is so close to smiling. Caught between her passion for new voices and the desire not to have her choir's thunder stolen by some foreigner who has given up his genitals in the service of court employment, Santa Caterina's radiant choir mistress is floundering. She sighs . . . 'From what I hear they have the ability to reach and sustain the highest notes with miraculous ease . . . but whether they can deliver the passaggio or the subtlety of decoration of a good soprano, well, those who witness them all say different things.'

Zuana glances towards Madonna Chiara, but the abbess's expression gives nothing away. She sits with her fingers curved perfectly over the ends of the carved mahogany arms of the great chair, her head bent to one side then to the other, the better to follow the discussion. The more seriously she is seen to take each and every opinion, the less those who lose the argument might feel they have not been listened to.

'Then how wonderful if we might be able to make up our own minds. It is Carnival, after all. We cannot pray all the time and can hardly avoid hearing what goes on in the streets.' Suora Apollonia is so excited there is even a hint of colour underneath her whitened cheeks. 'If seeing him is so corrupting then he could just come to the gate and we could stand inside and listen.'

'I agree.' Suora Francesca from the embroidery room is already aglow with the prospect of so much cleansing joy and laughter. 'Other convents go much further than this. Everyone knows that last year when Corpus Domini performed their Carnival play they "accidentally" left a portion of the main door open so that half the men in the city could see in.'

'Hargh!' In the silence that follows Umiliana's strangulated bark, everyone waits for the intercession of the abbess. A series of glances move like cross-currents through the room. Zuana seeks out Serafina again. Oh yes, now her eyes are shining. It suits her, she thinks, such unguarded pleasure.

The silence grows. Three, four . . . Zuana finds herself counting. She is good at timing, their spiritual leader. Five, six . . .

'You are absolutely right, Suora Francesca.' The voice, when it comes, is deep and commanding. 'Indeed they did. And ended with a severe reprimand from the Bishop for their pains – and the imposition of a penance that means that this year they will perform no play at all.'

She pauses to let the words sink in.

'When it comes to music I have no doubt that this "creature's" voice would be most interesting, though from what I have heard, Suora Benedicta is right and what he gains in range he gives up in subtlety. However, in this matter I think we should be led by our most reverend novice mistress. We would not want to be seen to be so eager for praise that we seek out competition from such a dubious source. I do not have to remind you that it was not so long ago that the good prelates at Trent ended their Herculean labours of purifying the Church in the face of the grossest heresies by directing their attention to convents.' And here she looks directly at Suora Apollonia. 'While we are blessed that our own dear Bishop has seen fit to protect us from the fiercest of the restrictions, it would be unfortunate indeed if some "misdemeanour" on our part drew attention to that which should be beyond reproach.'

While the words are mild, the message is clear. Apollonia's perfect eyebrows meet now to form a perfect frown. But she bows her head and holds her tongue. When one is outmanoeuvred in chapter it is better to accept graciously.

'Besides,' the abbess says, more lightly now, 'I have it on good authority that his Carnival calendar is fully booked. I dare say the only people outside court who will hear him will be those passing the open windows of Palazzo Schifanoia.'

A few stray titters rise up from the room. Palazzo Schifanoia is notorious for its great salon filled with paintings of pagan gods and goddesses enjoying the world – and at times each other. Though the rule of St Benedict is clear on the corrosive nature of careless laughter, it is also true that a healthy convent is a mix of the sweet with the sour. It is a skill the abbess excels in, Zuana thinks; offering titbits for those who thirst for novelty while at the same time supporting those who disapprove of it.

In contrast, Suora Umiliana remains stony faced, seemingly unmoved by her victory. Recently she has started to find public fault in every chapter meeting. While the abbess has both the power and the strength of character to overrule her, she seems to be giving more ground than usual.

Zuana glances around the room. How many others, she wonders, are aware of the change? If the last election had not been a foregone conclusion, based as it was on the power of family factions within the city, it is conceivable that Umiliana might even be abbess herself now, for she is not without a following. Had that happened, Felicità would no doubt be her novice mistress and together they would be tougher on all the souls in their care. There are a few, no doubt, who might have been brought to a deeper comfort by their rule. But for the rest, all those noble women for whom the walls were never a free choice, it would have been much harder. As it was, Madonna Chiara had won with an indisputable majority and the post of novice mistress had been Umiliana's consolation prize. While no-one had expected it to silence her, in a well-run convent it is better to have opposition inside rather than outside the fold. Though Zuana has begun to wonder if Madonna Chiara would still agree with that.

'Well, if that covers the entertainment, perhaps we might discuss the refreshments. Suora Federica, as cellarer, perhaps you will tell us your requirements? You will be needing to order extra stores, I think.'

'Oh yes, indeed.' Federica, a florid-faced woman who runs the kitchen as if it was her own vassal state, has been waiting patiently on her moment. 'For the cakes and puddings we will need two sacks of flour, extra sugar, vanilla and at least three dozen extra eggs. Those expecting more than eight visitors must supply eggs from their own birds, as the convent chickens will be hard pressed to lay enough.' She directs this remark to Suora Fortunata, who keeps half a dozen birds in and around her spacious ground-floor cell and has a reputation for being insufficiently generous when it comes to donating their produce. 'Also I will need more colouring dyes for the marzipan fruits. Suora Zuana?'

Zuana bows her head. In the years since she has been given an extra room to house her distillation equipment, Santa Caterina's Carnival fruits have become famous around town, as much for the veracity of their colours as their taste. 'I will look through my stores for you.'

'Most particularly the red. The strawberries disappeared within no time last year.'

As much into the mouths of the nuns as the visitors, Zuana thinks uncharitably. 'I will do my best but that dye comes from the Bishop, not the distillery, and I have almost none left.'

Now Zuana catches Serafina's eye again. They have already spoken of this in the dispensary: how in the outside world the cocciniglia dye is a prized possession, traded at exorbitant prices by the Spanish from the New World; so expensive that it is only since the convent took over as the Bishop's apothecary that Santa Caterina can rely on the occasional 'gift' of it from the palace. Its reputation is well earned, for it turns everything it touches — from cardinals' robes to women's mouths — the most vivid shades of red. Federica, no doubt, has her head too much in her own ovens to notice how those nuns who gorge on the marzipan strawberries enter the first days of Lent with lips the same colour as court ladies'.

Such transgression is not lost on Umiliana. But for now at least, this is too trivial a battle for her to fight. She frowns at Zuana. She regards her as her enemy in this, and she is right, though for the wrong reasons. Zuana is as eager for the dye as Federica but that is because she has recently come across accounts of remedies that use it — in particular one for breaking fevers — and until she has the opportunity to try it she is loath to give up her remaining stock for the sake of a few Carnival delicacies.

'Can't we get more?' The kitchen mistress addresses the remark to the abbess. 'It would be worth whatever extra trouble it took.'

'Oh, yes. We heard nothing but compliments in the parlatorio for months afterwards.' Suora Apollonia, uncrushed by her earlier defeat, is back in force.

'We shall do what we can,' the abbess says mildly. 'Suora Zuana is already at work on the Bishop's next order. I am sure His Holiness will be bountiful again in his thanks. How are you doing with the remedies?'

'They should be ready within the next week.' Zuana pauses. 'I am much helped in this by our new novice, who shows aptitude and dedication in her work.'

Some sixty or so pairs of eyes swivel to the middle row of the benches, where Serafina sits. As they do so Zuana catches a flash of anger in the novice mistress's face.

'Well, that is good to know. It seems Our Lord moves in wonderful ways to bring His beloved young lambs into the fold.' The abbess's voice drips like thick cream. 'We can only hope her ailing voice might recover in time to join us for the Carnival concert. It would be a great shame for a young woman to be otherwise so isolated and constrained in her cell when the rest of the convent is so joyfully employed. Wouldn't you agree, my child?'

And Serafina, taken aback by the sudden attention, drops her head hurriedly to hide the rising colour in her cheeks.

'It is a risky business, giving a novice cause for pride while she is yet to master humility.'

'I simply told the truth. She is clever and a fast learner.'

The chapter room has emptied but Zuana has been motioned to stay behind.

'Yes, well, the rebellious ones often are. Nevertheless, it would be better for the convent if all this "aptitude and dedication" could be redirected towards her throat. The two of you talk together, I assume.'

'When we need to, yes.'

'Only when you need to?'

Zuana notices the lion's head on the arms of the great walnut chair, the way the mane has been worn smooth under the movement of centuries of restless fingers. It is no small thing, guiding the fortunes of so many souls. 'If she is to be of help to me – to the convent – then there are things she must know, questions she must ask and that I must answer.'

'And?'

She pauses. 'And her voice is clear enough when she talks.'

The abbess nods. 'It is interesting. Even Suora Umiliana has time for her. More than one might have expected. Perhaps it is the challenge. She says there is spirit but that her soul is closed as tight as a fist.'

'If anyone can prise it open, then it will be our good novice mistress.'

'True enough,' she says drily.

At another time it is something they might talk about; Umiliana's disapproval and its possible influence on some of the choir nuns, but it is clear the abbess has other things on her mind.

'I have sent a letter to her father, informing him of her distress and asking if there is anything we should know about her that might help us with her reticence. But the family is away and not due back for some weeks. It seems there is a rumour of a marriage – the younger daughter and a noble from Florence.' She sighs, as if this was not what she wanted to hear. 'Tell me, the first night when you tended to her, did you notice anything in her dowry chest?'

'What kind of thing?'

'Lyrics, poems.'

'I . . . er . . . there were a few sheets of paper inside her breviary.'

'You read them?'

'No.'

'And you did not think to mention them?'

Of course she had thought about this since. But had she reported them and had they been confiscated as a result Serafina would have known beyond doubt that it was she who had betrayed her and any chance they might have had to forge a relationship would have been destroyed. Was that why she had said nothing?

'I . . . She came to us as a singer and I thought they might be copies of songs. Madrigals perhaps. Why? Has someone else found them?'

'In a manner of speaking.'

Of course. She should have known it. Augustina may have blunt hands but her head is sharp enough to know where the real power lies. Zuana can see her bent inside the chest, rummaging for things that it might be profitable to mention to others. As for the abbess? Well, unless she knows the things that are concealed, how can she decide whether or not they should be exposed? There are times when Zuana wonders if there are convents where godliness has expelled all trace of unwarranted commerce. If so, then she really cannot imagine how they work.

The abbess sits for a second, her fingers playing with the lion's mane.

'Possibly you are right. Certainly whoever wrote them had read his Petrarch extensively, indeed one might almost say swallowed it whole.' She pauses. 'I dare say they would make fine song settings.'

'What will you do with them?'

'I am not decided. Confiscation at this stage would risk burning them deeper into her memory.' She sighs, as if this too were a decision not quite yet taken. 'For now they are back in her chest.'

'And Suora Umiliana?'

Another stroke of the fingers. 'She is busy with her instruction. I am sure that once she hears the girl's voice praising the Lord she will forget what else she was brought up singing.' She pauses. 'Indeed it would be better for us all if this novice found her voice soon. We will have half the court of Ferrara in chapel on the Feast of St Agnes. Perhaps some form of penance might have more impact.'

'From what I know of her I don't think that will help.' Zuana's own first taste of penance had been sour to the mouth as well as the soul: table scraps laced with wormwood followed by an hour spent prostrate by the refectory door with the sisters stepping over her as they came and went, a few of the sterner ones deliberately miscalculating their stride and crushing flesh along with cloth underfoot. Her tears had been as much to do with memories of her father's balms as any new closeness to God. Since she has taken over the dispensary she has kept a pot of calendula ointment for those who might find themselves in need of it. 'I will do what I can,' she says quietly. 'I did not ask for this burden.'

'No, no, indeed you did not. I imposed it upon you – for your own welfare as much as hers.' She pauses. 'But then again, as burdens go, I do not think it is overpowering you. On the contrary, I would say that your spirit seems quite full with it.'

Now as they meet each other's eyes the abbess smiles for the first time. 'Well, we will not be downhearted.' She smoothes her skirts. 'At least we are not entertaining a gelding in the parlatorio. The Bishop would have had need of more than your suppositories to cure the fit of colic that would have brought on. Though it is a shame in some ways . . .'

'Is his voice so remarkable?'

'It would seem so, yes. Apparently he holds the high notes so long he creates his own chorus of vibrating crystals from the chandeliers in the Duke's palace. Imagine that. Perhaps our Lord will see fit to let a few of them enter Paradise just so we can have the pleasure of making – ah—' Her eyes dart off to the side. 'Ah, Suora Felicità. I did not see you hovering there by the door.'

'I am sorry, Madonna Chiara.' The nun moves sheepishly from the doorway inside. 'I did ask earlier if I might—'

'Yes, yes, so you did. Though I thought we had agreed . . . well, never mind, you may come forward. The dispensary mistress and I have finished our business now.'

ELEVEN

He is come! He has found her! He was here, last night, outside
the walls singing while she was asleep. Oh, it had to be him. He
said he would come and he has. Two voices, one as deep as a
chapel bell, that was what she said. If the other had been a perfect alto she would have known for sure, for there are few
enough men who can span all twenty-two notes from the bass to
the treble with such ease. How stupid she was to have fallen
asleep. If only she could find out the words of the song he was
singing she would know immediately. But she dare not ask the
old witch Felicità – anything said to her would get back to the
novice mistress within seconds.

She is so excited that she can scarcely keep her hands still as
she holds the candle. The flame flares and splutters. She forces
herself to put it down on the table until she can recover herself
a little.

It had to be him. Except . . . except such things happen at this
time of year. That is what everyone said: that men – on their own
or in groups – parade round the walls singing madrigals, love
songs. She remembers the madness in the streets around their
palazzo; sees herself and her sister (always less docile when she

was out of her father's gaze) leaning out from the upper loggia catching blown kisses and declarations of love until they are chased back to their beds by a tutting nurse, who has been enjoying it as much as they have. Carnival: the triumph of misrule and mischief . . .

Recreation hour after supper had been full of Carnival tales tonight, like the one told by Suora Apollonia – getting her own back on Umiliana, no doubt, for stopping the concert. How, many years ago, a group of nuns and novices had taken baskets of dried rose petals from the fumigant stores up into the bell tower and had thrown them down on to the crowds below, so that all the young men had started serenading them, singing love songs to Our Lord's pure and spotless wives – except that some of them were still only betrothed. A few of the men had tried throwing up purses, and in one case even a rope to help them climb down. It had been such a scandal that from that time on the tower had been locked permanently, with only the abbess and the watch sister holding the key.

Oh, if she could get hold of that key . . . the view from the tower would show her half the city. But there must be other ways. If she could work out the general direction of his voice – it must have been him – she could get to the inside of the wall there and throw a letter over. She could use the new, fatter stones. She could do that. Tonight even. Yes, tonight. She would stay awake all night if necessary.

She is far too agitated to sleep anyway. Oh, when Suora Felicità had said those words, 'a voice as deep as the chapel bell', it was as if a great fist had got into her chest and was squeezing her so hard she thought she would faint. Had anyone noticed? No, no, she didn't think so. Everyone was twittering and muttering by then. A castrato singing in the parlour. You would think it was the devil come in to share their pallets. Really – they are like children with all their bickering and flapping. A great family of beaked sisters squabbling like a sack full of crows.

Crows. Ah — no-one had mentioned birdsong. Maybe it was not him. Because if it was surely he would have brought the instrument with him. They had talked about it: how she would be sure it was him from the sound of birdsong soon after his voice. They had agreed, hadn't they? Except she could no longer quite remember. Those last few encounters had been so blurred with tears. It had all happened so fast. So fast . . .

The truth was that it had never been her intention to defy them all. When she was small she had been as eager as the next little girl that the angel Gabriel should be the first to pierce her heart. But instead it had been Cupid who had slid in through the window. And her father who opened it for him. By then he had already decided on the man she would marry — or rather the family name the man would bring with him. It had never occurred to him that a talented music teacher with no name might fly in and grab the prize first. It had been nobody's fault. Or rather if there was blame to be apportioned then surely it should fall on the wonder of his God-given voice and the beauty of his settings of Petrarch's sonnets, for the words of a great poet always encourage the seeds of love.

By the time the sanctioned suitor himself came to visit she was already so besotted that she could barely bring herself to talk to him, let alone offer him encouragement. He didn't care. The hour in his company was chaperoned by her sister, who excelled in flirtatious coyness — so much so that after a sleepless night (or so he claimed) he returned to announce that he would prefer the younger daughter instead. Since it was his name that was doing the choosing (the dowry would follow either girl), her father had been sanguine. 'Well, we had planned for the younger one to serve God, but if she is willing . . .'

They only told her after her sister had agreed. By then she was so deep in love that she thought for a moment it might even be good news. She and Jacopo – for this no-name singer did have a name and a beautiful one at that – would take the smaller dowry and be glad of it. It cost so little to live on song.

Her father's fury had torn the tapestries off the wall. Given the choice of an impoverished singing teacher or Christ, there was only one bridegroom. When she refused, he had locked her in her room and refused to let her out until she gave in. Between her stupidity and her disobedience was the fear that she was already compromised. When he found the teacher at the door whispering to her, he had thrown him out of the house, then beaten her almost senseless, while her mother stood by howling. Within ten days she had been on her way to Ferrara, having bribed a servant to take the name of the convent to Jacopo so that he could follow her.

And he had . . . He had come for her. He was out there now waiting . . .

But . . . but . . . a worm of doubt remains. What if, after all, it isn't him? Oh, what if she is buried alive here for the rest of her life, listening out for every bird that sings at night while another bit of her withers up inside and dies?

She glances nervously around the cell. The nun who was here before her had died of something exploding in her head. Part of her brains had spewed out of her mouth. That's what one of the other novices had told her. Sometimes she thinks she can smell what happened here coming off the walls. She will go mad if she does not get out. 'It would be a great shame for someone to be so isolated and constrained in her cell while the rest of the convent is so joyfully employed.' As the abbess had said it, you could almost feel how much she relished the idea.

They had all been staring at her by then. She had been as

amazed as anyone by Suora Zuana's compliment. What words had she used? Aptitude? Determination? No, dedication. That was it. But she didn't think those things about her! How could she? In which case, she had said it to be kind. Yet kindness might skewer her worse than malice, since now they will be watching her even more closely. The abbess, the novice mistress, all of them . . .

Her mind is racing so fast that she feels almost sick from it. She has to stop, still this mad skittering inside her so she can think straight. She takes her hands and clasps them together hard, getting down on her knees and bending over, all the force of her thought and feeling going into the words.

'Dear God, please hear me. Please let it be him. Please make him sing again and let me find a way to contact him.'

Only now it feels like another kind of madness: to be in this place and praying to God for help. If the Lord cared for her at all why had He let them put her here in the first place? She had done nothing. Well, almost nothing. A few furtive kisses here and there, the moistness of hands moving over skin and the touch of swelling tongues. They had sinned more inside the music. Oh — their very souls felt joined there. But no-one could see that. Except God himself. Was it really so wrong to fall in love through voices? Was this His punishment? Could He really be so cruel?

'Talk to him. He is waiting, always, for the sign. We are his children, and He is listening.' Umiliana's exhortation slides into her mind.

'Forgive me.' She whispers the words. 'Forgive me. And help me. Please.'

She kneels in silence, waiting. The edges of the stone flags dig into her knees and she feels an ache from all the cleaning and scrubbing burn through her body. Gradually the noise inside her head clears, replaced by the throbbing pain, and she becomes a little calmer, more concentrated. 'Thank you,' she says, savouring the stab in her knees. 'Thank you.'

She gets up and goes to her chest. The excitement has been replaced by a sense of purpose. Under a cloth, next to the sheaf of papers, lie six stones, lifted from the edges of the herb garden when they harvested the figwort. She picks up the largest and weighs it in her hand. It is smooth and full, as if something in the earth had been polishing it. Ha! She sounds like Suora Zuana. Rainbows in the sky, rivers of gold and silver in the earth, the cosmic spirit vivifying everything . . . Even stones have wonder for her. What madness . . .

Yet after they finished work today, when Zuana had brought out that lodestone and held it close to the metal spoon and they had watched the two almost leap together . . . oh – well, that had been something. Something she could understand. A force from within. Almost like the pull of music between her and Jacopo.

She goes back to the chest, rummaging further till she finds what she is looking for: two petticoats, both silk – one red, one white. She lay them on the floor side by side. In the night on some cobbled path, which colour would stand out more? The white? She moves the candle over it but it looks grey and ordinary, while the red shines like a puddle of bright blood. Was this the colour they were all talking about, the dye that paints lips, breaks fevers and addresses melancholy? Wasn't that what it had said in that book written by the dispensary sister's father? Melancholy. Even the word is sad, like a grey fog suffocating everything it touches. There have been times these last few weeks when she has almost felt it creeping across the stones of her cell, lying in wait for the moment when she no longer has the energy to fight. But he has come and that is not how she feels tonight.

My lady's lips are red as rubies,
and her hair is like a cloud of gold
that is caught in the sun.
But when she turns her back to me
the day becomes night and frost is all around.

She takes the red petticoat and, tearing the fabric apart with her teeth, starts ripping it into thick strips. When she has finished she takes out two of the poems, turns them over and begins to write.

TWELVE

If Zuana has been expecting gratitude from Serafina then she is quickly disillusioned. In fact for a while she finds herself working alone in the dispensary, for things do not go well for the girl. That same night after chapter, the watch sister, who has been secretly instructed to increase the number of her rounds in response to the arrival of early Carnival singers, finds the novice skulking in the second cloisters trying to get back to her cell, her hands frozen and her sandals caked with mud from whatever part of the gardens she has been wandering in.

When questioned, first by the novice mistress and then by the abbess, she refuses to say where she has been or what she has done. In the absence of a confession a more serious penance is imposed. She is confined to her cell for two days with only bread and water. Before she returns there the room is searched by Augustina and another conversa and certain papers are removed from her trunk. That night, her howling reverberates around the convent again. Zuana sits in her cell over her books, listening but unable to do anything. She, like every other nun, is forbidden to go near her. When the sisters move in procession through the cloisters at Matins, they hear the girl fling herself against her door as they pass her cell, raining blows against the wood until you might think either it or she must splinter from the force. The other novices glance nervously as they pass, and one of them starts crying. But when they emerge from chapel later the banging and the yelling have stopped. From then on there is silence.

On the afternoon of the second day Suora Umiliana spends an hour with Serafina in her cell then accompanies her to dinner in the refectory, where the girl sits alone on the floor, her plate of leftovers thick with ash and bitter wormwood. The lesson, read by Suora Francesca with a slight quiver in her voice, is a teaching from St John Climacus, one of the desert fathers, who talks of repentance as the voluntary endurance of affliction, the purification of conscience, the daughter of hope and the renunciation of despair. It is beautiful in its way and a number of the nuns find their hearts lifting within them. When the meal finishes the abbess instructs the girl to lie down in the doorway while the others walk over her, not all of them as carefully as Zuana.

To make matters worse the next day is convent visiting.

It is not the first time Serafina has had to sit in her cell while others entertain (novices are forbidden outside contact for the first three months – a rule which in normal circumstances has kindness within its cruelty, since meeting loved ones too soon can rip raw the wound of missing before new skin has had time to grow), but the growing excitement over Carnival gives this visit a special energy. The day afterwards is the feast of St Agnes, when there will be a special meal and a court audience for Suora Benedicta's new psalm settings for Vespers. The parlatorio is full: almost two dozen nuns gathered in separate small groups, playing host to mothers, fathers, brothers, sisters, nieces, aunts and cousins, with such a noisy exchange of gifts and gossip that the casual passer-by in the street might think they were eavesdropping on some court function rather than the visiting day of the holy order of St Benedict. Zuana, working alone in her cell (what little family she has left is in Venice and has long since left her to her fate), can make out individual sisters' laughter and even once the gates are closed and the convent is silent again, those who have played host to the outside world seem lighter, a little more radiant than the rest.

That night, somewhere on the other side of the walls, a perfect lone tenor sings of a woman with hair like a cloud of gold and cheeks like rose petals. The serenade lasts only a few verses, followed by the trill of a nightingale and then the night silence returns.

The dandelion tea is already brewing in the pot as the girl walks, eyes down, limping slightly, into the dispensary. Zuana pours out a bowl of it and puts it down next to a spiced ginger ball at her place on the work bench.

'Welcome,' she says brightly, keeping her voice matter-of-fact. 'Sit and refresh yourself. We have a lot of work to do today.'

The rules of the convent are clear on such things. Penance, once over, is in the past, and nobody's business but the penitent's and her spiritual advisor's. And, of course, God's. It is not to be referred to and certainly not to be pitied or commiserated over.

The muscles in the girl's jaw tighten as she tries to swallow and Zuana knows she is on the edge of tears. It would be better if she did not cry, and if she did, it would better if Zuana ignored it. 'Drink the tea and eat the ginger,' she says quietly. 'I have added extra herbs. They will address the stabs of hunger and give you some energy.'

Serafina takes a breath, then picks up the ball and takes a bite. Zuana imagines the honeyed spices oozing into her mouth, counteracting the leftovers of the wormwood plant which can linger for days. When her father had first shown her the spiky leaves and made her chew a little to taste their foul bitterness, he had told her of the entry in the Book of Revelations when the third of the avenging angels throws a star called wormwood from the heavens to earth, poisoning the rivers and fountains so that men died of drinking from them. That such an instrument of destruction might come from a simple plant had amazed her then. She wonders if she should remind Serafina of that story now, but the girl is too absorbed in her misery to be distracted.

The tears start to fall as she chews, but it is clear she has not given them permission and she sniffs angrily to try to pull them back. After a while as she moves out her other hand to take the bowl Zuana notices her wincing.

She takes a small clay pot from the back of the worktop and puts it down next to the drink. 'Here.'

'What is it?' The girl's voice is flat and thin.

'It is an ointment for flesh that has been pinched or crushed. It will bring out the bruise fast and lessen the soreness.'

'I thought penance was meant to hurt?'

'It is meant to help. At the beginning the two are not always the same thing.'

'Ha! Tell that to Suora Felicità.'

Zuana drops her eyes. While one is not meant to acknowledge the nuns who step hardest, of course everyone knows who they are.

The girl finishes the drink and pushes the pot away. 'Was it you?'

'Me?'

'Who told them about my poems.'

And now they are trespassing into dangerous areas. Zuana says nothing, the shake of her head almost imperceptible.

'Who then? Augustina can't read . . .'

'No, she can't.' She pauses. 'However she has a good nose for secrets . . .' She trails off.

The girl nods. Nothing more needs to be said.

'Here.' Zuana takes an apron cloth from the side and hands it to her. 'Finish your drink. We have a lot of work. I prepared the ingredients for the syrups, but you are to do the mixing this time. That way you will be able to make the whole remedy your-self next time.' She is aware of the implication in the words but she does not flinch. 'Be careful, though. Boiling treacle sticks to any flesh it touches and can take a layer of skin off with it.'

The girl looks at her, finishes the drink in one gulp and takes the apron.

Over the fire, the mixture thickens as it boils but once she gets used to the weight she stirs it well enough. They work in silence, as they have so many other times over the last weeks and it comes as a relief to both of them. On the worktop the spices sit, grated, chopped and measured, alongside a small vial of brandy waiting to be added at the right time. As the ingredients fold into the treacle the smell of caramelising sugars suffused with cinnamon and cloves wraps itself around them. They are so much the aromas of Zuana's own youth that if she closes her eyes now she can almost imagine herself back in her father's company, even down to the sound of his shuffling and clattering as he goes about his work on the other side of the room.

'You must live more in the present and less in the past, Zuana.' The abbess's words move through her mind. 'It is for your own good. It will make you a better – happier – nun and bring you closer to God.'

She opens her eyes to find that the girl is staring at her. She moves her attention back to the mixture. A few moments pass.

'Those things you said about me. It was kind of you . . .' the girl says quietly, a mumble almost, keeping her eyes on the pan as she does so. 'I am sorry. I didn't . . . I didn't mean to let you down.'

The apology takes Zuana by surprise. While it is her duty not to feel any resentment towards the young woman, she has needed no effort to resist it. Neither – now she comes to consider it – has she felt any irritation or even impatience. On the contrary, there has been something about the girl's presence over these weeks – her very refusal to be comforted or managed that she has almost . . . What? Enjoyed? No, that cannot be the right word. Had sympathy with perhaps? Or at least understood.

'It is our duty to serve God humbly and quietly without worldly distraction, not to be blown off course by each and every scandal or petty novelty.'

Now it is Umiliana's voice she hears, coming back to her from the chapter meeting. Could this be what is happening to her? That she is being seduced by the novelty, the drama of it all? It is true that these days she wakes every morning wondering what the work hour will bring, even perhaps looking forward to its challenges. The idea disturbs her. It has been a hard-fought battle, the cultivation of serenity through the years, and she would not have it unwittingly undermined. Out of the corner of her eye she sees Serafina watching her again. 'Keep stirring,' she says, a little sharply. 'It is important that it stays moving at all times.'

The girl returns to the task. But after a few minutes she looks up again. 'I . . . I need to ask you a question.' She pauses. 'What kind of man is the Bishop?'

'The Bishop?' Zuana shakes her head. 'It would be better for you to forget the Bishop. He cannot help you.'

'He is the abbess's superior,' she says stubbornly. 'I think I have a right to know who he is.'

Zuana sighs. What were Madonna Chiara's words on his appointment years before, when she was still a sister rather than the abbess? 'As ugly as he is holy. But we will have to put up with him. Rome has had its eye on Ferrara ever since the last Duke's French wife Renata was found to be hiding heretics in her skirts.'

No doubt she would phrase it differently now but the conclusion would be the same.

Zuana is careful with her own words: 'He has a reputation as a godly man and a reformer.'

The girl frowns. She is, of course, far too absorbed in her own troubles to appreciate the magnitude of the shift taking place all around them: this war that is being fought within the faith in order to defeat the heresy outside it, bringing with it endless rules and definitions as to what is true thought and what is not. As yet, the nuns of Ferrara have been spared the worst of it (thanks be to God for the Bishop's ailments), but the future remains uncertain. It is better, perhaps, that she does not know the truth, for it would only make her journey harder, her passage to quiescence longer.

'He is also . . .' Zuana takes a breath. Ah well, she is long overdue a confession with Father Romero, asleep or awake. '. . . exceedingly ugly. Possibly the ugliest bishop Ferrara has ever seen. Keep stirring. It must not be allowed to set until all the spices are absorbed.'

The girl moves her hand but the stare continues. I know what lies behind that look, Zuana thinks: she believes herself too lost and angry to find anything in the world worth enjoying or delighting in. But she is wrong. Oh, how she is wrong . . .

'You think I jest? Believe me I do not. The Bishop of Ferrara is as fat as a wild boar, with jowls like slabs of pitted rock and a skin as thick as that of a rhinoceros.'

'A what?'

'A rhinoceros. You don't know this animal? Oh, it is a remarkable creation: a kind of overweight cow, with plates of gladiator's armour for skin and the single thick horn of a unicorn coming out of its skull. I am amazed that you and he have never become acquainted.'

'You've seen it – this thing?'

'On the page, not in the flesh. It is to be found in only the wildest parts of the Indies, though I believe they brought one back once on a boat and showed it in Portugal.'

She watches Serafina's eyes widening. Her father used to say that the world was full of young women with their heads stuffed with fabric and frippery, ignorant of the wonder of God's universe everywhere around them – and that he would not have his daughter wasted thus. Well, he had done a good job. When had she first learned about such creatures? Young enough that he had made her put her nose close to the page to catch the smell of the ink he claimed was still rising off it. 'This book left the printing press in Venice yesterday and has journeyed by boat all night and day to get to us. Imagine that, carina. Imagine that.'

But she had cared less about the freshness of the printing than the pictures themselves: page after page of the most fantastical plants and creatures as recorded by men who had voyaged to the very edge of the world to catalogue God's creation. In contrast, her father's interest in them had been as a source of medicine more than wonder; that great pointed horn from the rhinoceros was rumoured to have miraculous healing properties, as potent as the unicorn's. Years later, when she had caught sight of the Bishop's profile during service – the mass that accompanied his visit was endless, so that even the most saintly drifted off at times – the similarities had been immediate, even down to the horn of his mitre sticking out from the top of his head. She had shown the image to Suora Chiara that same night and they had laughed over it together. It had been barely a month later that the old abbess had taken to her bed with a running fever and the family factions had started gathering in anticipation of the next election.

'I dare say you have never heard of the lamia either.'

'Lamia? No.'

'Ah, if the accounts are to be believed this is the most astonishing creature. Half-tiger and half-female, a woman's face and breasts inside the fur, so that those who come across her in her natural habitat of the jungle don't see the tiger until it is too late. Besotted, they rush towards her until they are close enough, at which point she leaps from the undergrowth and embraces them in her claws. You really know none of this? What did they teach you, your tutors in Milan?'

'I was taught well enough. Poetry. Music. Song.' And her tone is suddenly fierce. 'The most beautiful things in the world.'

It is the first sign of a vivacity not bred from rage or desperation that Zuana has seen in her. Poetry, music, song. No, most certainly not bred for the veil, this one.

They work in silence for a few moments. The bait, however, has been too rich.

'You say you saw these animals in a book?'

'Yes.'

'Do you have it still? Is it in your chest?'

'In my chest?'

'Yes. Your father's books that you brought with you when you came.' She shrugs, glancing up at the shelves where the herbs and remedy books that she uses most often are kept. 'I mean, everybody knows that was what your dowry was made up of.'

While she may not be sharing her own secrets in recreation, she must be listening avidly enough to those of others.

'Will you show it to me?'

Zuana, of course, is caught now, since the thing she must say truthfully must also be a lie. Such images, wondrous or not, are no longer the stuff of a good dispensary sister's workshop.

'Even if I had such a book, Suora Umiliana would certainly not approve of its study.'

'Oh, she approves of nothing. Except prayer and death!' The words explode out of her. 'Really. That is all she talks about: how the flesh decays and how we must be ready, praying every moment, for we may be taken at any time. I tell you if she had burning nodules or gums full of pus she wouldn't come to you but welcome them in as God's messengers.' She shudders. 'She makes me feel as if my insides are already being eaten by worms.'

She is not the first novice to find herself gripped by such images. Partly it is their age: girls around puberty taste everything more sharply and though she might condemn poetry as the wordplay of the devil, the novice mistress, Zuana has noticed, is not above using some of its tools when it suits her, especially if she has smelt the poison of physical desire leaking out somewhere. Of course it is a great and honourable tradition within salvation; the elevation of the spirit through the vanquishing of the flesh. What had been Tertullian's words to converts to the cloth? 'If you desire a woman, try to conjure up an image of how her body will be when she is dead. Think of the phlegm in her throat, the liquid in her nose and the contents of her bowels.' He would have made a good doctor, along with a great scholar.

'I know Suora Umiliana can be fierce sometimes.' Zuana picks her words carefully. 'Yet she has a great flame of faith inside her and she cannot help but want others to be warmed by its heat. I am sure once you give yourself up to her you too will feel it.'

But the girl does not want to hear this. She turns back to the pans and the moment between them is lost. After a while across the courtyard the choir voices begin.

Zuana watches how once again, despite the resistance within the girl, her head and upper torso lift instinctively to greet the sound. To mark the celebration of the feast day of blessed virgin martyr St Agnes there are special chants and Benedicta's new psalm settings must be perfected in time for Vespers that evening. The abbess had her sights set on this service to introduce her songbird to the city and certainly the setting is lovely, even to Zuana's less discerning ears. Such young saints usually go down well with novices, for there is always a kernel of rebellion inside their godliness and while Serafina may not share the saint's proclivity for martyrdom it is clear that the drama of the music is already inside her.

By the time she was her age Zuana could recognise the tastes of most major herb ingredients within a given remedy, and identify each of their various healing properties. It would not surprise her if the girl was singing every note inside the silence now. Certainly she is listening hard enough. The haunting antiphon chant ends and the psalm setting begins.

'You know, I wonder why you choose to continue to give yourself such pain. It must be one of the greatest joys of life to have a beautiful voice.'

The girl shakes her head, staring down into the treacle. 'Songbirds don't sing when they are kept in the dark.'

'That is true . . . except for the ones whose songs bring on the dawn.' She pauses. 'I have heard a nightingale recently whose voice has the sweetness to ease an ocean of agony,' she says, thinking back to the moment in the cloisters when she had felt so at one with the world.

Serafina glances up sharply, as if the words have stung her in some way. The gesture causes the spoon to jump in the pan and a fat gob of boiling treacle spits up at her.

'Oah!' She yanks her hand back, dropping the spoon inside, her face contorted with the burn.

Zuana moves swiftly, grabbing her by the wrist, ripping the burning treacle off her skin and pulling her over to the water butt. 'Put your hand in!'

She hesitates, so that Zuana does it for her and she yelps again, this time at the fierce cold. 'Keep it there. It will stop the pain and hold off the burn.'

Back at the fire she sets about rescuing the wooden spoon while behind her she registers the sound of the girl's weeping. Once started, she is not able to stop.

Zuana finds herself remembering a winter afternoon in the scriptorium long ago. A young woman, furious and desperate by degrees, sits staring at her own tears splashing on to the page she is copying. And as she tries to wipe them away before they cause damage to the paper, she finds herself studying the great illuminated letter O that begins the text, inside and around which, following the curve of the gold leaf, she can now make out painstakingly tiny written words. Once read, never to be forgotten.

> My mother wanted me to become a nun
> To fatten the dowry of my sister.
> And to obey my mother I became one.

She repeats the words now, accentuating the patina of verse inside them.

> Yet the first night I spent in a cell
> I heard my lover's voice down below,
> And rushed down and tried to open the door.

Behind her in the room the crying has stopped now.

But the mother abbess caught me.
'Tell me "little sister",
So do you have a fever or are you in love?'

She turns to the girl. 'You are not the first, you know, to feel so angry or abandoned.'

'Ha? You wrote that?'

The incredulity on her face makes Zuana laugh out loud. 'No. Not me. My quarrel with these walls was different. But another novice – just like you.'

'Who?'

'Her name outside the convent was Veronica Grandi.'

'Was? Is she gone?'

'Oh yes, it was a long time ago. When I first came – a novice like you – I was apprenticed to the scriptorium. I found the words disguised inside one of the illustrations in a psalter. There was a name and a date: 1449, a hundred years before me.'

'What happened to her?'

'How is your hand?'

'I can't feel anything.'

'Then you can take it out.'

As the water drips off her fingers Zuana can make out a small welt of angry red skin. The numbness should stem the pain until the blister forms.

'Later I looked for her record in the convent archives. She took her vows a year later and became Suora Maria Teresa.'

'Oh. So she never left.' And her voice is hollow with the realisation.

'No. When she died thirty years later she had been the convent's abbess for nine years.' She pauses. 'Her entry in the convent necrology tells of her great leadership and humility and how on her deathbed she sang the praises of the Lord with a wide smile on her face. I think it possible that she had forgotten whoever was waiting by the gate by then, don't you?'

Zuana watches as the girl struggles to digest the wonder and the horror of it. If there had been someone waiting outside the gates for her, how much longer might it have taken? A dead father was an acceptable form of missing; even the sternest of confessors and novice mistresses found it hard to punish an excess of filial grief. But those who came with darker, more suspicious memories would have to keep them secret. It is not her job to ask questions. When the door closes behind a novice her past remains outside. Yet sometimes it helps to have someone listen.

'I cannot . . .' The girl stumbles. 'I mean if you . . .'

But whatever she is about to say is interrupted by a hammering on the door.

'Suora Zuana! Suora Zuana!'

The conversa who enters is young and plump, her face glistening with sweat.

'You must come – please – now. It's Suora Magdalena. I . . . I think . . . I don't know . . . I can't wake her.'

'What happened?'

'I don't know. I – I was crossing the courtyard with laundry when I heard voices coming out of her cell. It was work hour, but I thought – well, maybe one of the sisters was in there with her. There was laughter.' She stumbles over the words. 'Girls' voices – laughing. Then suddenly there was silence. So . . . I opened the door and . . . and there was no-one there. The cell was completely empty. Just Suora Magdalena on her pallet.'

Zuana is already reaching for the pot of camphor crystals.

'I am coming, Letizia.' As she turns she sees Serafina's face, alive with curiosity. 'Um . . . you are excused the rest of the work hour. Go back to your cell and wait for Vespers.'

'Can't I come with you?'

'No.'

'But . . . I am your assistant. That's what the abbess said. That I was to help you.'

'Yes, and the help I need is for you to go back to your cell. Letizia – find a conversa to come to take charge of this liquid until I get back.'

'But I could do that,' Serafina protests. 'I have studied the remedy. I know how and when to put in the herbs.'

Which is true enough, except that the rules forbid the leaving of a novice in an unattended dispensary. There are too many ingredients that could cause damage to others. Or herself.

'You are risking the charge of disobedience, Serafina. Go to your cell. Now.'

And whatever good work has been done between them is wiped out by the fury in her eyes. She pushes roughly past the conversa and the door slams behind her.

THIRTEEN

The work hour is still in force and the cloisters are deserted as Zuana makes her way swiftly across the courtyard. The choir has stopped but a few excited voices slip out from the embroidery room above, a dancing inflection inside them. This must have been the laughter that Letizia heard, she thinks; sound moves strangely through winter fogs and while it is not as dense as some days the air is still gauzy-grey around her.

The door to Suora Magdalena's cell is half open, as if it is waiting for visitors. She feels a strange prickling down her neck as she walks in.

Before her eyes have had time to adjust to the gloom (even in daylight it remains murky in here), Zuana is struck by the smell. She has prepared herself for sickness, even the tell-tale scent of death, but this is different: light, fragrant, like a wave of perfume; roses or even frangipani, summer smells in winter. It is almost as shocking as the sight that greets her on the bed.

Magdalena's pallet is on the floor against the back wall, next to a water jug and a plate, a bucket for excrement near by. Recently, Letizia has reported, there has been almost nothing in it to empty. But then the less one takes in, the less there is to evacuate, and in her relentless quest for God, over the years Suora Magdalena has been waging a steady war of attrition on her body, training it to survive on almost nothing.

When she entered the convent the century itself had been young and there are no other sisters left alive from that time. Everyone though – Zuana included – knows something of the story: how as a humble novice from the poorest family she had been able to go for weeks on end with only the host to sustain her, and that while she was in such a blessed state her hands and feet bled in sympathy with Christ's own.

Such godliness had been all the fashion then and Duke Ercole, a man with an appetite for holy women, who collected piety as others collected china or antiquities, had found her in a nearby town and installed her in Santa Caterina, where he and his family would visit, bringing members of the court to hear her prophesies – for sometimes she would go into ecstasies for them.

Rumour was that she had been small even then – some said she weighed so little that it wasn't hard to believe she could lift herself off the ground. It had been the time of the French invasions and the northern wars and every city was searching for a way to protect itself. Such humble, uneducated women – living saints as they were known then – who found God through prayers and their own goodness, were talismans of purity in a world of corruption. But once Luther and his dissenters started lighting fires of heresy across the mountains, such untutored salvation became suspect and after Ercole died the royal visits dried up – and so, it seemed, did Magdalena's stigmata.

By the time Zuana arrived, Magdalena was a forgotten figure who, by her own request, never left her cell, and even those who might have shared her hunger for God were wary of her reputation. Successive bouts of fasting had left her too weak to attend chapel and over the years convent confessors had proved either too tired or too forgetful to bring God's food directly to her, so that for some time now she had lived without the host. Her cell door remained closed and gradually even the memory of the memories had started to dry up. Since she had become dispensary sister it had fallen to Zuana to oversee her care, which she did as best she could, making sure that her food was delivered and interceding in the appointment of a servant conversa who would not be cruel to her. There was nothing more anyone could do. Magdalena's self-inflicted pariah status was a fact of convent life, unquestioned and secure. The rest was up to God.

Well, it seems He may have spoken now.

Her body is so wasted that Zuana can barely register the shape of it under the blanket. Her skullcap has fallen from her head and the stubble of white hair sits like frost on hard ground. But her face . . . oh, her face is vibrant: her eyes are fixed open, bright and shining in a sea of wrinkled skin, and she is smiling, a wild, exuberant smile, lips apart, as if she has seen something so wondrous that she has taken in a gasping breath in anticipation of laughter, only to find it caught in her throat.

Zuana uncorks the camphor salts and passes the bottle under her nose.

She remains transfixed, not a flicker of response.

The room grows dark again as Letizia's form blocks the doorway. 'Oh Sweet Jesus. He has taken her, hasn't He?'

'Is this how you found her?'

'Yes, yes. Oh, but you should have heard the laughter.'

'Move from the doorway. I need more light.'

The old nun's right hand is clasped over a crucifix, the knuckles bone-white. Zuana moves under the blanket to find the other. It lies loosely by her side, cold to the touch. When she brings it into the light she sees skin so thin and bruised and veins so pronounced they look like membranes on an animal's stomach. She searches the underside of her wrist for any sign of a life pulse.

'Oh Lord Jesus, take her soul, Lord Jesus, take her soul.' Behind her Letizia's moaning prayers fill the room.

Under her fingers she feels a faint fluttering beat. Then another. Slow, but there, surely. She slides a hand under the back of the old woman's neck to try to lift her up and her fingers register a run of vertebrae distinct as standing stones in a graveyard. But the body is rigid and will not move. Rigor mortis with a pulse? She looks back into the eyes, staring, unblinking, bright, with no film, no dullness at all. Dead, but with eyes that are still alive? She bends her cheek to her nostrils. Closer, the strange perfume seems stronger from the open mouth. And then, soft but unmistakable, she feels the heat of a exhaled breath.

'Lord Jesus, take her soul.'

The cell becomes gloomy again.

'Move, I said. I need more light.'

'What's wrong with her?' But it is Serafina's voice she hears now, harsh with fear. 'Is she dead?'

'What are you doing here?' Zuana does not take her eyes off the old woman's face.

'I . . . I heard someone running. And laughter. I . . . I was scared alone in my cell.'

If it is the truth it sounds disingenuous in her mouth. Such disobedience will mean penance if Zuana chooses to report it but there is no time to think about that now. Somewhere she knows that she would have done the same thing; the spice of curiosity overwhelming the blandness of prudence.

The light returns as the girl steps in closer. 'Oah . . . the smell . . . what is it? Is it death? Is she dead?'

Zuana picks up the jug by the bed and, lifting it high, splashes a thin stream of water on to the old woman's face. Nothing.

Except this time as the breath leaves her body there is the faintest 'aaaaah'.

'No, no, she's not dead.'

'What is it then?' Serafina's voice is as hushed as the room. 'What's happened to her?'

'I think she is in an ecstasy.'

'Oh! Oh, I knew it.' The conversa lets out a new moan. 'You should have heard the laughter. It was as if Our Lady and all the saints and angels of heaven were in here keeping company with her.'

'That's enough, Letizia,' Zuana says harshly. 'Go and fetch the abbess. Tell her I need her here now.'

In the silence that follows Letizia's exit Zuana can feel Serafina's fascination behind her. Maybe this disobedience has purpose after all. Even the most recalcitrant novice cannot help but be moved by the white heat at the centre of the flame.

'Come.' She turns to her. 'Since you are here, you had better see for yourself. There is nothing to be afraid of.'

'I'm not afraid,' she says boldly.

Zuana makes room for her by the pallet. And, of course, as soon as she sees the old woman's face Serafina cannot take her eyes off her.

'Ooh, she looks so . . . so joyful. And the smell . . .'

'It happens sometimes. It is the scent of flowers, but more than flowers.'

'How do you know she is not dead?'

'Here, take her hand. Don't worry – she cannot feel anything. Under her wrist where the great vein is . . . feel it? Feel the beat. Try again. Got it? Now see how slow it is. Remember how fast it was with the sister with a fever.'

'But doesn't that mean she is dying?'

'No. If it is like the last time then she can stay like this for hours.'

'The last time? You have seen it before?'

When had it been? Seven, eight years ago? Maybe longer. Summer. As hot as hell itself. Suora Magdalena had been upright on the pallet then, her arms bent out in front of her as if she were cradling a baby, her head flung back in what seemed like a paralysis of joy.

Of course Zuana had heard about such things – who had not? – but this was the first time she had ever seen it. As the newly appointed dispensary sister, she had been instructed by the abbess of the time to stay with her until it passed and so she had sat in the cell watching over her. Not that there had been much to see, unless you counted the fly that kept landing on her face, picking its way over her eyes and lips, even into her mouth, while all the while she remained oblivious. How long had it lasted? An hour, maybe less? But the journey had been longer for the old nun. She had been so dead to the world that when she first came back she could not understand where she was; not the time, nor the place, nor the day. But the wonder as to where she had been, and the sadness that she was no longer there, was painful to behold. With such sustenance for the spirit what need did the body have for food?

Next to her, Serafina reaches out a hand towards the old woman's staring eyes, but hesitates as she gets closer.

'Don't worry. She can't see you. Or hear you. You could stick a needle into her flesh now and she would not even flinch. She is not here.'

'So where is she?'

'I don't know. Except I think she has reached a place where her soul is as powerful as her body. So that she is able to move from one into the other for a while. To find herself with God.'

'With God!'

With God. Of course she would not know what that means.

But then who does? With God . . . When Zuana first came, the novice mistress of the day, a kinder though much paler force than Umiliana, would talk of the journey towards Him as a path that could be followed by everyone, as if obedience and prayer practised regularly would bring on divine love as surely as a dose of figs might regulate the bowels.

Except that it had never happened. Not to her nor, it seemed, to anyone around her. Oh, there had been souls who had grown gentler and more humble over the years, even a few who had come in like spitting cats but grown gradually into lambs, albeit with less spring in their steps. There were some who accepted suffering without complaint, and over-excited ones who might swoon occasionally in night chapel. Yet such elevation, whatever it was, was short-lived, and, to Zuana's eyes at least, always had the quality of a self-imposed state rather than sustained transcendence.

After a while it had been a relief to stop trying. Her books and her work brought their own rhythm, at times their own temporary loss of self. Still, one could not help but wonder at the idea: to be so consumed, so transfixed by joy . . . She glances at Serafina beside her, staring down at the old woman's face, and she knows she is feeling it too. Whatever the dangers within it, Suora Umiliana might do better to talk to her novices about ecstasy rather than contamination and decay. Such words would surely hook deeper into rebellious young hearts.

'What has happened here?' Madonna Chiara's voice from the door is clean and matter-of-fact. 'Is she transported?'

'It would seem so, yes.'

The abbess gives a small sigh, as if this is yet another unwarranted problem she must deal with in a busy day. 'How long?'

'I don't know. The conversa said she heard voices but when she came in she was alone.'

'Who is that next to you?' Her tone is sharp.

Serafina starts, half turning her head.

'What is the novice doing here?'

'I . . . I asked her to help.' Later, Zuana cannot remember deciding to say this before the words came out.

'Well, this is not her place. Go back to your cell, young woman.'

Serafina moves immediately in response. 'Ah!' Then stops. 'I . . . can't . . . I cannot move my hand. She is holding it too tight.'

It is true enough. Zuana can see it now. Where before the girl had hold of Magdalena's wrist searching for a pulse, now, suddenly, the old nun's hand has twisted to clasp hers back, claw-thin fingers, pressing so tight that they seem embedded into the younger woman's flesh, the worst pressure over the burn where the skin has been starting to rise.

'Aaaah!'

Serafina's pain and fright is apparent as the abbess moves across the cell towards her. Only as she does so, the figure on the bed starts to move too. Suddenly, it is all happening at once; even the smell in the air seems to be changing, the sweetness turning sour, as the old nun's face comes alive again.

'Hahaaahaha . . .' The laugh that has been held inside for so long is pouring out of her, high and girlish, full of pleasure and wonder, far too young for such a dry, wrinkled form.

Zuana tries to soothe her. 'It is all right. You are safe. You are here with us, Suora Magdalena.'

But her words are lost in the rolling moan that follows. The old woman with unexpected strength is trying to lift herself from the mattress yet she still has hold of Serafina's hand so cannot lever herself up. Zuana instinctively supports her until she is sitting upright, her body thin as a stick of wood. Her eyes blink hard in the gloom as if she is trying to expel some fleck of grit out of them and her mouth opens and closes like a fish, her lips making a dry slapping sound. Zuana lifts the jug carefully to her mouth and slowly she sips, coughs, gasps for breath, then drinks again. Water runs like spittle from her lips down her chin. Serafina, next to her, is whimpering slightly but whether from fear or from the powerful grip on her fingers it is hard to know.

'Suora Magdalena, can you hear me?' The abbess's voice is full and powerful, like the convent bell. 'Do you know where you are?'

The old woman seems to turn her head upward towards the speaker but she never makes it as far as Chiara's face. Because now she sees Serafina.

'Oh, oh, oh, my dear one, it is you.' The voice has returned to its fragile, cracked age now but the words are clear enough. 'Oh, oh, come closer.'

The girl throws a frightened glance at Zuana but moves forward anyway. Perhaps she has no option, for Magdalena's arm, a stick with a flap of crêpe flesh hanging off it, seems to have remarkable power. When she has Serafina close enough the old woman puts out her other hand and touches, almost caresses, the girl's cheek.

'Oh, welcome. Welcome child. I have heard you crying and I knew you would come. You are not to be sad. He is here. He has been waiting for you.'

Serafina looks to Zuana again, panic in her eyes. But there is something else too: a kind of wonder. How could there not be? Zuana nods slightly. The girl turns back to the old nun. And a great smile breaks out on the ruined face.

'Oh, don't be afraid – you must not be afraid.'

'Suora Magdalena!'

'He said I am to tell you that whatever comes, He is here and will take good care of you.'

'This is Madonna Chiara, your abbess, talking.'

'He will take good care of us all.' And she laughs again, the pearly, girlish sound echoing around the cell. 'For His love . . . oh, His love is boundless . . .'

'Can you hear me?'

It is clear Magdalena cannot. She sighs, her eyes closing as she finally loosens her grip. As Zuana helps her back on to the bed Serafina slides her hand away, but her eyes never leave the old woman's face.

Over their heads, Zuana and the abbess look at each other in the gloom.

Outside the bell starts to ring for Vespers.

FOURTEEN

It is only much later that Zuana comes to appreciate in full the power of the timing of that afternoon.

Certainly if there was a 'right' moment of the day for such a thing to happen it would have been at Vespers, since Vespers is the only office when the choir nuns can be heard, though never seen, by anyone who chooses to enter the public church. And as everyone knew, it was no ordinary Vespers that they sang that day either. As the feast of a virgin martyr, the service was marked by specific settings and prayers; indeed for those who knew their saints' calendar – and the city was full of them – the celebration of St Agnes was considered to be particularly affecting, so that devout men of business or great families at court with young daughters of the saint's age might make the journey especially that afternoon in order to be blessed by the heavenly sounds that flowed out through the grille behind the altar.

Even the weather played its part, for while the day had been foggy, miraculously, as the bell rang and the sisters started to make their way across the cloisters, the sky cleared, with a few rays of weak sunlight breaking through the clouds.

Then there was the impact of the afternoon's commotion on the choir sisters themselves.

Inside the cell, Letizia took her place by the old woman's pallet, and the abbess, the dispensary sister and the novice waited with her behind the closed door while the choir nuns passed into the chapel. Madonna Chiara's injunction to the three of them was instant and severe. 'What has taken place in here this afternoon is for Suora Magdalena and God alone to know. Is that understood? Any further mention of it to anyone apart from myself will bring down on the offender the strictest penance.'

But, as she no doubt knew, it was already a lost cause. Though the convent had been at work when it happened, there were those who claimed afterwards that they had heard the wild laughter, while others said they had followed the rushed footsteps through the cloisters, even down to one who, looking out from high windows, was sure she had spotted the open cell door.

All this certainty, though, only comes much later.

At the time, with the bells ringing out over the city and the nuns gathering in chapel, there is only a sense of slight confusion, as if something has happened to agitate the surface of the water, but no-one can tell what it is. With the doors shut in readiness for the beginning of the service, the nuns glance around them to see who, apart from the abbess, is missing.

This is the moment when Zuana and Serafina slip in quietly, heads down, eyes to the floor. As they enter, the girl grabs a breath, as if she might be about to cry, but her face is hidden from Zuana. The choir mistress, Suora Benedicta, is already seated at the small organ to the side from where she can both play and direct the singing and the curtain is pulled aside to reveal the great grille that runs along the length of the wall through which comes the soft glow of candlelight from the greater church beyond.

There are some convents where the nuns sing from a choir loft suspended over the nave of the church, so that sharp eyes might spot the odd movement or shaft of colour from below through the slits between the wood at their feet. But inside the choir stalls in Santa Caterina while they can see little they can hear everything – the shuffling of bodies, the clearing of throats, the odd raucous male cough or low chatter of voices. That evening they make out more unrest than usual: Santa Caterina's reputation and the fact that the city is still celebrating the d'Este wedding means the church is full, with many arriving early to find good seats and restless now for the service to begin.

From her place at the end of the second row Zuana tries to keep Serafina in her sight. The girl is in shock still. She is deathly pale and has not said a word since being freed from the grip of Suora Magdalena. Even before she had walked into the old nun's cell she would have been light-headed from the lack of food and sleep but now her disorientation is obvious. She stands stock still, staring straight out at everyone and no-one. Next to her, old Maria Lucia, she of the toxic breath, sits hunched over her breviary, her chin trembling in anticipation.

At last the abbess enters and quickly finds her place. She nods to Benedicta and they both rise, the body of nuns following them. The rustle of cloth alerts the rest of the church and beyond the grille the congregation quietens in readiness for the music.

Discounting the few sisters who are too simple or – in the case of Suora Lucrezia – too physically damaged to sing, some fifty earthly angels now stand waiting to bring glory to God, and perhaps a little to themselves. The diminutive figure of Benedicta raises then drops her head as the sign, and the voices lift into the air, the words of the order clean and clear, plunging the audience immediately into the drama of a young woman's martyrdom . . .

Blessed Agnes, in the middle of the flames,
spreading her hands wide, prays . . .

In the beat of silence that is her cue, the choir's best songbird, Eugenia, head held high, draws a breath, ready. But before she can open her mouth to let it out, the voice of Agnes herself, ripe with youth and sharp as a golden spear, soars up from the fire into the air and out through the grille.

O great father. Respected. Worshipped. Feared . . .

In the choir stalls there is an involuntary flick of heads towards the novice. Zuana registers a skewering in her stomach; though how far it is shock or pleasure she cannot tell. Serafina's face remains pale, her eyes are still focused somewhere in the middle distance. But she, or that other she that has been hidden for so long, is here now. The novice has found her voice.

Through the power of your great son,
I have escaped the threats of a sacrilegious tyrant.
I have crossed over filth of the flesh,
And lo — I am left undefiled.

Within the great equality of God's love, it is not considered healthy to pick out the single from the several, the particular thread from within the weave. The very purpose of convent life is to iron out the sense of the individual, to blend the one into the many and, from there, the many into the sublime oneness of God. And nowhere is that ideal more powerfully realised than in chapel, where the voices of the choir meld into one coherent, seamless sound, praising God and His infinite bounty.

There are, however, moments. And there are voices . . . And

when the two come together it can be impossible, even undesirable, to resist.

Behold, I come to you:

As the phrase dies away in preparation for the next, Zuana watches the abbess secure Eugenia's silence with a single glance; though the poor girl is so stunned that it is unlikely she would have tried to take back her place. She closes her half-open mouth and drops her eyes. Whatever lesson she is learning now is made more potent by the fact that, in that instant, even her humiliation is irrelevant.

You, my Lord whom I have loved,
Have sought, have longed for — always.

Many of those present will talk later of it as a small but perfect miracle. On both sides of the grille they will search for words to describe the sound of the voice they heard, likening it first to the concentrated sweetness of the honeycomb or warm grain inside the wood, then contradicting themselves to speak of the burning flash of a comet, the purity of ice, even the shining transparency of heavenly bodies. But those who will do it most justice will speak not of the voice itself but how it made them feel.

The old and the pious will speak of a piercing of their heart so that they found it hard to breathe; a penetration which, though painful, unleashed a flow of love like Christ's blood gushing under the centurion's spear, or the joy of the Virgin Madonna as the words of the angel Gabriel enter her breast. In contrast, the young will recall feeling it most powerfully in their gut, which is where another kind of love resides, though they will claim the arrow entered through the heart, and both young and old will, without noticing, hold their hands to their hearts while recalling the moment. And once they have tried to outdo each other in hyperbole they will sit back exhausted, quietly satisfied that their city is indeed a musical paradise, so much so that God sees fit to send new angels into its midst to guide its citizens on their way.

None of this word-spinning will mean much to Suora Benedicta. Though she might be a visionary in her composi- tions, she is also a choir mistress with a pragmatic understanding of the tools of her trade. The exuberant sweetness she has heard before (and can make good use of, for there can never be too much purity in a convent choir), but what she could never have predicted is how such a young body – still a girl's as much as a woman's – might produce a voice of such extraordinary range and control. How her lungs might hold so much within a single breath. How she might encompass so many registers, or move between them so effortlessly, betraying no hint of strain nor even the smallest of impurities with which the onset of men- struation can often infect the vocal cords. And then – most of all – how, when the choir reaches the new psalm settings in four or even six block parts, this single voice can know and travel between them all with equal assurance, though she can only have heard the notes once, at best twice, through half-closed win- dows. So that by the time the service ends, Benedicta is already halfway in her composition of the next, her mind filled with a voice that seems to be writing its own parts.

And meanwhile, what of Suora Zuana in all of this? Zuana, who remains as ignorant of the subtleties of vocal technique as she is impervious to the poetry of exaggeration. Zuana, who has been bred to observe and consider, to make sense of what her senses tell her. Except that everything that her senses tell her now seems wrong. In front of her she is seeing a young woman, apparently suffused with joy. She is hearing a voice singing its heart out to the glory of God and the joyful sacrifice of a virgin in the fires of martyrdoms. But who is she, this girl? How can such a transformation have taken place? How can the strong-willed, recalcitrant, rebellious, angry young woman that she knows – a figure of much power but dubious spirituality – have disappeared so entirely, to be replaced by this new creature: absorbed, distilled, so consumed by the music she is making that she seems not even to be aware that any change has taken place.

Surely at some level she must know what she is doing. What, in effect, she has already done.

The service moves triumphantly to its close. Yet as the last notes fade into silence – Serafina's voice now plaited into, though not lost within, others – no-one on either side of the grille moves.

The abbess, whose rising will mark the sign for others to do so, sits still in her seat. Around her the choir is caught, some looking down as they are instructed, others watching for the sign, a few staring more openly at the novice, who has dropped her hands and eyes and looks only at the floor.

The silence in the choir stall is matched by that in the body of the church. Not a sound can be heard through the grille now, no clearing of throats, no coughs nor whispers. The good citizens of Ferrara are either unable or unwilling to accept that the experience is over.

Then, out of the silence, comes a man's voice, clear and loud. A single word: 'Brava!'

The shock of it runs through them all, so that now the abbess is spurred into movement and quickly the others follow.

And the girl? Well, for a moment the girl does nothing, just stands staring at the floor. But as those around her start to move she lifts her head up and for a second her eyes meet Zuana's.

What is it the elder woman sees there? Exhilaration? Satisfaction? Even joy? Certainly. But also the unmistakable flash of triumph.

It is this last that Zuana registers most powerfully, for though the girl has reason to feel gratified by the impact she has made, she must surely also understand that she has pronounced her own life sentence. Because, whatever happens, they will never let her out now.

PART TWO

FIFTEEN

The smells from the bakery are almost overwhelming. It has been building up over the last few days, this assault on the senses, from when the first trays of ginger biscuits, followed by cakes and fresh herb breads, went into the ovens, releasing their yeasts and sugars through the cloisters. Some sisters have even confessed to salivating as they pass by the kitchens (winter meals can become sparse and repetitive), but their confession only makes others more aware of the sin in themselves, and impatience is the mildest of transgressions. They will all be allowed to taste the results soon enough.

In the kitchens, Suora Federica has been excused the more exhausting of the daily offices, as she and her cohort of nuns and converse struggle with the extra work needed to produce the specialities that will feed a small army of visitors. Packages are delivered to the gatehouse every other day and the chief conversa in charge of provisions is run ragged with journeys to and from the river storerooms to collect deliveries and further supplies. That very morning two barrels of wine have arrived from a new benefactor. One is to be opened and decanted, the other put into storage. The abbess has sanctioned the use of

Suora Ysbeta's private store of glasses. As a nun from one of the great families she has a passion for Murano glass as well as small dogs and came with a dowry chest full of it. There has been the annual discussion in chapter as to how far the uses of such luxuries might count as ostentation or even vanity, with the vote going – though less smoothly this year – in favour of the demands of hospitality. As a consolation to the novice mistress and her followers it is decided that the glasses will be used only to serve benefactors and the highest rank of visitors, and that should there be any breakages the convent will not be responsible for replacing them.

Soon the gilded goblets will be sitting next to full jugs of wine on the covered trestle tables along one side of the parlatorio. The room has been transformed: the small organ has been moved from the music chamber into one corner with two high-backed chairs placed near by for the lute and harp players and space for the choir. There are candles (beeswax of the highest grade, from the stores) on spiked stands, branches of evergreens with winter berries have been woven together with garlands of herbs across the ceiling, and fumigants in metal pomades hang suspended ready to be lit, the air already fragrant with their scents. The room gives off such an appearance of a great domestic salon that those sisters who entered the flock late enough to recall feast-day gatherings with their families are flooded with memories as they stand in the entrance and marvel.

One end of the refectory has been cordoned off ready for the construction of a platform stage upon which the martyrdom of St Caterina of Alexandria will be performed before a specially invited female audience, and a storeroom nearby has been opened to hold props and costumes. Some are being made by the nuns themselves, but the more exacting – doublets and hose for the emperor's courtiers, boots and swords for the nun soldiers and the wheel itself, which must appear solid only to be broken by divine intervention before St Caterina can be tied to it – have to be brought in from outside, courtesy of the nuns' families. Those sisters and novices involved can often be found during recreation walking briskly in the garden or around the cloisters reciting their lines, either to themselves or to one another. Santa Caterina herself will be played by Suora Perseveranza, whose habit of self-mortification does not prevent her from the pleasure of occasional performance, to which, everyone agrees, she brings a tender verisimilitude. In years past her portrayal of such shining saints have brought tears – and flowing donations – from many of the female benefactors who have seen them.

After a long spell of bitter cold the city has grown a little warmer, though not enough to drive off the mists. The change has come too late for Zuana's fingers, which are raw from mornings spent in the herb garden fixing hoods of rough hessian over her more vulnerable plants. While the collection of garlands and herbs and the making of the decorations and the fumigants are her responsibility too, she has been afforded some help with this, though not of the calibre of which she had grown accustomed over the last months.

With everything finally prepared, the sisters of Santa Caterina can look back and feel satisfied with their work, not least because the weeks behind them have been difficult in many ways, peppered with events that have brought sorrow and crisis as well as celebration. Events in which Zuana has found herself more affected than most.

It had started a few days after the Feast of Agnes, when the young sister Imbersaga, whose bleeding Zuana could not staunch, was finally taken by God. She had been growing weaker for some time, until one afternoon during Vespers she had fallen into unconsciousness. She had received extreme unction from Father Romero that evening after Compline (a heroic feat considering his sleeping patterns) and had died before Matins when the convent was at its stillest, while in Suora Umiliana's care.

When Zuana had come to relieve her fellow sister so she might get a few hours' sleep before the office, she had found her kneeling by the body, hands clasped and tears of joy streaming down her cheeks. With no words allowed or needed, the two women had knelt together side by side praying and keeping vigil until the bell called them to Matins. Zuana couldn't help but wonder at the depth of the novice mistress's devotion; no young nun could have asked for a more faithful companion for her last hours on earth.

Early next morning the body was cleansed and dressed in fresh robes and, after the rest of the convent had paid their respects, buried in a simple wooden coffin in the small cemetery at the back of the gardens. A mass was said for her, in which Serafina's voice brought more sense of God's grace than all of Father Romero's mumbled words, and her obituary, composed by the abbess and inscribed in perfect hand in the convent necrology by Suora Scholastica (whose own dramatic composition was already being memorised by half a dozen eager players), spoke of her chastity, obedience, humility and forbearance in the face of suffering.

As such it was almost identical to every entry before it, though no-one would suggest it was untruthful: at barely twenty-two years old Suora Imbersaga had not had a great deal of life in which to fall prey to temptation.

In her own records, however, Zuana is less forgiving, at least to herself, noting down the various compounds that had failed and suggesting a few others that might help if and when the same

symptoms should occur in others. If she had had more time perhaps . . . but she had not. She wonders if maybe she had been
wrong to concentrate on the womb, and if the location of the
pain might instead have indicated a tumour within the bladder or
the bowels, for she has come across such a case – too late now –
noted from a dissection done in Bologna. But in her limited
experience such tumours are the ailments of the old rather than
the young and anyway, whatever the cause, she will never know
for the secret had died with her. In contrast to Umiliana, whose
exultation remains a scalding memory, Zuana is left with a persistent, almost painful, disquiet, so that she gives herself the
penance of extra prayers to try to exculpate it.

Within a few days, however, another form of penance is visited on her, when a powerful infection slides into the convent, an
epidemic of wheezing and sneezing, followed by a high fever
and vomiting. Once in, it moves like water, with six choir nuns
and one conversa brought down by it in as many days. While
such maladies are common enough during winter, the virulence
of this one takes Zuana by surprise and to avoid further contagion she quarantines each afflicted nun to her cell, with only
herself and a nurse conversa to tend them while she searches for
remedies. Together they use cloths soaked in balm mint and
vinegar water to keep down the fever and a tonic of ragwort and
penny royal in wine to feed them when their stomachs have been
purged. By the time the first sufferers are on their feet again, a
further three sisters and a novice have fallen prey to it, and the
conversa is complaining of aches and fever flushes.

Zuana, who by then has barely slept for nights on end, asks for
a meeting with the abbess to request that she be granted more
help. Or at least to enquire as to whether the help she once had
might be returned to her.

SIXTEEN

Sometimes at night inside the cell she has to stop herself from dancing. He is here . . . He has come . . . They will find a way.

Though the pages of poems have not been returned to her, she knows the words – and his music for them – off by heart and when she twirls her body to the sounds inside her head she can feel the swish of soft petticoats beneath the serge and the silk of her hair, washed and brushed under her loosely tied scarf, sliding over her shoulders. With her chest unpacked now, the stone floor has grown softer and there is colour against the grey: the weave of the rug, the gold threads of the tablecloth, the glint of the silver candlesticks, the painted blues and scarlet within the Madonna's robes and the cherub-pink flesh of the baby on her lap in the small wood panel painting hung above her little table in the second chamber. Though the space is small, and even in daylight still half night, with the glow that comes from an extra candle the atmosphere is almost welcoming. Until you let your mind move to the walls and locked doors outside it.

But she no longer thinks of that. And she will not be mean with her good fortune, either. When she goes she will leave all this here for the next one; an altogether kinder legacy than vomit and death.

Much of this new comfort is thanks to her conversa. Two days after the feast of St Agnes, the malicious Augustina had been replaced by Candida, a sturdy young woman who knows her way around convent restrictions, and who for a small sum (or the equivalent in clothing or trinkets) can make a novice's life less bleak in so many ways: extra candles, special soap, even leftover delicacies from the kitchen, from which she takes her own cut before delivery. But Candida's finest gift is her hands, for though they are not those of a lady – too much scrubbing and washing for that – they have a gentle touch to them and sometimes, in the private hour before Compline, when she has finished brushing the river of Serafina's hair, she plays a little at arranging the locks, and her fingers move across Serafina's shoulders, sending a cascade of tiny shivers down her back. The first time it happens it lights a fluttery fire of memory in Serafina's belly, as much for the playful hands of her younger sister as for the wilder caresses of her imagination. The next night, when Candida stands behind her waiting, as if for further instructions, for an instant Serafina's mind goes to the gargoyle twins, who can often be spotted hand in hand and are rumoured to compensate for each other's deformities in the strangest of ways. The novice who told her that had a half-smile on her face as she did so, and as Serafina turns towards Candida now she registers something similar in her look and it makes her confused. Whatever sweetness she is being offered it would no doubt come at a price; and there are more important things for Serafina to spend her trinkets upon.

What she really wants from her, though, is impossible, for even corruption has its limits and Candida's influence, it seems, does not extend outside the gates. She cannot, for example, spirit lovesick young men inside under piles of laundry as the romance stories would have you believe, nor even redirect letters over the heads of the censor nuns who scrutinise and vet every communication coming in and out. This much Serafina has learned casually, while exchanging tall tales of convent gossip, since she has no way of knowing if the payment that has already changed hands between her and Candida has bought loyalty or only goods. But in among the prattle, small seeds of information fall which she hoards away for later consumption: the whereabouts of the chief conversa's cell (such is her status that it allows her a cell of her own outside the servants' dormitory), the hours she keeps in her busy work day and, most notably, the existence of her own set of keys to the river storeroom, which she carries with her almost constantly.

Though there is still a fast stream of excitement running inside her, so fast that it sometimes feels like panic, Serafina keeps it deeply buried, feeding off its energy. When she walks in the garden with other novices during recreation, the walls are still as high as they were but she no longer wants to scream or howl at them. Instead she uses the time to memorise the fastest short cut from her cell to the place by the walls from where she had thrown the first stone. Knowing he had received it, she now makes the journey there and back within the space of the night-watch rounds, dropping sprinklings of white pebbles from under her robes as she goes in the hope that it will make the route easier to spot in the dark.

It still makes her shake to think of how on that first night she lost her bearings trying to get back to the cloisters in time and was caught by the watch sister. It had been black as hell out there with all manner of noises and scratching in the under-growth, so that when she hit the tree root it felt as if something had grabbed her foot and her stumble had sent her sprawling into thick mud. For the next two days she had stunk of its filth and her own sweat as the walls of her cell squeezed in around her. Still, she would go through it again just to hear that trill of the bird whistle, followed by his dancing voice. Dear God, she had thought then she might die of that feeling, the wild erupting sweetness of it. By the time they had let her out she was terrified that he might not have found the message she had lobbed over into the dark, or have given up waiting. But if she could no longer hear him, then at least now he could hear her.

'*Behold I come to you, you whom I loved always.*'

And then came that single word echoing back through the chapel grille: 'Brava!'

It had been all she could do not to shout back to him: 'You have come. Oh you have come. We will find a way . . .'

Instead, though, she had put her head down and become a nun.

Oh, they must be so proud of her, of what they think they have achieved. She is proud of herself. The transformation is every-where: in the way she walks, eyes to the ground as if God were to be found in every flagstone, or the way she sits in chapter or refectory, shy as a young Madonna. But the best is how she behaves in chapel, for there is a whole world in this performance when you choose to savour it: the prostration before the crucifix, the stretch in her body, the cold stone through the warm cloth, fol-lowed by sitting, alert and straight, so straight that she even registers the indent of the slivered wood pictures of the choir stalls against her back. And then, depending on the hour of the office, the constantly shifting daylight on the frescoes – paintings of Christ as humble as he is divine; carrying children on his back across raging streams, helping souls to clamber out of their graves, even climbing up on to his own cross by way of a ladder. Though all these images have been around her, she has been too angry or wounded to have looked at them properly. Now they help her to quieten her mind, for she cannot sing well if she is elsewhere in her head and it is her voice that is buying her freedom.

It still amazes them. You can see it in their snatched glances, even in Suora Eugenia, whom she has displaced, and whose envy and fury rises off her like smoke. She would feel sorry for her – for she knows something of that turmoil – only there is no time. Well, she will get her place back soon enough.

And then there is the grille – that wall of braided iron between them and the outside world; so close and so far. She has flirted with its possibilities often; once she even went into the chapel during private prayer hour in the wild hope that he might be able to know what is going on in her mind and that very same moment be standing on the other side waiting for her . . . their thoughts then their fingers entwining through a lacework of metal. She had even sung a few notes to alert him but the sound had been huge and haunting in the empty space and she was ter- rified that if there was anyone there they might report her and she would be incarcerated again. And that she couldn't bear.

No, there will be no further punishment. She is a good girl now, as good as she was once bad; obedient, humble, sweet- natured. Of course they are still judging her, even when they pretend they are not. Suora Umiliana is by far the worst: '*There is no hiding place from His Divine Majesty. His gaze burns wood, breaks rock, melts iron.*' Even when, as happens sometimes, the pleasure of singing in chapel overwhelms everything, including for a moment her own dissemblance, Suora Umiliana's stare is still there when she surfaces, piercing straight into her. '*How easy is it then for Him to penetrate through human flesh to the spirit?*'

The choir mistress knows it, though, or rather hears it, for it is a knowing that moves through the ear not the eye; this sense of calm at the centre of one's being, stillness in the middle of a great wind. If she were asked to describe it she might say it was almost an absence of self; though not an ecstasy as such. Oh, no, not like that. Not like the corpse woman in her cell. Not like her at all . . .

Serafina tries not to think of that afternoon, because when she does her body goes hollow and her hand starts to throb as if the old woman's nails were still buried in her skin, piercing her palm, drawing enough blood so that when she had entered the chapel she had had to wipe it off on her robes for fear that someone might see it and think she had done damage to herself. In fact the wounds had healed fast, almost as fast as they came. But sometimes at night when the churning inside her is such that she cannot sleep, then she could swear she hears the mad old nun's voice seeping through the wall of the cell, talking to her, calling her name. 'Serafina, Serafina? Are you there? I knew you would come. He is here. He has been waiting for you.' And she sees those eyes again, fathoms deep with wonder, and feels the melting, the falling away inside herself. It sparks such panic in her that she has to put her fingers in her ears to stop it, as if it were some siren song pulling her on to the rocks for though she was witchold and half dead there had been an intensity and ardour – yes ardour – in that wizened face greater than that of the rest of them put together.

She would like to know more about her, understand what took place in that cell, but the abbess's imposed silence is law and she must be seen to obey her now. Even Suora Zuana will tell her nothing. Perhaps if they worked together still . . . but that is over too. Her voice is deemed too precious to be put at risk from the rank smells of distillation or the contagions of the flesh, especially as there is an influenza taking its toll within the choir. Suora Zuana looks so tired that she is almost asleep over her plate at meals. She imagines her, head bent over the crisp pages in candlelight, words and drawings blurring in front of her closing eyes as she searches for the right ingredients with which to stew up health again.

She thinks about it sometimes, that room, at moments almost misses its particular strangeness: the cold, the fire, the books, the smells, the taste of the dandelion tea, the spiced heat of the ginger balls and, in the middle, this even stranger woman, broad face and gnarled fingers, content inside her passion for it all, as if there was no world but this one and it was God himself rather than crows' eggs or boiled roots inside those fat little pots. Mad, certainly, but not without wonder, even comfort.

Still, better to be without it. She has no friends in this place, whatever they like to pretend, and the traps are everywhere. God knows there were times when Suora Zuana's caring was harder to bear than cruelty and though she may be crazy in some things she was sharp enough in others. When she had talked of the power of the night songbird, for instance . . . what if she had heard more than the song, if she knew more than she claimed? And that poem of the old nun with its rattling of the convent doors and the lover's voice outside. Maybe she had picked it deliberately, or made it up to draw some truth out of her? Even before the penance it had become harder to lie to her; she recalls moments when the temptation to confide had been like vomit rising in her throat and she had had to clamp her lips together not to let it out. How would it be if Zuana could see inside her now – understand what lay behind the excitement in the same way she had started nosing her way in behind the pain?

No. Better for them both to be alone. When the convent wakes up – as it will – to find her gone, she wouldn't want the blame to fall on the one person who has shown her kindness; the one who has, without knowing it, already given her much – though not yet all – of what she needs to get out.

She lifts up the mattress and slides her hands under until she locates the tear in the material. Inside, deep within the straw and padding, her fingers find a lump of material. She extracts it carefully. The petticoat silk is stained dark and oily. She unwraps it to reveal a roughly fashioned pad of waxy ointment, scooped from the pan when it was cool enough to be touched but not yet set too hard, and squirrelled away under her robes. In chapel the morning she had taken it, the smell of the rancid pork fat had been so strong she had been terrified someone would know, and she had had to press herself close to the gumless old bat with the vicious breath to cover up her own stink. Thank God, she has a new seat in chapel now, while the smell of the pork has faded as the ointment set harder.

Under the light she puts the pad on to the table and presses the nail of her index finger deep into it. The surface gives a little to take the imprint. When she lifts it off the shape of her nail is etched perfectly, even down to the slight ridge of skin around the cuticle. She rubs hard to make it smooth again. Then from under her shift she pulls out a silver medallion of the virgin on a chain around her neck. She takes it off and embeds it face-down into the ointment, pressing it heavily, equally on all sides. When she prises it loose the image of the metal face in the candlelight is clear, each line and the curve perfectly reproduced.

Thank God for the Bishop's pustules and the mad correspondences of figwort and pork fat. It can indeed cure all manner of things.

He is come. He is waiting. They will find a way . . .

SEVENTEEN

When Zuana meets the abbess in her chamber that afternoon it is the first time since Suora Magdalena's ecstasy that the two women have been alone together.

Inside the old nun's cell the routine of prayer and sleep has returned and she has been largely forgotten again. Whatever the initial excitement, the rumours of some kind of transcendence have been extinguished by the lack of firm facts plus the drama of Vespers and the death of Suora Imbersaga, with no less a figure than the abbess herself encouraging the distractions. Letizia still keeps her fed and watered as before and reports to Zuana that though she grows weaker, there are times when the old woman will close her eyes and rock to and fro, suffused with what seems like quiet joy, after which she often asks about the young novice and how it goes with her. But when Zuana visits, as often as her duties allow, there is no such excitement. Instead Magdalena lies silently on her pallet, her expression dreamy, as if she is only half present. Her flesh is now so paper-thin that Zuana is almost afraid to touch her in case bits of it might peel away in her hands. If the decision were hers she would move her to the infirmary now, for a soul so close to death deserves better care. She wonders if, when Suora Scholastica comes to inscribe this particular entry in the convent necrology, her life might warrant more or different words.

The abbess welcomes her in and seems pleased to see her. The formerly errant curls are now scooped back under the wimple but then she has hosted a number of eminent visitors recently and is always careful to fit her style to their differing expectations.

'I am glad you are come. I have been concerned that the work might be proving too much for you . . . I had wanted to see you earlier but the passing of Suora Imbersaga and the communication with her family took up my time, along with everything else. You did a fine job of tending her.'

'I did nothing except fail to stop the bleeding. It was Suora Umiliana who eased her passage into the light.'

'You are hard on yourself. You have also been managing an onslaught of fever. We are grateful to you for your dedication.'

'I would do it better if I had my assistant back.'

'I am sure. And I would be the first to send her to you if the demand from the choir mistress was not so great.'

'Does it take so long to learn a few psalm settings? She has an excellent memory.'

'You are very forthright today,' the abbess says mildly. 'Would you like to sit down? Or take a small refreshment of wine perhaps?' She gestures to a decanter that sits on the table, its ruby colour lit up by the firelight. 'It is from the Duke's own vineyard.'

'No. Thank you.' Zuana bows her head. 'I am sorry for my open tongue, Madonna abbess. My mind is somewhat beset by problems.'

'I am sure it is. And let me assure you if it were only Carnival I would give the novice back to you now, for you did a wondrous job with her.' She pours herself a glass, then holds it up before taking a sip, as if raising it in Zuana's praise. 'But as you know, after Carnival comes Lent and then Easter. We will have full churches for quite a while and Suora Benedicta is up all night scribbling.' She pauses. 'Sometimes I wonder if God has somehow singled Santa Caterina out – unworthy as we are – for special responsibilities: Suora Scholastica with her writings, Suora Benedicta with her passion for music, you with your pursuit of dispensary knowledge.'

It is a subtle reminder – which Zuana does not fail to register – that not every convent offers such freedoms. But while the words are humble they are also fat with pride. How could they not be? Following St Agnes' Vespers her chambers have been filled with visitors: relatives come to share the triumph (any accomplishment of the convent is also a success for the family that runs it), benefactors from the court, representation from the Bishop, even a wealthy father from Bologna who had been visiting friends during St Agnes' Feast and is thinking of where he might place his second daughter – a young girl whose voice, he assures her, is as sweet as her disposition. Then the letters start arriving, from other abbesses and more notably from her own brother in Rome, secretary to Cardinal Luigi d'Este, rich with church gossip and congratulations to his little sister for keeping such a wondrous songbird in hiding until the perfect moment for her debut. In this way, Santa Caterina has stolen a march on all the other convents around. With each appearance at Vespers the story grows. For a city that prides itself on its musical sophistication, the talk now is more of the simple wonder of God's instrument than of the novelty of men with no balls. And through all this, Madonna Chiara must keep her feet on the ground, though she must surely be allowed a little pleasure.

'While I appreciate your plight – and will, as soon as I can, find you another conversa to help with your nursing – my first duty must be to the interests of the convent. I cannot allow the novice to risk infection or wear herself out with other work as well as all the extra hours in the choir room.'

'And the interests of the convent are also the interests of the novice herself?'

Zuana intends this as a statement, though the question is there for both of them to hear. She surprises herself with her own forthrightness.

'Ah! I am indeed a blessed abbess. It seems as well as our great Bishop to watch over me, I have been given two other consciences to supervise my decisions. No less figures than the dispensary and the novice mistress.' While her tone is amused it does not preclude a certain tartness. 'I think, Suora Zuana, it might be better if you sat down after all. Please.'

Zuana does as she is ordered.

The abbess pours another glass of wine and hands it to her.

'It was sent explicitly for *all* the choir nuns of Santa Caterina, with the Duke's compliments. You may drink less of it at dinner if you feel unfairly honoured now.'

Zuana puts it to her lips. There is a flavour of rich berry underneath its smooth surface. How strange, she thinks, that it has taken the life of a nun to teach her such secrets of the grape; but then her father's knowledge of wine was as much about the remedies he mixed within it as a pleasure to be savoured in its own right.

'So. I wonder if your fears for the novice are the same as Suora Umiliana's. Is it the effects of pride on such a vulnerable young soul? Or perhaps the lack of time for proper prayer and instruction now that her choir duties are so demanding? Suora Umiliana is exercised by both. Though it is possible that neither of you appreciate the discipline that comes from using one's voice in chapel to sing the praises of the Lord. As our great St Augustine said, "To sing is to pray twice.""

Of course, Zuana has thought about this – how far her concern about the girl is born out of her own selfishness. For yes, she has missed her company. More than she had expected. More than she finds it easy to admit. But it is not only that. Watching from the outside, there is something about the girl herself, an almost fevered energy in the way she seems to hurl herself through each and every day – as amenable as she was once intransigent – which makes Zuana think of illness rather than health.

'It is not so much her singing that worries me as the sudden perfection of her behaviour.'

'Hmm. First she is too bad and now she is too good. Our novice mistress mistrusts her motives for starting to sing at all. She thinks she is using it as a way of gaining privilege and that underneath she still remains resistant to God's love. I have wanted to know for a while what you think.'

The wine has a slight metallic aftertaste to it. Zuana cannot tell whether it is pleasant or not. How much there is to note even in a single mouthful of liquid. One lifetime barely scratches the surface of experience.

'I think . . . I think she could have started singing earlier if that was the reason. She would have saved herself a lot of trouble.'

'So why did she choose to do so when she did?'

Zuana is silent. It is something to which she has given a good deal of thought over these last weeks, like the study of an ailment whose cause she is struggling to understand.

'Let me ask you another question. How far do you think your tutelage may have helped?'

She shakes her head. 'I simply taught her how to make lozenges and ointments.'

'Ah, Zuana, if you have the temerity to accuse your abbess of the sin of pride, then you would do well to address the mote of false modesty in your own eye first.' And now for the first time they smile. Sitting closer to her, Zuana can see the pull of sallow skin under her eyes and the furrows across her forehead. With all the triumph she is not without worries. 'It's clear that some kind of bond developed between you. I had wondered if perhaps she came to identify something of her own journey within yours.'

'Mine! Oh, no . . . I was never so . . . so accomplished. Or so eligible.'

'No, but you arrived with a similar anger and resistance.'

'Is that why you sent her to me?' she says quickly.

'I think you know why I sent her.' The reply is equally quick, almost brusque, in its tone. She gives an impatient shake of the head, as if to deny the inferred intimacy of the comment. 'A good nun learns as much as she teaches.'

Zuana drops her eyes to her hands, which are folded in her lap, the correct position for a choir nun when in the presence of her abbess. Behaviour. Order. Hierarchy. The power of obedience and humility. How many times must one learn the same lessons over and over again?

'I did what I could to show her how she might make a life here for herself, how resistance was . . .' She is lost for the word for a moment: futile – though it nudges around her tongue – will not do. '. . . was . . . fruitless. But I didn't expect . . . I mean that afternoon in Vespers I was as taken aback as anyone. Except for—' She stops . . .

'Except for what?'

'Nothing. It is a matter that is not to be discussed.'

'Ah! We are talking of Suora Magdalena?'

Zuana nods. Though she can make no sense of this, she has found herself returning to it: the look of awe in the girl's face as she watches the old nun's sublime joy; the way those talon-like fingers flick over and embed themselves in her flesh. And those words: 'He told me you would come.' As if the novice had in some way already been marked out by Him.

'Has she spoken to you about it?'

'We do not work together any more.'

'No, but you have seen each other.'

'Once.' Once, if one does not count the glances across the refectory table or the passing of one another in the cloisters.

'Suora Zuana, if you know something that I don't about what happened in Magdalena's cell that afternoon then I need you to tell me. Despite this new . . . humility, the girl is still highly strung and, while I thank God constantly for her new-found . . . energy towards life here, with Carnival coming the last thing we need is further trouble.'

'She did speak of Suora Magdalena when we met, yes.'

'What did she say?'

'She asked me who she was and why we could not talk of her outside that room. She was concerned that if it was indeed an ecstasy then people should know of it. I told her that all those who needed to – God and yourself – already did. And that it was our duty to obey your instructions.'

'It was well said.' The abbess smiles and leans over and refills Zuana's glass.

EIGHTEEN

While Zuana has answered the question honestly, as is her duty under the rules of obedience, she is aware that there are things she has not told. The fact is that the meeting between her and Serafina had not been an easy one, though how much that was to do with the girl and how much herself Zuana does not fully understand.

On the surface it had simply been another work hour in the dispensary, the task in hand being the finishing of the Bishop's lozenges. However, given that it had come the day after the drama of Suora Magdalena and Vespers, with Madonna Chiara already in strict conference with the choir and novice mistresses over the novice's future, they had both been aware that it might be their last together, at least for a while.

All morning the convent had been alight with excitement over the girl's voice. She had sung sublimely in both of the early offices, eyes bright, manner open, the transformation so complete as to be almost miraculous. Yet when Zuana had turned to find her standing in the doorway, the young woman who greeted her was reserved, almost shy, unsure how to behave, dropping her eyes as she came in quietly and took her place at the work bench.

The table had been laid out in readiness for the final stages of the lozenge making and initially neither of them referred at all to what had gone before, busying themselves instead with slicing the cooled treacle and fashioning it between their fingers into mouth-sized bits, which they then rolled in a sprinkling of sugar and flour to make them more palatable and stop them from sticking, ready for packing together in the rough wooden box.

They worked quickly and efficiently but whereas at other times the silence would have stilled them, now it felt messy with unspoken words. Zuana could not work out to whom they belonged, for though the girl was clearly nervous – edgy, almost skittish, as if her heart was beating too fast – she could feel a tension in herself, too. As the lumps of treacle grew into a hill of smooth sugared balls they caught each other's eye once or twice and the contact served to break the ice. It was Zuana who spoke first.

'So, you have found your voice at last.'

The girl's responding smile was small and hurried. 'Uuuh – I . . . yes' – the words half-swallowed.

'The convent's night songbird may be struggling with feelings of jealousy today.'

'Oh, the night songbird!' She laughed nervously. 'Singing to bring on the dawn, yes?' She ducked her head back to the treacle. 'You are right. I mean . . . I am grateful to you . . . for telling me to sing. It has eased my turmoil . . . helped me to find some peace being here.'

Though there was more agitation than peace in her as she said it.

'It had nothing to do with me. The Lord has worked within you. It is His love and His mercy that we should praise.'

'Yes . . . yes indeed,' she murmured, her fingers moving restlessly over the balls of treacle. For the first time Zuana found herself almost uncomfortable in the girl's presence. The realisation troubled her more than she cared to admit. How could it be that all the spitting fury and rebellion, all the pain and tears, were easier to bear than this new-found harmony? If indeed harmony was what she was feeling.

Zuana was fashioning some form of question that might go deeper without seeming to intrude when the girl spoke again.

'I . . . I need to ask you something.'

When she had used those same words less than twenty-four hours before they had found themselves in a jungle of fabulous animals and the poetry of disobedience. It already felt like a lifetime ago.

'That old woman in the cell. Who is she?'

But this Zuana was ready for. 'She is a humble nun intent on her journey to God.'

'So why is she hidden away as if in prison? And why did the abbess forbid us to speak of it?'

'I . . . I think that is for the abbess to know.'

'But what happened to her yesterday . . . the ecstasy? I mean it was an ecstasy – you said so yourself . . .'

Mindful as she must be now of Madonna Chiara's injunction, Zuana hesitated. 'She was transported in some way, yes.'

'Then shouldn't other people know about it?'

'The only ones who matter know already. As Madonna Chiara said, it is no-one's business but her own and God's.'

'But those things . . . that she said to me . . . I . . . I mean if she was in ecstasy, then . . .'

Of course. Who would not have been affected, alarmed even, by such prophetic testimony?

'Serafina, there is nothing to be frightened of. The things she said to you were full of love. Her own and God's. Of that I have no doubt. And neither should you.'

And for a second Zuana saw what she would swear was a look of anguish pass over the girl's face before she clenched her jaw (a gesture that recalled her rebelliousness) and gave her attention back to the worktop.

They returned to work, side by side, their hands moving swiftly over the table, cutting, rolling, finishing.

'I do feel . . . more loved.' The girl's voice was quiet but firm as she pushed another sugared ball towards the box. 'As if I am . . . am looked after.'

'Then let us pray that feeling continues. Thank Him for His infinite mercy.'

'I should thank you, too.' The words came out in a rush, though she kept her eyes fixed on the bench, her right hand palm-down on the wood. 'I mean for all that you have done. You have . . . well, you have been good to me.'

'I have done only my duty through God's love.'

'You say that – but I think you have done more than that.'

Zuana said nothing, for there was nothing to say. They stood silently, their hands close together, resting on the wood of the work bench. Tomorrow she would work here alone, the room her own domain again. The things she had grown used to over these last weeks – the girl's quickness and curiosity, the unpredictable, unexpected companionship that had developed between them – all this she would grow used to being without again. That is how it must be. She knows that.

The girl flexed her palm downwards so that her fingers splayed out across the wood. There was a dusting of flour on them at points where the treacle had stuck and acted as a glue. Despite the work they were still lovely, fine and tapered, the nails smooth and pink, with perfect pale crescent moons rising out from the cuticles. In contrast Zuana's own looked more like newly dug vegetable roots, thick and stained. Staring at them side by side, it made her think of the youthful moistness of the girl's cheeks as she had loosened her head scarf the first morning and the plump softness of her body as she had supported her from the floor to the bed that first night. Though there was less flesh to her now (an excess of emotion and the repetition of convent food had sculpted her more finely), she was still lovely. Yes, along with the club-footed and the squinty-eyed, Our Lord takes the most luscious young women into his care to keep them from the defilement of the world beyond . . . The spiritual treasure of virginity. The words of St Jerome came into her mind: 'If you walk laden with gold, you must beware of a robber. We struggle here on earth that elsewhere we may be crowned.' For those novices who enter yearning for God, it was an inspiring text. Though why Zuana should have alighted upon it now she did not quite understand.

Beside her, Serafina's breath flowed out like a fluttering sigh. Zuana glanced across at her, and as she did so she registered the girl's right hand moving again, rising slightly, then falling, the last three fingers coming to rest lightly on the back of her own.

Zuana snatched her hand back sharply, as if the touch had scalded her.

'Oh – I am sorry.' The girl's voice was light, surprised by her surprise. ' I . . . only wanted to show you . . . I mean—'

'Show me what?'

'What you have done for me. My hand. Where I hurt it yesterday on the treacle. See?'

And now Zuana was seeing. Or rather she wasn't. For there was nothing to see. The back of the girl's hand was clear, the skin smooth, no sign of a blister nor a mark of any kind.

'It's healed. See? No burn, nor even any marks where Suora Magdalena grabbed me with her nails. Your ointment is miraculous.'

'It is not meant for burns. I gave it to you to bring out the bruises from your penance.'

'Oh – but they are gone, too.' And the girl's face lit up, as if the healing had somehow gone deeper than her skin. 'Really. I am completely healed.'

But Zuana was not thinking of her ointment now. She was seeing instead the old woman's face, hearing that strange, pearly voice: 'He said I am to tell you that whatever comes, He is here and will take good care of you.'

Was the girl hearing it, too? Sweet Jesus, look after this child. Do not burden her with more than she can bear. Zuana, who was not prone to prayer creeping up on her unannounced, found herself suddenly unnerved.

'Come. There is no time for chatter,' she said roughly. 'You roll the last lozenges while I start packing them.'

If she felt rebuffed, the girl did nothing to show it; simply dropped her head and moved her hands back towards the treacle.

When the noon bell started to sound it was Serafina who left the bench first, washing her hands in the bowl in readiness for chapel and wiping them on her apron cloth before taking it off and putting it carefully back on the hook on the wall where it came from. Habit. Familiarity. It does not take long to establish itself.

'God be with you, Suora Zuana,' she said, bowing her head humbly and offering the customary sisterly greeting as if it was something she had done all her life, rather than the first time she had spontaneously used it.

'And with you, novice Serafina.'

They were now dismissed from each other's company. Yet she did not leave.

'I – I think I will be required at choir practice this afternoon.'

'Yes. I would think so, too. I wish you well with it.'

'I . . . I have a book to deliver back to you. On correspondences and remedies. You said I could borrow it, if you
remember. I shall bring it later if that is all right.'

Zuana nodded. The girl moved to the door. Then turned.

'It was most interesting . . . the book, I mean. I am sorry not
to learn more.'

And then she was gone, leaving Zuana glancing at the shelf for
the place where the volume had been and wondering why,
although she remembered making the offer, she could not
remember her taking it.

NINETEEN

'Suora Zuana?'

In her chambers, the abbess's voice is gentle now.

'Is all well with you?'

'What? Oh, yes, yes. I am sorry. My mind is full at the moment.'

'And you are weary. I can see that. Do you feel fever or aches within your body?'

'No. Thank you. I am quite well. Just tired.'

'Are you sure?'

'Yes.'

'Good. That is good. We need you well while others are ailing.' She stops. 'I wonder if being so close to Suora Magdalena's . . . transportation may have affected you, too, a little?'

'Me? No, no . . . well, at the time perhaps. Her ecstasy was very . . . profound.'

'Indeed. Such things are part of the marvellous warp and weave of convent life. I think of the way Suora Agnesina is so moved by Matins sometimes,' she says briskly, as if both occurrences were as ordinary as another delivery of salt.

Zuana says nothing. To her mind the two women are oceans apart – and when the abbess had been simply Sister Maria Chiara she would surely have thought the same thing.

'And Suora Magdalena herself? How is she now?'

'I think . . . I believe she is dying.' Zuana pauses, seeing the old woman's rheumy eyes and face, the skin like a dried-up river bed. Well, it is what she thinks, so she might as well say it . . . 'I would like to move her to the dispensary. She would be more comfortable there.'

'As always, your charity towards her is admirable. However, as you know, it is Magdalena's own wish that she remain segregated, and in that she is still supported by her abbess.'

The sudden sharpness of her tone takes Zuana by surprise. She must remember to ask forgiveness within her prayers for the implied disobedience. She straightens her back and feels a singing ache move through the left side of her body and down one leg. Ah, now the idea of illness has been planted it seems she is experiencing it, too. It is interesting how the mind plays such tricks sometimes, making the body feel things that it has no business to feel. Her father would have things to say on this subject if she could find more time to spend with him . . . Perhaps that explains some of the weariness and loss she is feeling – since the arrival of the novice everything in her life, even the comfort of her father's presence, has been subject to change.

The abbess is looking at her carefully. 'You find me hard on Suora Magdalena.'

'I . . . I do not think about it.' Now she must note the fault of lying as well. Some days it seems there are no thoughts that don't contain the seed of an offence. Even the one that follows: that she is wasting her time sitting here discussing things she cannot change when there is so much she should be doing outside. She pulls herself back into the moment. 'Perhaps . . . well, yes, I do find it strange. I mean whatever happened in the past was a long time ago and she seems so . . .' – she gropes for the words – 'harmless now.'

Madonna Chiara puts her glass down carefully on the small table by the fire, then brings her palms together, lifting up her hands until the tips of her fingers reach her lips. In any other of Santa Caterina's nuns Zuana would be reading prayer now but with her abbess she knows better. She watches as the thoughts – whatever they are – clarify themselves.

'There is a further chapter to the story of Suora Magdalena that you do not know. Indeed there is no reason why you should since it happened long before you arrived, but it might help to know it now. Some years ago she became briefly powerful again in the convent. The story is that that all stopped when she was young and the second Duke Ercole died, and certainly no-one from the court visited her after that time and for some years she was confined to her cell. However, when all the fuss had died down and she had grown well enough – for despite all her fasting she was still a strong woman – she began to join in convent life again and the abbess of the time, a good and humble soul, did not have the heart to stop her.

'After some months, it seems that she began to suffer fits again – what appeared to be paralyses of holiness, not unlike her state in the cell. And once or twice in chapel – always at Matins, it seems – her hands and feet would start to bleed. In the middle of the service she would open her palms and there would be blood, dripping out from wounds that no-one could see. Those who witnessed it said she never made a sound, simply stood with tears rolling down her face. She would say nothing, ask for no help, only go back to her cell and close the door.'

Now Zuana is no longer fretting to be at her work, for this is indeed a convent secret she has not heard before.

'Of course it caused a stir. How could it not? Especially with the novices. They were most taken. Even the confessor of the time was affected, but then he was a very simple fellow. Anyway, news got out through the parlatorio and people started to talk about how Duke Ercole's humble little bird had started to sing and that Santa Caterina was housing a living saint again.'

'When was this?'

'When? The spring and summer of 1540, I believe.'

'1540? But you were here by then. You must have seen it for yourself . . .'

'The convent was only my school then, not yet my home, and the nuns who taught us were forbidden to speak of it. No, the things I am telling you I did not learn until many years later.'

Nonetheless she would surely have noticed something. Such drama would have played havoc with convent discipline and the clever ones always sense it. Zuana has learned to spot them over the years as they trip along behind the choir nun on the way to their classroom: the little ones whose curiosity is greater than the rules, their faces round and shiny as bubbles, mischief and good-ness at war, the outcome as yet undecided. Oh yes, she would have known something.

'The date will mean nothing to you now but it was a disas-trous time for such a thing to happen. The Duke's French wife, Renata, was causing a scandal at the court with her heretical sympathies. There were apostates eating at her table and stories that she had even given refuge to the arch-heretic John Calvin. The great Church council was meeting again at Trent and the rumour was that the inquisition was on its way to Ferrara. An uneducated peasant woman like Magdalena becoming a conduit to God again without the proper tutelage of the Church could only bring the city the worst sort of attention at such a time.'

'What happened?'

'After some . . . discussion within the convent, the old abbess — who unfortunately had a sister at court inside Renata's entourage — was removed and a new one, Madonna Leonora, appointed. With help from the Bishop a more exacting confessor was brought in and it was decided that it would be better for all if Suora Magdalena was returned to the confines of her cell again.'

Returned to the confines of her cell. In effect walled up within the walls. How had it taken place? Had she protested, howled, hammered on the door? Or simply curled up on her pallet and turned her face to God? Even if He had been there to welcome her, the image sends a shudder down Zuana's spine.

'So it was not her own decision. She was imprisoned.'

'No . . .' The abbess hesitates. 'She was confined to her cell. And everyone — herself included — accepted it, because for the good of the convent it was better that way.' She pauses. 'It is . . . noticeable that since then, without an audience, she has again remained without stigmata or any regular ecstasies.'

'You are saying she is a fraud?'

'No.' She shakes her head impatiently, as if this whole conversation is unsatisfactory in its use of language. 'Though when she was younger it is true that she was accused of that. No, I am simply saying how it has been. Only God knows what is taking place within her.'

But while that is sound enough, Zuana also knows what she saw. And a bird-boned old woman with skin like over-rolled pastry should not have the strength to manacle a strong young woman with her grasp, let alone be so transported that she allows flies to walk over her eyeballs.

'The story I have told you was only fully explained to me four years ago when I was elected abbess and my duty to the convent with regard to Suora Magdalena was also made clear to me.'

Your duty to the convent . . . Zuana thinks. But also to your family. For what the abbess does not say – because they both know it, anyway, as does every other choir sister with half a brain – is that those same tumultuous years of the early 1540s had also been ones of shifting allegiances within Santa Caterina, and the appointment of Madonna Leonora to the position of abbess had seen the power returning to Madonna Chiara's family – where, despite graduations of opposition, it has remained ever since.

'I see.'

'So, if she is indeed dying then as infirmary mistress you can perhaps find other ways of caring for her within these rules.'

'And what if . . .' She trails away.

'What if?'

Zuana hesitates. 'What if God really is talking through her?'

'Then He would do well to find other means,' the abbess says quietly. 'Though you are not the most holy sister in Santa Caterina, Zuana, you are certainly one of the more astute. This is not gossip I am sharing with you. Nor even old history. I am telling you these things now because once again we are voyaging in stormy waters.'

'But . . . but I thought the worst was passed. The Duchess Renata is long returned to France, we have a new duke, a new pope and the inquisition has moved on. Surely the city is out of danger now?'

'The reprieve is temporary. Our new Holy Father still has his eye on Ferrara. Without a legitimate heir the city will return to the Papal States at the Duke's death, though God willing that will not happen. But there is a more immediate threat. You will know among the final decrees passed by the council at Trent was one directed at convents to purge them of any impurities or scandals by enclosing all nuns, regardless of their order or status.'

'Yes, but that doesn't affect us. As Benedictines we are an enclosed order already.'

'That is true. However, it seems that there are meanings and meanings of the word "enclosed". And what is becoming clear is that the decree was passed so quickly – some might say deliberately so – that it is a blunt sword, which, if wielded equally bluntly, could change all our lives.'

Zuana is silent. For most nuns the inner workings of Church politics hold more twists than a knotted intestine and there is always another piece of gossip sliding in over the walls, the next more scandalous than the last. Which is where a brother in the Church proves more reliable – and more useful – than any mystic in a cell.

'I don't understand. What do you mean?'

'I mean that within that idea of enclosure the decree empowers bishops – should they see fit – to limit or close down almost all contacts between convents and the outside world. It means that they can, if they so choose, stop plays or concerts, cut down the number of visits or visitors, sever trade connections with the outside world so that we become dependent on charity rather than our business endeavours. There is even talk that letter writing should be restricted as "not conducive to the tranquillity of our state".' She pauses. 'It does not take much to imagine the impact of such a decree upon us here.'

Except she is wrong – to imagine Santa Caterina so changed, so shrunken, so constricted, is surely impossible. 'But . . . but how can they do that? It is against the understanding on which women entered.'

'I think that when faced with the fear of heresy such "understanding" was of little interest to the good cardinals and bishops who worked at Trent,' the abbess says tartly. 'However, a decree is only words on a piece of paper until it is implemented, and not all church officials are so stoked with the fire. For now, at least, Ferrara's own bishop is open to the entreaties of the city's great families, and is more liable to execute the reforms in the spirit than in the letter. But to make sure of that we in turn must be seen to be above reproach, avoiding the scrutiny of those who would destroy in order to purify.'

Now, of course, Zuana understands it all better: the subtle changes in atmosphere in the convent over these last months; the abbess's work to secure even bigger dowries to push the balance books into credit; the insistence on getting the novice settled and singing as fast as possible; the damping down of the more liberal faction in chapter, while holding Umiliana's fierce fire in equal check. And now the blanket suppression of gossip concerning an ecstatic Magdalena . . .

It has always been impressive to Zuana, this sharpness of Chiara's when it comes to the balance between the work of God and the work of man, especially when as an unwilling novice she had found it hard to disentangle the holiness from the hypocrisy of convent life. If she is in some ways the product of her father's teaching, then surely the abbess's talents, too, have been bred in the bone. The names of Chiara's ancestors run through the history of Santa Caterina like a rich seam of gold in the earth: women of shrewdness and distinction, perpetuating the family influence through a convent rather than children. The only question is — and it is one that Zuana has asked herself before without ever putting it into words — were such a woman to find herself having to choose between God and the power of family, which one would call loudest?

'It will, I am sure, be clear to you now how it is wonderful for us to be offering the city a young virgin songbird. The re-emergence of a living saint, however, having ecstasies with no proper confessor to control her, would be another thing entirely.'

She pauses before picking up her glass from the table. 'I hope that lays to rest any worries you might have in this matter.'

God versus family. It seems Zuana has the answer to her question. Perhaps it is not surprising that the realisation makes her feel a little feverish.

By the time she arrives back in the infirmary the morning work hour is almost finished. The mist seems to have found its way inside today as the room is gloomier than usual. She glances towards Imbersaga's empty bed and for a moment she is back in the still centre of that night, the young woman's face smooth as wax now that the pain has left, with Suora Umiliana's vibrant devotion all around her, spinning sorrow into joy. Suora Umiliana . . . How would she feel if the convent were to be purged according to the letter of the decree? More at home than most of them, no doubt. And what then of Suora Magdalena? If Umiliana were abbess now would she be so acquiescent in her imprisonment? Ah, these are not questions you are called upon to answer, Zuana, she says to herself firmly. As dispensary sister your calling is to care for the sick and that is what you will do.

She looks around the room. There are five beds empty now. Perhaps those suffering from the infection would be better tended here, where she could watch them more continually. But what if they infected the others? Three of the four remaining old women will probably die of natural causes soon enough – they are asleep most of the time, anyway – and even Suora Clementia seems to be fading. With the arrival of the pestilence Zuana has had to keep her restrained to prevent her wandering the cloisters all hours of the day and night, and the old nun has taken it hard. She spends most of the time now muttering into her bedclothes but as Zuana passes she raises herself up, suddenly agitated, trying to get off the bed.

'Oh, you are back. The angel of the gardens is waiting for you. She is with us again,' she says, waving her arms in the direction of the dispensary, straining against the straps around her chest.

'Shhh. There is no need to shout. I can hear you well enough.'

'No – but I think she is wounded. She came in so quietly. Her wings must be broken. You must let her fly again. We need her to keep us safe at night.' Since the restraints went on, her mind has been fracturing into even smaller pieces.

'Don't worry.' Zuana is by her now, gently moving her down on to the bed. 'There are angels enough already to guard over you.'

'No, look. There! I told you she had come. See – see – my night angel is returned.'

Zuana turns now in time to see Serafina coming out of the dispensary door, her newly washed head scarf a white halo against her head. An angel with broken wings? Hardly. But a novice with broken rules, certainly.

'What are you doing here?'

'Oh, oh . . . I have been waiting for you. I looked everywhere but no-one knew where you were.' She pauses. 'I . . . I brought you back the book I borrowed. I . . . I wasn't sure where to put it so I left it on the work bench.'

'You should never have gone in there on your own. You are no longer working with me and it is strictly against the rules.'

'Oh – I'm sorry. I didn't know . . . Suora Clementia said it would be in order.'

And the girl smiles now at the old woman, who waves back happily, madly. 'The angel – I told you – the angel is returned to us.'

'Oh, be quiet, sister. You will upset the others,' Zuana says tersely. 'And you . . .' – she nods at Serafina – 'I will speak to you inside.'

With the door closed, Zuana casts a quick glance around the room. Everything seems in its place, apart from the book, which is on the worktop. Clementia's celebration continues in muted tones through the wood behind them.

'What did you say to her?'

'Nothing. Nothing, I swear. I thought she was sleeping so I came in quietly, but then she woke up.'

'Why are you here, anyway? You should be in choir.'

'Suora Benedicta let us go early. She is working with the lute players on some new arrangements. She is very excited by them.'

So excited that she, too, thinks nothing of bending the rules. 'In which case you should have gone back to your cell.'

'I am sorry. Please – I meant no harm. I told you. I just brought back the book. I thought you might need it now.'

Zuana stares at her. Ten weeks ago she did not even know of the existence of this young woman. She worked alone amid her plants and her remedies, and kept her thoughts, such as they were, to herself. But now her whole life, even that of the convent, it seems, is full of her, as if the journey of this single novice is somehow a test in which they must all participate.

'The dispensary is out of bounds to everyone but myself. What you have done is a reportable offence. You could find yourself with grave penance upon you again.'

'Then you must report me for it,' she says quietly, the slightest of tremors in her voice. They stand for a few seconds in silence. 'I know I did wrong but . . . I mean . . . I also came because I wanted to ask if I could help. So many people are ill now. I know there is just you and the conversa, and you cannot do it all alone. I could tend them with you. You have taught me something of fevers and vomiting.'

Zuana sighs. 'It is charitable of you to think such things—'

'No, it isn't charity. Well, I mean, I hope it is. But you helped me. Now I would like to help you.'

If I felt better would this be easier? Zuana thinks. What am I do to with her? What is for the best?

'I . . . I wondered if you had thought of using cocciniglia?'

'What?'

'The dye. We talked of it, remember? About its powers. Wasn't that one of the things you said? That as well as turning the world red it could be used to break fevers.'

'You have a remarkable memory, Serafina.'

The girl bows her head. 'The things you said interested me. Is it a good idea?'

'No, it is . . . it is an untried remedy. But I thank you for the thought. You have the makings of a good dispensary assistant.'

There is the beat of a pause before Serafina looks up and says, 'I wondered if you might have asked for me again.'

Only now Zuana is visibly taken aback by the pride implicit in the comment.

'Enough! Your presence is required in chapel. That is the abbess's decision. And you are her novice.'

The girl drops her head again. 'I am sorry. I just . . . well, I do not understand why but . . . but I miss it here.'

'I am sure Suora Umiliana will be able to help you with that.' She takes a breath. 'If you are lucky you will get back to your cell before the bell for Sext.'

The novice's eyes slip upwards. 'Does that mean you won't report me? I really didn't mean any harm.'

Zuana closes her eyes with impatience. She thinks back to the madrigals in the girl's chest and her unbidden arrival in Suora Magdalena's cell. There are those who would say that ignoring the transgression of others is a transgression in oneself. 'Just go now. Go.'

The girl does not need telling again. Zuana hears the door closing behind her.

In heaven, they say, the body of a saved soul is so pure and with powers so alien to those on earth that not only can it travel faster than lightning across the sky but its senses are so heightened, so crystal-clear, that it can hear the beat of a bird's wing a hundred miles away and see through the densest of forms as if they were made of air itself. It is almost a shame, then, that Zuana is still mortal. For it means that she does not hear the noisy sigh of relief that Serafina blows from her lips as she closes the door behind her, or see that under her robe her right hand is clasped over a bottle of dark liquid.

As she moves through the infirmary, Clementia calls out plaintively to this unlikely angel, who passes her by without even a sideways glance.

TWENTY

Ah! She can barely breathe with the thumping in her chest. Her chest and her head. She runs her fingers over the rim of the bottle under her robe to make sure the stopper is still in place. It would not do to be leaking poppy syrup in her wake.

This is not how she had planned it. She had intended to decant some of the liquid into another vial so as not to leave a gap on the shelves but she could not find any empty ones. There had to be a store of them somewhere but for the life of her she could not remember Zuana ever using it, so frugal is she with all her supplies. As it was, when she heard the voices outside she had barely had enough time to rearrange the other bottles and slide it into her pocket before propelling herself out of the door.

She had not expected Zuana back before Sext. The spreading of the illness was disrupting the patterns of the convent and when she had seen her go into the abbess's chambers after breakfast she had known she would not find a better time. After Benedicta had dismissed them early (that much of the story was true — the choir mistress has indeed been overflowing with new notes, so many that it is hard even for her to follow them) she had noticed that the shutters were still drawn on the outer chamber, which meant they were still in conference.

How close . . . She swallows to get her saliva back. She is out of the infirmary now, moving back into the cloister courtyard. She remains so agitated that it is hard to know whether she is relieved or still scared. What might have happened had she not heard Clementia warbling about her angels and Zuana's voice answering does not bear thinking about. She must be more careful. But then she had not foreseen the time it had taken to get past the crazy one, who had heard her even though she had moved on tiptoe.

'Oh, it's you. Where have you been? How is it out in the night? Is the holy army gathered yet?' Such a river of nonsense she spouted . . . 'I cannot count them any more, so you must do it for me.'

As she spoke she had yanked against the restraints like some lunatic shackled to a prison wall. See – see what happens when they keep you against your will: eventually the mind curdles, sprouting fancies like mould on old cheese. But they will not keep her. Not for a moment longer than she can help. Once she has the keys and they agree a plan she will be away from here. However great a scandal she unleashes. And no-one will stop her. Not even Suora Zuana . . .

That is the only worry now: how much she knows . . . The rest of them she can fool. Even Suora Umiliana seems to have stopped picking on her, so intent is she on the welfare of the rest of her flock now that the fever of illness as well as Carnival is in the air. But Zuana . . .

'What are you doing here?'

She sees again her face as she confronts her coming out of the room. She had been so fierce. Had she somehow guessed that she had not come back only to deliver the book? What if she had known she was lying? What if she could smell the syrup leaking out of the bottle, or see its shape through the folds of her cloth?

At least the threat of it had made her fight back . . .

'I came because I wanted to ask if I could help.'

Zuana had believed her then. Or if she hadn't, she had wanted to enough to let the suspicion go. And she'd been right. Though it had been born of cunning it was not without feeling. Serafina would have helped her if she could (*her*, not the others – she couldn't care a fig about them) because it was clear she was not well. She had wanted to offer to make her some dandelion tea, to sit down with her and watch the draught warm its way into her vital spirits while they talked of possible remedies for the contagion.

'Just go now. Go.'

It was as if Zuana had almost been frightened of her. She knew then that she had won. That she would not report her. There would be no penance. Surely God is on her side after all. Somewhere He has understood how unfairly she has been treated and how she deserves to be free.

She sings to herself quietly to calm the thumping in her chest. Her head is full of new music now: lines of prayer that swoop and soar like evening swifts, their phrases full and lovely as any madrigal. When she is alone she can still hear the other parts in her mind, rising, fading, joining, curling around her own. Never in her life has she been inside so many voices before, and it surprises her sometimes how much it calms and yet excites at the same time. There are moments after Vespers when if she were not incarcerated she might feel almost satisfied; when she can almost imagine how it must be for Suora Benedicta, spending every moment of her life pulling melodies out of her head. Oh, to so live for music. She cannot wait to see his face when she sings for him again, for there are things she has learned here that not even he could teach her.

Inside her cell, with the door closed behind her, she takes out the bottle from her robe and turns over the mattress to locate the hiding place.

Her cunning in such things amazes even herself. She has gone through it all a thousand times. How, when, where . . . If someone were to ask her now she might almost say she was enjoying herself, for as a child she always liked best those bits of learning that could be applied rather than simply memorised. 'You have the makings of a good dispensary assistant.' That is what Zuana had said to her just now. Well, perhaps she does . . . But she is bound for greater things. What they are she cannot quite imagine, for some days there is barely time to think of that – of him – at all, she is so full of it; the planning, the preparations.

At night, to blot out the voice of Magdalena, she tries to imagine herself out of here. She gets as far as a room (Ferrara beyond the convent walls is an unknown city to her), not as rich as her father's house, but comfortable enough, with a fire in the grate and musical instruments all around and she and he in each other's arms, the music they have been making suddenly stopped by kisses. She tries to imagine his mouth, lips soft like the inside of a ripe plum, and to find it again she brings her own open lips to the back of her hand, feeling the wet heat of her own saliva, the probe of her tongue, the ridge of teeth pulling playfully at her own skin. It brings with it a pinching in her gut that leaves her slightly breathless. In her mind their embrace is so close that she cannot see his features and she has to step back to try to reacquaint herself with his face, only the image of him remains blurred so that she feels a twinge of disappointment, almost a sense of shame, which unnerves her a little.

Never mind. Soon it will be different. Soon she will see his dear face again and remember why she loves him so.

She has made her plan. The best time will be during Carnival. With so much distraction and the excitement of performance they will have too much on their hands to police the comings and goings of a single – and now radiantly obedient – novice. And with all the activity revolving around the cloisters and the parlatorio – she has thought this through, step by step – no-one would be even thinking of the storehouse by the river, where on the other side a boat could surely loiter in the darkness without causing suspicion.

But for him to come in or for her to go out, separately or together, they will have to get through two sets of doors: one from the river to the storeroom and another from the storeroom into the convent. And for that she needs copies of the keys. Here lies the next challenge. Apart from the master keys held by the abbess there are two sets. The first, kept by the cellulare, is impossible; Suora Federica has a face to match the rock in her soul and everyone knows she wears the keys next to her skin day and night. However, the gossip is that the chief conversa is less amenable to the imprint of sharp metal between her breasts and so sleeps with her duplicate set under her bolster instead. Although the story has it that, like all good dragons, she sleeps lightly to protect her treasure.

In which case she would no doubt appreciate a good night's rest – a touch of that same relief as is sometimes generously offered to those on their way to the gallows, though it would provoke dreams that would torment them further should they ever have the good fortune to wake up again. It is not easy, even with the poppy syrup in her hands, for she has to find an innocent way to administer it. Candida has the wherewithal but she is too savvy for her own skin to take on something that would almost certainly end with her exposure. No, there has to be another way.

She slips the vial through the tear into the mattress, next to where the wax block is already nestling amid the horsehair and straw.

The bell for Sext sounds.

TWENTY-ONE

Perhaps if Zuana had had more time. With time she might have thought further about the abbess's story. With time she would have checked the supplies and samples in her room more rigorously. But a few minutes later the bell for Sext sounds, and between prayer and work and more prayer sometimes there is simply not enough time . . .

Over the next twenty-four hours the malady spreads further, strengthening as it goes, and in one of the infected sisters the fever becomes dangerously high. With the convent concert and play only a few weeks away there is a growing concern that Santa Caterina will be too ill to participate or – more importantly – to entertain and impress others.

The next morning's work hour finds Zuana in the dispensary sucking on a wad of ginger root to counteract the nausea that is rising in her stomach and ignoring the way her head is burning. She is ill, that is clear enough. But she is not yet incapacitated. Either the contagion will prove too strong for her or she will resist it. There is no point wasting time wondering which it will be. It is more important that she finds a way to fight back.

She has seen all the symptoms before in varying computations, the rhythm and severity transmuting over the years. One winter such an infection might come early, moving like a fast wind across a field, bending but not breaking any of the crop. Another year it might wait, feeding off the damp and fog until it is fat with fetid water, and affecting the oldest or those with moist humours worst, drowning more than a few in their own phlegm – only to be replaced next year by one that favours heat rather than water, burning up rather than pulling down.

'Remember, it is always best to try to contain rather than rely on curing, since by the time you have found a treatment that works the malady has often done its worst.' During his lifetime her father had kept notes through the most virulent outbreaks, comparing the ages and constitutions of those who died against those of the ones who survived.

'That is all very well, but once started it is easier said than done,' Zuana murmurs as she mixes up another batch of mint and rue vinegar water for the fever.

He had found that those people who nursed others – mothers, doctors, priests – were often most affected, which was not so surprising, for as well as their proximity it could be that God chose to take to Him the kindest and therefore those He loved best. Except that He also took at least as many sinners as would-be saints. While some resisted with tonics, others remained healthy without, as if they held the cure already within themselves. Then there were the ones who were not helped at all, even when they took anything and everything available.

As to the causes, well, the answers were as plentiful as the contagions. In his last years he had been drawn to the theory (which, like many, was built on an ancient one) of a physician colleague in Verona who argued that such diseases travelled by means of tiny malevolent seeds in the air that sat inside clothing and materials and, having entered the body, attacked and overcame the healthy seeds they found there, turning them into an enemy force within. Yet if they were so small as to be invisible how could any doctor tell where they were hiding? Why were some more dangerous than others? And how, short of burning everything, even the air itself, could we destroy them? To the lack of answers he had brought only more questions. In the end, the outcome was the same: if it was not actually the plague or the pox, whatever it was eventually moved on, only to be replaced by something the next year, then another, not entirely unlike it, two years after.

In some ways Zuana is lucky to be kept so busy, for if she were not she might find herself thinking of that winter, sixteen years ago, when her own life had started to unravel. The weather itself had been unusual that year, mild right into the beginning of February, and the infection, when he contracted it, had seemed benign enough, though he was old by then – over seventy – and already no longer quite as boundless in his energy. He had sneezed and wheezed, then turned hot and cold, but after two days in bed with a fever, which she had treated according to his instruction, he had got up again, declaring himself to be cured and with the appetite of a horse.

They had dined at table – he had had broth, roasted meat and a bottle of good Trebbiano wine – and they were sitting together by the fire companionably reading as was their habit. He was studying one of the recently arrived volumes of Vesalius, as he often did those days, and was deeply absorbed.

When it had happened it had been so quick that she could barely remember it. She had heard a fast intake of breath, as if he had come across something that annoyed or amazed him – recently he was as much in dialogue with his younger colleague's findings as he had first been in awe of them. She had looked up to see or ask what it was that had incensed him in time to register a frown on his face as his head slumped down on to his chest. For a second it seemed as if he had simply fallen asleep, as he did sometimes those days after a good dinner, but then, slowly – so slowly that it seemed as if time itself might have stilled to mark the event – he had leaned to one side and keeled over on to the floor, his hand sliding off the book heavily enough to tear the page as it went.

She had got to him almost as he hit the ground, screaming out for the servants and trying to raise him up. She had done all that he taught her: loosening his collar, calling his name, rolling him on to his side – though his body was as heavy and loose as a great sack of grain – and pouring water from the jug into his slack, half-open mouth. But already it felt as if there was nothing there. He, her father, was gone. No movement, no breath, no hint of a pulse, nothing. It was as if life, not wanting to cause any fuss or bother or the need for remedies or nursing, had slipped out of him in that one single exhalation of breath.

Later, when the priest had come and the body had been lifted and carried out to lie on the table in his workshop, and the place was full of servants and people wailing, she, who had been too stunned to cry, had gone back to the book on the table to find that it was the sixth volume, dedicated to the thorax, and that the torn page was an illustration from the dissection of the heart showing how the blood moved from the left to the right side. It had been a subject of some vexation to him, this chapter, since it exposed an apparent contradiction between the authority of the great Galen and the evidence of Vesalius' own knife. Vesalius himself later went so far as to publicly declare Galen wrong – the blood did not, could not move that way, as it was evident to his own eyes that there were no holes in the wall of flesh through which it could travel.

When, many years on, the news of this reached her through

the grille she wondered if perhaps that was what her father had been thinking about when the fit took him, or if the correspondence between the dead organ on the page and the loss of his own vital spirit was a more simple affair, left there deliberately so that she might in some way understand this death better. Certainly with the silence of his heart came the silence of everything, from the sound of his voice to all those thoughts and words from the great library of his experience not yet written down and therefore lost for ever.

'Get up now, Faustina. You have mourned enough and there is work to be done.'

And he had been right. She could not grieve for ever and there were things to be done. Almost before the priest had said the last prayers you could hear the flapping of vulture wings in the antechambers and if she didn't stop crying soon, how else would she notice when his most precious volumes started to slide off the shelves, or how his papers were disturbed by teachers or ambitious students coming to pay their respects and take back a few things they had 'left with him for safe keeping'? It was flattery of sorts. A doctor with connections at court left a hole waiting to be filled by others; and what young woman – even if she could command any offers – could possibly want books of herbs and remedies as part of her dowry?

But the real communication didn't start until some time after the funeral, days before she was due to leave for the convent, when the kitchen girl had been struck down with the most monstrous stomach cramps and headaches that had had her vomiting with their ferocity. She was a long, gangly strip of a girl from the country, at that age where she seemed to be growing too fast for her own flesh, and when Zuana had found her she was in such agonies that she could barely uncurl herself to show the source of the pain.

'Come on! Have you forgotten everything I taught you so soon?' he had said in her ear as she had bent down beside her.

She had been so nervous that her hand had been shaking as she took the girl's pulse. When she couldn't find it in her wrist she went to the neck, behind her ear, where he had taught her, and there she located it, forceful but not so fast as to suggest dangerous fever. She had set to work on the headache, making up a crown of verbena leaves in vinegar and wrapping it around the girl's forehead, then dosing her with basil water and eau de vie to settle or expel whatever was wrenching her gut. And because she would not have slept even if she had gone to bed, she had sat with her through the night as she had tossed and moaned.

'Well?' he had said just before dawn, at that hour which seems to suit the dead more than the living. 'What is your opinion now?'

She had laid her hand on the girl's forehead. 'Whatever fever she had is gone. But the cramps continue. I would have expected bowel evacuation by now if there was gut poisoning. Perhaps I should increase the eau de vie to help expel whatever is there.'

'Perhaps. And what if there is nothing to evacuate?'

'But there is something. I can feel definite tenderness.'

'Where? Show me.'

She put her hands on the thin shift that covered the girl's body, moving them down from her stomach gently towards the pubic bone. But the truth is she didn't know exactly where, for while she had seen woodcuts of the insides of a woman, this was the first time she had actually had flesh under her hands.

'Here.'

But by now he had fallen silent.

The girl moaned, arching her body in response to the pressure and the pain. And now, through her shift she noticed for the first time the fat buds of new breasts. She got up from the bedside and went up into the workroom, pulling down a bag of St Mary's mint and some bugloss leaves, infusing them in a mix of hot water and wine. How stupid! No wonder he had stopped talking to her.

Back at the bedside she helped the girl upright so she could sip it slowly.

'Oh, ooh. Oh, I am dying.'

'No, you are not,' she said. 'The problem is more that you are growing.'

Some time next morning the girl passed small clots of black blood, followed not long after by a more recognisable menstrual flow.

'I should have realised.' Back in her room she was almost too tired to undress. 'How could I not realise? It was so simple.'

'It is the simple that is sometimes hardest. That is why you have to continue to ask questions and keep looking.'

'Perhaps if I had had a mother . . .' she wanted to say – but if she thought about this now she would have to accept the loss of two parents.

'You did well enough. So go to bed now, Faustina. You need the sleep as much as your patient.'

'No! Don't go. Please don't go.'

'Do not worry. I will be here when you need me . . .'

'Benedictus.' The voice behind her in the dispensary is loud and real.

Zuana turns too suddenly, which causes her head to throb so that she has to steady herself to avoid falling. The novice mistress, Umiliana, is standing almost directly behind her, her cushion-fat cheeks red and veined from exposure to the winter winds.

'Deo gracias.' Has she been talking out loud to herself? Surely not.

'Do I disturb you, sister?' The older woman pauses. 'I heard voices.'

'No. No, I . . .' Zuana stumbles, unsure of what or how much she has heard. 'I was . . . praying. Is there something wrong?'

'A novice has been taken ill during instruction.'

'Who?'

'Angelica.'

'Angelica? She suffers with her lungs.'

'God has seen fit to afflict her that way, yes. But she bears it well.'

'I . . . I will come to her.' She turns back to the worktop as if to find something to give her but the move makes her dizzy again.

'I would not worry yourself. She is recovered enough for a while. I have sent her to the chapel to pray.'

But Zuana is thinking of how the infection might mix with the asthma and what they would do if the girl starts to find it hard to breathe. 'It would be better if she were resting.'

'What? And make the chapel even emptier?'

She hesitates. It would help no-one to have them bickering now. 'It is only that the contagion moves more swiftly in places where we are gathered together.'

'So I have heard said. However, when it comes to the greater well-being of the convent there is some disagreement as to what brings most relief.'

Zuana watches as the novice mistress's gaze shifts away from her face down to the open books behind her on the worktop: woodcuts of the upper chest and respiratory system, with a commentary to the side of them. She is struck once again by the intensity of Umiliana's concentration. It is no wonder that her novices find her so intimidating; it seems there is little, inside or outside the soul, that she does not notice.

'You use interesting prayer books, sister.'

'They are records. From a physician in Verona who dealt with an influenza similar to the one besetting us now.'

'And did he know the cause of it?'

Now that Zuana thinks about it, she cannot remember a time when the novice mistress has come to her in the dispensary like this. Certainly, she does not need to be here. News of a novice's illness could have been sent easily enough via a conversa.

'He had some idea, yes.'

'What was it?'

'He was of the opinion that it is connected with semina morborum.'

'Semina morborum? Bad seeds? What – that come from the ground?'

'No. No. They are all around us. In the air.'

'Where?' And Umiliana looks about her now with such innocent immediacy that Zuana can detect no hint of mockery.

'They are incorporeal and therefore invisible to the eye.'

'Then where do they come from?'

'They exist within nature.' As she says this she becomes suddenly aware of how ill she is now feeling.

'So they are created by God, then? On which day of creation did he make them?'

'I think there was not a particular day.' Maybe a vinegar and rue water cloth on her forehead would help. 'The great St Augustine himself has this same idea within his work.' She will make up a further batch as soon as Umiliana leaves. 'Perhaps I have not explained it well.'

But it seems that the novice mistress is not that interested in leaving. 'Well, I am only a simple nun. I do not have your . . . education in such things.' She pauses. 'But I have another idea as to why such things happen. Of course, it is not as . . . newfangled as yours.'

And as she says this she smiles, as if to show her business is not quarrelling after all. Only it is hard to tell what she is really feeling since when she smiles her eyes are swallowed up into cheek flesh.

Zuana leans back against the bench.

'You are sure I do not disturb you? I would not so presume if the welfare of the convent was not at stake.'

Zuana glances to the hourglass, which is pouring sand towards the end of her work hour. If the novice mistress has come simply to debate God's place in medicine, she could have done it within chapter. It would not be the first time they had wrangled over such matters and in chapter she could have been sure of having an audience to play to.

'No. You do not disturb me at all. Please – I would very much like to hear.'

Umiliana takes a step towards her now, as one might do if the intention was to share a special confidence. Her gaze slips over Zuana's head to the wall of vials and pots behind her. My choir of cures, Zuana thinks, then checks herself. Never once has the novice mistress had recourse to use them. Whatever pain she may encounter, she keeps it to herself. If that is strength, does that somehow make others' suffering weakness? Umiliana's eyes move back to connect with her own. Certainly something is happening here, and she would do well to pay attention to it. She tries to concentrate.

'It seems to me that God may use such contagion for a purpose, sending it into people and places where He feels He is not worshipped properly.'

Their faces are close now. If the seeds are indeed turning more potent inside me, I must be careful not to breathe them out directly on to her, Zuana thinks. She looks away to the side. 'Yes. Well, that . . . that can also be true.'

'Ah! So – you are aware of it, too?'

'Of what?'

'The way He feels towards Santa Caterina. About what is happening here – how the convent is changing.'

'Changing? I . . . am not sure . . .'

'That night when Suora Imbersaga died – you did not sense something? You did not feel His blessed presence in the room?'

Certainly she had experienced something. 'I . . . I felt His great compassion, that He had seen fit to end her suffering.'

'Oh, yes, indeed. But more than that. You did not feel that His taking her to Him was a sign of how He felt about Santa Caterina? That such a good soul would do better in His care?' And now she pulls back slightly. 'You were much moved that night, Suora Zuana, I could tell – I would say more than I have seen you for years.'

'I was . . . I . . . yes . . .' She breaks off, not knowing what to say.

A soul as smooth as a bolt of silk. Those are the words her supporters use about Santa Caterina's novice mistress. Though others might add 'and a tongue as sharp as a toothpick'. Yes, Zuana had been in pain that night, though it had been more about what she could not feel than what was revealed. Had God really spoken to Umiliana and not to her? There was no question but that there had been an intensity of sweetness in her sorrow. No question either but that the young nun was deserving . . . But does that make Zuana so undeserving that she had noticed nothing?

She is aware that the silence is growing, can feel herself sweating further under the heat of Umiliana's concentration. My work is to tend the plants and alleviate suffering, she thinks stubbornly, not to dabble in convent politics. If the abbess were here she would know what to say now. Particularly with the welfare of the convent at stake. Well, it seems she must say something.

'The convent has grown in numbers in recent years. I think all change brings more change with it.'

'Yet Our Lord Jesus Christ does not change. His love . . . His sacrifice . . . And neither does our duty towards Him. We are bound to serve Him in obedience and humility, not look to the outside world for sustenance and praise. The great bishops of Trent warned against such contamination. Yet look around you, dear sister. Do you not think that in our hunger for ever more dowries and glory we take in too many young women who love themselves more than they love God?'

Ah, so it is the problem of young souls. Everyone knows it has been a source of distress to her for some time. Not to mention this latest challenge. 'If you are talking of the young novice Serafina . . .' She pauses, not sure for a second what she is about to say. 'I think . . . I think with your help – and God's music – she is slowly finding her way.'

'Do you? I am not so sure. I think the Lord is crying out to her but that now she uses her voice to stop her ears against Him. And why not? These days Santa Caterina is more interested in training voices for profit than for prayers. Perhaps you do not see it because you do not remember. But this was once a convent of great devotion. Novices would feel it all around them. Angels would wrap Suora Agnesina in their arms during Matins, and Suora Magdalena had only to open her hands in chapel for blood to pour out from her wounds. But she is locked and forgotten in her cell.' She pauses. 'Though I am sure that He still comes to her. Does He not?'

Ah! So even the novice mistress is not immune to the power of gossip. Surely this, too, is its own form of contagion, Zuana thinks: how words once spoken have no need of repetition, since instead they can travel through the air, invisible, incorporeal, becoming potent as soon as they are ingested. She has a sudden image of the world as it must be seen by the angels, vibrating with a cornucopia of unseen matter, a mix of the benevolent and the malign. On what day was all of this created? She wishes her father were here so she could ask him. But that is not the matter in hand. The matter in hand is Suora Magdalena and her possible transcendence. Is this what the conversation is really about? Could it be that the holy novice mistress is simply using the welfare of the convent as bait to catch a bigger fish? Such cunning seems, well, somehow unworthy of her.

Thank God, Zuana is safe from it, though. Unquestioning obedience is the greatest discipline a nun can aspire to. And the instruction of one's abbess is the instruction of God himself.

'The last time I tended her, the good sister was quiet in her cell.'

For that second the disbelief in Umiliana's eyes is so naked that Zuana is startled; more so as she watches the tears starting to flow down the plump slopes of the sister's cheeks.

'Oh, oh, I know you have a good soul, Suora Zuana. I see it in the way you treat the sick. Our Lord Jesus Christ himself was a healer and you have been given a gift from Him in your work. But I fear we have failed you by not training your spirit to find His great love through prayer. I would have given much to have had you as my novice . . .'

'I . . . I would have liked that, too,' she says, and suddenly it feels as if the words have been wrenched out of her heart, which now feels as hot as her forehead. It may be that she even sways a little.

'Are you all right, sister?'

'Oh, yes, I am fine. I . . . well, I just have much to do to help the sick.'

Umiliana regards her solemnly, as if wondering how much more she should say. The tears now reach the deep creases around her mouth, slipping down towards the pitted pores of her chin. Zuana watches them, half mesmerised. She is so lovely and so ugly. If Suora Scholastica were to compose a play about the birth of Christ then surely the novice mistress would play the part of Elizabeth, her withered old womb filled by God's grace . . .

Enough, enough. I must concentrate, Zuana thinks again.

'I am trespassing upon your work hour. God needs you for other things.' The elder nun takes a step back, but the gaze remains. 'I thank you for this . . . this talk between us. You are always in my prayers. I hope I have not . . . disturbed you too much.'

'No. Not at all. I . . . I will come to Angelica soon.'

But she makes a dismissive gesture with her hands. 'Do not worry. I will let you know if you are needed. If the prayers do not help. God be with you, Suora Zuana. You are precious to Him and He is watching your journey.'

'And with you, Suora Umiliana.'

TWENTY-TWO

As soon as she is alone again she mixes up the vinegar water and rue, then moves on to some fresh eau de vie and basil. Though she knows she is ill, she is determined at least to finish the work hour.

How many batches of these remedies has she made up in this room? Twelve, thirteen years' worth? How many more to come? What will be her allotted span? Fifty, fifty-five? Certainly there are nuns who live that long. Even sixty. Sixty years . . . She thinks of time almost as a weight. She sees a set of scales, with the years like bags of salt on one side, balanced on the other by good works and prayer. Perhaps when the two are in perfect harmony she will be ready. But how does one measure goodness? And does all time weigh the same? Surely not . . . Days spent in prayer or sacrifice would surely be worth more than those taken up in watering plants or distilling juices. Perhaps the point is not balance after all but the tilting of one side in favour of the other?

She wonders if this is something she already knows but has simply forgotten because she feels so strange. Yet she cannot shift the thought that recently her progress has seemed so slow. Sister Imbersaga was barely twenty-two years old when she was taken. On the surface she had been just another nun, in truth rather ordinary. So why her? Unless it was that very ordinariness that had made her the chosen one.

Chosen. Even the word smells of carrion these days. That is what the heretics believe: that God has chosen some and not others; and that His choice is more important than a life of good works or a convent full of nuns interceding for your soul. Of course they will burn in everlasting fire for such thoughts – though hell must be overflowing now, for the sickness is still spreading, crossing mountains, seas and borders, taking villages, universities, towns, even nobles and princes with it, almost as if it is another form of malevolence moving through the air. No wonder the true church is grown so nervous for its flock. What had been the abbess's words? *They would even stop us writing letters for fear that it disturbs the tranquillity of our state.* How, though, could they do that? Such isolation would surely start another kind of fever.

The basil and eau de vie is barely mixed when she hears footsteps and turns to find a young conversa, whose name she cannot remember, in the doorway, a package in her hand.

'I . . . Madonna abbess sent this for you.'

The girl steps forward hesitantly. She is new to convent life and finds the infirmary the strangest place of all, inhabited as it is by mad crones, with the dispensary sister, flush-faced and sweating, suddenly the maddest of them all. Zuana holds out her hand but the girl ducks by her and leaves it on the work bench, moving away so fast that she knocks against a table as she goes.

The package bears the Bishop's seal, though it has been broken. The abbess will have already checked the contents. No doubt there will have been some flowery message from his Holiness, thanking the worthy sisters for their kindness and offering them this gift of cocciniglia in recompense for their goodness. Inside the cloth wrapping is a small hessian bag. Zuana holds it in her palm, weighing it up quickly. Ten grams, maybe more. Together with what she has put by, enough for both the kitchen and the dispensary. She pulls open the strings and lifts it to her nose. There is a dusky quality to its scent, of something grown and dried in great heat a long way away. How far has it travelled to get here? Carefully she pours a small quantity of it into her hand. The small granules are a dark, dull red. You would never think that they could contain such fiery colour. Red gold, that is what people call it. What little she knows of it comes from one of her father's books: a history of New Spain written by a doctor who had followed the army there. He told of how the dye was made from worms that sprouted out of a cactus, grown in a desert somewhere where they had never heard of the Garden of Eden or the name Jesus Christ, but where the colour produced was strong enough to paint His blood as if it had been shed that very day for them. The book had shown a drawing of the plant, soft and spiky at the same time, but not the men who cultivate it, so she has to imagine what they look like: naked, painted skins, or lips stuck out like plates into the air, as she has seen in drawings elsewhere.

It worries her that she is offending against modesty by even thinking such thoughts and she moves on instead to the contemplation of how, with the help of God's missionary fathers, these men – and women – would have found Jesus Christ by now. Some of them, she has heard said, are even taken into the Church as monks and nuns themselves. Thus does the glory of the Lord bring light into dark places, especially ones where nature has fashioned an entirely different prism of wonders. What would she give to have seen some of those wonders herself?

Oh! But the illness is making her thoughts run wild. In her palm she sees that the edges of the granules are moist from the sweat on her skin, leaving a dark mark, and when she brushes her forehead with her other hand she finds it burning to the touch.

'I wonder you have not thought of using the cocciniglia?'

Of course she has thought of it. 'To be taken to break a fever.' That is what her father's notes had said. But although she remembers him writing about such a remedy in theory, he had left no measurements, for he had never had his hands on the dye, and therefore she has no way of knowing how strong would be too strong or what too strong might mean when taken internally.

She knows very well what her father would have done had he had the opportunity. 'The only thing to be aware of is that for such an experiment it is well to err on the side of caution and always be sure to note each and every step, so that when you look back you can mark its course with certainty.'

His voice seems so close in her ear now that she turns her head to see where it is he might be standing, only to find her vision blurred by the speed of the gesture. I am more ill than I realise, she says to herself. I must be careful how I do this.

She moves slowly, notebook open to the side with a new heading, date and time, while she measures out a portion of the granules into a clay bowl, before wrapping up the rest and securing the bag within a drawer, ready for delivery to Suora Federica during the afternoon. Then she takes a measure of hot water and slowly mixes it into the grains, noting the proportions in her book as she goes. The resulting liquid is too dark to distinguish what depth of colour it might be making. It occurs to her that this may mean it is too strong but the work hour is almost over and if she wants to have time to test this, it would be best done now. What does not occur to her is that she is so feverish that she is no longer capable of deciding what is and what is not best for herself.

She takes a few sips. Under the heat of the water the mixture is bitter to the taste. The shelves in front of her look strange suddenly — as if something is wrongly placed or missing, but she cannot think what. Her head is spinning. As she drinks the rest she wonders if it will stain her lips in the same way as the marzipan strawberries, and if so what Suora Umiliana will make of her new-found vanity as they sit opposite each other during the midday office.

Because so many of the choir sisters have been struck down in the last days, Suora Zuana's absence is not immediately noticed in chapel. It is not until everyone is settled and the office has begun that the abbess, counting her flock and duly marking the return of Suora Ysbeta, pale but clearly better, seeks out her dispensary mistress to communicate her silent congratulations on the recovery, only to find that she is not there.

In her place amid the sweetest-voiced, sweetest-breathed choir sisters, it takes Serafina even longer to notice, for she is caught today between her singing and her thoughts, which are still wrestling with the problem of how to get into the cell of the chief conversa. As soon as her eyes fall on the gap at the end of the second row, however, she knows straight away what must have happened. She glances around surreptitiously to see who else has spotted it. But the abbess has her eyes on the crucifix and seems, at that point, unaware of her flock.

When the office ends she files out of the chapel into the courtyard with the others, then loiters a little as the rest disperse to their cells. The midday service is followed by personal prayer. Given her new-found compliance it would not be fitting for her to be found guilty of disobedience at this stage. But among the many things she owes to Zuana is her silence on a matter that might even now have had her incarcerated on bread and water. Anyway, if the dispensary sister is ill, it would surely be better if it is known about sooner rather than later.

In the infirmary Suora Clementia is fast asleep, her snores reverberating round the room as intermittent growling. She does not wake even when a few moments later the abbess herself enters, walking swiftly between the beds, her shoes clipping fast across the flagstone floor.

As she opens the door into the dispensary the sight that greets Madonna Chiara makes her forget momentarily that she has a duty to note at once the transgressions of any of her flock. In the middle of the room the novice Serafina is kneeling by the body of the dispensary mistress, who is slumped on the floor, blood dripping from her mouth.

TWENTY-THREE

For a while now it feels as if time itself changes its form, becoming liquid as opposed to weight, moving faster for some than it does for others. And for Serafina it moves fastest of all, so that there are moments when it seems to her as if God himself must have taken a hand in her well-being, so powerfully and smoothly does she find herself negotiating the rapids, anticipating, reacting, her eyes fixed on the horizon ahead regardless of the tilt and trembling of the world around her.

'What's happened?' The abbess's voice has none of its usual velvet nap. 'Suora Zuana . . . can you hear me?'

'She has fainted. It's the fever.'

'But the blood . . . look at the blood.'

'I . . . I think she has vomited it up.'

'There must be a wound inside her.' The abbess's hand touches close to Zuana's lips and her fingers come back bright with what looks like the reddest of blood. 'We must get her to bed. Help me.'

But Serafina is staring at her own hand, equally stained from where it has come into contact with the liquid on the floor. She gets up quickly and moves to the work bench. She notes everything: the empty vial on the side (so she does have a supply!), the clay bowl next to it, its insides dark with the left-over of some mixture. And nearby, the open notebook. The last entry marks a time: a half hour before Sext, followed by some figures, but the writing is too small to make them out. She puts a clean finger into the remains in the bowl. It comes out a fierce crimson. She lays it on her tongue, grimacing at the taste, then looks back to Zuana's body and the red stain around. If you didn't know you might think she was indeed dying in a lake of her own blood.

'What are you doing, girl? Either help me or get a conversa here now.'

Serafina has a sudden image of herself turning back to the abbess, her mouth wide open, her bloody tongue flashing out like a viper's. But instead she is already at the sink, finding a cloth and dipping it into the bowl of mint and rue vinegar water Zuana must have been mixing when the fit took her. Back on the ground, she lays the soaked material across Zuana's forehead.

'Are you mad?' Madonna Chiara's hand snaps out to take the cloth. 'That is no use. She is bleeding to death.'

'No, Madonna abbess, I think not.' And as she says it she thinks how calm her voice is compared to that of her superior. 'I think she has swallowed some grana and it has reacted badly with the disturbance in her stomach.'

'Grana?'

'Cocciniglia. It is a remedy made from the Bishop's dye. She spoke about how it might work to bring down high fevers. Look – that is what is staining her lips.'

Now the abbess is catching up with her, seeing herself filing away his Holiness's note in her leather ledger where she keeps all the testimonies of the convent's benefactors, before sending the package off to Zuana, who she knows has been waiting for it. 'Oh! She has tried it on herself first,' she says, because of course she knows her dispensary sister's ways better than most. 'Do we know how it long it takes, or what it can do?'

'No, though I think she must have known or she wouldn't . . .' She trails off. 'Anyway, she still has the fever, so the vinegar and mint will help.'

The abbess moves her hand back from Zuana's face. The girl is right. Though the skin is flushed she looks quite serene, not like someone who has vomited up her own insides. Chiara pulls herself up, her composure regained. 'We must hope you are right. Go and get a conversa so we can carry her to her cell.'

Now she is back in control there is no opposing her. Serafina rises meekly from the floor.

'And when you return you will tell me what you were doing in the dispensary in the first place.'

But Serafina is not so easily disconcerted. 'I came to bring back a book of remedies that Suora Zuana lent me to read and which she had need of now.' And she points to the notebook sitting obviously on the work bench, as if it had just been placed there.

As she moves by the unconscious Zuana she slips it quickly back on to the shelf.

In the second cloister, the laundry room is belching steam into the courtyard but inside there is only one conversa at work and she is as old and gnarled as a dead tree, barely able to lift a wet sheet, let alone a sturdy nun. Moving to the kitchens, Serafina finds Letizia shedding tears over a mountain of half-chopped onions. Suora Federica howls when she thinks she is going to lose her, until she hears the reason.

'God in heaven, what a day! First the chief conversa, now

Suora Zuana. I will be cooking for a convent of corpses if we are not careful.'

'Don't worry. We will bring them both back to health soon enough.'

And such is the young novice's certainty – even joy – as she delivers this, that Federica marvels at the transformation that has taken place in her over the last few weeks, and wonders if she had, perhaps, been a little heavy-handed with the bitter ashes she had mixed into her penance scraps.

As the two young women move swiftly back across the courtyard into the main cloisters together, Letizia glances at Serafina with an undisguised curiosity.

'What is it? What are you staring at?'

'Nothing.'

'Then keep your eyes to yourself.'

Back in the dispensary they lift Zuana off the floor and move her through to the infirmary. The intention is to take her to her cell but as they go Serafina says, 'Madonna abbess, perhaps we should put her in one of the beds here? That way whoever takes over the dispensary can also keep watch over her. And as she recovers she will be able to advise and help. She would not want to be separated from her patients.'

Possibly because it is a sound idea, or maybe because the body is so unwieldy and heavy (knowledge must weigh more than flesh, Serafina thinks, as they struggle to carry her), the abbess agrees.

They move her on to the nearest bed, the one left empty by Imbersaga's death.

As the abbess returns to the dispensary Letizia makes a move to tend to Zuana but Serafina elbows her out of the way, covering the inert sister with the thin blanket and dabbing her forehead with the cloth.

'Dear Mary, Mother of God! What is happening here?' In the doorway the novice mistress is a sudden wind of anger. 'Novice Serafina. You are meant to be at silent prayer. This is—' Then she catches sight of Zuana on the bed and, at the end of the room, the abbess emerging from the dispensary.

'Do not disturb yourself, Suora Umiliana.' Madonna Chiara's voice makes it clear that the situation is under control. 'Suora Zuana is taken ill and the novice is helping, as she knows the cause of it.'

But the novice mistress now glares at both of them, her undisguised disapproval making it clear that a convent beset by such troubles is a convent in need of more than the help of a rebellious novice. Oh, Serafina thinks triumphantly, but you have no idea how much trouble is still to come.

After a while Letizia braves the silence to ask if she may be allowed to leave. 'Suora Federica has no-one else to help her now. She will skin me alive if she is left alone much longer.'

'I would very much hope that she does not resort to such an undue punishment.' Now the moment of crisis has passed the abbess is almost gracious again. 'You may go. Tell me, how is the chief conversa?'

The girl shakes her head. 'Very poorly. Suora Zuana had said she would come to her later.'

'Ah, we are beleaguered on all sides.' The novice mistress's cry has a note of anguish in it.

Letizia ducks out of the room, as Suora Umiliana falls on to her knees by the bed. 'Oh, Lord Jesus, help us in our hour of darkness and bring respite to this good sister who works in your name.'

She bends her head, deep in prayer, as if pointing out that amid all the drama this is the work that should really be done. Serafina hesitates for a second then sinks to the floor next to her, eyes closed, praying silently but so hard she fears the words might be spraying out of her. Please, God, please, God, help me, too . . .

There is silence for a while. It is unclear whether or not the abbess herself is praying but when her voice comes it is remarkably matter-of-fact. 'I think that will do now. Serafina, you may go to your cell.'

The girl rises, eyes down, meek-voiced. 'Mother abbess, do I have permission to speak?'

'Very well.'

'I want to offer my help to the dispensary. To nurse the sick.'

She feels the novice mistress's cluck of impatience behind her. It is not easy, having to charm two such different mistresses – though charm them she must. If she has learned one thing over these last months it is that her own sister's simpering brought her more joy in life than all the natural defiance she herself displayed.

'I could help. Suora Zuana taught me how to treat fever . . . I mean I know I am unworthy . . . that I have behaved with gross selfishness . . .' And here she glances at the novice mistress. 'For which I am deeply sorry. I . . . I have even feared that Santa Caterina may be being punished in some way for my bad behaviour and I—'

'Don't talk nonsense, girl.' Madonna Chiara cuts across her sharply, but not before Serafina has registered how her comment has affected Umiliana. 'Half the city is infected and our Lord has better things to do than to take notice of a puffed-up novice. If there are amends to be made you can make them in the choir.'

Serafina looks so genuinely anguished now that even the abbess is slightly taken aback.

'Madonna abbess.' She hears Umiliana's voice over her head, quiet but firm. 'Might we have a word?'

There is a small pause. Serafina keeps her eyes to the floor. She must not be seen to be part of this, and when the abbess orders her to leave the room she is up and out within seconds.

She stays close enough behind the door to hear the murmur of voices, though not to make out the words. She wonders what Zuana would have to say if she could join in with them now. Would she have been able to fool her, too? She hears the footsteps and backs away from the door as it is opened by the novice mistress. But it is impossible to tell anything from her face.

Back in the room she stands before the abbess, eyes to the ground.

'You are to go to your cell directly and spend the rest of the hour in private prayer.'

'Yes, mother abbess,' she says with perfect meekness.

'If the convent has need of you we will call you later.'

'Thank you.'

And thank you, Suora Umiliana, she says silently. She could not have planned it better herself: this way before she is given the chance to slip her hands under a certain mattress, she has time to retrieve something from beneath her own.

'Suora Umiliana,' she says, quietly. 'Might I come to you for further instruction sometime today? I feel myself in the greatest need.'

TWENTY-FOUR

And so it happens that in preparation for caring for others, Serafina finds herself first addressing the sufferings of Christ himself.

The old nun and the young novice meet together that afternoon in the chapel, with the great crucifix in their sights. Outside the weather is grown almost clement for the time of year but the chapel remains as cold and damp as the grave. Umiliana, in contrast, heats the air with words, never letting her eyes move from the girl's face while she describes passionately the ways in which beside the pain of Jesus Christ all the pain of the world is as nothing; how every drop of blood He shed was like a flood washing over the surface of the earth, taking man's wickedness with it, so that through His sacrifice we are given the chance to live again, whatever our sins.

Then, to reinforce the message, she gives the novice a passage to read out loud from the teachings of Santa Caterina of Siena. It is a clever choice, for in her way Caterina had been a great rebel herself, pursuing her ardent love for Christ against the more conventional marriage planned for her by her parents. Hers was a disobedience, however, that was exquisitely rewarded, as the passage shows: decribing how after years of self-mortification and prayer the Lord saw fit to come to her and offer her His wounds to kiss, opening His side for her so that His blood flowed like milk and as her lips tasted it she was filled to the brim with love, as if the spear had gone into her very own flesh.

Serafina has a good voice and the novice mistress listens attentively, joy like a soft sweat on her skin, almost as if the miracle is happening to her then and there. The saint's words are powerful, so visceral that even the girl herself is affected – so for that moment she stops thinking of the pad of ointment concealed under her shift, or the white pebbles strewn in the grass to mark her way to the spot by the wall where, having taken the imprint of the conversa's keys, she will throw the package over for him to catch.

Later, when the convent is on its way to supper and she is called instead by the abbess and given dispensation to miss the meal in order to assess the condition of the chief conversa, she is surprised by how calm she feels at the prospect. She remains unperturbed when she walks into the tiny, dank cell, buried away in the corner of the second cloister and reeking of sweat and old menstrual blood, to be presented with the sight of the woman who lies there, arms as thick as ox legs and her face puffed up with fever. No doubt it helps that the patient is barely conscious, for it means that as Serafina leans down to listen to her breathing it is easy to slide her hand under the pallet far enough to locate a thick metal stem, then a wedge of key teeth. She still has to be careful, though, since the conversa Letizia stands directly behind her, assigned as an assistant but no doubt also a spy to report back anything that is worthy of reporting.

She removes her hand and goes to work on the woman's wrist, searching for a pulse amid the fat flesh. She has no idea how ill she is but she smells as though she is dying and there are specks of froth around the edges of her mouth.

'She is in need of eau de vie and basil.' She turns to Letizia. 'There is a bottle on the work bench. Suora Zuana left it there just before she became ill. Can you bring it to me?'

At first Letizia is having none of it. While she may be a good nurse, she knows when she has been given power of her own. 'I have to stay with you at all times. That's what the abbess said. Anyway, I don't know which bottle you mean.'

'You will smell it clearly enough. Look at her. See how sick she is? If we are to help her I need that bottle. Get it. Now.' And she takes her tone from the one Zuana used when they were in the cell with the mad Magdalena. 'Unless you want it known that you were the one who allowed her to die.'

The girl hesitates, then turns and goes.

It is done fast enough in her absence. The keys are big and heavy, and there is a moment when she fears that the waxy block will not be long enough to take the imprint of both of them. She is possessed by a sudden urge to slip them under her garment and walk out with them. It is the end of the working day – surely no-one will have need of them until tomorrow morning at the earliest. But if she takes them now then she must use them tonight. And that is not the plan, and there is no way that she could tell him, or even if she could that he could get it organised in time. No – if it were tonight she would have to do it alone, and when she tries to imagine herself moving through both sets of doors and standing alone out on the dock, an ink-black expanse of water in front of her, she knows she couldn't do it; that there are limits to even her courage.

She uses the ball of her palm to push the keys evenly into the pad of wax. They sink satisfyingly deep, which means it is not easy to extract them without muddying the imprint. She cannot rush it but she also cannot waste time. As it is, she barely has time to push the keys back then wrap the pad in the strips of silk petticoat and slip it under her robe before she hears Letizia's footsteps behind her.

Together they lift the woman's head off the pallet and administer the dose. Afterwards she still seems more dead than alive. At least there has been no need for Serafina to use the poppy syrup.

'There is nothing more we can do for her now but let her sleep.'

She stands up and as she does so feels the package slip from under her breast and has to bring her hand up to hold it through the cloth to stop it falling. She worries that Letizia may have spotted the movement but the girl is on her knees by the pallet still, busy with the patient, smoothing the grubby sheet and tucking its edges, pushing her hands so far under the mattress that surely her fingers will have found the cold metal of the keys by now; almost as if it had been part of her job to make sure they are still there. She glances up at Serafina and for a second their eyes meet. Oh, yes – this place is full of cunning. How right she had been to resist the temptation.

Nevertheless, she is sure she must have seen something, for as they walk across the scrubby courtyard back to the main cloister she keeps staring at her – small, keen glances. 'What is it? I told you, don't look at me like that.'

'It's nothing.'

'If it is nothing then why do you keep looking?'

The girl shrugs, then looks shyly back to her. 'I just wonder what she sees in you, that's all.'

'What do you mean? Who?'

She purses her lips as if she knows she should not talk but the opportunity for gossip, or maybe the taste of revenge, is too much for her. 'Suora Magdalena. The way she keeps asking after you . . .'

'What?'

'She thinks I am you . . . Every time I bring her food or go in to empty the bucket, it's the same: "Serafina. Serafina, is that you? Are you come again? I knew you would." And she makes her voice go high and wobbly as she says it.

'She says my name?' And Serafina feels a hollowness open up inside her again, as if someone is scraping at the bottom of her gut with a knife.

'Oh yes, though I don't know how she knows it, for as Jesus himself is my judge, I never told it to her.'

'What else does she say?'

The girl shrugs again but there is no time for further revelation as they are already in the main cloister, busy now with its traffic of silent sisters on their way from the refectory back to their own cells for prayer or recreation. Letizia bows her head and disappears back whence she came, leaving Serafina struggling to make sense of her words. She looks again into those rheumy, unblinking eyes and the wild, frozen smile. Had Christ offered Suora Magdalena his wounds to kiss, too? Tasting the blood, sucking up strength from his overflowing love? No wonder her grasp had been so strong. Uugh! No, no, she will not think of this now. The old woman has nothing to do with her. Soon she will be out of this place, leaving all its holy madness behind. All she has to do is play the humble novice for a while longer.

She slides into the throng, passing one then another silent figure. When the fog mingles with the twilight as it does today it is almost like a gathering of phantoms, the hushing of skirts and padding of feet offering up its own kind of spectral conversation. She lifts her head in time to catch Suora Apollonia's ghost-white face moving past her in the thick air. Their eyes meet and she drops her gaze, as is the rule, but Apollonia keeps on looking, as if she is seeing something of interest there. During recreation this most worldly of choir nuns sometimes holds court in her cell, gathering together the more fashion-conscious sisters to play music and tell stories over glasses of wine and kitchen titbits. Novices are not allowed but it won't be long before some of them are sisters in their own right and she is always on the look-out for the next generation of rebels.

Serafina passes the entrance to the infirmary. She has not seen Suora Zuana since the morning, after chapel. The wax seal needs a safe home, but if she is quick she might check on her now. And also perhaps manage to replace the syrup on the shelf. Once in her cell she will not be allowed out again except for Compline.

Inside, she is amazed to find the dispensary sister not only conscious but propped up in the bed, her head resting heavily back against the wall. She finds herself smiling, even laughing a little, as she hurries towards her.

'How are you?'

Zuana stares at her as if trying to orientate herself. 'Serafina? I . . . what are you doing here?'

'I . . . I have dispensation from the abbess. I . . . we were fearful for you.'

'What happened? Did I faint?'

'I think so.'

Her skin is almost grey, though her lips are a rich scarlet. Not the mark of God's love but of her own experiments, Serafina thinks as she pulls the cover over her.

The move upright seems to have exhausted her. 'It was the cocciniglia,' she says wearily.

'Yes. You threw it up all over the floor. We thought you were bleeding to death. Everyone was very worried. You had the most terrible fever.'

She shakes her head. 'I . . . I remember drinking it, then feeling very ill.'

Serafina hesitates, then reaches out her hand tentatively and places it on Zuana's forehead, first with the back and then with her palm, as she has seen the older woman do with other patients.

'Oh!' She takes her hand away, then brings it back again to confirm, as if she cannot quite believe it. 'But you are cool! The fever has gone.'

Zuana frowns up at her; touching her own forehead she locates the pulse on her wrist, registering it for a few seconds. 'So it would seem.'

'But how? I mean — it couldn't be the cocciniglia. You vomited it up.'

'You said there was some on the floor — did it smell as if it had passed through my stomach?'

'I . . . er . . . I don't know. It smelt . . .' and she tries to remember. 'Musty? There was a little left in the bowl. That's how I realised what it was.'

'I didn't drink it all. As I fell, the rest must have fallen with me. Did you give me anything else?'

'No, no . . . just bathed your head with the mint and vinegar. I was scared to do more in case you vomited it up again.'

'What time is it?'

'The hour before Compline.'

'What day?' she says impatiently.

'Oh, still today.'

'So — six hours. The remedy takes six hours. I have to write it down.' And she makes a move to get up.

'No . . . I mean, you're not well yet.'

But she is still moving. 'I am well enough.'

'Wait. I'll get the book for you.' She gets up. Then hesitates. 'Am I allowed to go into the dispensary alone?'

Zuana puts her head back against the wall and smiles weakly. 'It seems you have been there anyway.'

'Oh, only with the ab—' She breaks off. No, that is not true. She was there before the abbess. But she does not want to draw attention to it now.

Inside the dispensary she spots the stain on the floor and feels – what? – almost joyful? Yes, joyful. Suora Zuana is better. She will not die. Had she really been so worried for her? It seems that in some part of her she must have been.

But there is no time for that now. She slips the bottle of syrup out of her robe and quickly transfers some of it to the waiting empty vial, then slips the original back on the shelf. The row of bottles nestle up to one another again. It has been missing for twenty-four hours. She can only hope it was barely noticed. Now she still has to get back to the cell with the wax imprint, for the bell is ringing for private prayer and the cloisters will be deserted soon enough.

'How is the convent?' Zuana says as soon as she returns with the book. 'What of the chief conversa?'

'Her fever is high. I gave her a dose of basil and eau de vie a while ago.'

'You?'

'I told you. They gave me dispensation to help. The novice mistress said it would be good for me.'

Zuana stares at her. 'Well . . . we will make a dispensary mistress of you yet.'

But Serafina's duplicity is now so far advanced that the compliment makes her uncomfortable rather than pleased.

'Santa Caterina doesn't need another healer,' she says quietly.

'It already has you.' The feeling is made worse by the awareness that the block of ointment wax under her robe is growing ever warmer from her skin and that she cannot afford for the imprint to be less than perfect.

Zuana starts to pull herself out of the bed again. 'Give me the book. I will write the notes while you prepare another draught.'

'I . . . I must go. The bell is ringing.'

'It will only take a few minutes and I will make sure the abbess knows why you are late. Come. Help me get out of here before Clementia realises she has a new companion.'

Later, when Suora Zuana arrives for Compline, weak but nevertheless on her feet, the rest of the convent is amazed, for everyone knows by now that she was found half dead from bleeding on the dispensary floor. If speech were allowed they might congratulate her, even marvel a little at how, despite her pale face, there is such a ruddiness of health to her lips. As it is, Federica is the only one who regards her at all suspiciously – but then she is impatient to start her marzipan fruits and is alert to the colour of strawberries wherever she sees it.

Others express their gratitude through the words of the office, for Compline, which marks the end of the day and the beginning of the Great Silence of the night, begins with penitence but moves towards joy. Even Suora Umiliana seems relaxed, almost satisfied, and the once so troublesome novice Serafina, who it is rumoured was given special dispensation to tend her former mentor, offers up the words of the twenty-ninth psalm: '*Thou hast turned mourning into dances, put off my sackcloth and girded me with gladness. O my Lord I will give thanks to thee for ever,*' in purest voice. Those sisters – and there are a few of them – who have been as suspicious of her sudden goodness as they had been tired of her outright rebellion find themselves giving extra thanks that the convent has regained its balance. And that there is nothing now to interfere with Carnival, with all its opportunities for pleasure and performance.

The abbess, as ever impeccable in her formality and avoidance of favouritism, waits until the service ends to show her delight, pausing briefly in front of her dispensary sister and bowing her head to welcome her back to the flock. Those who are close enough to note the encounter are struck by the deep warmth in Madonna Chiara's eyes, not to mention the way she offers the lightest of nods in the direction of the young Serafina herself, who seems so taken aback that the blush is evident behind her veil.

Three hours later, when the convent is deeply asleep, that same young novice slips out of her cell, a parcel concealed under her robe. Not long after, the voice of a perfect male tenor, moving along the street to the river wharf, lifts up and over the walls. It sings of young love and a woman whose hair is a cloud of gold, Petrarch's words set to haunting music. When the song ends It is answered by a single high, vibrating note, female rather than male, and then a heavy thud as something hurled from inside the walls lands somewhere on the other side.

Three days later the same procedure takes place the other way round. That night Serafina is especially fortunate. With the Carnival spirit on the move again, the watch sister has changed the timing of her rounds and the novice barely reaches her cell before the footsteps hit the flagstones outside.

She lies on her pallet, fully dressed, heart thudding, the heavy package clasped to her breast, as she hears the footsteps stop by her door, hesitate, then go forward again. In the dark when all is silent once more she pulls open the wrapping and feels underneath her fingers the shape of two newly forged iron keys and the fold of a letter around them.

There is nothing they can do to hurt her now. She is ready. It is only a question of waiting.

TWENTY-FIVE

With Zuana back on her feet it takes less than a week for the contagion to be halted. The fever passes naturally from the remaining sisters (in the city, the severity of the attack is already waning), while the chief conversa, in whom it proves more stubborn, emerges three days later with rosy lips and renewed strength; a happy outcome, since her trips to and from the storehouse are even more frequent.

The rehearsals for the play enter their final stages. Perseveranza comes out of her cell word-perfect, having been heard reciting her lines while in the midst of her delirium. Except for meal hours the refectory is now strictly out of bounds, as workmen are brought in from outside to build the stage and set. For three days their sawing and hammering offers a background percussion to the daily orders and their presence, invisible though it is, introduces a level of exhilaration into the convent, with the novices and boarders closely chaperoned on every journey. There is a story, so often repeated that it is almost certainly apocryphal, of how a particularly beautiful postulant from a convent in Prato had her lover dress up as a workman to come in and fix the pews in the church and then at the end of his time he smuggled her out in a great bag of his tools. The very idea is enough to have a few of the younger ones swooning with excitement – but it is Carnival, after all, and when the body is incarcerated the mind cannot help but play a little.

Outside, too, the city has come alive. Family visits to the parlatorio tell of a wave of new arrivals: visitors from Mantua, Bologna, Padua, Venice; even a few from Rome itself. Ferrara has a reputation for good living as well as beautiful voices and celebrations are already in full swing. It is said that if you walk by the palace you can hear the trumpeting of elephants brought in especially for the d'Este marriage feast and kept on for Carnival. The ducal garden has been transformed into a huge stage set, lit by a thousand candles, with grottoes and temples and even a great pyramid, all part of an elaborate game of valour in which a group of knights must win their ladies' hands by slaying dragons and answering riddles – though since the Duke must triumph there are rumours of the riddles being adapted to fit his somewhat limited knowledge.

Meanwhile, the streets outside the convent have become their own stage for debauchery. All over the city young men are trying on their Carnival masks and once disguised how can they possibly stay indoors? Disturbing the city's peace is an accepted part of the celebrations. Disturbing its nuns is a more serious affair, a crime against God as much as the women themselves, but even here a little leeway is granted in the name of high spirits. Soon the odd slingshot is arriving over the walls, to be picked up by the watch sister after Lauds: balls of paper scrawled with madrigals and bad poetry. Madonna Chiara sighs as she reads them and feeds them to the fire. The sentiments are predictable: unrequited love like evergreen laurel for ladies whose virtue is so fierce that it freezes the sun itself, alongside a handful of scurrilous verses offering a more instant heaven on earth for those with the wit to imagine it.

Any abbess worth her salt has seen it all before. Most men are tempted by what they cannot have and the truth is that it is not just heretics who are greedy for tales of lustful nuns, that, like bad confessors, they can both enjoy and denounce at the same time. If anything, she thinks, this year's crop is somewhat tamer than the last. Surely the city's poets used to be wittier and cleverer than this? Or perhaps she, like Suora Umiliana, is becoming nostalgic for times past.

When the great annual procession takes to the streets, the whole city stops to watch. The road outside the main entrance of the convent becomes a moving wall of people. At different times throughout the day small groups of converse and the more adventurous of the choir nuns crane their necks out of the few available high windows to watch as the biggest floats go by. From this vantage point they see giants, dwarves, mermaids, goddesses, angels, popes and devils. By now most of the performers have spent so much time waving and shouting up to the noblewomen on the balconies that they have permanent cricks in their necks. The convents, however, are always a challenge, especially for the key-makers, who have a float of their own this year and who make a special effort, strutting up and down waving huge counterfeit keys and shouting out verses about their tools being especially useful for women behind locked doors, and inviting anyone who wants to come down on to the float and handle a few for themselves.

With the cocciniglia at last delivered to the kitchen, the first marzipan fruit bowls are now complete. There is a tradition within the convent that the kitchen mistress is allowed to choose one sister and one novice to sample the first batch. After supper one evening Suora Benedicta and Serafina are called to the back cloisters, where Federica gives the choir mistress a fat green pear – 'Because your melodies bring us closer to God' – while

Serafina is presented with a somewhat misshapen but exceed-ingly red strawberry: 'And your singing gives more pleasure than your howling ever did. Also as the last novice to come inside, you can still remember the tastes you left behind and can judge how this compares.'

While it is probable that the recipe for marzipan remains con-stant whichever side of the convent wall one lives on, Serafina's reaction — she is clearly affected by the intensity of the taste — satisfies even Federica.

'Here. Wipe your mouth,' she says, handing her a cloth. 'We would not want you getting into trouble now you are doing so well.'

And doing well she is. With every passing day Serafina grows more radiant, despite her humble demeanour. She shines even when she is silent, as if God's great love were trying to burst out of her heart, and her voice in chapel, especially at the darkest point of the night, entrances everyone. When she is not singing she is at prayer. She has even dispensed with her conversa and taken on the duties of cleaning her own cell, washing the floors, making her own bed, changing her own linen. There are those who whisper behind her back that she is only trying so hard in the hope that she will be allowed to stay and join in the visiting in the parlatorio after the concert is over (the rules are clear that she is not yet eligible to entertain or be entertained). But if that is her aim then she says nothing about it. In fact she says almost nothing at all these days.

Serafina's behaviour might be more remarked upon were it not for the drama that takes place within the convent in the days leading up to the concert and play.

Following some urgent exchanges of letters and out-of-hours visits in the parlatorio, Suora Apollonia's sister, the lady Camilla

Bendidio, arrives late one night with a maid servant and a small bag, and is quickly settled in the guest house to the side of the main cloisters. It doesn't take long for the news to spread that there is trouble in the marriage and that she has asked for refuge away from her husband while negotiations take place within the family to try to bring peace. Apollonia is given special dispensation to spend time with her and that same night Zuana is called by the abbess to attend her. She has a deep cut at the hairline of her forehead, as if something has been thrown at her, and sits without movement or murmur while Zuana cleans and tends the wound. When asked if there is anything else she needs help with she removes her shawl and upper bodice to reveal a set of large, ripening bruises on her arms and shoulders, and sits weeping silently as Zuana rubs ointment gently into the damaged skin.

She was a pretty woman once, Zuana remembers, but she is grown gaunt now, older than her years. Those young nuns who cry themselves to sleep at night for want of a man's hands on them might find pause for thought here, for this is not the first time she has used the convent as a haven. Her husband, the eldest son of the splendid Bendidio family, is one of the Duke's most favoured courtiers and by all accounts a man with a quick temper. There might be more sympathy for his long-suffering wife were it not for the fact that in seven years of marriage she is yet to produce a child. He, in contrast, has had no such problems, having already sired half a dozen illegitimate children. If it continues much longer she will be under pressure to allow the marriage to be dissolved so that he can get himself a sturdier, more fertile bride – in which case she will find herself coming back to Santa Caterina permanently, as there is nowhere else that would take such a cast-off. Perhaps that would be a relief to her. Looking at Apollonia's healthy young body and her rebelliously fashionable courtier face, Zuana cannot help but think that

Bendidio married the wrong sister. But it is too late now. For both of them.

The next afternoon their father, along with the abbess, meets with a representative of the husband's family in the guest-house parlour to discuss her future, while the parlatorio overflows with the last visit before the Carnival concert.

Zuana, in contrast, sits alone in her cell with her books. She has more than enough work but cannot concentrate on doing it. It has been like this for a while now. The time of year has much to do with it. While many of the inhabitants of Santa Caterina find Carnival an exquisite distraction, for Zuana it is more a disruption than a pleasure. During her long and painful assimilation into convent life it was the rhythm of routine that became one of her greatest solaces and to have it so rudely interrupted makes her almost nervous. Perhaps it would be different if she was more connected to the outside, if she had family to visit and entertain; mother and aunts, cousins or sisters with an ever-expanding brood of little ones to cuddle and coo over. But all she has is her herbs and her remedies, and while they keep the convent healthy they count for little in the world beyond.

This much she is used to, has grown to understand. Yet there is something else going on now. Over recent weeks, even before the illness, if she is honest, she has detected in herself a strange restlessness that she cannot entirely explain. While it is possible that the contagion may have exacerbated it, with the exception of the blood-red urine she passed for two days after the draught (a shock in itself until she realised it was the drug and not her own insides pouring out of her), she has felt well enough since.

No, it seems that it is not her body that is ailing but rather her mind.

She finds herself feeling sad – yes, sad is the right word – for no reason. It is as if for the first time in her life her own company is not enough. She prays, of course, each and every day, but often her mind slips in and around the words, so that they never rise high enough for Him to hear.

The healer in her has witnessed such things in others; convents are full of nuns who become lethargic or tearful or distraught by turns. Winter sadness. Summer madness. Monthly moon cycles or the more persistent melancholia that comes with their ending. There are as many terms for it as there are states of mind. The stricter nuns – the novice mistress and Suora Felicità (even her name marks her out as immune) – regard it almost as a rebellion against God, and counsel stern treatment of work and prayer. But over the years Zuana has tested and used other remedies. Her father's books are full of them: infusions, pills, fumigants; wine steeped in borage, St John's wort, fumigants of incense and hypericum, with mandragora and poppy syrups to ease the insomnia that often accompanies such distress. Then there are other treatments that involve no simples or compounds: kindness, sympathy, a little relaxation of the rules of solitude. In the darkest cases the best is a combination of all of these. Prayer, work, sleep, and care. God, nature and man working together as they were meant to.

Of course Zuana is not so distressed herself. Nowhere near. More likely she is simply tired. She disciplines herself through duty. The parlatorio needs more perfumed herb tablets to place on the brazier during the concert and she busies herself preparing them. When ordinary prayer does not work, she uses recitations from the psalms.

> *The voice of the Lord is powerful,*
> *I will praise Thee, My God, with my whole heart.*
> *And show forth all Thy marvellous works.*

She says these particular phrases over and over again under her breath, wrapping them around her like a blanket, leaving no room for the cold draughts of distraction to slide in around the edges.

For God is Good, His mercy is everlasting
His truth endureth to all generations.

After a while, the simplicity and the repetition bring her a certain calm. Like tonight . . .

Somewhere outside the walls a muted roar goes up. They must be lighting the Carnival bonfire in the piazza in front of the cathedral in time for the sunset. Her father took her to see it once when she was very small. There were so many people they could barely move and he had to hold her up amid the crowd. She remembers that the smoke made her eyes water and her throat sore. At least she thinks that is what happened. Recently she has noticed that she is less sure of things she was once certain about, as if her life before the convent is slipping away altogether. Her father's face, for instance: the broadness of his forehead, the shadows under his eyes, the way his bottom lip always seemed a little pulled downwards by the weight of his beard. All this she had assumed was imprinted in her for ever. Yet when she studies the face of Christ on the cloister crucifix sometimes she could swear she sees the same features in Him too; as if the familiarity of one face had simply blended into another.

Yet there are a few memories that have become, if anything, almost more powerful. Like the stone carvings in Ferrara cathedral. There must have been twelve of them, one for each month of the year, but if she closes her eyes there is one that she can still see as clearly as if it were in front of her now. In it, a small, naked child is crouching on all fours under a goat, suckling from the animal. She can see his mouth, clasped almost lewdly over the fat teat, the fullness of his stone cheeks, the roundness of his belly as the milk pours into it. It surprises her, the power of this memory, for in other ways she does not care much for children; certainly she is not one of those nuns who yearns for the babies she could never have, bringing in Jesus dolls in their dowry chests or imagining themselves taking the suckling baby from Mary's arms and offering him their own breasts instead. Nevertheless this less than holy child – with its evident greed for nourishment – has stayed with her.

She pushes back her books and closes her eyes. These are hardly thoughts befitting an infirmary sister with a history of convent infection to write up. If she cannot work then she should be praying. Why is it that her mind spirals away from her so easily these days?

'*The voice of the Lord is powerful . . .*'

She closes her eyes.

'*The voice of the Lord is full of majesty . . .*'

By the time the knock comes at her door she has managed to pull herself deep enough inside the words, so that at first she does not hear it.

'*I will praise thee, my Lord, with my whole heart.*'

It comes again, sharper.

She turns, and as she does so she wonders if it might be the novice. Since the day of Zuana's illness and recovery in the dispensary they have not spoken a word to each other and when their paths do cross, on their way to chapel or in the cloisters, the girl keeps her head bowed as if she is afraid to meet Zuana's eyes. Over the years she has watched other young women come in angry and rebellious, hysterical even, only to soften gradually, but she has never seen a change as swift and strange as this. It is as if all the molten fury that had been erupting out of her has simply changed course and is now directed towards God. It should be cause for celebration but when she thinks about it – which she tries not to – it makes her uncomfortable. And that, in turn, adds to the restlessness to which she seems so prone these days.

The door opens. If it is the novice she will have to chide her for disrupting prayer, but she will still be pleased to see her. She thinks this at the same instant as she sees Madonna Chiara standing in the doorway.

'Good evening, sister.'

'Am I needed?' Zuana is already on her feet. 'Is someone ill?'

'No, no . . . far from it. The convent is exceedingly well. As you can hear for yourself.'

'How is our guest?'

'The meeting between the families has ended and there are signs of progress. It is agreed that she will stay with us until Carnival is ended. The break between them may bring back a little . . . fondness.'

She does not need to add that this way, when Bendidio drinks himself stupid on the Duke's wine cellar, he will not have his wife to take it out on.

'I could look in on her again if you think it would help.'

'No. She is with Suora Umiliana at the moment and Suora Apollonia has dispensation to join her afterwards.' She pauses. 'It seems they were not so close as children but her troubles have made them fonder. It is a wonder to see. Thus doth the Lord bring comfort out of adversity.'

'*For His mercy is everlasting and His truth endureth to all generations . . .*'

'Indeed it does.' The abbess sounds mildly surprised. She glances down at the open books. 'I have come to offer you some respite from your work, Suora Zuana. The rest of the convent is at recreation with their families and it is only right that you should enjoy the same privilege.'

'Oh, no, I . . . I am . . .' The words 'well' and 'content' battle with each other to be the first out of her mouth, and as a result neither of them succeeds. The abbess, who cannot help but notice the struggle, smiles.

'What is the phrase that Suora Scholastica has written for the prologue to the play? "As the body needs food to thrive, so the spirit also needs recreation and rest."' She laughs. 'You have not heard the speech? Oh, it is most charming and will bring us many pious plaudits, I am sure. I think even Suora Umiliana would find it hard to fault its advice.' She pauses. 'So, if you have a cloak to protect you from the breeze, I wonder if you would like to see something that I think will bring you pleasure . . .'

'Thank you, Madonna,' Zuana says, for it is clear that the offer is also an order. 'I would like that.'

Outside, the air is crisp and the sky clear. The final week of Carnival often marks the end of winter fogs, though Lent will deliver some bitter days of its own along the way. She follows the abbess across the cloisters and into the chapel. Inside, on the left behind the choir stalls, is the door to the bell tower. The abbess brings out a key and slips it into the lock.

'They are setting light to the Carnival bonfires. We will get a particularly good view of our great city from the top of the tower. God has given us a wondrously clear night for the proceedings.'

Aware of the privilege she is being offered, Zuana bows her head and starts to climb. Halfway up she reaches the wooden platform where the ropes for the great chapel bells hang down for the bell ringer. This is as far as any sister is allowed without special permission. If the nun in charge of the bells ever disobeys the injunction it remains her secret. Given the wrecked back and damaged hearing that comes with the office, some compensation is perhaps deserved.

The abbess takes the lead. The bottom of her robe sends out a cloud of dust around her. The stone steps are narrower now, the walls and ceilings thick with cobwebs. Zuana has a sudden image of herself thrusting her hands into the corners and harvesting the gauze: the deathly stickiness of spiders' silk mixed with honey has a reputation as a miraculous salve for flesh wounds. '*I will praise the Lord with all my heart, and show forth his marvellous works.*' Even the best-trained apothecaries find some preparations difficult, however. Another day, perhaps.

They reach the top and step out into the open bell chamber. Their arrival disturbs a host of roosting pigeons, which rise up in a squawking fury of feathers and beating wings. The abbess waves her arms in wide circles, shooing them away, and the two women let out their own squawks of laughter as the birds swoop and clatter around their heads before lifting off and out into the air.

'I wonder how they stand the noise of the bells,' the abbess shouts above the flurry of their wings. 'We should put up pigeon traps. The kitchen could use a few extra fowl in winter, though I cannot imagine Suora Federica coming up here to collect them.'

With the birds gone, the tower becomes theirs. The two great bells sit suspended above them, their fat clappers hanging heavy underneath. Around them the wall reaches to their waists, high enough to protect but low enough to reveal the city far below.

The abbess is right. The view is breathtaking. Zuana registers a sudden dizziness, less from the height than from the exhilaration of the perspective. In the twilight to the north and west she can see right across the old town, a jumble of burnt ochre roof tiles and cobbled streets, to the great cathedral and its piazza, the two parts of the castle with its crenellated towers and moat, then out into the new Ferrara with its grid of wide modern streets and palaces laid out by the second Duke Ercole in his role as great humanist ruler and town planner. And all around it the massive brick walls marking the boundaries of the city.

'It is beautiful, yes?' The abbess smiles at her.

Zuana nods – for the moment she cannot speak. The abbess, understanding, looks away, giving her time to compose herself.

Bricks and cobbles. That was how her father had once described their home town. There were other cities, he said, more full of stone and marble, with great domes and towers and every surface plastered and painted, and they were in their way fabulous enough; but to appreciate the power of the humble brick, so small yet so mighty and filled with so many colours of the earth, then a man had to come to Ferrara on a summer's evening when the very fabric of the city was alight and glowing.

'See the fires?'

As yet there are only two of them: one great plume of smoke rising up from the main square, another smaller one from within the courtyard of the palace. Outside the ring caused by the blaze, people, small as ants, are milling and flowing everywhere. Zuana follows one of the larger streets back from the cathedral square into the old town, trying to locate where she once lived. She can get as far as the long, thin space – not big enough for a piazza – in front of the main university buildings but then becomes tumblingly lost in the curling alleys that branch off all around.

'You are looking for your father's house?'

'Yes.'

'You should find a landmark and work backwards; or perhaps a journey you remember taking.'

But the one she had vowed she would never forget – the walk from the house to the doors of the convent – has gone completely.

She shakes her head. 'The streets nearby are too muddled. They all look the same. And you? Can you see your home?'

The abbess spreads out a hand towards the north. 'The new city is easier. It is a few blocks to the west from the Palazzo Diamante. There is a garden in the middle – see . . . I used to play there with my brother when I was a small child. At least, so he tells me. I don't remember it myself.'

She says the words lightly. The youngest boarder in Santa Caterina now is six – no, five – years old. If she were to stay and take the veil at sixteen as Chiara had done, then there would be precious little past for her to forget. What one has never had, presumably one cannot regret losing.

'How much do you remember?'

Zuana does not look at Chiara as she asks this. Instead the two women stand side by side, their arms leaning on the parapet, looking out over their city, as if this is no longer a convent but simply a high balcony in a rich house where two noble wives have chosen to take the evening air for a while, gossiping about this and that.

'Less as the years go by. Though a few things strongly. Being inside a carriage at night going across water, with the noise of the wheels on wood and the torches on fire at the end – the draw-bridge over the moat of the castle, no doubt. And there is someone telling me that if the ground were to give way now we would all drown.'

'Were you frightened?'

'No . . . no, I think I was excited.' She smiles. 'And a room – I remember a room I was taken to, with a painting all over the cupola ceiling of a round balcony, with the sky above and people and cherubs leaning and peering over the painted parapet as if they were in danger of falling. It was so lifelike. One of the men had black skin and there was a monkey perched on the edge next to him, holding a necklace as if it was about to drop. I remember standing underneath with my arms out waiting to catch it, I was so sure it would fall.' She laughs. 'As a young nun I used to dream that when I became abbess I would commission a work by that same artist for one of the chapels. Imagine! The Bishop or our benefactors looking up to see our Lord and all the apostles leaning over a balcony as if they were about to tumble over.'

As she says it, Zuana can think of a good few sisters who would be there waiting to catch them.

The sunset is moving faster now, throwing up great gaudy streaks of pinks and purples. No cherubs or monkeys, though; only a high-pitched chorus of evening swifts darting like showers of arrowheads across the sky. After a while Zuana turns from the view across the city towards the other side, to the world they do not need to make up, the one they cannot forget.

From this height, Santa Caterina resembles a palace rather than a prison. She looks down over the swooping nave of the chapel into the two cloister courtyards, alive in the golden light, then out over the side houses, by the vegetable and herb patches into the sweep of the gardens and great bow-shaped pond, onwards to orchards backing on to the river, a thick, silver ribbon of mercury, with its sluggish traffic of boats and barges. And around the edges the long run of brick wall, so low from up here that one might think all one had to do was to step over it to reach the world outside.

Oh, but there is beauty in here, too, Zuana thinks: the richness of the earth, the warmth of the bricks, the coolness of stone. Beauty, space and, once you stop wanting it to be different, peace, a relief from the madness outside. If someone were to open the doors now what point would there be in walking out into the world? Where would she go? Who would she be? The house where a young woman called Faustina grew up is home to another family now, while the city that surrounds it is a maelstrom of people who neither know nor could care less about her. That infinitesimal space in the world that was once hers has long since disappeared – and to appreciate quiet one must accept less excitement.

No, whatever restlessness is going on within her it is a cloud passing across the sun, the temporary blindness that comes with a morning fog. In all of the gossip that filters through the walls she has never heard of a well-born woman with her own apothecary shop or her own list of patients. '*I am like the green olive tree in the house of the Lord. I trust in the mercy of God for ever and ever.*' The cloud will pass, the fog will lift. For the first time in many days she feels quieter.

As her eye moves back across the garden to the cloister it picks out what looks like a broken line, no, more of an arc, made up of random pale stones on the grass and in among the leafless trees, moving from the edge of the wall close to the river to the path leading past the outhouses back to the cloisters. At this distance it resembles a run of uneven stitches on the hem of a garment or a long necklace of white rose petals fallen on to dark ground.

Far below them on the street in front of the convent a clash of young men's voices rises up: laughter, shouts, what sounds like playful barracking of one another. Rose petals. Zuana moves to face the town side again. She has an image of herself, both arms held wide over the parapet into the air, opening her fists and letting loose cascades of rose petals on to the crowds of spectators below.

'May I ask you a question, Madonna abbess?'

'If you wish, certainly,' the abbess says, almost surprised at the return of formality in her former friend.

'Is it true, the story that Apollonia tells about the tower?'

'Which story is that?'

'About how one year at Carnival a group of novices came up here with dried petals from the storehouse and threw them down on the revellers in the streets below.'

'And what happened then?'

'It seems the young men went mad. Shouted, threw up ropes, tried to climb up to reach them.'

'Hah. I have always thought Suora Apollonia should be writing plays alongside Scholastica,' she says mildly.

She bends down and picks up something from the ground. As she straightens up her fist uncurls over a handful of moulted pigeon feathers. She leans over the edge and lets them go.

'Certainly such a thing might have driven young men mad.' The feathers dance coquettishly in the air before floating down. 'But as you can see yourself . . .' And now she leans further out and over, so far that Zuana has an image of the painting inside the cupola ceiling and begins to feel anxious. 'The height of the wall and the angle of the tower over the ground are such that you cannot see directly down to the street immediately below. Or from there up into the tower.' She pulls her body back again. 'So, though the petals might have seemed like a shower of grace from heaven, there was little chance of anyone actually seeing the angels that threw them.'

She wipes her hands on her robe. 'However, it is true that when the authorities found out it caused a scandal, such that new locks had to be fitted to the tower door and a rule was instituted that neither choir nuns nor novices were allowed to enter without the express permission of the abbess.' She sighs. 'I cannot tell you how many years it took me to find my way up here again.'

They stand together for a moment, watching the bonfires throwing up broad ribbons of smoke against a luminous sky.

Zuana finds herself smiling. Of course she would have been one of them. She should have guessed. The Lord punishes but he also forgives. The world is full of saints who began as sinners. Or, if they were always good, found their goodness pitted against rules others imposed upon them. She thinks of the novice with her incandescent anger, Benedicta with her mad music, Apollonia with her fashion-white face and stock of stories. Even the holy ones: Magdalena and her visions that are not allowed; Umiliana who, if she could, would break the rules by having even more of them. Without the rebels there would be no stories to tell, no fellow travellers to identify with.

In front of them the sky is now on fire. She thinks of the cocciniglia. Using a dye to treat a fever might be seen by some as a breaking of the rules. While there is wisdom in authority there must always be room for questions. Though you must also know how to question the answers you find. 'Are you listening, Faustina? There is a lot to learn and I will not always be here to teach it.' She has not heard his voice since before the illness. So which answers should she be questioning? The dye broke the fever, yes. In doing so it turned her urine red. But what if it also stained her spirit a little? Such things have been known to happen: a good remedy having another, bad effect. Those who take mercury for the pox suffer as much from the cure as from the illness – everyone knows that. She must ask the chief conversa how she feels now she is better. If she has time she will write an entry before Compline.

'It is amazing how beauty offers sustenance to the soul as well as the eye, don't you think?' the abbess says, as if this has been a conversation between them, rather than she alone who is doing the talking now. 'On the few occasions I have stood here with a sister since I became abbess, I have watched it bring God's peace back into some of the saddest of hearts. Or refresh some who are simply tired and in need of rest.' She pauses. 'Though of course it is not something to be talked about with everyone.'

The sunset is burning itself out now, the reds already shading into grey. Zuana glances at her. The lines on her face have been smoothed by the twilight and her skin has almost a glow to it.

'Thank you, Madonna abbess,' she says quietly.

'Oh, I only do as the Lord bids me. If He sees one of his flock dispirited or buffeted, it is my job as abbess to bring them back into safe harbour again. Come,' she says briskly, turning to her. 'The light is going and the staircase will become treacherous in the gloom. Oh, I almost forgot. There is something I need you to do, for the well-being of the convent. It concerns the novice . . .'

TWENTY-SIX

In the darkness Serafina shifts her weight, registering a sharp lump along her upper thigh. The pallet mattress has so little stuffing in it that she can feel the imprint of the keys wherever she turns. She likes the discomfort. For a while it brought her only terror, for with her chest unlocked there was no hiding place where she could be sure that her treasure would not be found. She could have tried to buy more stuffing, of course – such a thing is possible – but it might have brought suspicion. The discovery of a little poppy syrup or an extra lump of wax was one thing – Candida was being paid to make her life easier – but a duplicate set of keys to the outside doors . . . well, the profit to be made from that information would far exceed any paltry gain she could offer her. So instead she had had to pay the conversa off with a good piece of cloth when she took over cleaning the cell herself. Who would have thought it? A noble young novice scrubbing out her own cell. Well, it gives her something to do to make the time pass quicker.

Time. There is so little of it left and yet what there is seems endless. She closes her eyes – but knows she will not sleep. Her public docility has come at a cost. While her head stays bowed and her face remains serene, there are moments when the insides of her gut feel so twisted into knots that it is hard to walk upright. This state of constant excitement has become almost a pleasurable pain. She remembers it from before, at home – how every moment between their singing lessons was like a torture of waiting, sometimes so bad that she could barely breathe with it. Now the idea of him – the freezing, burning anticipation of it all – blots out everything; sleep, thought, hunger.

She has had precious little appetite since her arrival but recently she has come to enjoy the feeling that comes from not eating: the hollowness, the gnawing and fizzing in her stomach, is a kind of excitement in itself, like having something alive dancing inside her. Even her voice sounds purer, with less to hold it down, and when she is made to eat – when Federica calls her to the kitchen and presents her with the marzipan strawberry – the syrupy sweetness is so strong that it is all she can do not to vomit it back up again.

It is not easy, though deliberately contriving not to eat. You might think a convent would be happy to have its sisters starving a little – didn't the saints live on air? – but here there is moderation to everything: enough prayer, enough work, enough sleep (well, once you get used to the mad clock they live by) and enough food. The rule is that each nun must finish what is on her plate, and disobedience is a matter for penance.

Of course there are ways. Deceptions, pretences. She is fooling them in everything else; why not in this as well? At meals she comes into the refectory and finds her seat at the long table quickly, bending low over the plate, hands clasped under her chin for grace. When the grace is over she keeps her left hand close to her mouth while her right holds the spoon. In this way it is simple to transfer the food into her hand before it reaches her lips. No-one is watching, anyway. Those who are not intent on stuffing their faces are too busy listening to the readings: stories of mad men and women living in caves in the desert, vying with each other to endure the worst suffering. It is a technique – this squirrelling away of food inside her habit – that she had perfected after she had started singing. It was as if she had been in need of some minor disobedience to reassure herself that she was not becoming one of them. She liked the way the fear of being caught mixed in with the guilt and the fury; sweet and sour at the same time. She had hidden the scraps away in her cell and eaten a few of them later (how dare she – a novice eating in her cell when she should be asleep!), or used them to pay Candida, for the trade in titbits moved both ways.

Now she holds on to them until recreation, then surreptitiously lets them fall from under her robe as she wanders in the gardens. She is not the only one doing this. She spotted Eugenia doing the same thing the other day. They exchanged shy, sly little looks as they passed. At least they will not betray each other. The evidence is gone within seconds, thanks to the birds; the pigeons pecking away the finches and sparrows then pecking at each other. Today they swooped down from the bell tower even before they had dropped anything. Still she must be careful. Suora Umiliana, though she might approve of fasting and would no doubt love to see their flesh withering on their bones, is hawk-eyed when it comes to any infraction of the rules, however small.

Well, it is only a few days before it is over and she is gone from here for ever.

Only a few days. The thought slices into her belly. Sometimes it is hard to tell the hunger from the excitement. Gone from here. But to where? How? Oh, if only she could sleep. You could die of waiting here. She slides her hand into the mattress and extracts the keys from the cloth. The iron is cold to the touch.

She runs her fingers over the cut of the teeth, clean and smooth. Of course he would have found a good blacksmith. Like those men on the Carnival carts. When she had heard the stories of their songs she had felt her cheeks burning. She had died a thousand deaths that night he had brought back the keys. He had been so late she had thought he wasn't coming. She had barely made it back to her cell in time to avoid the watch sister. When she had unwrapped them there was a scrap of paper inside with the confirmation of the day and time upon it. That was it. No endearments, no poetry, no words of love. Since then there has been nothing. His face has long since blurred in her mind and now she cannot even hear his voice, so that when she thinks about the future sometimes all she can see is the black ink of the river at night.

She lives so much in her own head now (with so many novices involved in the play, the religious instruction has been reduced until the performance is over). Even at her most rebellious as a child she was never so alone. The only contact she has is within the choir and while the actual singing steadies her a little, the rawness returns as soon as it stops. There are moments when she craves company, a way to soak up some of the tension inside her, only she is terrified of what someone might spot in her, even though most of them are half mad with Carnival anticipation themselves. Except for Suora Zuana. The dispensary mistress seems oblivious to it, distant almost. Yet out of all of them Zuana is the one she cannot see, the one she fears most. She goes out of her way to avoid her and when they pass each other, on the way to chapel or in the cloisters, she is certain she can feel her watching her, probing to see what is going within her.

Their time spent together in the dispensary feels like a lifetime ago. The ointments, the spitting treacle, the ginger balls . . . She thinks about it more than she wants to. She tells herself that it is because the older nun is clever that she needs to be careful of her in case she suspects something. But it is more than that. What started as anxiety has turned into something more uncomfortable, a gnawing that has nothing to do with hunger but comes instead from guilt. Guilt that the one person who has helped her, shown her kindness and understanding (God knows, more than her own mother ever did), will be seen to have failed with her and brought disgrace upon the convent – perhaps even be blamed in some way for her escape.

These feelings make her angry and she tries not to think them but when she is awake at night they return. What if they punish her? Take away her privileges, stop her working on her remedies, even confiscate her books? How would she live then?

Serafina considers leaving a letter saying that it is nothing to do with Zuana, relating how much she has helped her. Except she knows that would makes things worse. She would pray for her, only prayer is not possible any more. How can she ask God's help for anything now? Whatever the wrongs done to her they are nothing compared to the one she is about to commit.

She closes her eyes again and tries to sleep. From somewhere in the gardens comes the screeching and yowling of a cat fight. She relishes the noise, finds it exhilarating rather than alarming. She brings her right arm up and lays it across her belly, feeling the flatness of her empty stomach, the ridge of her hip bone, as a hot and cold shiver runs down into her groin. So be it. Even if she brings the world down upon all their heads there is no going back now.

TWENTY-SEVEN

O, you will never be His bride if you go by the easy path.
You fool yourself that you can fly to heaven without wings.
But there is no value in being good after death.

The voices die away and the harp brings the song to a close. An audible hum of appreciation moves through the audience. The parlatorio is packed, all the best seats taken by the women visitors; a sea of jewelled hairnets, starched ruffs, slashed sleeves and pinched waists with such expanses of satin and brocades flowing around them that every time they settle themselves they bring their own rustling accompaniment to the music.

In front of them, on a set of benches, Zuana sits with those few choir nuns who are not called upon to perform. They face the stage and keep their backs to the audience so that there is little risk of them making eye contact with the men, who are crowded in at the back, unrecognisable in cloaks and masks: brothers, fathers, uncles, cousins, not to mention a sprinkling of those who, though they will have argued family status at the gatehouse, have just come for the singing, their Carnival calendar taking them around all the best concerts in town, with Santa Caterina high on the list this year.

At the front the choir and convent orchestra face each other, as if to pretend that they are performing for themselves alone. Suora Purità has her head and hands poised over the organ, Lucia and Perpetua are bent over lute and viol, while Ursula keeps her fingers cupped around the strings of her harp as if she is still cradling the notes she has just released. At her feet sits a flute, which she will play later. Its presence in the room has already caused a lively debate in chapter since there are those – some outside as well as in – who would consider it almost indecent for a woman to be seen in public playing any instrument with her mouth. The fact that it is there at all is testimony to the passion of Benedicta's arguments, along with the thinly veiled threat that her arrangement of one of the more popular song cycles might not be able to be performed at all without it.

Across from the orchestra sits the choir itself, each of its forty sisters in freshly laundered robes and pressed black veils over wimples newly starched with egg whites left over from the baking. And in front, marked out by their white robes with the echo of the angelic about them, a handful of novices, easy on the eye as well as the ear. One especially.

Benedicta gives her a signal. As she takes in her breath it seems as if everyone else holds theirs.

> *Here am I, a little lamb,*
> *A new bride of God,*
> *I live in splendour*
> *And celestial ardour.*

The words are from Rome, written by one of the Pope's new favourites, though the setting – as joyful as Serafina's own voice – is Benedicta's. Even Zuana, who is not generally susceptible to such over-sugared sounds, is charmed. She glances to the carved wooden seat (brought especially from chapter for the occasion) where the abbess sits, ramrod-straight, her hands like a pair of resting white doves in her lap. It had been she who had suggested the text as a suitable one for Carnival, during the same chapter meeting at which tempers had flared over the use of the flute. Not surprisingly, with the exception of Umiliana and Felicità everyone had been won over by it.

> *I cheer the holy angels with my song.*
> *My eyes are fixed on*
> *the sun of Paradise,*
> *And my life sustained*
> *by an infinite beauty.*

Certainly it is perfect for the occasion: the mix of innocence and fervour irresistible to any prospective novices in the audience and also – more importantly – their parents. 'Christ is the one son-in-law who will not cause me trouble.' The words had been those of Ferrara's great Isabella d'Este, when she had married two of her own daughters to the Church. The nunnery that had received them had been lucky indeed, since there had been no greater patron in the whole of Italy. However, with a songbird such as this one Santa Caterina will do well enough.

And it is not yet over. There are still Petrarch's sonnets to the Virgin to come, in a new setting that shows the girl's voice at its finest, then, after refreshments, the play in the refectory before an audience of female relations and benefactors. If the performance goes as well as the concert – and the only concerns are that Suora Lavinia finds her courtier's costume, which has gone missing, and that the nun in charge of special effects gets the moment right so that the thunder coincides with the miraculous breaking of the wheel rather than rumbling irrelevantly two or three speeches later – then the convent will surely have delivered up its finest Carnival entertainment ever. Yes, Zuana thinks, the abbess has every right to look satisfied.

As the song draws to a close all eyes are fixed on the girl. She glances up quickly towards the audience then drops her gaze demurely to the ground. Though some will see a glow of performance about her, to Zuana's eyes she looks gaunt and exhausted, almost feverish with the excitement of it all. Perhaps it is no wonder. Extreme goodness can be as taxing as extreme rebellion. Once Carnival is over and normality has returned she will find convent life gentler and more soothing. If, that is, gentleness and soothing are what she really wants.

In the orchestra Suora Ursula picks up her flute and brings it to her lips as the audience settles itself for more pleasure.

The concert ends and the singers disband. Behind a screen a table is now revealed laden with refreshments: fine wines next to fine glasses, hand-painted ceramic plates piled high with biscuits and sugared almonds; and, in the middle, a glass bowl full of the glowing colours of marzipan fruits. The families and visitors surge forward to meet and congratulate the performers, and a few of the younger men are so eager to get to the front that there is some shoving and pushing along the way (protected by their masks, there is now the chance for a little Carnival courtesy as well as compliment). When they arrive, however, they are disappointed. The songbird herself is already gone, whisked out through the back door by Umiliana, who, having been a veritable lioness in her protection of all her novices, now sacrifices her visiting rights to chaperone Serafina in the interval between the concert and the performance.

They go first to the chapel, where they are joined by Suora Perseveranza, excused from the festivities to spiritually compose herself for her ordeal at the hands of the pagan emperor. From prayer they move to the refectory, where it becomes Serafina's task to arrange the remaining chairs and light the candles in readiness for the performance. Though it is humble work for a young woman whose voice has just captivated some of the city's most discriminating music lovers, she exhibits no resentment or impatience at her fate; simply does everything she is instructed, occasionally glancing out through the window to where the day is gradually dying.

By the time the watch sisters in the gatehouse have counted out the last male visitor and closed and secured the doors against possible intruders (a procedure most rigidly observed today of all days), and the abbess has accompanied the most noble women, sashaying across the courtyard like a fleet of well-rigged galleons, into the refectory, the twilight is advanced enough for the candles to light up the stage, leaving just enough remaining natural light for the actors to move behind the curtains.

The novice mistress's attention is now divided between those of her charges who will perform and the others who will be spectators, and everyone is vying for the best seats behind the benefactors. Such is the bustle and chatter that Serafina finds it easy to slip away from the throng and select a place for herself at the far end of a row at the back.

There are still a few empty places elsewhere when Zuana takes a seat to the right, almost directly in front of her. She turns a little to survey the room and as she does she catches Serafina's eye.

'Your voice was heavenly in the concert,' she says lightly before the girl can drop her gaze. 'The parlatorio was ringing with your praises.'

Far from taking pleasure in being complimented, the novice looks confused, almost anxious. 'Thank you,' she says with a half-smile. Zuana glances back towards the stage across a sea of elaborate veils and tall head dresses. 'I fear you will not see much from here. You should find a place closer to the front.'

'Oh, no, no . . . I am happy here.' The girl shakes her head. Zuana notices how her hands are clasped tightly in her lap, one on top of the other as if to stop them trying to escape. 'I . . . am, well, I am very tired now.'

Her voice trails away as the noise level in the room rises. With the men gone the women are more animated, rowdy even. She would not be the first young novice to yearn for company after solitude only to find it hard to be amid so many people and so much clamour.

There comes a sudden hushing and shushing as Suora Scholastica emerges from behind the curtain and stands waiting patiently, her full-moon face beaming with nervous excitement. Someone claps their hands to signal silence. She clears her throat.

'Welcome, dear friends and benefactors of the convent of Santa Caterina, to this, our humble entertainment.' Behind her the curtain rolls and twitches as someone moves along against it.

In the same way that the body needs food and sleep to thrive,
so the spirit also needs recreation and rest.

She pauses, smiling broadly, and around the room people smile back, for it is impossible not to be affected by her enthusiasm.

For this reason those wise men who established convents
saw fit to allow the sisters to put on sacred plays and comedies
by which to aid learning and to enjoy a little spiritual fun.

Someone in the audience lets out a little cheer and a ripple of laughter moves through the rows. A few of the noblewomen of Ferrara will no doubt have heard stories of convents where such entertainments are banned or curtailed following the new rules from the council of Trent, and are concerned lest the same thing should befall their owns sisters and daughters here.

'The first scene . . .' Scholastica raises her voice to make it heard. These words have taken her many months to compose and she is determined that people are going to listen to them. 'The first scene of our presentation of the martyrdom of Santa Caterina takes place in the emperor's palace in Alexandria.'

The curtain parts, pulling slowly back from either side to reveal a wooden cut-out of an entrance with two painted pillars to either side. To the left stand a few noble courtiers and scribes, draped in fabrics and hats, and opposite them the emperor, tall and imperious, though still recognisable as Suora Obedienza, in a velvet cloak and a gold diadem, with a fuzzy black beard clinging precariously by two straps to her chin. A spirited interchange takes place between them about the pleasures of pagan living and the power of the gods and then the music starts, with the courtiers giving a short dance, the steps of which most of the nobles in the audience could execute with their eyes shut.

Everyone now is craning their necks to see. Even Umiliana, who of course must disapprove in principle, cannot help but be a little curious in practice. Zuana glances back towards Serafina, who sits upright, eyes to the stage with an almost fierce attention. This time next year she could be behind the curtain herself, for there are ample opportunities for good voices during the musical interludes. Next year. How many Matins and Vespers and prayer hours will have come and gone before then? There was a time when Zuana knew the answer to that; could compute the number of offices, even the number of psalms sung, between each and every feast day. Everything becomes easier when you stop counting. Has the girl reached that stage already?

The dance is interrupted by the banging of a drum and

through the back entrance two soldiers appear, their brass helmets picking up the flare of the candles. They pull with them a figure in a long white shift and a wig of golden curls down to her shoulders. This arrogant young girl has been found defying the will of the gods in favour of her own Saviour. The audience gives a little gasp of pleasure. She seems so small, too fragile almost to be God's messenger. Yet she must debate with the emperor's scribes and either recant her Christian beliefs or be tortured.

She – Perseveranza – opens her mouth and a breathy singsong voice comes out. She is not the convent's greatest actress but there is a passion to her when it comes to portraying martyrdom and once given the stage she is not afraid to use it.

The emperor claps his hands to begin the debate. The scribes open their books and pontificate but Santa Caterina passionately rebuts every argument. From offstage comes a loud crash, followed by a cry. The actors momentarily freeze, glancing nervously in the direction of the noise. The audience hears a stifled giggle and hushing. The debate starts again. Words fly. Caterina trumps her opponents, and the emperor claps his hands to mark the end of the debate, only to trap part of his beard between his palms so that it pulls away from his face and he/she has to hold on to it as the curtain closes in front of them. The smiles are everywhere now. Everyone, except the actors, yearns for such mistakes, for in a world so finely ordered they offer a taste of splendid, infectious chaos.

Out from behind the curtain three young women in peasant costumes emerge to talk about the wonder of the young virgin (and give the converse behind time to move the scenery). One of them, Eugenia, offers up a song about the joys of nature. The audience is entranced. She is a pretty thing and with her veil and habit gone she moves her body elegantly to the music. It is as well that there are no men in the audience to admire her, though they might find her a little thin for the fashion. Before Serafina's arrival she had been the nightingale of Santa Caterina and she has taken her dethronement hard. I must mention it to the abbess, Zuana thinks. She moves her head to try to spot Chiara – she will be in the front somewhere, next to the most influential of the guests – but the crowd is too thick.

The song ends and the audience offers up a little gasp of pleasure. On the stage Eugenia positively glows with her triumph. Zuana glances back to see what Serafina is making of the challenge.

But Serafina is not there. Her seat is empty.

Zuana turns and looks further along the row – perhaps she has moved to get a better view – but it is hard to tell, as the room outside the throw of the candle flames is gloomy now.

In the twilight beauty of the bell tower in Zuana's mind's eye the abbess turns to her again. 'Officially, as it is within the first three months, she should not be allowed to watch the play but she has done the convent such service with her voice that I feel it would be cruel to deny her the entertainment . . .'

Could she have left? Become so tired that she must retire to her cell? Surely not. No novice, however fatigued, would miss such entertainment. Though if she had slipped away no-one would have noticed, for the whole audience, especially those towards the back, are transfixed by what is taking place on the stage.

Zuana acknowledges a sharp twinge in her gut.

'Of course usually the novice mistress would look after her but she will be too busy with the other performers. So I would like you to keep a watch on her . . .'

She slips out of her seat and moves behind, to the back of the refectory, to check more thoroughly.

'Though it would be better if you did not make your observation too obvious. She has worked hard these last few weeks and I would not like her to think we do not trust her.'

There is no-one there. The girl has disappeared.

Zuana makes her way towards the door, trying not to disturb those around her. The last thing she sees is the curtain opening to reveal two of the converse scuttling offstage too late after setting up the wheel.

Outside, the upper loggia of the cloisters is growing dark and it takes a few seconds to adjust her eyes. Once she does she is surefooted: down the stairs and across the courtyard towards the girl's cell in the corner. The door is shut, no light from underneath.

She turns the latch and pushes it open.

She has not been in here since that first night almost three months before. She has an image of a young woman flattened against the wall, hair wild, howling, howling for her lost freedom. 'I am buried alive in this tomb.' The snarl of fury. So much rebellion. So much life . . .

In the deep gloom she makes out the shape of a figure in the bed. Where has it all gone? She remembers the weight of her body as the draught started to work. 'It will not make me give in.' And now what? Was she really so broken? So ready to curl up and die here, just like all the rest.

'Serafina?'

She moves towards the bed. But even before she reaches it she knows what she will find, realises suddenly what is happening here; understands it exactly, deeply, completely, as if she had known it always but chosen not to look. And a wave of cold and hot wonder runs through her.

'The words came from my mouth, not from my heart.'

She rips back the bedclothes. The fat bundle of cloth roughly fashioned to the shape of a human figure looks pathetic even in the gloom. She picks it up and it unrolls to reveal a Christ doll in the centre. There are those that would see the use of the baby as a blasphemy.

She is moving fast now, out of the cell along the corridor towards the gatehouse. The parlatorio is dark and the gateroom empty: there is no sister on duty here, as everyone is given dispensation from their work to see the play. But both outer doors are locked and bolted, and the only keys will be in the pockets of the gate sister and the abbess.

So if not here, then where? And how?

As she crosses the courtyard into the second cloisters a great crash of thunder explodes into the air. In the refectory, God is entering the drama. The noise is such that it penetrates the infirmary and a few seconds later Clementia's voice rises up, moaning, straining against her cords. Will it be angels or devils this time? But it brings with it another glancing memory: the girl coming out of the dispensary, hands hidden in her robe. And behind her Clementia's insistent voice: 'The angel from the gardens is waiting for you . . . See – see – my night angel is returned.'

Inside her ranting what had she been saying? Yes, Serafina had been caught once out of her cell after dark. And had suffered penance for it. But now Zuana thinks about it, that had been after Clementia had been put under restraints, surely? In which case . . . in which case, how often might she have seen her before then?

'She has worked hard these last few weeks and I would not like her to think we do not trust her.'

Has everyone been so fooled?

Through the second cloisters she moves into the grounds. This is forbidden territory after dark, and though she has done it once – no, twice, with special dispensation to collect a herb that was needed urgently – she is less sure of her way. She recalls the image of the convent from the perspective of the tower: the gardens, the pond, the fruit trees, and out to the walls. And with it comes the straggling line of pale rocks and stones, like ragged stitching, moving from the edge of the second cloisters to – where? A point near the wall by the river's edge. Pale stones. On the ground in daylight no-one would notice them but at night, unless there was no moon at all, their brightness would mark a path, which once picked out could be navigated swiftly enough.

Now she knows what she is looking for it is easy to find and as she follows the line, lifting her skirts to avoid the undergrowth and brambles, she remembers an angry young novice picking up a handful of stones and hurling them into the pond, while she, her appointed guide and mentor, showed her around the grounds, describing the wonders of a convent with its walled river storeroom, through which a great wealth of trade moves in – and out – through double-locked doors to the world beyond. Sweet Jesus, has the girl remembered and used everything?

By the time she reaches the storeroom doors, she is panting and breathless. She can hear sounds from the streets around but the wall near to where the line of stones ends is deserted and the doors themselves are closed. No sign of life. Nothing. She leans against the wood, gasping to get her breath back. As she stands there, her mind racing, she becomes aware of something, some scratching or sliding noise, from within. She turns her head so that her ear is hard against the wood and listens. Beyond is the inner storeroom, with another door that leads to the outer store and from there to the river. Is there someone there? Yes? No?

She puts out a hand to the iron handle above the keyhole, then as quietly as she can she pushes against it. It holds firm. Of course, it is locked. As will be the one beyond, no doubt. No.

She is imagining the noise. Who could possibly get their hands on these keys? The abbess apart, both the cellulare and the chief conversa are diligent beyond words.

Aaaah! Sweet Madonna. The chief conversa . . .

'I dosed her with basil and eau de vie. They gave me dispensation to help . . . The novice mistress said it would be good for me.'

Even Zuana, who knows nothing, knows that at night the conversa – a light sleeper – keeps the keys under her own weight beneath the mattress. In a fever, however, how easy would it have been to slip one's hand under and . . . But her illness was almost two weeks ago. If the keys had gone missing then everyone would know by now. So what? Could she have had them copied? But how? By whom? The more Zuana thinks, the less she understands. But something is happening here. The girl's absence and the wrapped body of clothes is proof enough. That and the rolling panic in her own stomach.

By the time she gets back to the refectory the spectacle has finished. The nuns are lighting candles all around now and there is excited chatter and laughter as the audience mingle with the performers. The chief conversa is nowhere to be seen but the abbess is prominent enough, basking in the glow of success with two or three finely dressed women grouped around her. While this is hardly the time to announce that they may have lost a novice over the wall, it is clear that she has to know.

A good abbess has eyes in the back of her head and long before Zuana reaches her she has registered her arrival in the room, flicking a glance and then a frown in her direction. As she approaches, Zuana hastily wipes the sweat from her face.

'Suora Zuana.' The abbess turns and welcomes her easily. 'Lady Paolo, Signora Fiammetta, this is our beloved dispensary mistress. It is she we have to thank for the health of the convent and the splendid aromas that rise up from our pomades and hanging baskets.'

The women glance at her, politely uninterested. They are both so thickly painted that the slightest smiles would crack their faces. Ambergris and honeysuckle, Zuana thinks. And a hint of musk underneath. It would cost the convent a small fortune to produce their smells. She bows her head.

'I ask forgiveness for the interruption, Madonna Chiara. But I need the keys to the river storehouse.'

'The river storehouse?' The abbess's voice is light. 'What? Are we in need of more supplies at this time of the evening?'

'Yes . . . something for one of the . . . younger novices.'

She watches the abbess's eyes narrow. 'I see. Of course then. Do you need help? I . . . I am not sure who I can spare for you at this moment.'

'No. No, I . . . I'll be fine alone.'

The abbess moves her hands inside her robe to the belt that she wears underneath, always, whatever the occasion, and from it unclips a ring with two solid iron keys.

'Here. At this hour you will need a candle and a taper. Take one from the stage.' She continues brightly, 'And come back to us soon, yes?'

The flash in her eye belies the comfortable smile she gives as she turns back to her painted guests.

TWENTY-EIGHT

Once down the stairs and across the courtyard Zuana quickens her pace, the taper protected in her hands, until she is half running through the second cloisters, out along by the herb and kitchen gardens, then bypassing the stones to go instead around the pond and out across the small orchard towards the river.

'Though do not make your observation too obvious. She has worked hard these last few weeks and I would not like her to think we do not trust her . . .' The abbess's words, thrown over her shoulder as they descended the stairs of the tower, had been casual, almost an afterthought.

Except how was one supposed to watch over someone who must not know she is being watched? Dear God . . . The girl had been out of her sight for what – five? – maybe ten minutes at the longest. Zuana's skirts catch on brambles and she has to wrench them free, feeling the material snag and tear. Had the abbess herself known something when she said that? Suspected, even? In which case who is not trusting whom here?

In the gloom she misses her step and almost trips. She forces herself to slow down. Running within the convent is strictly forbidden except in the case of fire, as the very act of it gives birth to panic. More importantly, she cannot afford to sacrifice the light of the taper, for the dusk is turning to night fast now . . .

The brick façade of the storehouse comes up ahead of her, the convent walls rising up behind it. At the doors she bows her head. 'Dear God,' she begins again. 'Dear God, I give myself into your . . .' But the prayer is interrupted by what is definitely the sound of something moving on the other side.

She slips the key into the hole and feels it bite against the lock, then turn heavily. There is a flat clunk as the bolt moves and the door cracks open. The noise sounds enormous. She pushes the door further and steps inside. The yawning gap reveals only darkness. She stands for a moment, registering the silence. She feels stinging like a thousand needle pricks running through her body and knows it is fear. If there is someone in here . . .

On the ground nearby comes a sudden scrabbling and something heavy scuttles fast over her feet, and it is all she can do not to cry out. An animal – it is only an animal running, Zuana, she tells herself. Most likely a rat. Was that what she had heard? Has she come all this way just to trap a water rat, gorging itself on convent supplies? She brings the taper to the candle and is pleased to find that her hand is steady as she lights it.

The flame jumps up into the darkness to reveal a room that is already mapped out in her mind: one wall stacked with crates and sacks, another with wine barrels and a salt container, and at the back a locked door, which leads to the outside store and from there to the river itself. Everything is as she imagined it. Except for one thing. The door in the back wall is not locked. Indeed it is not even properly closed.

She takes a few steps towards it. Her sandals are soft on the floor but not so soft that she can conceal the rustle of cloth over grit and straw. As she stops so does the noise. There is no sound anywhere. But there is something stronger than sound now.

There is feeling. Someone has been here. Is still here now. She knows it.

She reaches the door. It opens inwards and as she pulls it quietly she lifts the light so that she sees everything at the same time. The room is empty save for a few crates. But straight ahead, the double doors that give out on to the river are open. She can hear the slap of the water and the thud of the convent's old rowing boat bumping against the small dock. And in the middle, in silhouette, is the figure of a woman dressed in full skirts, tucked bodice and piled hair. The missing donated courtier's costume, no doubt, out of fashion already but wealthy enough to denote status on the body of a young woman, and one with such a fine head of long hair that if anyone were to pass her on a Carnival street now it would never occur to them to see her as a fugitive from a convent.

The figure is already turning as she crosses the floor.

'Serafina!'

'Oaah!' The wail she lets out echoes out over the water.

'What are you doing here?'

'No! No! Stop. Don't come near me.'

And such is her anguish that for a second Zuana hesitates.

'Be careful. Step away from the water's edge. What are you doing?'

'What does it look like?' And her voice is all spit and panic. 'I am getting out. He is come for me. He is taking me away.'

He? Zuana glances quickly around her. But the room behind is empty and there is no-one on the dock. The girl is clearly alone.

'Who? Who is come?'

'He will be here directly.' She waves her hand wildly. 'I can hear the boat. It is coming. Don't move, I tell you. Just go away, go back now and nothing bad will happen.'

But instead of going back Zuana walks towards her. Close to, the water is choppy, butting angrily against the wood. If someone is out there then they will still have to negotiate their way to the wharf and moor in the semi-darkness. And if there is no-one, then surely she will be able to pull her back.

'Don't move. I told you – if you move . . . I'll . . . I'll jump.' And she shifts her weight closer to the deck's edge.

Zuana stops. How long has the girl been standing here in the darkness waiting? Half an hour? No, by now surely it would be more. There is a wind building and the air smells of rain. 'Serafina, Serafina,' she says, and she keeps her voice gentle. 'Listen to me. It doesn't have to be like this. At the end of the year you can—'

'I will never get to the end of the year. And even if I d-did no-one would listen to me. You s-said so yourself. Not the abbess, not the B-Bishop.'

'But what you are doing here will only bring catastrophe upon yourself. You cannot live alone outside. The scandal—'

'I don't c-care about scandal. I don't care about sc-scandal. I can't stay here. I'll die in this place. Don't you see? I am not like you. It will k-kill me.' The depth of her terror is sending stammer tremors through her voice. 'He is coming. He – he – he will look after me.' She stares out quickly over the black water. But the truth is that there is no boat to be heard or seen anywhere. 'He – he is coming,' she repeats. 'He is coming. He is waiting on the other b-bank.'

She moves towards the old rowing boat.

'No!' Zuana steps forward instinctively. 'There is nothing for you out there. Only disgrace.'

But the girl is crouched already, fumbling with the ropes. There are probably only three or four arm's lengths between them.

Zuana stretches out her hand to her. 'Come. Take my hand. It will be all right. I will help you . . .'

The girl glances up at her, and in the flickering candle her eyes for that moment shine out. 'I can't. Don't you see? I can't,' she hisses. 'Please, leave me, just turn and go away. W-when I am out of here I will never tell a living soul that you found me. Even if they c-catch me and put the screws on me and break all my fingers I will never tell them. I swear. Just turn around and go.'

'And what if you drown?'

'I don't care.' And now suddenly the girl's voice is calm. 'Because whatever happens it is better than slow death in here. Please. I beg you.'

Zuana stands paralysed. She knows she should move, take hold of her, bring her back, but . . .

The moment stretches out around them.

The girl smiles. 'Thank you,' she says simply.

She turns her attention to the ropes – and as she does so there is sudden movement behind them.

'Get hold of her. Stop her – now!'

It is the voice of the abbess.

Zuana responds involuntarily, throwing herself across the wood, grabbing the girl's arm, pulling her back while she flails and kicks and yells. Within seconds the abbess is with her, grasping the other arm, wrenching the girl's fingers off the ropes, and then both of them are dragging her away from the river's edge, inch by inch back from the boat towards the open doors. Inch by screaming inch, until they cross the threshold into the room. Anyone within listening distance will be hearing bloody murder now, though being Carnival it could easily be mistaken for an over-enthusiastic courtship.

'The keys. Give me the keys, Zuana.'

The abbess lets go of the girl to lock the doors behind them.

'NOOOO!' the girl howls in the darkness, breaking free of Zuana again and throwing herself towards that disappearing sliver of freedom between the closing doors. But the abbess is there blocking her way, and Zuana grabs her back.

'NOOOO! Jacopo! Jacopo! Where are you?' The desperation bounces and echoes off the walls.

The door bangs shut, the key turns and suddenly the outside world is gone; no lapping water, no expanse of night sky, no open air, nothing. Nothing.

'Haa-aaagh! No-oooo!'

The girl sags, suddenly such a dead weight that Zuana has to let her down on to the floor. The abbess recovers a hooded candle from by the door and, lifting it up, moves over to where the girl is lying, slumped and moaning in Zuana's arms. She stares at her for a moment, then shakes her head. 'It is over,' she says quietly, almost wearily. 'It is over.'

But the girl is moaning to herself and does not seem to hear her.

She raises her voice. 'You should thank me. You could have waited out there all night and he would still not have come.'

Now she has her attention. 'What? What do you mean?'

'I mean he is not here any more. He left Ferrara two days ago.'

'No! No. You are lying. You don't know anything about him.'

'On the contrary, I know a great deal. I know for instance that he – Jacopo Bracciolini – that is his name, yes? – is a very fortunate young man. His composing and vocal talents have been recognised and he has accepted an offer of work in Parma as assistant capelle master. You should be happy for him. It means he is saved from the prosecution and imprisonment that would certainly have followed an attempt to kidnap a novice of one of the city's greatest convents.' She brushes down her skirts, as if this is an ordinary matter of convent business she is now attending to. 'Indeed he is doubly lucky, since I cannot imagine any other employer would have taken him, given that he was dismissed from his last post for the attempted rape of one of his noble pupils.'

'Noooo . . .' the girl moans.

The abbess waits. She looks at Zuana and shakes her head slightly. While there are things they must talk about, this is clearly not the time.

She bends down and offers the girl her hand. 'Come. It would be best if you walked back yourself rather than having to be carried.'

But the girl recoils fiercely from her.

'You think me cruel, no doubt.' And her voice now is almost friendly. 'But I am less cruel than he has been. You should know it was not hard to persuade him to abandon you. He does not really care, you see. He may say he does, he may have sworn everlasting love — I am sure he did — you were fruit ripe for picking and had he been able to trick your father into marriage there would have been money in it for him. But in the end you are not worth the trouble you would cause him. The trouble you would cause all of them. Do you understand?'

But the girl does not answer, just moans quietly to herself.

'The truth is that God will care for you much more than any man ever will. And so will we — however much you might hate us now.'

Now the girl looks up. 'You're wrong. You're wrong about him. He loves me. He wouldn't just leave.'

The abbess sighs. 'Believe that if you will. But believe this also.' Her tone is harder now. 'For the welfare of your family and the convent, this, what happened here tonight, never took place. Is that clear? And if one word of it should become gossip, then I will make sure that however good his voice, Jacopo Bracciolini will spend the rest of his life rotting in a castle prison for gross indecency.' The girl stares at her. 'I think you know by now that I can do this.'

She gets up, making a gesture to Zuana to do the same, leaving the girl curled on the ground like a broken doll.

They move quickly into the outer storeroom.

'I must return to the refectory. I have been away too long. You will have to get her back to the cloisters on your own.'

Zuana nods, though it may be too dark for it to be seen.

'Take her to her cell and stay with her until I decide what to do with her . . . Can you do that?'

It is only a short pause. Nowhere near as long as the one when Zuana had stood paralysed on the deck, with the abbess somewhere in the room behind her. But now, as then, the air is too gloomy to know for certain what anyone could have seen. Or heard.

'Yes,' she says flatly.

'Good.' The abbess moves out into the gardens, the door swinging behind her.

But inside, on the floor of the inner storeroom, the girl has already made her own decision.

While the two women have been talking Serafina has had her fingers inside the pocket of her skirts. She has drawn out a glass vial and removed its stopper, careful not to lose a drop of the liquid as she takes it out. By the time Zuana turns back to her she has it to her mouth and is gulping greedily.

Zuana reaches her fast and smashes the vial out of her hand so that it jumps and clatters on the stone, the glass too thick to shatter. Immediately she is on her hands and knees feeling for it, a barrage of images instantly assaulting her. She is standing in the dispensary mixing up cocciniglia and water, a fever cooking her brain — and there is something strange about the arrangement on the shelves in front of her. Yet when she is well and upright again, and studies them more carefully, there is nothing missing; every ingredient is in its rightful place and there is no reason for her to check the level on each and every bottle.

Her fingers close around the glass. She brings it to her nose. God help us now. The ground is dry and the bottle is empty. She crawls back over to the girl, grabs her by the shoulders and pulls her up, bringing her face so close to her own that she has to look at her. 'How much, Serafina? How much was in there?'

But in answer the girl only licks her lips to make sure there is no drop left.

'Tell me!'

She shakes her head. 'It's one of the ingredients they give to those going to be tortured to death. Isn't that what you told me that night?'

'Oh, Heavenly Father,' Zuana says under her breath. 'What have we done to deserve this?'

She puts out her hand and strokes back the hair from the girl's face. She looks so tired and worn. Too much youth. Too much emotion. The lunar madness that can strike some young women at the onset of menstruation. This is how it started all those months ago. Please God, don't let it be how it finishes. 'Come,' she says gently. 'Come. Let's take you somewhere more comfortable.' She picks the girl up and hauls her to her feet, noting as she does so how thin her body feels beneath the robes, so much lighter than the one she lifted up from the floor of her cell all those months ago, and she wonders how this weight loss will increase her susceptibility to the drug. But none of this shows in her voice, which is kind, loving almost. 'So, Serafina, can you help me? Can you walk with me?'

The girl nods and starts to move her feet obediently. In the gloom she offers up what seems a crooked half-smile. 'I think it was enough not to feel pain. I hope so.'

TWENTY-NINE

The vomiting and the evacuation go on through that night and well into the next day.

Because Zuana has no idea how much poppy syrup she has drunk, she must assume the vial was full. The dose of hellebore she gives must be enough to empty her stomach but not so much that it will kill her. It is a balance that no apothecary, however experienced, can be sure of.

At least she is given the freedom of a night without interruption to start the process.

With the visitors gone, the abbess brings her flock together and congratulates them on the wondrous performances of the day and the glory they have brought to Santa Caterina, and announces that tonight of all nights they have earned a rest that will not be disturbed, even by prayer, so there will no service of Matins. The convent bell will remain silent until dawn. It is a popular dispensation, for now the excitement is over they are exhausted; indeed a few of the younger ones even weep a little at the news. If the novice mistress does not entirely approve of the decision, she is as tired as everyone else and says nothing against it.

As the convent slides into satisfied, deep sleep, the abbess and the dispensary mistress meet in the corner cell of the main cloister, where one of them holds open a young woman's mouth while the other pours into it a draught of poison made from pulped apple saturated with white hellebore root.

It does not take long for the first spasm to hit. Though by now she is almost unconscious, the agony is sharp enough to wake her: she opens her eyes in a kind of drugged terror and an unholy groan comes out of her mouth. Together they drag her from the bed on to the floor. For the next however many hours they must keep her sitting up with her head bowed over, to facilitate the evacuation but also to stop her drowning in her own vomit. It might be better if they could pray and the abbess is quick enough to find the right psalm on her behalf . . .

> *O God rebuke me not in Thine indignation*
> *Neither chasten me in Thy wrath*
> *For I am weak and my soul is in anguish.*

But once the spasms start in earnest they are so violent and fast that there is no time for speech, let alone prayer. It is physically exhausting work. The bowls Zuana brings fill and refill. When the diarrhoea begins the girl's body is racked by double agony. The stench fast becomes almost unbearable. They roll up their sleeves and tuck their habits into their belts to avoid the worst of the contamination. They strip her down to her shift so she will soil herself as little as possible and wrap her hair in a piece of material to keep it from falling over her face into the vomit. But they can do nothing about the sweat that pours off her or the way her limbs shake uncontrollably from the spasms that crack through her body.

There are those who swear to the efficacy of hellebore as an aid to exorcism, since any demon trying to bury itself deeper to escape the burns inflicted by holy water will find its hold on the body severed from within. While Zuana has never had cause to use it in such a way, she has seen it work enough to understand what that might look like: the torso so gripped by spasm that it can go as rigid as wood, lifting the backbone high off the bed as if some spiteful spirit is controlling it from within. But what she has never witnessed before is its effect on top of such a powerful soporific. The battle between a body wanting to let go and the eruptions seizing it from within is truly terrible to watch, so that there are times when the girl feels like a rag doll held between the teeth of a great dog who shakes her to and fro before flinging her down on to the ground, only to pick her up and start the whole thing again minutes later.

'Don't be frightened, Serafina,' she finds herself whispering to her as they lift her back up in anticipation of the next wave. 'Remember how we said that sometimes one must use a poison to cure a poison. It will not last for ever.'

But the poppy and the hellebore have her too deeply in their grip and it feels as if there is no reaching her. Across the girl's body Zuana meets the abbess's eyes and sees in them a look of such unashamed admiration that she feels almost shy. On the wall above the bed the figure of Christ looks down from a wooden crucifix. Suffering upon suffering. Who is to know how much is enough? Which sins can be forgiven and which remain?

As she falls backwards into Zuana's arms again the girl murmurs something.

'Srree – m srre.'

Zuana puts her head close to her mouth to try to hear more but it is gone, swallowed up in a long growl of pain as her insides contract again.

Somewhere towards the end of the night the abbess leaves.

She will have to appear at Lauds and before then she must return the stolen costume to the props cupboard, cleanse and dress herself, and get at least some sleep. By now the spasms have become less frequent and for a while Zuana wonders if the worst may be over. But almost as soon as she leaves a new wave of vomiting begins and it is all she can do to manage her on her own.

They had pulled the thin mattress down on to the floor to give the girl some respite from the hard stone and once the spasm has passed she lies flattened on it, her breathing fast and shallow, her skin covered in a mist of sweat which returns however many times Zuana mops her. How successful the hellebore has been will only become clear when the spasms finally stop and she becomes conscious again. But she has no idea if – no, she will not hear that word – when that will happen.

Out of the deep I have called unto Thee, O God
O Lord, hear my voice
Let Thine ears be attentive unto the voice of my supplication.

Outside, it starts to rain, gentle at first then much fiercer, with a wind driving the water. Whoever is still out after the madness of Carnival will be chased home by it. Our Lord is washing the streets clean in time for the beginning of Lent. Tomorrow the city will wake with a collective hangover and turn its face to abstinence and repentance. And if the repentance is sincere then surely He will listen.

If Thou, O God, shall mark iniquities, then who shall stand unaccused?
Yet there is pardon of sin with Thee, that Thou mayest be feared.

The downpour is so relentless that soon she can hear water from the roof gushing out in streams through gargoyle mouths on to the flagstones in the courtyard beneath. She has a sudden desire to be out in it, to be standing in the middle of the deluge, drowning in its freshness.

The cloth of her habit is stiff with vomit and traces of faeces and the smell is so pungent that the girl's condition will surely become obvious to everyone as soon as they wake. She turns her on to her side in case another spasm should take her and quickly slips out of the cell into the courtyard, taking the bowls with her. She puts them on the ground and the water hammers down into them. She washes them out as best she can, then lets them fill again as she lifts her face into the rain. The night is black, the half moon that was there before engulfed in thick cloud. Within minutes she is soaked, gasping with the cold. But she is also awake. On the river the wind will be smashing the rowing boat against the deck, the convent doors behind closed and locked. But then nothing happened there tonight, did it? Did it? She will not think about that now.

She goes back into the cell with the fresh water and washes the girl as best she can.

Purge Thou me with hyssop and I shall be clean
Wash Thou me, and I shall be whiter than snow
Turn Thy face from my sins and wipe out all my misdeeds
Make Thou unto me a clean heart, O Lord
And renew a right spirit within me.

There are a dozen other psalms she could recite: verses of supplication, cries of shame and guilt, calls for repentance, for forgiveness, for God's boundless mercy. But sitting over the novice's unconscious body now she is suddenly no longer sure about their efficacy; while the words are fine enough, none of them says what really needs to be said here.

The truth is that forgiveness can only come to those who are repentant. Yet the girl lying on the pallet is sixteen years old, in love and incarcerated against her will. What if, when she wakes and finds herself back in her cell for the rest of her life, she is not sorry for what she has done — only sorry that she has failed in the doing of it? The list of her sins is long: deceit, cunning, rage, lies, lust, disobedience. But the worst is surely despair. Sworn to silence now, where will she go for relief? Without the intervention of God's grace as well as his penance, what reason will she have not to fall prey to desperation?

'Forgive me, Lord. For not seeing what was in front of my eyes.' The girl is not the only one in need of grace and forgiveness. Zuana bows her head on her own behalf.

'Forgive me for not recognising her despair. For thinking only of my own sadness when I should have been listening to that of others. For not keeping guard over the poppy syrup in the dispensary. For my loss of concentration during the play. Forgive me for being too proud or too blind or too busy. For all these sins send me penance and, in your infinite mercy, if it be possible, save this young woman from further torment.'

After a while she notices a muddy line of light under the door of the cell; it is dawn already, muted this morning by the rain. She hears the bell for Lauds, followed by the watch sister's steps and the slapping of sandals on the soaked stone. She sits back against the wall and closes her eyes.

She has no idea how long she sleeps for. The day has already begun when the sound of groaning and the smell of fresh faeces wake her.

Outside, the sisters go about their daily business, moving quietly around them. The news has travelled fast. Santa Caterina's songbird has been taken ill with fitting and from where a lovely voice once came, now there is only a river of vomit. Her condition is grave. There is talk of how the cell itself is cursed; of how its predecessor, Suora Tommasa, had been healthy – and sweet-voiced also – until one day she was found throwing up her life all over the walls. This story is given more credence by the fact that the cell, even the cloister corridor close to it, is strictly out of bounds, as if there was indeed some contagion at work there.

Before the midday meal the abbess returns, bringing Zuana a change of robes and food and fresh water from the kitchen. She stands looking down at the girl. The face is calm now, the mouth slack, lips blistered where the poison of the draught has scorched them.

'When was the last spasm?'

'A while ago. Half an hour, maybe longer.'

'So the remedy has worked?'

'I don't know.'

The abbess glances up at her. 'But she is not going to die?'

'I don't know.'

'She is not going to die,' she says firmly, the words as matter-of-fact as the announcement of the menu for a feast day. How wonderful, Zuana thinks, to be so certain of everything. How wonderful and how terrible. 'I will sit with her if you want to rest.'

'No. I must watch still.'

After she leaves the girl's breathing becomes noisy through her parched mouth. Zuana puts a few drops of rosemary essence into the water and lifts her head while she moistens her lips, then pours a little gently down her throat. It is her father's remedy: once the body has no more to evacuate one must start to put something back, for with so much liquid gone the organs can dry up and no longer work properly. She chokes on it, and this time does not throw it back again immediately. But there is no sign of her regaining consciousness.

A few hours later Suora Umiliana comes to the cell, given permission by the abbess to say prayers over her most troublesome novice. Her distress at the sight that meets her is palpable. She sinks to the floor, hands clasped, lips moving almost before her old knees have found purchase on the hard ground.

Zuana feels a lurch in her stomach. Does Umiliana see something she does not? Perhaps she knows she is dying, senses it as she did with Imbersaga. Has she missed some change, some sign within the body? But the girl's pulse, when she finds it, is still the same weak but steady beat.

The room settles around the novice mistress's whispering intercession . . . God's love, His horror of our sins, the depth of His suffering, the wonder of a sinner returned to the fold. The joy of the final reunion even in death, the power of the light, the pull of the boundless, boundless sea of love.

Zuana listens, mesmerised by the older nun's flow. If only I could pray like that, she thinks: pray with my whole being poured into each and every word. Pray as if I could hear Him listening.

The prayers end, and Umiliana leans over and puts her finger gently on the girl's forehead before rising. 'Shall I ask the abbess to bring Father Romero?'

'No. No.' Zuana's voice is clear. 'She is not going to die.' The abbess's words have become her own now. 'This reaction to the remedy is to be expected. She will wake soon.'

But while Umiliana has been praying Serafina's face has moved from pale to a kind of grey and though her lips are open it is hard to know if she is still breathing. It was too much, Zuana thinks. If not the poppy, then the hellebore. I gave her too much . . . God help me.

'We must keep praying for her. That is all we can do.' The novice mistress takes hold of Zuana's fingers and squeezes them.

'Do not despair,' she says, as if she knows that this is one of Zuana's darkest temptations. 'You have done all that could be asked of you. He will know that.'

Oh, but I haven't, Zuana thinks. Not at all. And He will know that, too.

Time passes. She strokes the girl's head and pulls a cover over her. The bell sounds for supper and once more she hears the shuffle of feet across the cloisters. She pinches herself to stay awake.

'There is nothing more to be done, Faustina.'

She shakes her head. 'There has to be. There has to be something.'

'You are only a healer. There comes a point when you must give it up to God.'

'Ha! You sound like Umiliana.'

'Why don't you leave her for a while? Walk out in the air. Maybe take something to give you energy. Do you keep infusion of angelica root? I think you must do.'

'Yes, yes I do.'

'Then take a dose of it, with some peppermint essence. Make it strong. It will help you to get through the night. But before you go, give her some more rosemary water.'

'What if she vomits it back up while I am gone?'

'If she does there will be only a little bile. Not enough to choke on if she is on her side. At least it will show some sign of life.'

'Papa, Papa, I don't want her to die.'

'I'm afraid you are grown too fond, child. It does not make for good healing. Go now. You have done all you can.'

It seems days since she was last in the infirmary. The two elder nuns are asleep, while Clementia lies in her bed, singing quietly to herself. The room is clean, the floor washed, the hanging baskets fresh and the night candle already prepared on the small altar. Letizia has done a good job. Life, it seems, must go on. The very thought makes her want to cry. You are tired, Zuana, she says to herself sternly. And too much tiredness makes one maudlin.

In the dispensary she finds the angelica root and mixes it with a little wine and peppermint. It has kept her awake before and it will do again. She swallows the preparation and feels it moving into her stomach. It will take a while to work. She transfers more to another vial. She will need something for the second night. If indeed there is going to be one.

The bell marking the end of supper is already ringing as she leaves the room. She must hurry. The sisters will be returning to their cells and this is not the time to meet anyone, however kind and sympathetic.

But as she crosses back over the courtyard she sees something that makes her heart pound. In the corner of the cloisters, the door to the girl's cell that she had closed so carefully behind her is now wide open.

There is no way the girl could have done it herself. So who is in there? Has the abbess returned, bringing her supper? In which case why hasn't she closed the door?

She runs across the courtyard, regardless of the rules. And as she nears the open door she hears something, more a sound than a voice: a whining, like a line of taut thread vibrating in the air.

Inside, on the floor by the mattress, a figure is crouched, so small and bowed that it looks more goblin than human, the head larger than the body and naked save for a covering of white stubble over scabby skin.

For a moment Zuana stands transfixed in the doorway. Then as she goes closer the keening turns into words.

'See — oh yes, you can see Him. Yes, yes, I know you can. He is come to welcome you back. Oh, see how He bleeds for you, Serafina. Feel His breath on your face. If you open your eyes He will be there. Oh, He has been waiting for you to find Him. He has been waiting so long for you.'

'Suora Magdalena . . .' Zuana tries to keep her own voice gentle.

But the old woman does not turn, simply tilts her head to one side, like a beady-eyed bird detecting a sound. 'Not yet, not yet. I am with the child. See – she is better.' She gives a sudden girlish giggle. 'See what He has done for her.'

And as she comes closer, Zuana does indeed see. For the girl, lying on her side on the mattress, is awake, her eyes open and blinking.

Zuana takes a sharp breath and moves towards her, dropping down on to her knees next to the old woman.

'Serafina!' she says urgently.

The eyes are huge in her thin face, and there is a strange blankness to them, as if she has woken to something she does not yet understand. Three months ago she had come in young. Well, she is not young any more. But she is alive.

'Welcome, welcome.' Zuana cannot stop smiling. The girl stares at her, then seems to give a small nod.

'What happened?' Zuana's question is directed at the old woman – but she is not listening, simply rocking to and fro, singing to herself, the holy goblin returned.

Behind, out in the courtyard, Zuana can hear people moving. She must get up and close the door.

It is already too late.

'Oh, Sweet Lord Jesus. She is alive!' Suora Umiliana is standing in the doorway, a few brave souls, willing to risk disobedience, gathered behind her. 'Suora Magdalena has brought her back to us.'

But Magdalena is not listening to her, either. She has taken hold of the girl's hand now, thin claw on soft flesh, and is stroking the skin. 'See, see, I said He would come.'

The girl tries to pull herself up on the mattress but does not have the strength. Zuana supports her until she is almost sitting.

Umiliana is inside the cell now, others crowding in behind her.

Serafina opens her mouth a little, moving her tongue around her blistered lips. She looks at Zuana, then out across the room.

'I saw Him,' she says — and though hers is a sad little voice now, its silky beauty all burned out of it, it reaches everyone in the room. 'Yes, I do think I saw Him.'

THIRTY

In the beginning there was nothing. Just darkness, blessed darkness, deep, soft, like being wrapped in swathes of black velvet and held within the silence of an eternal night sky. No past. No future. No present. And it was good, this nothingness, an oblivion of mercy with no pain.

It had descended upon her as she moved across the gardens. She did not have to do anything. After all that had been done, nothing more was asked of her. She was not even scared. Zuana's arms were around her, her voice was in her ears and she was safe.

'Help me, Serafina. Walk a little, yes? Oh sweet child, I am so sorry.'

She wants to tell her that it is all right. That it doesn't matter any more. She wants to say that she is the one who should be sorry, not her. To thank her for what she has done, and to ask forgiveness, for she is not yet so lost that she doesn't know that what took place on the deck between them will bring trouble on her head.

'No, no, don't try to speak. Save your strength. Just a little further. We can talk later.'

Only there will be no later. Because when the drowsiness

comes it is not to be argued with. Behind it she feels the pull of the darkness, with its deep, rich velvet touch.

'We are nearly there. Keep walking, keep walking.'

And she does walk, because she does not want to disappoint her, not again. But after a while she has to stop, because the nothingness wraps itself around her and takes her away. And, just as she hoped, there is no pain.

Except, except – how can this be? – it does not last. How long she floats in the velvet black she has no idea. But she knows when it ends. Knows when the dark is torn apart by scorching white pain. Someone is hammering a long nail into the centre of her stomach. After the first there is another, then another. Once inside, the nails become scissors, slicing and chopping her innards into pieces small enough to be able to come out of her mouth. It happens so fast that she barely registers the nausea before the stuff is already up in her throat. The force of it sends her reeling so powerfully that if something or someone had not been holding her she would have fallen over. She watches in horror as her insides explode out of her mouth. The shock is almost worse than the pain. The next time the hammer hits the nail goes through her stomach into the bowels beneath. The sound of her groans and the smell of her own decay are everywhere.

She tries to breathe, to find her way back to the blessed darkness, but when she gets there it isn't blessed at all. She sees herself suspended, arms and legs dangling uselessly on either side, a spiked pole rammed through her, anus to mouth, like an animal on a spit ready for roasting. And when she looks around she is not alone. There are hundreds, even thousands, like her, figures stretching into the darkness as far as she can see, their bodies eviscerated, roasted, grilled, sliced and diced into bleeding bits by an army of squat, grinning torturers, black as the night they are born out of. There is flesh and pulp everywhere, and the terrible emptiness of silent screams, each soul locked for ever in their own suffering.

'Oh, but we did not sin like this,' she hears herself say. 'It was love, not lust, I swear. Bodies singing together, that was all . . . Oh Jacopo . . .' But even as the words form, her offending lips are wrenched open and another stream of bile pours out.

Now as she looks around, instead of devils in the darkness she sees a water rat, sleek, wet fur like a black veil around its head, face pale and twitching, teeth drawn, ready to sink into her insides. It looks up at her and smiles.

'Sometimes you must use a poison to cure a poison. Don't be frightened, Serafina, it will not last for ever,' it says, before the fangs go back in and the agony returns.

Further into eternity, when her guts are on the floor and there is nothing more to lose, she comes far enough out of the pain to open her eyes to the inside of her cell. She knows it must be her cell from the crucifix on the wall.

She fixes her gaze on it to stop herself sliding back into hell. She studies how He hangs there, slumped forward against the nails, ribs pushing out against his skin, each muscle singing in agony. Oh yes, He understands pain. He knows what it is to be consumed by suffering, the terror and the terrible aloneness of it. Oh, no-one should be so alone. She keeps Him in her mind after her eyes close. His bloodied face, His lacerated body. He would be so beautiful were He not in agony. She sees a young man standing tall, hair falling and curling over broad shoulders, the smooth, unblemished skin of his chest and the fine, fine face: high forehead, full lips and clean, clear gaze. If one loves him broken, how much would one love him whole? Oh Jacopo, where were you? A good saviour. Such strength, such goodness.

'He does not really care for you. You are not worth the trouble you have caused him.'

No. No. No. But He cares. Look at Him — oh yes, He cares. Always. Whatever the trouble, He cares enough to climb up the stairs on to his own cross and hang there in agony for an eternity waiting for her.

'I'm sorry. I am sorry . . .'

She tries to say the words loud enough for Him to hear but then the slicing starts again and all that's there is the long groan of her own voice.

The darkness returns, changed again. No bodies now but also no velvet. Instead just parched stone, hard, unforgiving, stretching up and out all around her, and she must lie on it for ever and ever. At least she has no bones. They have been ground up and vomited out or melted in the furnace of her insides. Her limbs are filled with sand, so heavy that it means she cannot move at all unless the pain does the moving for her. And everywhere is so dry — no moisture anywhere, only sand. In her body, in her mouth. She cannot swallow. She is so thirsty. So thirsty.

Now someone lifts her head and puts a finger across her lips, moving droplets of water inside her mouth. How it stings! After so much agony it is wonderful to be able to feel such a small, distinct pain. Then there is more water. It dribbles into her mouth, burns down the back of her neck. She chokes. It hurts but not enough to stop. She takes more, would be greedy if the hand did not gently resist her. Her insides start to groan and heave as it hits, and she feels herself retching, but nothing comes out.

Later — is it days or only hours? — she realises that the pain has stopped.

She is flooded with relief, the utter joy of feeling nothing. Serenity like a flat surface of water; no ripple, no wind, nothing, just the wonder of being still. How is it possible for it to have gone? For there to have been so much of it and now none at all? How does that happen? How much care does it take? What kind of miracle?

'Dominussalvedeigracias.'

The singing is high and thin. She moves her eyes up from the still surface of the water to see a bank of reeds moving in the wind. And there is light now, she thinks. Surely it must be the sun, because she can feel warmth on her skin. In the distance there is a heat haze across the world, and inside it something – a figure? – walking towards her.

'See – oh yes, can you see Him, Serafina? Oh, He cares so much. He sent me to wake you.'

It is a strange voice, childish except for the cracks of age in it. She knows it immediately, feels it inside as a familiar hollowness. She concentrates on the image ahead of her. The air is so warm. No wonder everything shimmers so. Within the shimmer a figure forms, tall, flowing hair, then seems to un-form again, as if he has stumbled and the haze has engulfed him again.

'See how His poor hands and feet bleed. But He smiles for you. He has been waiting for you. He is come to welcome you back.'

Back. She feels a sudden terrible ache inside her, as if after her innards they have scooped out her womb. But she keeps on looking and He is closer now. Yes, yes, she sees Him: that beautiful broad forehead pierced by a line of fat little wounds, the eyes clear, filled with so much understanding. *He* cares. *He* would not leave. He loves me.

'If you open your eyes He will be there.'

She lets out a slight cry. She knows she must wake now. Knows that is what He wants her to do.

She opens her eyes. It is grey in the cell. No shimmer or light here. The smell is foul and stale. On the wall Christ hangs forlornly off the cross. Next to her the shrivelled figure of Magdalena, her face like a pickled walnut, is rocking and laughing with girlish delight.

'Serafina?' And now Suora Zuana is on the floor next to her, her face close to hers, tired, but smiling, smiling like the sun. 'Oh, welcome, welcome.'

Beyond, in the doorway, she sees Suora Umiliana, with Eugenia, Perseveranza, Apollonia, Felicità and others peering in around her.

'Sweet Jesus! She is alive! Suora Magdalena has brought her back to us.'

The novice mistress's happiness is so complete, so infectious, that a few of the nuns behind her start to laugh, too.

The room fills up as she tries to move, but of course her bones are weak and she cannot raise herself off the bed.

The old woman puts out her hand. 'See,' she says, with a toothless grin. 'See, I said He would come.'

She opens her mouth a little, moving her tongue around her blistered lips. No – she did not escape, did not find a way to get free after all. She looks at Zuana, then out across the room. They are all here, this family with whom she must now live until she dies, until the white hairs grow on her chin and her skin shrivels up like old leather, each and every drop of juice squeezed out of her.

Except she is not dead yet.

'I saw Him,' she says, so softly that the voice barely reaches to those inside the room. 'Yes, I do think I saw Him.'

'Oh, but it is a miracle.' In contrast, Suora Umiliana's voice carries far out into the courtyard beyond.

PART THREE

THIRTY-ONE

In their respective cells Zuana and Serafina sleep their way through the first days of Lent. The cleansing of the city continues around them. It rains so much that the gutters and the gargoyle mouths cannot keep up with the flow and the cloisters run with filthy streams. The water seeps under the doors of the cells and the bottoms of sisters' habits grow sodden as they walk. Even the convent cats retreat indoors, curling themselves inside the warm wood of the choir stalls, to be shooed away at the beginning of every office.

The Murano glass goblets and the ceramic plates are packed back into their dowry chests, the dresses, boots and wigs returned to their owners; and the sounds of the stage being dismantled are nowhere near as thrilling as those of its construction. In the kitchens the roasting and the baking pans are shelved and the sisters contemplate their first fasts, encouraged, no doubt, by the prevailing aromas of boiling vegetables and watery soups.

It is a time for quiet contemplation and considered abstinence. Yet no-one is downhearted. Far from it. While Lent usually brings a sense of anti-climax, this year it has been

replaced by a bubbling excitement. In the aftermath of the revelation in the novice's cell something is happening in the convent.
Everyone, novices as well as sisters, is praying more (what else is
there to do?) and there is a building anticipation towards the
coming chapter meeting.

The girl is cared for by Letizia and her old conversa, who
clean the cell around her and, on the orders left by Suora Zuana,
hang the leftover pomades from the refectory to freshen the air.
When she finally wakes, too weak to walk, Federica brings the
kitchen to her. Novices are not required to fast during Lent (it is
not recommended for any nun under the age of twenty-five)
but though Federica has saved her titbits from the last of the
feast, Serafina eats almost nothing. The illness has hollowed out
any appetite and it would be better if she took some sustenance
but she is adamant and refuses everything but liquid. When visited by Suora Umiliana she begs that she may be allowed to take
confession in preparation for the host. The novice mistress, in
turn, speaks to the abbess. It is hardly a request that anyone can
deny her. As she is clearly too ill to go to Father Romero, he
comes to her. It is a while since he has set foot in the cloisters and
the abbess sees to it that he has a flask of wine to sustain him on
his long journey. He stays inside her cell for some time. It is a
matter for conjecture whether or not he remains awake for all of
it.

As he leaves the abbess stands watching him pad across the
cloisters, a conversa holding up a covering to keep him from the
worst of the rain. Whatever he has just heard he cannot tell and
she will not ask. She wonders how long it will be until he dies.
He barely remembers any of the sisters' names, anyway.

Madonna Chiara folds her hands and gives a little sigh. She has
a busy few weeks in front of her. Whatever work Carnival entails
there is always more to be done afterwards: account books to be

checked, outgoings to be set against offerings, supplies to be reordered and letters of thanks to be written. Her attention had been elsewhere when the 'wondrous event' in Serafina's cell had taken place, so that by the time she had arrived it was already over and she could only hear about it secondhand.

She has no illusions, however, as to its possible importance. Lent is a period when traditionally the convent falls back on its own resources, spiritual as well as material, and any abbess must be alive to the undercurrents and tensions that might surface. Having lived for thirty-seven of her forty-three years inside Santa Caterina, there is not much about her convent and its sisters of which Madonna Chiara is not aware, and even without the extended drama of the novice or the re-emergence of Suora Magdalena, Umiliana's challenge to her authority has been building for some time. With the outside world taken care of – relationship with the Bishop good, the benefactors fed and entertained, and a list of requests for new entrants with dowry offers, to be negotiated upwards if demand continues to be so healthy – it is time to look inwards.

In her cell, given dispensation to miss the morning offices, Zuana finally wakes during the afternoon work hour. Her sleep has been deep and dreamless. She washes in a bowl of warm water, which one of the converse has delivered outside her door along with a new pad of rich-smelling soap and a fresh washing towel. As her own dowry is not sufficient to fund such regular luxuries, she understands this to be a gift from the convent stores. She is grateful for it. The smell of the girl's bodily expulsions still clings to her and she washes herself vigorously. She takes special pleasure – yes, she accepts the word – in lathering up the soap on her head. Her hair has grown during the winter months and she likes the wet weight of it, the shiver of massage as her fingers move over her scalp. She leaves her head bare as she uses the cloth to wash her arms then her body under her shift.

Working as she does in the infirmary, she is less of a stranger to women's bodies than most nuns but in general she takes little interest in her own. Of course there have been moments in her life when she has wondered what it is she will never feel, even once or twice explored her own dark sweetness, but her battles with the flesh have proved to be, at most, passing cravings, absorbed and subdued as much by the challenges of work as the discipline of prayer.

The soap is soft on her skin and lathers up like sea foam. She can detect a hint of almond and calendula within it – perhaps it comes from the abbess's own stores – and she registers a quiet delight in the way the smell and the softness complement each other.

She understands that the fight with the flesh is not always so easy for others. Serafina is far from the only young woman to have brought her virginity to Jesus while in the grip of desire for a more carnal husband. Of course there are ways to earth such lightning bolts. Over the years there have been nights when, unable to sleep because of some problem or remedy, she has detected a sudden wind of rushed breathing and moaning sliding out from under one cell door or another. Sometimes it is hard to tell the pain from the pleasure; but either way it is a sound that can ignite yearning in those who hear it and Zuana has become adept at increasing the volume of her own thoughts to blot it out. It is not up to her to damn or save the souls of others.

She rinses and dries herself quickly, rubbing her hair until it sticks out like a spiked halo around her, though with no mirror in her cell she will never see the effect of it.

If, or when, such transgression becomes obvious – and in the end it always does – the induced confession will be a private matter, the sister, or sisters, finding themselves subject to penance and regular discipline. Either it passes – the excess of energy transmuted into the love of Our Lord – or they become better at concealing it. Amid the filth of heretic propaganda, the most popular scandals are those of priests and nuns scaling the walls or squeezing their way through the confession grille to reach each other. The idea of women sinning with themselves or each other is too poisonous even for those who would wash away the structure of the Church along with its sins.

She dresses herself in a clean shift and robes, then kneels down by her bed. She has missed almost two days of offices and is long overdue on prayer but her mind fills up fast and it is hard to stem the flow of thoughts. She does what she can with words rather than contemplation then makes her way into the cloisters to check on her patients.

Back in her own cell, Suora Magdalena lies like a corpse on her pallet, the bones of her head so prominent as to seem already half skull. Her sleep is so deep that Zuana has to put her ear next to her mouth to discern any breath at all. It seems inconceivable that this . . . this wraith . . . could ever have found the strength to get up and walk to another cell, let alone sing and pray over a sick girl. Well, it is gone now, drained away along with her life force. Whatever she may be seeing behind her eyelids, Zuana prays that it is a landscape full of light and joy, for there is nothing left for her here. She moistens her lips with water and changes her position a little to ease the worst of the bed sores. She can do no more.

Inside Serafina's cell there is more to celebrate. The air smells of fresh herbs and by the bed there is bread and vegetable pie, along with a single bright green marzipan pear. The girl is asleep between clean sheets, her body washed, her hair brushed and flowing around her. Zuana wonders if she should wake her to check on her progress but her pulse is steady and after such a powerful purging sleep is often the kindest remedy. There is a stillness in the cell, a sense of peace almost, but whether it is the relief that comes with the cessation of suffering or something more she cannot tell. She thinks of Suora Magdalena crouched by the bed, transfixed by her vision of Christ . . .

Her vision – but not mine, thinks Zuana. However much she might wish it differently, the cell had remained empty for her.

And what of Serafina? What had she seen when she had first opened her eyes? Zuana understands her medications well enough to know that anyone in the grip of poppy and hellebore would already have been careering between heaven and hell. In such a softened state, Suora Magdalena's intensity may indeed have reached inside her, for everything is close to the surface when body and mind melt into one another.

The girl's skin is pale and there are hollows under her eyes. She will need feeding up if she is not to find herself permanently weakened by the viciousness of the evacuation. How could she not have noticed such loss of weight before? Though convent robes conceal all manner of sins, surely the novice had not been so gaunt when they had last worked together? Was this the result of love sickness, too? Ah, it seems so obvious now. Had Zuana been so preoccupied by work, or so much in need of a younger companion, that she had missed what was in front of her eyes? Would it have been any different if she had known? If the abbess had taken her into her confidence earlier – whenever that might have been, for she has no idea when she found out.

No. She glances around the cell. It had been here all along, everything she needed to know. The fury and the lushness of that young body as she carried her to the bed that first night, the love madrigals hidden away in the breviary, the man's voice singing behind the walls, that single 'Brava' after Vespers, the way the girl's eyes had grown large as she recited the poem found in the scriptorium manuscript. 'Tell me, little sister, do you have a fever or are you in love?'

Oh yes, this conflagration of the flesh had been there from the beginning, burning fiercely enough for her to risk everything – disgrace, social exile, even death – to find a way back inside its flame.

Zuana looks down at her. A slight frown flickers over the girl's forehead. What will she do with all that fire now? All the despair and shredded dreams?

Love. There is no illness like it, nor anything in her herb garden or her notebooks to address it. No, this disease must be left in God's hands, to kill or cure as He sees fit. Instead of comfort the thought sends a shiver through her. She bows her head in prayer but the bell for chapter interrupts before she can find the right words.

As she crosses the courtyard she passes Umiliana, her novice flock trotting behind her. A few of them stare openly across at her, a mix of admiration and curiosity on their faces.

THIRTY-TWO

'With God's grace we gather in this the first chapter of Lent to prepare ourselves for the beauty and discipline of abstinence. But before we speak of what we will give up, let us celebrate for a moment what we have.'

The abbess rests her hands lightly on the carved lions' heads and looks out over a sea of eager faces. The room is full to capacity: choir nuns, novices, converse, all in their place. The only ones missing are the old and the infirm, most notably the oldest and the most recently ill.

'In the last days I have received letters from guests and benefactors thanking us for our hospitality. To read them all would spark a contagion of pride that would take another period of Lent to address . . .' She smiles to allow the humour to penetrate. 'However, a few words, I think, are in order. They come from no less a personage than the Duke's sister, Leonora, who rose from her sick bed to attend with members of her family.'

Clearing her throat, she lifts her body a little higher in her chair. The small touches of flamboyance encouraged by Carnival are put aside now: the full petticoats have been removed, her wimple is severe, with no lace trimmings to it, and a plain silver crucifix is substituted for the jewel-encrusted one. She looks for all the world like a woman who can take care of her flock.

'"To all the holy sisters in your care, please convey the joy and deep spiritual sustenance felt by myself and my companions during your Carnival concert and theatrical performance. We left the convent gates secure in the knowledge that our beloved city is in safe hands with such loving and holy women interceding on our behalf."

'And so it goes on with the same glowing sentiments, before ending thus: "I must also say that while my soul sings, my lips are still rosy with the taste of wild strawberries. If it does not take you away from your duties to God I would be grateful for the recipe, so I might instruct my own kitchen to deliver such delicacies." Suora Federica — I believe that is directed at you.'

The kitchen mistress, however, is less than delighted. 'Must we tell her? She has a niece at the convent of Corpus Domini. If the recipe goes to her then it will also go to them and by next year everyone will have it.'

'In which case perhaps you might modify it a little to ensure our primacy is retained.' The abbess gives a small, tinkling laugh and the room answers in kind. Zuana glances towards Suora Umiliana, who is watching the others though not joining in herself. She is handling her impatience gracefully.

'Meanwhile, Suora Scholastica, I have to send two copies of *The Martyrdom of Santa Caterina* to sister convents in Venice and Siena who have heard that we were performing a new work. And Suora Benedicta, I have received a letter from Rome, from no less a figure than Cardinal Ippolito d'Este.'

In the second row, the choir mistress's face lights up like a star.

'It seems that news of our settings for St Agnes's feast have reached his ears and he is sending as a gift to the convent a score for *The Lamentations of Jeremiah* commissioned from no less a person than Giovanni da Palestrina, with the hopes that we might perform it during Easter week.'

Benedicta shakes her head but whether in disbelief or to tease up some new threads of music it is hard to tell.

'In terms of donations received and promised, assuming that the new dowries come in on time I can now confirm that we will be able to start work on The Last Supper for the main wall of the refectory next winter.'

Someone claps their hands and a few of the younger nuns actually cheer. It has been almost forty years since a fire caused by a candle left burning after supper wiped out the original frescoes. This will be an opportunity for Santa Caterina to have a great work in the fashion of the day, along with the excitement of a fashionable artist installed behind screens for the time it will take to complete it. Zuana is less enamoured of the latest style of painting, which seems to her to be interested more in exploring the violent contortions of the body than in finding the anatomical truths beneath. Nevertheless she cannot help but be impressed. Such large-scale commissions are expensive. She finds herself wondering what might have happened if Serafina had not survived the treatment. The death of a novice before taking her final vows would trigger the return of a proportion of her dowry. A successful escape, however, would surely render it all forfeit. It is not something Zuana has thought about until this moment.

Perhaps she is not the only one to note the connection between the girl's health and the fresco; a couple of the choir sisters have been glancing towards the side seats where, amid the row of novices, a small space marks out her absence. The abbess, who is better at reading minds than souls, lifts her hands to recover everyone's attention.

'Finally, before we move on, we should pay tribute to another sister to whom we owe particular thanks. As you will know by now, following the success of the concert and the play our youngest novice, Serafina, was taken suddenly and gravely ill with fitting and fever. Without the intervention and vigil of our dispensary mistress it is likely that we would have lost her. The art of healing is one of Our Lord's greatest gifts and Suora Zuana's expertise and devotion enriches all our lives inside Santa Caterina.'

This is remarkable praise indeed and the room responds with a rustle of appreciation and smiles. Zuana is so taken unaware that all she can do is smile and drop her eyes.

The abbess, however, has picked her moment well. All present – choir nuns, novices and converse – are happy to acknowledge their dispensary mistress. The fact is that even before Carnival Zuana's star had been rising. Her part in taming Serafina's rage and delivering her to the choir, her handling of the contagion – including her own illness and now the drama around the novice's illness, ending, as it did, so theatrically . . . all this has brought her naturally to prominence. After years of seeking ways to fit in unnoticed, Zuana has unwittingly become a player in the drama of convent life. And, it would appear, an acknowledged favourite now of the abbess herself.

'So, I think it is time to go on to the rota for Lent fasting. Yes, Suora Umiliana?'

'Madonna Chiara. If I may?'

In the middle of the second row Umiliana stands, hands clasped together, and turns to address the choir sisters behind her.

'Before we move on we should surely mark a further wonder, one that more than all the others shows the glory of God within our midst . . .' She pauses until she is sure she has everyone's attention. 'I speak of the arrival of Suora Magdalena in the novice's cell and the part she played in this . . . miraculous, marvellous recovery. For those of us who saw it for ourselves it was as if Our Lord Jesus Christ Himself was in that cell helping to guide the young woman back to life.'

The room is very still now.

'If I may continue . . .?' She glances to the abbess once more, who nods her head almost imperceptibly.

Umiliana now turns to Zuana. 'Suora Zuana, you arrived there before any of us. Perhaps you might recount for us what took place.'

Zuana, the centre of attention for a second time, looks up into Suora Umiliana's piercing gaze.

'I . . . I am not sure I saw any more than you, dear sister. I had been in the dispensary making a potion and when I returned Suora Magdalena had left her own cell and was at the bedside of the novice, praying.'

Though the words are entirely truthful it is clear that they are not what Umiliana wants to hear.

'And was there not something of . . . of wonder about her? Some vision of the Lord that touched both her and the sick girl?'

Zuana picks her words with special care now. 'The novice was certainly much comforted by her presence. She opened her eyes for the first time since the remedy had sent her to sleep.'

The novice mistress stares at her coldly. How quickly enemies are made, Zuana thinks.

'Oh, but the girl was dying. It *was* a miracle!' Suora Felicità's words burst out as if she can no longer keep them within, for fear of them exploding inside her.

There is a tiny, shimmering silence, as if the whole assembly is now holding its breath. This is indeed a chapter meeting worth waiting for.

'Suora Felicità . . .' The abbess's voice is gentle and measured by contrast. 'Those are strong words to describe an event that, as far as I am aware, you did not yourself witness.'

'I? Well, I . . . not exactly.'

The abbess turns her attention to Zuana, her gaze cool, professional. 'Suora Zuana, you treated the novice and you were in the cell with her all night and before anyone else arrived. It is most important to know if you saw or noted anything – felt any sense of this . . . this "vision" that is being talked about.'

'I . . . what I saw . . .' And she struggles towards the right words, ones that tell the truth in her heart as well as her head. 'What I saw was Suora Magdalena praying over the young girl – praying most devoutly, and speaking of the Lord and how He was there with her.' She pauses. 'I myself did not see anything but I cannot help but think He was listening to her prayers.'

'Indeed,' the abbess says gravely. 'As He will have listened to all our devotion and intercession. Thank you.'

Umiliana moves as if to speak but the abbess has not finished yet.

'And if I remember correctly our conversation this morning, Suora Umiliana – for this is an important matter – when you yourself came into the cell you did not experience any "vision" either.'

Umiliana frowns. It is hard to know with whom she is most upset: the abbess, Zuana or Suora Felicità. Or even perhaps herself.

'I saw Serafina – who had been gravely ill only a few hours before – recovered. And I heard her say that she also had seen Him.'

Again there is the slightest murmur in the room.

'But you yourself did not?'

The novice mistress hesitates. Then shakes her head.

'And those other sisters who were present in the room afterwards – is there anyone who saw anything?'

The novices glance nervously at one another and among the choir sisters it is clear that Perseveranza would dearly love to be able to speak but knows she cannot lie. In the row in front of her Zuana sees both of the twins shake their heads in unison. The silence grows.

The abbess nods. 'Thank you, all of you. And particularly you, Suora Umiliana. You do us a great service to bring up the matter of Suora Magdalena now. I had intended to speak of it later but perhaps this moment is opportune.

'Suora Magdalena, as we know, is an old and chaste soul who would give her last breath for the welfare of a young sister. She has always been the most humble of nuns with no wish to draw attention to herself. In fact it has long been her fervent wish to be left alone and undisturbed to serve God as He saw fit. As a few of the older sisters in the convent can testify – Suora Umiliana, you yourself are one of them – that wish was granted many years ago by both the abbess and the bishop of the time, and the convent has been bound by it ever since.'

Zuana is busy with numbers now. The novice mistress is older by how many years than the abbess? Five, maybe ten; though caring as little as she does for her appearance it is hard to tell. Either way, in 1540 when all the fuss had happened she would have been either a novice or a young choir nun. And it is always the young who are most affected.

'However, as you point out, it seems that she has of her own accord broken that vow now. In the light of which, I think perhaps we must look to her welfare. She is exceedingly frail, certainly not well enough to be moving around the convent on her own without help. It seems to me that the best course of action is for us to transfer her to the infirmary, where Suora Zuana can give her the personal care she needs as she approaches the end of her life.'

This change of mind is so perfect and expressed with such sincerity that Zuana is rendered speechless for a moment.

Umiliana, however, has no such problem.

'If she is now to leave her cell, if the convent decides that is best for her, then surely she could also be allowed to attend chapel and mass, and take the host. I am sure there are sisters who would happily carry her there if she so desired.'

There is an audible gasp now. On the surface it is the drama of the sparring between abbess and novice mistress but there is something else going on here: some of the older nuns, the more natural allies of Umiliana such as Agnesina and Concordia, will no doubt have memories of the services where Suora Magdalena's appearances coincided with weeping stigmata. And, given the excitement in the convent, some of the younger ones will surely have heard rumours by now.

'Suora Umiliana, you have spoken my own thoughts aloud. However, such is her fragility I do not think that will be possible,' the abbess says smoothly. 'In fact I have discussed the matter with Father Romero already. Indeed he visited her this morning when he came to hear the confession of the novice.'

Whether he did or did not visit Magdalena, there is no-one in the room to contradict her, since they were all at work hour. Anyway, why should anyone doubt the word of their abbess? Although at that moment Zuana finds herself doing just that.

'She was, alas, unconscious and so not able to take confession or receive the host. But he has promised to come again.'

'Oh, is she dying? Are we to lose our holiest soul having only just re-found her?'

Suora Felicità's voice is now tearful, so that a few of the young ones look positively alarmed. Umiliana glances at her sharply. It is one thing to pit your wits against a skilled opponent, another entirely to find yourself undermined by your own side.

'We must all die in the end, Suora Felicità,' the abbess says gently. 'And we must not be selfish. For Magdalena herself it will be the greatest celebration to be taken by God.'

The words, so humble that in other circumstances they might have been spoken by the novice mistress herself, still the room. In her chair on the dais the abbess sits upright and graceful.

'Suora Zuana? As dispensary mistress you have seen our dear sister the most recently of all of us. Perhaps you might give us your thoughts on her strength or frailty?'

She turns to Zuana and her eyes are shining. To look at her you would think she was positively enjoying herself. At recreation the more mischievous nuns sometimes speculate on what a perfect wife for a great noble she would have made, running his family and his palace as efficiently as she runs the convent. They do her an injustice, Zuana thinks. It is not a mere palace she should run but a state. For surely in its way that is what she is doing here. Right down to a network of spies and agents to help keep her authority intact.

'When I saw her this morning she was unconscious and most weak. She is also suffering from chronic bed sores. In my opinion it would be kinder if she was moved as little as possible.'

A network in which Zuana appears now to have been granted a position of considerable authority.

'And if it was so decided, would you take over her care in the infirmary? You have in the past expressed grave concern over her state, I know. '

But how much does Zuana really want the role? It is not a question she can answer now. She bows her head.

'If it is the will of the convent, I would be honoured to do so.'

The abbess smoothes her skirts and turns to the audience.

'So, let us put it to the vote then. The motion before the sisters of Santa Caterina today is whether to move our aged and beloved Suora Magdalena from her cell into the infirmary, where we may ease her passage unto God's hands.'

The novices watch as the choir nuns come up one by one to the front and, with their backs to the rest of the room to ensure anonymity, pick out a small wooden ball from the bucket – white for yes, black for no – and drop it through a hole into the voting box.

When everyone has voted, the box has been emptied and the balls have been counted by the sacristan, witnessed by the gate mistress, the motion is declared duly carried. It is noticeable, however, that among the winning white balls are a greater than usual number of black.

THIRTY-THREE

She is empty. Quiet. Still. Maybe stiller than she has ever been in her life. It must be the aftermath of the poison. During her time in the dispensary she had wondered about the drama of the helle-bore: what it might feel like to have one's insides ripped apart, scraped out nigh unto death. To be so purged. So emptied out. Almost as if one might be able to start again. Another Serafina. Newer, lighter, cleaner, with no hand gripping her heart and twisting her guts. No man to love and yearn for any more. Because it seems, after all, that he never loved her.

'He does not care, you see.'

He does not care. Yet how could that be? What of all the poetry? The music? The harmony of voices, the starburst sweet-ness of mouth on mouth, skin on skin, the mingling of souls that made them for that instant pure, afraid of nothing? Ah – now, now it is too late, she knows that she did really love him; that amid all the rebellion and hot blood, the very exhilaration of being alive, separately and together, that Jacopo had been a man worth loving, himself, generous, filled with song and no malice.

Except, it seems, he wasn't. Instead, he, like she, had been a master of deception. Yet how could that be?

At any other time these thoughts would have been like hooks in her flesh but there is nothing left to lacerate now. She is so tired. Too tired to think properly. Certainly this new cleansed Serafina cannot hold on to anything for very long. Her head feels as light and empty as her body. It is not so awful; more like dizziness, like holding on to a high note for longer even than your longest breath allows, hearing it vibrate, shimmer inside your head.

Perhaps this sensation is the result of her confession? The scouring of her soul as well as her stomach. She had told the old priest everything. With the screams of the pierced and the sliced still inside her, how could she not? Everything: the bliss, the rage, the terror, the disobedience, even the self-destruction; such a fast flowing river of sin. How much of it he heard she has no idea, for both their eyes were closed as she spoke. But at the end he had prayed for her, imposed a penance of confinement with bread and water fasting for two weeks, and given her absolution.

Two weeks' confinement and fasting. It is not such a torment. In fact she welcomes it. In the time since she opened her eyes on the cell full of nuns, she has relished the solitude. How could she bear to face people again? As for the fasting, well, the hunger is so familiar to her now that even when she does feel the need to eat, she feels a greater sense of triumph when she overcomes it. Her gut has been full of undigested pain and rage and panic for so long that to be without anything inside her seems a marvel in itself.

Whether it comes from the quiet or the exhaustion, she prays more: simple prayers held inside simple phrases. I am sorry. Help me. Forgive me. Childish, almost. Each time she sleeps she wakes to the sight of the crucifix on the wall but often when she looks at it she sees instead the figure of the man in the marshland, walking towards her with the sun as a radiating halo behind him.

The moment when he first came she had thought it might have been Jacopo, because his hair also fell curling round his shoulders and he, too, walked with a long stride. But she knows now that it was not him but Christ himself and that He came to her through Suora Magdalena. Why and how this had happened she does not know. She is certainly not deserving. Yet oh, He brought her such comfort then. And now. For He, too, is generous, filled with song and no malice.

As for the future, tomorrow and tomorrow and tomorrow . . . well, she does not think of that. How could she?

'Serafina.'

She knows she is in the room. She heard her come in, registered the noise of something being placed on the table. But once she opens her eyes she will have to speak to her, and of all people she is the one who will surely make it all begin again. Nevertheless . . .

'Serafina.'

She turns her head and blinks.

Zuana is sitting on a small chair close to the bed. Next to her is a wooden plate with bread and cheese, and a bowl of hot soup. She had forgotten how familiar this face is: the broad, open forehead with its furrowed lines of thought and those clean, clear eyes, smiling now along with the mouth. No malice here, either. Despite everything, she is pleased to see her.

'Praise be to God for your recovery. Do you have pain in your stomach?'

'No.'

'Any nausea?' She leans over and takes the girl's pulse, red-stained fingers on the thin, pale wrist.

The smell of the cooked food brings a rush of saliva into Serafina's mouth but she swallows it down again. Only when I think of eating, she thinks. 'No.'

'What about dreams? Are you having bad dreams?'

'No.' And she sees the man in the mist striding towards her. 'No, not any more.'

'Good. Here, I have brought you some cheese and fresh soup and bread.'

'I am not hungry.'

'Still, you should eat.'

'I can't.' She shakes her head. 'I am given penance.'

'Penance?'

'Father Romero. He heard my confession. My penance is confinement and bread and water for two weeks.'

A frown moves across Zuana's face. 'Did no-one tell him that you had been ill?'

'I don't know.'

'Can you sit up?'

She attempts to pull herself up but it is an effort.

Zuana goes to help and as her hands touch her, Serafina is pulled back into the maelstrom of that night – hanging suspended in strong arms as her bowels open and her stomach screams. Such intimacy makes her embarrassed now, almost ashamed. She moves away, pulling the blanket around her.

'I am sorry . . .' She keeps her eyes on the blanket. 'If what I did got you into trouble.'

Zuana shakes her head. 'There is nothing to be sorry for. You have confessed your sins. And you are forgiven.'

'I told him everything,' she says, looking straight at her now, the words thrown down like a gauntlet. 'All of it.'

'I am glad,' Zuana says gently.

'Do you think it a fair penance?'

'I can't say. Though it is not healthy to starve yourself after such violent purging.'

'It doesn't matter, I am not hungry,' she says again. Then: 'Suora Magdalena has not eaten for years.'

'That is not true. She just eats exceedingly little, so that over the years her body has grown used to it. I think she is not someone to emulate in this regard. Not at this moment.'

'That is not what Suora Umiliana says.'

I wonder what else Umiliana says, Zuana thinks to herself, though no doubt some of it she can guess. 'Who else has visited you?'

'Suora Federica came. She brought me a pear – look, here.' She pulls it out from under her pillow, the green marzipan collecting tiny particles of dust. 'I don't want it. You take it.'

Zuana shakes her head. 'Keep it until the end of your penance. It will be something to look forward to.'

To look forward. Such a simple idea, like waiting for the sun to rise again in the morning. It is a grave sin for any novice to try to escape the convent. And an equally grave one to aid or abet her. This girl has confessed her part and been forgiven. Zuana should be looking to her own soul now. There is nothing more she can do for her. Still . . .

'Serafina, listen to me. The hellebore along with the poppy is a poisonous evacuator and the dose that I gave you was not small. You will feel strange for a while. There will be lethargy and sadness; some confusion in your mind, even.'

'I don't feel anything,' she says flatly.

'That will be part of it. But it will pass.'

She stops because she does not know what else to say.

The girl puts her head back against the wall. 'I did see things,' she says quietly. 'Terrible things.'

'It was the drug. Remember that: only the visions of the drug.'

'Have you ever seen such things?'

As she looks at Zuana her eyes are huge in her face. And black, black as lumps of charcoal.

'Yes, I have.'

'And wondrous ones, too?'

'I . . . yes, in a way.'

'But you have never seen Him?'

Zuana does not wait long on this. 'No.'

'Why not? You are a good nun.'

'No. I . . . I am—'

'Yes, yes, you are. I know.'

'Well . . . I . . . I think there are many levels of goodness. And only the fewest of the few are given such an honour.'

'But *she* is given it. *She* sees Him.'

They do not need to give her a name. We are not allowed to speak of this, Zuana thinks. It is forbidden territory. But then so much has changed over these last weeks. The list of secrets inside the convent is growing ever longer and there seems no point in denying this one, especially since she has been witness to it more profoundly than anyone else.

'Yes. She does.'

'She's always seen Him, hasn't she?'

'It appears so.'

'Why her? One of the novices told me she was just a peasant girl from a village whom the old duke found somewhere. No family, no study, nothing. Was she born holy? Is it how she prayed? Or was it the fasting? Is that how she did it?'

'I don't know.'

'I think I saw Him, too.' She shakes her head. 'Just for a moment.'

The poppy: it can show you anything and everything. 'It is possible that this, too, was the drug, Serafina,' she says softly.

'How do you know?' Her voice has a tremble in it. 'If we all saw Him maybe it would be all right to live and die here.'

Yes, something has changed in her, Zuana thinks. But then how could it not have? Please God, it might bring her to peace.

'I think Our Lord is always here, even if one does not see Him directly.'

Serafina is silent for a moment, as if considering this idea.

'She was wrong about him, you know,' she says at last and her voice remains small, with none of the edge or energy from before. 'The abbess said he didn't care. But it's not true. He did love me.'

She should eat something, a little bread at least. That much is permitted. Zuana breaks off a small chunk, dips it in the water and holds it out to her. 'Here.'

The girl stares at it and shakes her head.

'I am not hungry.'

THIRTY-FOUR

The bell for work hour is beginning to sound as Zuana comes out
of the girl's cell and moves along the cloister. Directly in front of
her she sees Suora Umiliana walking towards her. She drops her
head, intending that they should pass without words – the novice
mistress practises silence even when it is not called for – but
instead the elder woman meets her eye. Her manner is welcoming, almost joyful.

'You have come from the novice? How do you find her? The
change is powerful, yes?'

'I . . . yes, yes, she is different.'

'Praise be to God, He has seen fit to cleanse her of her anger
and pretence, and plant in their place a seed of humility. Thanks
be to Him. And also to you for the care within your remedy.'

Zuana stares at her. Since their encounter in chapter she has
expected, even prepared herself for, hostility, but there seems
none here. She wonders what the novice mistress would say if
she knew why the 'remedy' had been administered in the first
place. Of course Zuana cannot tell her that. Just as she cannot
tell her what went on in Suora Magdalena's cell all those weeks
ago. Secrets within secrets – they grow like mould in a badly run

storeroom. But does that also make it a badly run convent? How much deception is permitted in the pursuit of peace? She realises that she does not know any more.

'She is grown quieter, that is true. But I am concerned about her health. The remedy has left her very weak. She should be eating, not fasting.'

'In unquiet souls the body must be subdued sometimes to give room to the soul. She will come to no harm, Suora Zuana, I will see to that. These are wondrous times we are living through in Santa Caterina, would you not agree? The Lord has answered our prayers and is come among us. Come through both the old and the young. I fear you have not seen it yet but it is here, as clear as sunshine on water. You must look to your own soul, Suora Zuana. He is longing for you to find Him, too. And you will. I know that. All you need is to——'

'I thank you for your good wishes, Suora Umiliana.' Zuana smiles as she cuts across her words. 'I long for Him, too. But still I think the girl should not be fasting.'

The novice mistress claps her hands together and pulls them back under her robe. 'Neither you nor I have the right to question the wisdom of our father confessor,' she says, the old Umiliana re-emerging out of her certainty. 'She is in my care and I will tend to her as if she was my own child. God be with you, sister Zuana.'

'And with you,' Zuana replies as they pass each other. Ah, if only the love of God moved like the bad seeds of infection through the air, she thinks. Then perhaps we would not need so much continual saving. The boldness of her irreverence takes her by surprise. I am tired, she thinks, and in need of air for my body if not my soul.

The bell for the work hour is still sounding as she puts on her cloak and goes to the herb garden, taking her hessian bag of forks and other tools. The great rain has finally passed, leaving the sky as washed as the earth, and the day that has emerged from it is cloudless and almost warm. In summer after such storms the cloisters steam as the sun burns off the moisture. There is nothing so dramatic today but in the gardens the ground will have been softened by the long downpour and whatever early growth has started under the soil may now have had a chance to push further through.

She has not been out of the cloisters since the night in the storeroom and she is amazed by the difference it makes to her spirits to be in the open again. It will do her good to be working in the garden, surrounded by plants rather than people. She walks briskly, feeling the wind fresh on her cheeks, and as she does so she lets go of her anxieties about the girl, and Umiliana, and the abbess, all the tangled threads of convent politics and conspiracy, and remembers instead what it is that she does here: how the work of a good dispensary mistress is as much about tending plants as tending people.

The garden is probably no bigger than the abbess's chambers (though Zuana has expanded it by half since she was voted into the post), yet it is home to close to a hundred herbs and medicinal shrubs. There are days between spring and autumn when the workload is such that she barely has time for mental prayer – when the fecundity of nature will fill her with wonder and thanks but the words will be waylaid by the attention, even devotion, that the plants require: weeding, splitting, staking, pruning, feeding, harvesting, dead-heading; even waging war on their behalf, picking off and crushing small plagues of slugs and snails, which grow out of putrefaction and dampness to lay waste to her most tender and precious herbs.

This winter has been harsh, on both her fingers and the plants, but the worst is over now. She can feel it as soon as she moves into open ground. Protected on one side by the back of the smaller cloister and on the other by the vegetable garden wall, the herb patch is a sheltered enough space for spring to make an early appearance. During a clement March she will see most of the more robust or courageous plants poking their heads above ground. This mass arrival is one of the most powerful memories of her childhood, for before the university instituted its own medicinal garden (spurred on, no doubt, by the fact that Padua and Pisa were already famous for theirs), the courtyard of her father's house was a field of old buckets, pots and wooden trays filled with seeds and cuttings. He would take her out sometimes in the first days of warm weather and make her listen to the silence.

'There are scholars, great men of the present as well as the past, who believe that God created man because only through us could He celebrate the power of His vast creation. And thus it is both our pleasure and our duty to witness the wonder. You cannot hear it, can you? But even now as we stand here, under the earth a thousand bulbs and seeds and roots are budding and cracking and sprouting, an army of small tendrils and shoots rising up, moving through the earth towards the light, each one of them so tender that when you see them you will marvel at how they could have moved such a weight of soil above them to emerge. Imagine that, Faustina. Each year the repeating miracle of it . . .'

The picture he painted was so strong – and he had such awe in his voice – that whenever she reads about or imagines the Second Coming, she sees graveyards like vast herb gardens, with bodies, as tender and young as those new shoots, pushing up against the rotten wood of their coffins and rising up towards the light of God to the sound of trumpets. Flesh incorruptible. She had told him of this vision once and he had smiled in that way parents do when their children are wiser or more charming than their years.

But she could see that for him it was in some ways no more impressive than the more humble version of God's glory that nature presented.

Given the complexities of the world around her, she has need of such a simple miracle today.

Save for the occasional drops of rain coming off the evergreen shrubs and trees, it is quiet in the garden. The lavender and the rosemary, bruised from the downpour, are thick with aromatic pungency as she rolls her fingers along their stems and leaves. In the early beds, the calendula and fennel and hypericum are already reviving. She clears a space and softens the soil around them so that the shoots can expand. Next will come the belladonna and the betonica and the cardiaca, the plant that strengthens the heart, which once it starts will grow as thick as nettles and as fast as weeds. She used to wonder whether in the very beginning someone had plaited together the alphabet and the seasons: marking the first plants as Bs and Cs, then Fs and Hs, leaving the poppy, the valerian and the verbena to come later. By then the garden will have gone wild so there will be barely an inch of space left.

She slips her fingers under the newly sprouting fennel, with its lacy, feathery fronds. Her father was right. It is indeed a wonder how something that can barely hold its head up in the air has the force to break through heavy, sodden earth. Yet give it another few weeks of good weather and its stem will be proudly upright, thick with its own juice. Soil, light, water, sun. Growth, death, putrefaction, regeneration. No need for confession or forgiveness or redemption here. Life without soul. So clear, so simple. Oh, Zuana, you were bred for plants, not convent politics.

'I thought I might find you here.'

She turns quickly. The abbess is treading her way carefully through the undergrowth.

'So – how are all your new children doing?' She gestures to the garden around.

'It is early days. But I think we will have good crop of calendula.'

'Possibly you will be able to harvest some off your cheek.'

Zuana puts her hand up and wipes away a streak of mud. The abbess, in contrast, is clean and newly pressed, though it is her complexion that gives her away most obviously; the choir nuns who live in cloisters stay pale and smooth without the aid of Apollonia's powders, while those who work outside find the sun and the winter winds excavating rivers of broken veins in their cheeks and noses. How much this releases them from the sin of vanity is hard to know, though an inspection might find fewer silver trays doubling as mirrors in their cells.

'I am come to talk to you about the novice. To explain what happened that night at the dock.'

'You don't have to explain anything, Madonna abbess.'

'No, I don't have to, that is true. Rather I choose to.' She smiles and looks around. 'Tell me – where is the hellebore?'

Zuana points to an evergreen shrub towards the back of one of the beds. The abbess lifts her skirts and moves over to it.

'It looks so . . . innocent.'

'The poison comes from the root, not the foliage.'

She nods, studying it as she starts to talk.

'After I wrote to her father he took an unconscionably long time in replying. By the time he did she appeared to have settled, which is why I did not think fit to communicate his answer. To his credit, he was as frank in his responses as I had been in my questions. He told me that his daughter had always been of strong character, clever and full of passion, first for one thing then another, and it was this . . . volatility that had decided him that although she had initially been chosen for marriage she might be better ruled by God than by any husband. Unfortunately he had omitted to inform her – and us – of this decision until rather late in the proceedings.'

Zuana moves her eyes over the garden beds. Strong character. There are plants like that, ones that survive no matter what – frost, rain, sun, insects – while others born from the same handful of seeds wither away beside them. They are the ones you should nurture and take cuttings from, rather than putting them behind walls to die without propagating. 'And the young man?'

'The music teacher? Unfortunately, he was less than frank about him. By then, by God's grace, I had other information. It seems it was a considerable attachment. When it was discovered there were accusations and violent scenes, and the man was dismissed. Hence the decision to send her to us here in Ferrara rather than Milan, to separate them with distance and avoid further scandal. It was only later that I found he had made his way independently to the city so he could stay in touch with her, by a form of communication the manner of which they had decided earlier.'

'That is a great deal to have discovered,' Zuana says, for there is no way she cannot be impressed.

The abbess shrugs. 'In a good family there is always someone who knows how to find things out. An impoverished stranger in a foreign city warms to friends who open their purses – and a young man who has made a noble conquest likes to boast about it.'

She knows so much about men, Zuana thinks, admiringly. How could that be? She has never seen the inside of a tavern, never sat and drunk wine with any man, let alone wooed or been wooed by one. Yet she talks of them, talks of all of it, as if she has imbibed the wisdom of the world with her mother's milk. Perhaps there was some manual passed down in her family, too, hidden away in her dowry chest. She would need to protect such a volume against the long noses of Church inspectors.

'And these "friends"? Are they the same ones who found him the post at Parma?'

'The same.' The abbess nods, her attention now distracted as she brushes some piece of dirt or insect carefully from her skirts. 'I would have told you this before but I did not want to compromise your relationship with the girl. You seemed to have such a . . . a connection with her that I hoped, despite it all, that she might change her mind. I involved you that night only because I was not privy to what had been arranged between them and because I could not watch her all the time.'

'I should have seen it myself. It was in front of my eyes.'

'No. The level of deception was too great. I would not have seen it if I hadn't known.'

Zuana shakes her head. 'I was thinking more of the poppy syrup missing from the dispensary bottle.'

'As always you are hard on yourself, Zuana. You had been ill and the convent was mad with Carnival. There is no reason to blame yourself.'

'The thing I do not understand is why, having gone to such trouble to find and contact her, he had no qualms about suddenly deserting her.'

She plucks a leaf from the hellebore bush and crushes it in her hand. 'As I said, such young men do not care a fig for anything but their own pleasure. If he had had his way he would have taken her, ruined her and cast her aside. We must thank God that He saw fit to let you save her from herself.'

Zuana sees the two of them standing on the dock, the black water in the background, Serafina fumbling with the ropes on the boat, while she herself offers no resistance. The abbess had known all along that there would be no-one there to meet her. It had never been Zuana's job to stop her escaping, only to bring her back from the edge when she realised she had been betrayed. 'Thank you.' She hears the girl's voice low in her ears. Surely the abbess must have heard something, too.

'Madonna Chiara, there is something I must tell you.'

'Actually Zuana, I think that there is not.' She lets the leaf fall, wiping its juice off her hands. 'As far as I am concerned whatever faults you have committed in this matter, you paid your penance in the room with her that night. Anything else that burdens you, you should take to Father Romero.'

It is clear from her tone that the matter is closed.

Yet there are so many frayed ends.

'What happens now? To the girl?'

'She will take the veil and in time become a valued and valuable sister of the convent.'

'And if she is still unwilling?'

'I do not believe there will be any further rebellion. Not now.'

Again the conversation seems finished but Zuana hesitates. 'I am concerned that she is fasting so quickly after the evacuation, I—'

'And I am concerned that she continues to take up so much of your – and this convent's – time.' Her tone is sharp now. 'If she is to settle she must accept her lot as an ordinary novice and taste a little bitter fruit like everyone else. Given her sins, it is hardly an onerous penance and it will do her no lasting harm. Suora Umiliana can tend to her "needs" for a while, not you.'

The abbess's evident anger, and the fact that Zuana is being forbidden access to the girl, are confirmation in themselves that she had seen or suspected what took place on the jetty that night. Zuana bows her head to show obedience. It occurs to her that she might mention Umiliana's evident joy in the novice's 'conversion' but she knows that this is not the time. In the life of any nun, criticism must be accepted with the same humility as praise. 'You must look to your own soul, Suora Zuana.' Umiliana's words come back to her. Maybe they are both right: she has given too much of her journey to this volatile young woman. There are others who need her more.

'Anyway, you will have your hands filled in the dispensary looking after Suora Magdalena,' the abbess says more kindly. 'I cannot tell you how good it will be for her to be in your care – how good it will be for all of us.' She pauses, rubbing her hands together hard. 'Ooh, it is cold out here. You must have grown a second skin in your work. I think I shall go back in time to see Suora Federica before the Sext bell. Perhaps we might walk as far as the second cloisters together.'

Zuana packs her fork and trowel into her bag and they make their way along the wall of the vegetable garden.

'I meant what I said in chapter yesterday, Zuana,' the abbess says as they go. 'You are a beloved sister of this convent. Your work enriches all of our lives. As do your obedience and loyalty.' She pauses, as if to decide whether to continue. 'In that spirit I would like to share with you some news I have received – disturbing news. It seems that Bishop Paleotti in Bologna has sent notice to all the convents in the city that there will be no more public performances of theatre, for fear of contamination between the nuns and the outside world. And in Milan Cardinal Borromeo has forbidden any musical instruction between nuns and musicians from the outside world and is threatening the removal of all musical instruments other than the chapel organ.'

This is indeed shocking information and though Zuana might question the abbess's motives for telling it now, there is no reason to doubt its veracity. She sees Benedicta's and Scholastica's faces, shining with the pride of their achievements. No more plays and no more orchestras. It is unthinkable . . . except perhaps in a convent run by Suora Umiliana.

'You really think such things could happen here?'

'It is happening already in quiet ways. As Benedicta starts to arrange her "gift" of the *Lamentations* she may find that the music that delights Rome these days is a good deal starker than that which pours out of her soul. For the rest, though, we are not lost yet. Our Bishop may be a reformer but he is also of excellent family and will be open to the entreaties of others. It is, however, essential that we give him no cause for concern.'

They continue silently for a bit. At the cloister entrance they pause, the abbess turning to her and smiling.

'Given the circumstances, you understand, I am sure, how it will be better for all concerned if Suora Magdalena remains confined inside the infirmary until she dies . . .'

. . . rather than wandering the corridors having revelations everywhere she goes.

The words are there even though they are unspoken. Zuana sees the demented Clementia straining her arms against the night straps on the side of the bed. A decrepit old woman, unconscious and covered in bed sores, strapped down like a prisoner. Is that what she is being asked to do? For the good of the convent . . .

She bows her head but cannot bring herself to speak. Please God, it will not come to that.

THIRTY-FIVE

They move Suora Magdalena that evening before the office of Compline. Zuana makes up a stretcher from garden poles strapped to a mattress and she and three of the convent's strongest converse lift the old woman carefully from her pallet bed on to it. When they pick it up and start to walk her eyelids flicker a little as her sores rub against the stretcher but she does not protest.

In the infirmary Clementia is muttering as usual but falls strangely quiet at their entrance. They slide Magdalena on to the newly prepared bed and Zuana administers a poultice of calendula to the worst of the bed sores. The abbess comes to pay her respects, joined almost immediately by Suora Umiliana, who kneels and prays at the bedside. From across the room Clementia's sing-song voice joins in the prayers.

Later, while the convent sleeps, Zuana stays at her bedside. In her experience more souls are taken by God during darkness than in the light, which makes the infirmary a potent place to be at night. There are times when the end comes in an agony that not even her potions can soothe, when the night candle on the altar seems barely strong enough to keep the darkness at bay. But not tonight. Tonight the room is safe and sweet-smelling, as if the perfume of the fumigant is stronger than usual. Magdalena's deep sleep seems to affect those in the beds around her. In contrast, Zuana herself feels perfectly awake, as if she could sit there for ever. She keeps vigil until the Matins bell and when the divine office is finished checks one last time before allowing herself to sleep. The morning finds the shadows gone and all her patients still aslumber. From then on when she is in chapel she has Letizia sit with the old woman so that she is never left wholly unsupervised. There will be no straps and restraints here. She has made her decision on that, whatever the cost.

On the surface at least, convent life returns to normal. The weather remains clement as the daily offices of Lent unfold, with their prayers of abstinence and repentance. After so much excitement the re-establishing of rhythm comes as a balm to all.

In accordance with the abbess's injunction, Zuana does not see Serafina. While this causes her anxiety, she accepts it. The abbess's words were not without wisdom. If the girl is to forge any life for herself here then like every other novice she must find her own way to God. And to do that she must make peace with herself. While Suora Umiliana may not be the gentlest of guides, nor the abbess's greatest ally, it had been she, out of all the nuns, who had remained the most sceptical about the novice's earlier false goodness, and with humility and discipline as her credo she will surely be an honest, steadfast watchdog over any young soul.

As for the fasting, well, it is a route they have all taken at some point in their journeys towards God and as long as the girl is careful not to exceed the penance she should not be too damaged by it.

*

'As the body grows thin, so by as much the soul waxes fat.'

The lump of bread is delivered to the cell every morning along with a jug of water mixed with a few spoonfuls of wine. Like everything in Santa Caterina, fasting is encouraged in moderation and the daily ration is designed to prick hunger, not cause starvation.

Serafina, however, is not interested in moderation. Her hunger, curled inside her stomach like a great tapeworm, lies in wait for the delivery. She drinks some water in slow sips, feeling it move down her throat, then tears the bread into a dozen small pieces, arranging them carefully on the wooden plate. She eats a single piece, washed down by more water, then places the plate in the centre of the cell so that it is always visible wherever she moves, as a reminder of temptation. At some point during the day she will perhaps take another of these pieces and break it into even smaller bits, a few of which she will put in her mouth, letting her saliva work on it until it is soft enough to swallow. At the end of the day whatever is left she secretes somewhere around her cell to hide it from the nun who brings the next day's ration, and in case she might need it later, though she never does. This much is her choice, in her control.

It is a cause for some wonder, how quickly this change has taken place: the way the fasting, the idea as well as the fact of it, has become her life. She carries the hunger with her every moment of the day. When she is praying she prays to withstand it – and when it is at its most acute it moves her towards prayer. The only time she does not feel it is when she is asleep. And yet – and here is the strangest thing – she is not in anguish over it. Instead, this concentration, this absorption in the act of not eating, is so strong that it has begun to wipe out all other feelings and thoughts that might pursue her. There is no room now to pine for voices reciting poetry or to yearn for the touch of a hand upon hers. No time for fury at her incarceration, nor the indulgence of despair. Even the music that used to soften the silence in her head has stilled now. She is too busy with the business in hand, decisions to be taken, challenges to be faced: how many sips of water, when and how many slivers of stale bread, how many times each mouthful must be chewed to make it last, whether at the end she will swallow it or perhaps spit it out. And though there may be setbacks, there are also triumphs. The simple fact of controlling what she does or does not put in her mouth gives her a strange sense of power. It also makes her feel less alone. For in this struggle another voice is becoming louder.

'As the body grows thin, so by as much the soul waxes fat.'

The novice mistress's words have become her poetry now. While Suora Zuana was intent on pushing the bread into her mouth, Suora Umiliana understands the satisfaction that comes from crushing one's own resistance. Suora Umiliana, who has always offered her cold comfort, is now kindness itself. Each day she gives up her recreation hour to sit and pray with her. Her instruction, which once seemed so joyless, becomes full of substance and meaning.

'Give it up to Him. The struggle, the temptation. Your weakness and your unworthiness. For no-one can do it alone.'

It is as if the novice mistress has been waiting for this moment, to see her so reduced and defeated that she can be rebuilt. Her voice, once so harsh and prodding, has grown gentle in this companionship.

'Hoard your hunger, taste the ache, feel the emptiness. Give it all up to Him, Serafina. He has felt it all and worse. If you are truly humble He will not reject you. Ask Him for His help. "I am not worthy, Lord, but be with me now in this fight. Fill me with emptiness. For you are my only food, my only sustenance. Purge me so I will be ready for you."'

*

'My only food.' 'My only sustenance.' When she is not thinking of the stale bread she is thinking more and more about the host, constructing the moment, wondering what it might taste like on a clean conscience. Even as a child, when she tried to be good she was often distracted by small sins of thought, like flea bites on her soul. But it is different now. Now, with nothing else in her life to long for, she begins to long for this: the sacrament, laid out like a banquet in her imagination, the tang of the wine, the incomparable melting sweetness of the host on her tongue. But only if she keeps herself pure for it.

So the days begin to blur together and under Suora Umiliana's tutelage, she waxes fat while she grows thin.

Meanwhile, through the parlatorio come mangled rumours of visitations, changes and troubles inside other convents in other cities, so that many nuns bow their heads in prayer and give thanks to God that here in Santa Caterina they are not so oppressed.

Many nuns . . . but not all.

THIRTY-SIX

On the third Sunday of Lent, after two weeks of confinement and penance, the novice Serafina is given leave to attend mass and take communion, and so rejoin convent life.

Zuana takes her place early in the chapel. She has not seen her former assistant since the morning of her recovery. The girl arrives supported on the arm of young Suora Eugenia. Even at a distance Zuana is disturbed by what she sees. The girl is hunched and withdrawn, eyes to the ground, each step small, considered. Beside her Eugenia stands slender and proud. Like a number of the younger nuns, she has been much affected by the story of the illness and semi-miraculous recovery, and now seems content to offer herself as the novice's acolyte rather than her rival. They make an arresting pair: the convent's two songbirds, both in their way highly strung, and both worn thin by the intensity of being alive. How susceptible the young are to such storms of emotion and drama, Zuana thinks. It is as if their very hearts beat faster than others'. She keeps an eye on them as they settle in their seats. Theirs has been an entrance as much as an arrival and she is not the only one watching through half-closed eyes. 'There will be no more rebellion.' The abbess's words sound in

Zuana's ears. As Madonna Chiara will be the last to take her seat, she is not here to witness this moment – which is unfortunate, for it is perhaps something she should take note of.

Except . . . except, Zuana thinks, while I know this young girl to be a dissembler of extraordinary talent, there is no deception in what we are seeing now, surely? How could there be? Installed in her choir seat she looks so small, curled in on herself, eyes dull, her expression almost dreamy. If, on top of her drug-induced voiding, she is starving herself more than the allotted penance, there will be precious little stamina for deception in her now. A better confessor would never have imposed such a rigorous penance, for younger girls are known to be more susceptible to the drama of fasting than their older counterparts.

Still, it is possible some good will come of it. She thinks of Suora Magdalena, dried up in her bed like a piece of salted meat. While she represents the extreme, degrees of hunger are necessary – even beneficial – to convent life. In readiness for the host Zuana herself has not eaten since last night and there is a familiar, almost pleasurable hollowness in her stomach. For those who find themselves distracted by the world around fasting can be a wondrous tool. Indeed, this is the time of year for it; Lent after Carnival. Carne vale: farewell to the flesh. Most of the nuns will be feeling the growl of hunger in their stomachs at some time over the next six weeks. Disciplining the body to free the soul – with the convent still so upside down there will be those who will actively look forward to it as a way of returning to a state of greater calm.

When they are all seated, Father Romero enters, flanked by the sacristan sister and the chosen choir nun who will aid him in the business of the mass. In contrast to the ceremony celebrated in the public church, mass in the convent chapel is an intimate affair: a simple altar set below the great crucifix with the nuns gathered in their choir stalls close by; the greatest privilege as well as the greatest pleasure.

If they are honest they might admit that it is not, alas, always a transcendent experience. Father Romero's surplice, embroidered by the sisters themselves, is so heavy with gold thread that he can barely walk underneath it. Zuana watches him fumbling with the objects on the altar. In the sixteen years she has been here there has been only one confessor whose inner light matched the gold on his robes. He had lasted a mere seven months, taken when a sudden wave of pestilence hit the city, and in the years that followed they had all been either too fierce or too feeble. In the lives of the convent saints, the journey of the most holy women is marked by the wisdom and charity of their confessors. How would Caterina of Siena have learned to speak so clearly to the world if the first human ear had not been that of Raymond de Capua? But here they must fend for themselves spiritually – what is it that Suora Umiliana says – 'like lambs bleating with hunger in need of a pasture to nurture them'. Though Zuana does not want to live in a convent run with her strictness and ferocity, there are nevertheless moments when the novice mistress's eloquence speaks to her. How many other choir sisters, she wonders, may have felt the same?

The service begins. While Father Romero's voice is cracked and wheezy, the nuns' responses are full and joyful and the chapel resounds to eager voices.

'God be with you.'

'And with you, too.'

And despite Father Romero, surely He is.

Zuana bows her head. She has lived among these women for almost seventeen years. Recently even her father's voice has been growing quieter compared to theirs. The thought does not frighten her as it once used to. The abbess is right: through the rhythm and discipline of prayer eventually comes acceptance. How many of them could that be said of? She glances across the stalls and senses Suora Umiliana's eye upon her. Ah, she always has an uncanny way of knowing who is not properly concentrating.

Zuana gives her attention to the altar. They are reaching the moment of the blessing of the Eucharist.

'This is my body.'

'This is my blood.'

She glances up at the great crucifix, the trickle of blood unfurling like a scarlet ribbon from His tortured side. And as she studies it the body seems to tremble forward against the nails. Zuana narrows her eyes to look more clearly. I am tired, she thinks. It makes my vision untrustworthy. She glances around her but, with the exception of Agnesina, whose faulty vision makes even the closest things unreliable to the eye and who is now staring fixedly upwards, no-one else seems to have noticed. The bell rings and all of them bow their heads for the elevation of the communion.

Father Romero turns to face the nuns. The moment has come. The women file out of their seats towards the altar, led by the abbess. She is grace itself at such times, hands folded, back straight, gliding more than walking. Those who come after her try to match her, though with the elder nuns it returns to shuffling soon enough. They kneel one by one in front of the stooped figure, heads back, mouths wide open, like hungry birds waiting for the mother's food. It is as well that Father Romero keeps good hold of the chalice, for a few of them are almost greedy for the wine. His blood. His body. How could you not want more of it? When Zuana's turn comes she clasps her hands and empties her mind.

'Accept the body and blood of Christ.'

'Amen.'

The wafer slides on to her tongue. She feels its cool, familiar weight, the way it starts to disintegrate as it mixes with her saliva. To take the Lord thy God inside you. To be filled with His grace. His sacrifice. His love. The essence of goodness. There is no simpler or greater miracle.

She returns to her place in the choir stalls, head bowed, eager to hold on to the loss of self for as long as she can. At the altar Suora Umiliana kneels, followed by each of her novices in turn.

It is not clear exactly what moment it happens – whether Serafina is actually receiving the communion wafer or if the priest has already moved on to the next young girl. What everybody does agree on is that the noise comes first. A sharp, angry crack, as if the very flagstones of the church are splitting open; indeed those who have lived through such quaking of the earth swear that they even felt a shiver. But the ground stays firm enough. It is the world above that changes.

'Aaaah —'

'Our Lord . . . Jesus!'

'The cross. The cross!'

Above their heads the left hand of Christ has pulled away from the horizontal bar of the crucifix and the torso lurches forwards. For a second it seems as if the whole body might tear itself off the wood but the right hand and the feet stay anchored, so that He remains, hanging, suspended, His left arm stuck out into the air, the nail still embedded in His palm, His face staring down in agony towards the altar. At the same time a thin rain of wood dust pours from the exposed hole, showering Father Romero's robes and head. The priest gives a strangled cry and his hands let go of the psalter and chalice. They bounce off the stones, scattering the remaining hosts and spilling the wine across the floor. And suddenly everyone is wailing and screaming so that it feels as if the beginning of the end of the world might be nigh, right there in the sanctuary of Santa Caterina's convent chapel.

In the vacuum left by Father Romero's dithering, the abbess is immediately in charge. She retrieves the chalice and sets it back on the altar, though she does not touch the hosts, for even she is not so blessed.

'Sisters, sisters, be calm . . .' Her voice is clear and penetrating. 'There is no danger. One of the nails on the crucifix has come loose, that is all. But we must be alert in case Christ's dear body falls further on to us. Return to your cells, all of you. Suora Umiliana – will you guide the novices out of chapel?'

But Umiliana is still on her knees and does not move.

'Suora Umiliana. Look to your novices.'

It might have ended there, for when she chooses Madonna Chiara delivers not just comfort but unmistakable authority. Yet even as she says it the chapel door is opening and the figure of the conversa, Letizia, stands inside, the morning light bright behind her.

It is possible that Zuana sees her before the others. Certainly she recognises her faster. She does not even need to make out the look on her face to know there is more to come . . . Oh sweet Jesus, she thinks. What is happening to us here?

'Can someone come . . . please! Suora Zuana – the old sister is dead.'

The abbess closes her eyes briefly. While she may have indeed been bred for this, there are still moments when the testing seems more than she can bear. She does not have long to rest, however, as at that very moment, behind her, with no fuss or drama at all, the novice Serafina slides quietly to the floor.

THIRTY-SEVEN

Fourteen days and fourteen nights.

During one of them she dreams of Jacopo, his body washed up in black river water, small fishes darting like coloured musical notes in and out of his mouth. The dream scares her so much – not for the violence as much as for the very thought of him – that the day after she eats nothing at all, making do with only a dozen sips of water, and the fixation of her mind on food – or the lack of it – erases any further thought.

She is tired much of the time now and would sleep all day if she were allowed. There are times while she is awake when she feels so light and giddy that she wonders if she might even be lifting off the ground. The closer it comes to the day of the mass, the more she fears that if anything should pass her lips it might sully the purity of the sacrament. She listens carefully to Umiliana's instruction leading to this moment, on her state of unworthiness and His boundless grace, the need to approach Him in complete humility, but there are times when she finds it hard to concentrate and more than once she finds herself crying with the effort. When this happens the good sister does not chastise or criticise but rather takes her hands and draws up her gaze to meet her own, pulling her back into alertness.

> *My soul longeth, yes, even fainteth for the court of the Lord*
> *My heart and my flesh crieth out for the living God*
> *For the Lord God is sun and shield*
> *The Lord will give grace and glory*
> *And no good thing will He withhold from them that walk uprightly.*

There are times when her words are so warm that Serafina is tempted to confess everything to her, but she is frightened that the depth of her sins might make Umiliana reject her.

For her part, if Santa Caterina's novice mistress is curious as to the reason why such a rigorous fasting penance has been imposed upon her young charge, she does not ask. Some of the holiest journeys begin with transgression and she speaks of the penance only as a blessed chance. Serafina has been given a great gift, she tells her, and she must treasure it.

Some questions, however, she does permit herself. She is eager to know what happened when the old woman entered the cell as the girl lay there half dead. What had the blessed Magdalena said to her? What did she herself see? And what about the time before then, that afternoon before Vespers, the incident that no-one speaks of but which everyone in the convent knows about, when Magdalena experienced some form of rapture?

Serafina answers as honestly as she can. When she describes how it was for her in the cell, how as the old woman had grabbed her hand and spoken to her she had experienced a terrible hollowness, as if someone had taken a scalpel to her innards and emptied her out, Umiliana's crumpled face lights up like a lamp and she tells her that this in itself was a sign, that for all her unworthiness the old sister had seen in her the possibility of grace. And for this reason it is even more important that she continue her fast for goodness. Though Serafina has no idea what grace feels like, she knows she is moving towards something, for in all of her life she has never felt so . . . so consumed, so dense and yet so full of air.

The night before mass she prays and prays until she falls asleep on her knees. In place of the gnawing hunger there is now only a dull ache and a certain tingling and numbing in her fingers and her feet. Though the weather remains quite warm she often finds herself cold and has to add another shift and shawl under her habit. As she changes her clothes she is struck by how strange and large her body looks, as if starvation is making her grow rather than reduce. It is God's way of telling her she must try harder. She thinks of Suora Magdalena and how the host was her only food. She knows more about her now, for in exchange for Serafina's acquiescence Umiliana has her own convent stories to tell. She describes how Santa Caterina was once a place of miracles and marvels, nurturing its own living saint, who lit up each and every office with her goodness and even bore the marks of her own stigmata, blood dripping from her hands and feet. How there was not a single novice or young nun who was not thrilled and exulted by the experience. And her eyes shine with rising tears as she says it.

The light outside in the cloisters on the morning of the mass is almost dazzling after the dimness of the cell. As Serafina walks towards the chapel supported by Suora Eugenia she feels a sudden cramp in her stomach. The cloisters bring back a flood of memories and for a moment she cannot keep at bay the horror of all that has taken place in her life. She tightens her fingers on the young nun's arm and Eugenia stops for a second. Serafina looks up at her. Whereas in the past she has seen envy, even anger in her eyes, now there is wariness, even a little awe. What is happening to me, she thinks? Panic, like a jet of water, rises then subsides. They start to walk again.

Inside the chapel she avoids Suora Zuana, though she feels her eyes on her as soon as she comes in. She takes her place in the stalls and sits with her hands on the arm rests to keep her sense of balance. On the other side of the pews Perseveranza and Felicità throw curious little glances in her direction, while old Agnesina stares openly, not even pretending not to look. What do they all see? Maybe they are fasting, too, all equally hollowed out ready to be filled with God's grace. How long could one continue? Weeks, months? Longer? Suora Magdalena lived on the host for years. Isn't that what Umiliana had told her?

The mass begins. When the time comes to sing the responses the breath she takes makes her dizzy and her voice reverberates so far inside her own head that she is not sure if the sound reaches out at all. By the time they reach the blessing of the Eucharist she feels as if her whole body is vibrating. She can barely stand in order to make the short walk from the stalls to the altar. She fixes her gaze on the bowed figure of Umiliana in front of her to keep herself steady. She kneels and in readiness tilts her head backwards, opening her mouth and closing her eyes, only the sudden darkness makes everything start to spin and she has to open them again. There is a throbbing in her head. She holds herself still, anticipating the moment, ready to hear the words, which take an age, it seems.

'Accept the body and blood of Christ.'

'Amen.'

And now at last the host is on her tongue. She waits for the explosion of sweetness. The crack is so harsh and sharp that it pulls her head further back again and as this happens she feels a terrible dizziness. She sees the figure of Christ tear away from the cross and start to fall, coming straight at her. Oh – He has seen through me, she thinks. He knows that I am not penitent nor empty enough. She tries to stand up and manages to get to her feet but the world is spinning. She hears voices, feels a rush of people around her and then she is falling, falling . . .

When she comes to, on the chapel floor, Suora Umiliana's face is close above her, the white hairs on her chin trembling like animal whiskers. 'What did you see?' she whispers urgently. 'Was Magdalena in the chapel with you? Did you see Him as He fell?'

THIRTY-EIGHT

'Termites.'

The chapter meeting is called by the abbess two days later. Suora Magdalena has been buried, the chapel is closed and a carpenter and a local sculptor have been brought in to assess the damage. But with the parlatorio open for visiting at the end of the week, it is time to make sure that the story told by everyone is the same one.

'It seems that large amounts of the wood have been eaten away around the iron fixings on the left hand and the back of the body where the statue was fixed to the cross behind. The crucifix is over a hundred years old. The carpenters say it has been going on for decades, perhaps longer. Such things are common enough in damp, hot climates like Ferrara's.'

The abbess looks out over the assembled sisters. It is true that most of them will have come across termite damage; rooms where the feet of rich desks or tables rest in bowls of water to try to ward off the worst of them. But Our Lord falling off his cross?

'But they are crawling insects. How did they get up there?'

There is a small silence.

'At times in the cycle of their life they have the ability to fly,'

Zuana says quietly, for that much she knows to be true. But she also knows that no-one really wants to hear this. And not simply because she is the abbess's favourite and might therefore say whatever she wants her to.

'They have had a hundred years to do such a thing,' Suora Umiliana says bluntly. 'Yet the moment it happens is that of our most holy sister's death.'

No-one can argue with that. A few of them look towards Serafina, who sits pale and hunched in among the novices. There seems no point in remarking that after fourteen days of fasting it had almost certainly been the lack of food that had made her pass out at that same moment as the death was announced. Though as she thinks this, Zuana realises that even she herself is no longer that sure.

The intervening days have been hectic ones, with whisper and rumour moving like wind round the cloisters and workrooms. With the chapel invaded by workmen, Suora Magdalena's body cannot be laid out in front of the altar as is the custom and so the humble coffin has to rest in the small room behind the dispensary that doubles as a mortuary. Zuana is helped by Letizia and Suora Felicità to dress her in a clean shift and new white skullcap and arrange her gnarled limbs as best they can, her hands crossed together over her chest, her frame so thin that it barely registers under the gold cloth, which is kept for this moment and will be returned to the stores when the body goes into the ground.

Left alone for a few moments before the night vigil begins, Zuana can only marvel at the corpse. Suora Magdalena looks as if she has been dead for years, half mummified already. That she has survived for so long like this is . . . well, if it is not a miracle, then it is certainly a wonder of nature.

Zuana does not ask – because she knows it would be refused –

but she would give anything to open up the chest and abdomen of the cadaver now to search for signs of further holiness. There are other places where this has happened; when a sister who was clearly saintlike before her death has warranted an autopsy in case the body might offer up its own evidence. How often has she thought of those nuns who rolled up their sleeves and took the convent's kitchen knives to the delicately perfumed corpse of the great Suora Chiara of Montefalco two hundred and fifty years before? Imagine the wonder when they discovered that nestling inside the chest cavity was a heart three times the normal size, with the clear sign of a cross made out of nodules of flesh emblazoned within. One of those same sisters had been the daughter of a doctor. That was what her father had told her. Oh, if she had been that nun, what a monograph she would have written on the dissection – fine and detailed enough to take its place on any library shelf.

But it is pointless even thinking of it. Suora Magdalena's secrets, whatever they may be, will be buried with her, for the good of the convent. 'For the good of the convent': the phrase is becoming a kind of liturgy.

In lieu of further miracles, the talk has been more of the death itself. The end, when it came, had been clear enough. Magdalena had opened her eyes wide, murmured a few words, then sighed her life out on a long, shallow breath. What she had actually said has been the subject of some debate, though after a conversation with Suora Umiliana Letizia now swears she is certain that the words were: 'I come to you, Sweet Jesus. God save us all.'

Though the parlatorio visit is not due until the end of the week, the news slips out fast enough in the pockets of the carpenters or through the mortar between the bricks in the walls. There are a few local Ferrarese old enough to remember Suora Magdalena's reputation for miracles and by the end of the first day a small crowd has gathered outside the gates. The abbess accepts a few scribbled condolences but is adamant (despite a protracted private audience with Suora Umiliana) that there will be no public showing of the body. Instead the convent holds vigil by the coffin but only choir nuns are allowed to attend and with the abbess leading them the atmosphere remains dignified and restrained. The burial takes place the next morning, immediately the twenty-four-hour laying out period is over: a simple, moving ceremony, with tears, prayers and words of joy and reassurance from the abbess and Father Romero.

It is not, however, over yet . . .

'I am not sure I understand your meaning, Suora Umiliana,' the abbess says coolly.

In chapter, Zuana, like the rest of the room, is trying to keep her eyes on both women at once.

'What I mean, Madonna abbess, is that the taking of the soul of Suora Magdalena at the same moment as the falling of our Blessed Lord from the cross is most surely a sign.' She pauses, but only briefly. Her mind is made up. 'I believe we are being told that there is not enough devotion in Santa Caterina. That with all our celebrations and public performances and fame, we are neglecting our true course, which is prayer and humility, discipline and obedience.'

She delivers it well; these days it is almost as if her piety has a natural performance within it. The chapter holds its breath. In all their years of sparring, the challenge has never been so direct.

In contrast the abbess smiles broadly. 'And yet I see a room before me filled with nuns who celebrate God with all their hearts and souls. There is surely no more joyful or productive convent anywhere in Ferrara.'

'There are those who would disagree.'

'Really?' She looks around the room as if they — whoever they may be — are about to speak. Suora Felicità opens her mouth but Umiliana silences her with a look.

'There are forces abroad greater than us or the city of Ferrara, Madonna abbess. I am talking about those within our Holy Mother Church, the good fathers of Trent, who might find all manner of faults within the convent of Santa Caterina.'

The abbess, who is done with charm now, stares at her coldly. Her eyes pass over the gathered nuns and a fair number of them at the back now look away from her. Apparently there have been some conversations within her convent that the Mother abbess, for all her acuity, has not been privy to.

'Ah! You would prefer to live in Bologna, perhaps. Or Milan, where they no longer play convent instruments and can sing only the plainest of settings when they perform to the outside world. You have, I assume, heard of these changes?'

Benedicta lets out an audible gasp. Arranging the score for *The Lamentations of Jeremiah* has been keeping her awake at night and she seems less joyful than she used to be.

The novice mistress gives a little shrug. 'There are sisters in those cities who would say there is more worship in the psalms they give up to God now than in all the fancy settings they once entertained visitors with.'

While a number of the choir nuns are now visibly alarmed, from the rows at the back of chapter there is a rustling wave of support.

Zuana finds herself imagining a ripe boil: the way it grows under the surface, swelling, hardening, gathering pus, and however many poultices are applied it will not soften or heal of its own accord. Such is the ailment within the body of the convent now.

'For a novice mistress whose greatest desire it is to close

down contact with the outside world, you seem to know a great deal about what goes on there.'

The abbess glances briefly at the gate/censor sister, who handles all the reading of the correspondence that moves in and out, and who has the decency now not to be able to meet her eyes.

But Umiliana holds her ground. 'Santa Caterina could be as great as any of those convents. He has already given us the purest voices with which to praise Him.'

And now she looks towards Serafina, so the rest of the nuns immediately follow the gaze. Not, however, the abbess.

'So – if I have understood you correctly, Suora Umiliana – you see the work of the termites in the chapel as God's message to us that we are failing in our duties towards Him?'

Zuana thinks again of the boil and how at such times the only way forward is to lance it, whatever mess and pain it might cause.

'I see it as a sign for us to mend our ways, yes,' Umiliana says again.

'A sign. Ah yes, signs – they are such a rich language.'

The abbess looks out over the assembled chapter. And her eyes are clear, no hint of fear in her.

'I have been in this convent serving God since I was six years old and what I have learned in that time is that His plan is wondrous indeed. While He would not choose to stop the appetite of termites, for nature must work by her own rules, He can certainly make His will felt.'

What is coming, Zuana thinks? Can she really do this?

'The left-hand nail that held our blessed Lord's body to the cross and the fixing in the back of his torso both worked loose at the same moment. Had the nail on the right side of the cross bar also given way the great sculpture would definitely have crashed to the ground. In which case we would be mourning the loss not only of Suora Magdalena but also of one or more of our sweetest novices; even perhaps Suora Umiliana herself, as they were all close to the altar taking the host.'

She pauses. Timing, Zuana thinks. The world is made richer by its subtleties.

'That, to me, is the true sign here. For I have to tell you that the carpenter has discovered that the wood behind the right-hand nail was even more badly eaten away. So much so that he and the sculptor are in total amazement that it should have held under the strain.' Another pause. 'It seems to me that far from damned, we were chosen instead to be saved.'

She waits again now, to make sure the room has taken on the gravity of what she has said.

'I have extracted an oath from the workmen not to speak of this outside the convent in case careless talk of a miracle should spread and we would seem lacking in humility in our desire to bring attention down upon us. But of course I have informed the Bishop and asked if perhaps a small service of thanksgiving within the convent might be called for.' She stops, smoothing her skirts again, though there is not a crease out of place, nor ever will be. 'If, however, Suora Umiliana, you are still determined to put another point of view, then His Holiness might be interested in hearing from you. If you compose a letter I will make sure that it is delivered.'

The novice mistress stares at her. Zuana watches her chin tremble slightly.

'I will write it today and bring it to you during visiting hour . . .' she says, absorbing the defeat as if it can only serve to strengthen her ' . . . when I would beg leave to talk of this further.'

A deep silence falls on the room. It is unheard of for a choir nun not to publicly accept the abbess's conclusion. They are entering uncharted waters now and that brings with it the taste of excitement as well as fear.

Among the sweet saved novices, some of them now seek out Serafina. She is sitting stock still, staring out on to the room, those sunken eyes not seeming to focus on anything at all. This is only her third day back within convent life but she had not needed Suora Umiliana's comment to draw attention to her. In contrast to the showy piety of before, her fasting penance has already had an impact, such that some of the sisters are beginning to wonder who this young woman really is. A novice with the temper of a gorgon and the voice of an angel is rare enough, let alone one who has been 'chosen' by the convent mystic as worthy of saving. And now, if Madonna Chiara is right, and the falling cross was indeed a symbol of God's grace rather than his anger, what should one make of the fact that it was she who was receiving the host at that fateful moment? Of the sweet saved, surely that makes her sweetest of all?

Zuana, in contrast, is concentrating more on the girl's body than her soul. She is thinking of how excessive fasting, especially when done too fast, can bring with it a strange intensity of self, which without proper supervision can become overwhelming; for emptiness is a place where one can get lost as well as found. She is thinking also that while the penance officially ended three days ago, she has not seen the girl eat anything since. And she makes a note to try to change her place at the refectory table so that she can get a better view of her.

THIRTY-NINE

On this of all visiting days, the abbess does not take any chances. She appoints two chaperone nuns to be present continually inside the parlatorio. This is not unusual – indeed a single chaperone is convent custom, since any contact with the outside world must be monitored – but the rule, as with so many others in Santa Caterina, is implemented lightly and the nuns generally speak, laugh and gossip with their relatives freely. Today, however, the presence of two overseers – both from within the abbess's family faction – will determine the conversations: in the unfolding drama of convent life, a holy sister has died and is much mourned, and though termites ate the wood of the great chapel crucifix, it proved an opportunity for the convent to be blessed by God rather than damned by Him. Added to that there is the news, come through that very morning, that the crucifix, now removed from the chapel, will be repaired and remounted in a few weeks, well in time for Palm Sunday.

That same morning Zuana is in the dispensary working when she receives a visit from Suora Ysbeta, distraught and cradling a silk-wrapped bundle, the snub nose and gummy, half-closed eyes of a small dog just visible at one end of the swaddling.

'He is sick, Suora Zuana. Very sick. Will you look at him?'

There is no point in telling her that the dispensary is a place for nuns, not animals. Ysbeta is a pure enough soul, compassionate and devout. In another world she might have been a follower of a stricter regime, only her love of animals is almost as great as her love of people and in a convent where she could not keep a pet she would surely wither up and die. As the dog is doing now.

Zuana places the bundle on the worktop and carefully unwraps the silk. The smell tells her much of what she needs to know. The animal is rank with sickness, its little body trembling, its coat, usually so sleek and groomed, matted and dull. She moves her hand carefully along the line of its stomach and soon locates a hard swelling near the groin. The dog whines and makes a feeble attempt to snap, but there is no fight there any more.

'He has not been himself for a while. Not since the feast of St Agnes. But it is only in the last few days . . . Can you help him?'

'I am afraid he is beyond my help. There is a growth, a tumour here. Probably not the only one. It will be sapping his strength and causing him pain.'

'Ah, I knew it. Even the pets are sick here.'

Zuana says nothing. She strokes the dog gently. It bares its teeth a little then gives up and drops its head heavily on to her hand.

'Surely God would not punish us so.'

'What do you mean, sister?'

'Felicità says there is a convent in Siena where, after a Church visitation, the inspectors took away the sisters' dogs and drowned them in a sack in the river.'

Since the chapter meeting the floodgates have opened on such stories.

'Oh, I can't believe they would do such a thing.'

'I can. I think Suora Felicità herself would do it if she could. Last week in the cloisters she kicked him.'

'I'm sure she did not mean to.'

Ysbeta will have none of this, either. 'Oh yes she did.' She nods her head vigorously. 'They are so pleased with themselves, she and Suora Umiliana. Just because they can live without comfort they think everyone else must be the same.'

Zuana has never seen Ysbeta so passionate before. 'Well, her kick did not cause this. Nor do I think it punishment for any sin. The fact is that the tumour will have been growing in his body for some time now.'

She stares down at the little animal. 'So you cannot do anything?'

'I could give him something to make him sleep, so he would not feel it so much.'

'What about the girl? Might she save him?'

'Which girl?'

'The novice, Serafina . . .' She hesitates. 'I . . . they are saying that Suora Magdalena passed her powers on to her when she died. That was why the cross did not fall on her and why she fainted afterwards.'

Indeed? Is that what they are saying? Zuana thinks. What kind of spy am I if I do not hear even the noisiest rustles in the grass?

'Who is saying such a thing?'

She shrugs. 'Oh, some of the sisters . . . Would you ask her? I mean – she is close to you.'

Zuana smiles gently. 'Suora Ysbeta, I am sorry, but there is nothing she nor any one of us can do. Your dog is dying. It is the way of nature.'

The old nun bows her head, nodding slightly. She moves to the worktop and, tender as a mother with an ailing child, starts wrapping up the shaking body again, taking care not to touch the animal's stomach as she does so. Zuana stares at her. Christ dolls, pets, babies in the parlatorio . . . some women find the barrenness of marriage to God so hard to bear.

She reaches for the poppy syrup.

She is thinking of the dog and how the convent is grown restless inside the winds of gossip as she sits at her dispensary desk that same afternoon marking down the remedies and essences that need replacing, when the knock comes at the door.

'Suora Zuana, the watch sister has sent me.' Letizia, bright and efficient as always. 'There is someone to see you in the parlatorio.'

'To see me?'

'Yes. The watch sister says it is the wife of one of your father's pupils whom you have met before. Her husband is very ill and she is come to ask you to pray for him.'

Zuana frowns. At the beginning she received a few visits from people who had known her father, women from the court whose children or husbands he had healed, but it has been many years since anyone had bothered to look her up and she has no memory of such a woman. Falling crucifixes, ailing dogs and dying, living saints. And now a visitor for a nun who knows no-one. These are strange times indeed.

Inside, the parlatorio is humming. While not as ornately decorated as for Carnival, it is still welcoming. Someone has cut a few green fronds and placed them in a vase on a table in the middle, and many of the separate groups have ceramic plates of biscuits and jugs of wine and water for the visitors to eat and drink. There must be near to twenty nuns (not counting the chaperones) entertaining, some with only a few guests, others with what seem like whole families gathered round. The noise level is high, partly because of the children, of which there are maybe half a dozen – two babies and the rest toddlers, climbing on to the nuns' laps and playing with their crosses or tottering around the room clutching sticky biscuits.

Zuana's visitor is sitting on her own close to the wall. She is a middle-aged woman, modestly dressed and a little self-conscious in such surroundings. Clearly she is not of noble birth but she has made an effort with her clothes, her shoes clean and her hair up as befits her married status, with a simple but stylish veil pinned at the back and falling on to her shoulders. Zuana has never seen her before.

'Hello, I am Suora Zuana.'

'Oh, it is a pleasure . . .' She starts to rise and holds out a hand as if unsure of the correct greeting for a noble nun.

'Please, don't get up. Forgive me – but do we know each other?'

'I . . . no.'

'But you are the wife of one of my father's pupils?'

'Yes, well, in a manner of speaking.'

'You are sure it is me you are looking for?'

'Oh yes. If you are Suora Zuana . . . My husband did know your father. We keep an apothecary store near the west gate of the city. In Via Apollonia. When he was a boy he met your father often when he used to come in there. He said he was a wonderful man.'

The woman is nervous. She smiles. It is a good smile: one that crinkles her eyes and without the restriction of a wimple lights up her face.

'So, how can I help you? He is ill, I hear?'

She takes a breath. 'There is illness, yes. But I am come on behalf of a gentleman.'

'Not your husband?'

'No, my husband . . . oh, it's not what you think. My husband knows I am here. This gentleman – he has been a patient. My husband found him. He was injured. Badly injured. We helped him. Without our help he would have died.'

While she is nervous, she is also determined. By rights, Zuana should not be listening further, for there is no connection here to justify the visit, but there is something about the woman that she likes. Or maybe it is the novelty of being here in this room, with a hubbub of people around her, as if this were not a convent at all but a receiving room in some great house where people gather to enjoy ordinary life. The chaperone nuns are moving between the groups. One of them looks over at Zuana. It is so unusual to have the dispensary sister here. Zuana smiles and nods at her. She smiles back and moves on.

'Perhaps you should tell me what happened,' she says to the woman.

'Yes, yes, thank you. Some weeks ago my husband was coming back into the city from collecting plants in the country. His horse had gone lame and he had had to walk the last miles so it was late in the night. He heard shouting on the river bank and when he approached he disturbed an attack. Some men ran away but there was another on the ground. He had been stabbed and they had tried to cut his throat. My husband stopped the blood as best he could – they had not severed any vital artery – and brought him back to the house. For many days we thought he might die, for he had bled a great deal, but my husband used casewort and yarrow on the wounds and he began to recover.'

'You help your husband with his work?'

The woman blushes. 'Yes. A little. We have no children; I was not able . . . so . . . well, it is cheaper than an assistant.'

'You like it?'

She gives a little laugh. 'Yes. Yes, I do.'

Zuana nods. Father, husband, even sister. Someone to talk to. Someone who is as interested as you are. It is all she has ever really wanted.

'And what is it about this story that has brought you here to me?' she asks gently.

'The young man told us that the men who tried to kill him had been his friends, people he had met when he came to the city, for he is a stranger here.'

'Then why did they try to kill him?'

'He didn't know. My husband said he must go to the city watch, for he could recognise his attackers. But he said it would be no use as they were from noble families and he would not get justice.'

Zuana can feel the cold moving through her. 'Did this young man tell you his name?'

'Yes. Jacopo Bracciolini. He is a singer. Well, I don't know if he still will be with his face and throat slashed. But he taught singing in Milan.'

Zuana shakes her head. She must get up now and walk away.

'Did he send you here?' she says more sharply.

'No. When I heard his story I offered to come. He is a good man and he nearly died.' She pauses. 'He has written a letter, which he asked me to deliver to you. It is for a young nun, a novice called—'

'I do not want to know who it is for. I don't know this man and I cannot take anything from him.' She is standing now. 'The novice has taken vows and will soon take others, and she is not allowed to receive letters.'

She spots the chaperone across the room looking over at her. The intensity of the conversation has attracted her attention. Zuana sits again and drops her eyes.

'But rest assured I will pray for his full recovery,' she says more calmly. 'And thank you for coming.'

'Please. Please . . .' The woman's voice is low but clear. 'It is difficult, I know. But this is a good man. I have spent weeks caring for him. He is not asking anything, only to say goodbye. He is going away and wants to wish her well. He will not bother her again.'

Zuana is shaking her head but it is partly to keep the woman's voice out of her ears. There is a great conviction in the way she speaks. If she was nursing you, you would surely be comforted by her strength as well as her gentleness. Or perhaps this love story has touched her heart. Certainly she would have reason to value love, for without the fondness of her husband a barren woman is easy enough to shrug off in favour of another.

'Have you read it?'

'No. But he is a good man, I swear.'

Now the chaperone has come up to them.

'How are you, dear sister?'

Zuana smiles. 'Oh, very well thank you, Suora Elena. Well, except for this sad news. This is . . . Isabella . . . Vesalio. Her husband was one of my father's most talented students at the university. He is very sick and she has come to me for advice. But more than any remedy, I think, we must all pray for him.'

The sister stares at the woman, reading the humility in her dress as well as her face. 'Rest assured, good woman, we shall add him to our prayers,' she says, smiling, and moves away.

Zuana keeps her head down, as if she is indeed in prayer. Opposite her, the woman holds her hands loosely folded in her skirts. Under her palms Zuana sees the edge of the folded paper.

'Why me? Why do you come to me?'

'Because he said you were a kind and good nun.'

'He does not know me.'

'He seems to. And he was right. You are . . . kind and good.

I wish I had known your father . . .' She trails off.

Zuana stares at her for a moment. Later she wonders when she made up her mind. Or perhaps she never did. Perhaps it was only her body that took the decision.

She moves her hands across the divide of their laps until they cover the woman's own. She is pleased to note that their fingers are as stained as each other's.

'Dear God, look down about your servants here and help this young man back to health so that he may use his voice to praise you.' And as she says the words the woman releases her grip on the letter and she takes it within her own fingers and holds it there.

'Amen.'

'Amen.'

Zuana pulls her hands back and folds her skirts around them. 'You had better go now,' she says quietly.

'Thank you.'

The woman stands and moves swiftly away.

'Oh . . . Signora Vesalio . . .'

The woman turns.

'Tell your husband to try honey and cobwebs mixed with white of egg on the neck and face wounds. It will help to salve the scarring.'

Zuana does not immediately leave but sits, her hands folded over the letter, looking out over the room. She watches Suora Perseveranza, her body held upright to compensate for the belt around her middle, in animated conversation with a well-dressed married woman of similar age and features. At her feet a child, a sweet little thing with a mass of fair curls, is balanced against her knees, her mouth grubby with biscuit crumbs, her hand picking at the wooden rosary beads that hang from her aunt's hips. How old is she? Three? Four? Already too pretty to be the next nun of the family. But there is time yet. Come an attack of the pox or some disfiguring accident, or even a gradually perceived slowness of mind . . .

Zuana slips the letter up inside her wide sleeves and leaves the room and the sound of laughter behind her.

FORTY

In the chapel she takes her usual place in the empty choir stalls and sits, her heart pounding. She closes her eyes and feels the wood on her back, registers the cuts of the craftsman's knife as a piece of walnut warehouse joins to a sliver of mahogany water. So much work here, so much devotion. After a while she opens her eyes on to the frescoes on the walls around her. As it is wasteful to have candles burning during the day the chapel is illuminated only by the progression of natural light, so that different parts are highlighted at different times. For this reason the cusps of the seasons have always been special for Zuana, as from her place in the choir stalls the afternoon light then favours two particular scenes. Over the years she has come to know them very well. Now she uses them to help steady her mind.

In the first, Joseph and Mary are returning to Jerusalem after the birth of the Christ child. Mary rides a donkey while Joseph walks beside her. The baby Jesus, already a sturdy infant, sits astride His father's shoulders, with His arms thrown out in recognition towards His mother, His childish glee so far away from the burdens of divinity yet to come. In contrast, the fresco to the side shows the cross on which He is to die, with a ladder

leaning up against it and the figure of the adult Christ climbing —
His step almost sprightly — up the rungs towards the lateral bar.

When Zuana first entered the convent, the novice mistress of
the day had pointed out these two images as representative of the
spirit of Santa Caterina: how they showed Our Lord reaching out
first towards life and then death. Even then the art was old —
over two hundred years — and considered special, she said, since
they knew of no other convent where Christ was depicted giving
Himself up for sacrifice in this manner. She had died a year later
from the fever (it was before Zuana was allowed to treat patients)
but her kindness and the power of the images had fused in
Zuana's memory and in times of crisis she has often found comfort being close to them. She sits and studies them now, the
letter resting in her hands, a modest dot of scarlet wax sealing it
shut.

So, Madonna Chiara's family had taken care of the young man,
had made sure that he did indeed disappear from the novice's life.
Dear God! But had they told her what they had done? Had the
abbess known all along that instead of a post at Parma there was
only the prospect of a corpse pumping blood from a dozen stab
wounds into the river? No. Surely not. How could she have
known? How could she possibly have condoned such a thing?
Except . . . except that in all of this story it had been the one
event that didn't make sense. Why, after risking so much to be
close to her, he should suddenly choose to desert her . . .

'Because such young men do not care a fig for anything but
their own pleasure. If he had had his way, he would have taken
her and ruined her.'

Is that what she truly believed? She, who has lived in the convent all her life, yet seems to know more about man than she
does about God. Zuana sees her standing in the herb garden, her
hands smoothing out the non-existent creases in her robes. It is

a gesture she knows well. But how well does she really know the abbess, this woman who has dedicated her life to the glory of God, the well-being of her convent and the reputation of her family? Until, that is, one of those loyalties comes into conflict with another . . .

In the chapel Zuana puts her head down and starts to pray.

The afternoon light moves around her. Eventually she lifts her head, takes the letter in her hands and breaks the seal.

It is almost the end of visiting hour when she crosses the court-yard to the novice's cell. By rights she should be studying or at prayer. Instead, she finds the girl lying on her bed, so deeply asleep that she does not even register her entrance. She is fully dressed, curled up like a small child, with a blanket pulled over her. Her face is pale, save for the lightly bruised skin under her eyes. The line of her chin is sharp now, the childish plumpness worn away. She will be feeling the cold, hence the body curled in on itself: before the spirit ignites its own fire, the lack of food drains away the body's warmth.

Under the bed Zuana notices a small bundle. She takes it out and unwraps it. A lump of bread sits inside. It is fresh, her daily portion from lunch, no doubt, concealed somehow in her robes. As her appointed spiritual guide it is Suora Umiliana's job to be monitoring her return from fasting to food now. Since there is no nun in the convent with a sharper eye for the infraction of rules, the very presence of the bread is evidence that Umiliana is encouraging the fast beyond the end of the penance. How convenient it would be for her if this sweetest of the sweetly saved souls now became a conduit to God. Her very own young mystic.

But how long does it take to truly subdue the body? At what point did Magdalena's fasting turn to joy? And what happens to

384

those who never manage to light the fire within, young women with no future, who in the end do not really care if they live or die? The letter lies folded in the pocket of her robe. She moves the blanket further up over the girl's body and leaves her quietly sleeping.

Back in the cloisters, the abbess's outer door is closed. It is a sign that she is either at prayer or in conference. Zuana lifts her hand to knock, then makes out muffled voices from behind the door. The mellifluous tones of the abbess's voice are instantly recognisable and in recent months she has become familiar with the harsher, more sibilant sounds of Suora Umiliana. She is about to turn and leave when she hears footsteps moving briskly towards the door. She barely has time to step back before it opens and the novice mistress comes out. The meeting is so abrupt and unexpected that it takes them both a few seconds to recompose their features – Zuana to disguise her discomfort at being caught at a kind of eavesdropping and Umiliana to cover up the unmistakable look of triumph in her eyes.

'What would she have us do? Drive nails into our own hands?'

Inside her chambers, Zuana has never seen the abbess so angry.

'If she is so in love with humility and poverty she should have joined the Poor Clares. Though even they might not have been strict enough for her.' She laughs bitterly, moving to and fro across the pile of the Persian rug. 'Ah! Who would have thought it? A younger daughter of the Cardolini family turning out so ambitiously pious.'

Zuana would prefer to leave now and come back when she is calmer, but she is already pulled into the orbit of her fury. Evidently she is the abbess's confidante as well as spy. 'What did she say?'

'That God has given her the courage to speak her mind and she can — or rather will — no longer be silent.' She shakes her head. 'Though I cannot recall when she was ever quiet, with or without His intercession.'

'Perhaps she feels there are more who agree with her now.'

'And who are they? Agnesina, Concordia, yes, Obedienza, Perseveranza, Stefana, Teresa perhaps, and a couple of the novices and younger nuns — I have not seen Carità so enthusiastic at the idea of deprivation before. Still, I would not give her more than maybe fifteen or twenty in total. Twenty out of sixty-five choir nuns; that is hardly the convent. Santa Caterina is home to some of the city's noblest women. Their families did not pay good dowries to have them living like paupers, fasting and praying twenty-four hours a day.'

She moves to the desk and opens the glass decanter, pouring two glasses of wine. Zuana takes hers without a murmur. She has no idea when she is going to speak and what she is going to say. Strangely, it does not worry her.

'Ha! She is playing with fire. She knows nothing of what is really going on out there. Once a bishop or a cardinal is determined, the inspections can take place with barely any warning. Apostolic visitors, they call themselves, and when they leave an army of ironmongers and bricklayers come after them, building walls and fitting grilles and gates wherever there is a glimpse of open air. I have heard of one place where the parlatorio is being redesigned as a prison, so that the nuns can only see their families through iron grilles covered with curtains. Is that what she wants? We would have half of the city's fathers hammering on the Duke's door complaining that their daughters were suffering ill treatment.'

'In which case the city's families will protect us, surely?'

'They will try, but it seems Rome is committed to taking on

even the authority of the families: those final statutes of Trent call for elections of abbesses to take place every four years.'

It is a rule that up until now has been honoured only in the breach, giving many abbesses and therefore also their families power down through lifetimes. If it were to be imposed now Santa Caterina would be voting for a new leader.

'And what if they did? You would still be re-elected.'

'What? Even though I underestimate her support?'

'I didn't say—'

'You did not need to. I saw it in your face.'

'I . . . I just think there may be a few more than twenty.'

'Who are they?'

'I do not know names,' she says quietly, for she is no longer anybody's spy. 'It is more a feeling.'

'Hmm. How much is this to do with the girl?'

'What do you mean?'

'Come, Zuana, naivety does not suit you. She has done nothing but shake the walls of the temple since she arrived. First the fury, then the acquiescence, then the escape, then the drama with Magdalena and now this showy fasting and the fainting in chapel just at the right moment. Do you think she is eating on the sly?'

'No, I don't. In fact I think she is become ill with it.'

The abbess is silent for a moment, then sighs. 'Ah . . . Suora Umiliana. I fear I made a grave mistake leaving her alone so much with her. Though at the time . . .' She stares at Zuana. 'Well, we have come too far to have her die on us now. You must see her and get her eating again.'

Zuana hesitates. This is the moment. There will never be another.

'I think it would do her good, perhaps, to have some news of her lover.'

'How could that help? It would only make it worse.'

'Her sense of abandonment is acute. I feel it might address her despair.'

The abbess shrugs. 'From what I hear, there is nothing to tell. He is well enough; singing his heart out with a bevy of pretty girls on his arm.'

'Madonna Chiara, I don't think there is a more remarkable abbess than you anywhere in Christendom,' Zuana says quietly. 'The things that you know.'

She shrugs it off, but it is clear she is pleased. 'I know only what I have to know to help the convent.'

'So you have no fear that he might try to come back to claim her at the vow-taking ceremony?'

'None at all.'

'Well, perhaps you should have. Because he isn't dead.'

It is immediate and perfect: the way the abbess now stares at her, the expression on her face changing not one iota. 'Dead?' Her voice is light. 'No, of course he isn't dead.'

'However, it seems that the knife wounds to his face and throat might make it hard for him to take up the post at Parma. If it should ever have been offered.'

Zuana feels her mouth dry. She lifts the glass and takes a sip of the wine. Her hand is very steady. Across the room the abbess's face remains impassive. Then suddenly, she gives a sigh; light, almost playful.

'As always you do yourself an injustice, Zuana. It is not I who am remarkable but you. I do believe that if you had been born into a better family you might be ruling this convent now.'

'I don't think so.'

'Oh, such a thing is not impossible.' There is a pause. 'Indeed, with the right people behind you it might yet happen. Imagine the great dispensary you could build then.'

'I am happy with the one I have,' she says quietly.

'Yes, I believe you are.'

It is strange but there is almost a sense of calm inside the room. How amazing, Zuana thinks. When confronted with such danger to herself, this woman still seems at ease, confident. Does she feel it always? When she is praying? When she is in the confessional? How early would she have had to catch Father Romero to be sure that he was sleeping through this admission?

'It seems now I must ask you about *your* sources, Zuana.'

'I had a visitor.'

'So I heard. Who was she?'

'It doesn't matter.'

'Oh yes, it matters. My nuns do not accept visits from just anyone.'

'What? Do your rules now squeeze harder than Umiliana's?'

The abbess stares at her, then sits back heavily in her chair, her natural grace deserting her for an instant. This time there is no smoothing of creases or removal of fluff from her skirts.

'I did not have anything to do with it,' she says at last. 'It was never . . .' She breaks off. 'It was not my . . . well, sometimes one does not always have control over what one unleashes. But it was never – never – what I wished.'

Zuana puts down her glass of wine. She has no idea whether she believes her or not.

'Do I have your permission to treat the novice?'

'If you do, what will you tell her?'

'That he did not desert her.' She pauses. 'I believe knowing this will lessen her despair.'

'No. No. I cannot allow that.'

With the exception, perhaps, of the girl herself, the woman in front of her is the nearest Zuana has come to a friend in her life. She has admired, respected, enjoyed, even at moments sought to emulate her. Most of all she has obeyed her. For this is the first and most powerful rule of the Benedictine order: to obey one's abbess in all things.

'And what if she continues to refuse to eat? What if she starves herself to death?'

'Then to make sure we do not lose half her dowry we will just have to arrange for her to take her vows before she does so.'

To Zuana's astonishment, the abbess laughs. 'You look shocked! Yet those are the words you wanted to hear from me, yes? Proof that as your abbess I care only about money, not souls. Oh Zuana, do you know me so little? Is that what they say about me, this small army that is raised up now behind Umiliana? That I think more about reputation than I do salvation? Is that how it is?'

Zuana does not reply. There is nothing to be gained from false comfort now.

'Well, in some ways they are right. There may be times when my methods seem cruel. But believe this, if you believe anything. The battle we are fighting now is not just for the honour of the convent or the influence of one family over another. If Umiliana wins, if she creates enough noise and rebellion to bring the inspectors in, then it will affect everyone.

'After they have stripped us of our income, after they have walled us up, even in our own parlatorio, after they have banned Scholastica's plays and taken away the instruments from the choir orchestra, they will come to you. You, who have found such unexpected sanctuary inside these walls. They will not care about your remedies and your herbs. They will break the bottles in your dispensary and take away every book in your library, and after that they will find the other ones, the ones that are hidden in your chest. That is what my "cruelty" is trying to avoid. That – the great and the small of it – is what is at stake here.'

Zuana feels her heart moving fast against her ribcage. She will not think that far ahead. No, she could not live without her books or remedies, in a convent ruled by Umiliana. Yet how can it be acceptable to so offend God in order to be able to continue to serve him? She, who can solve the most difficult riddles of the body, feels lost in the face of such complexity.

'I am still the abbess of this convent, Zuana. And until I am not you must obey me, or I must impose penance on you.' She pauses. 'As I have done already on Umiliana. Which, of course, was exactly what she wanted me to do.' She sighs. 'Think of it: the abbess's enemy and her favourite both lying in the doorway of the refectory for the other nuns to walk over. What a gift it will be to her.'

But this last appeal to the sister who used to be her confidante is too little too late.

'If you will excuse me, Madonna abbess, I must return to my dispensary.'

She gets up and moves to the door. The abbess watches her go.

'Zuana,' she says as she reaches the door. 'She is only a young woman who did not want to become a nun. The world is full of them.'

FORTY-ONE

At supper, Suora Umiliana accepts only scraps, with a generous layer of wormwood sprinkled on top. The rest of the choir nuns and novices watch nervously as she carries it with her to the table. Once there, she chews each mouthful as if it were filled with honey, a smile playing around her lips. While it is forbidden to look at anything but one's plate during the meal, it is almost impossible for people to keep their eyes off her. Serafina does not even need to worry about the squirrelling away of her food at this meal, since no-one is looking at her. Except Zuana.

The meal and the reading – which no-one hears a word of, though Scholastica has been especially picked for her strong voice – finally end, and the novice mistress rises and kneels at the feet of the abbess, before going over to take her place in the doorway. She takes a while to get herself down on to the floor. While she is adept enough at kneeling, it seems harder for her to lie prone. But then she is not a young woman any more and bones at this age become brittle and if broken heal badly.

The abbess leaves the room first, graceful as ever, bringing her left foot to rest on Umiliana's robe but carefully avoiding her flesh. In her wake, each and every choir nun and novice makes it her business to walk over rather than on the prostrate old nun, though whether it is out of respect or fear for her it is hard to tell. Either way, as convent martyrdoms go it is a fairly painless business. Now the lines have been drawn, it seems, everyone is nervous of what might happen next.

That night it takes a long time for the convent to settle. In her cell Zuana turns over the hourglass and watches the sand fall. How many times in her life has she sat here, trying to wash away the business of the day in readiness for the prayer before sleep? She has always envied those sisters who live lightly in the world, giving themselves up easily to the silence and stillness of God's love. She needs that stillness more than ever tonight, for how can she take the next step in her life without His guidance?

Her first spiritual guide, the novice mistress who had showed her the paintings in the chapel, had alerted her early to the pitfalls of intoxication with her work. 'Your knowledge brings you great solace, Zuana. But knowledge alone has no substance. Our founder, the great St Benedict himself, understood that well enough. *"Let not your heart be puffed up with exaltation. Everyone that exalteth himself shall be humbled, and he that humbleth himself shall be exalted."'*

And she had tried; truly and honestly tried, so hard that sometimes, despite the nun's kindness and patience, she thought she might go mad with the effort. Eventually she had come to accept a level of failure. What point was there in dissembling? He would know it anyway. *'God always seeeth man from heaven and the angels report to Him every hour.'*

How much easier it had become when the kind old novice sister died and she had found herself in the company of her assistant, Suora Chiara. Chiara, with her smooth skin and dancing eyes and her bright, confident relationship to God and the world around her. Chiara, who seemed able to inhabit both the mind and the spirit without fearing His displeasure and who, even then, enjoyed an almost unnatural standing in the convent itself; much more than other women of her age with fewer aunts, cousins and nieces around to support their rise through the ranks.

Yet she had been generous with her power. Without Suora Chiara arguing her case Zuana might have languished for years in the scriptorium, decorating the word of God with calendula leaves or fennel fronds. It was she who had helped Zuana to find work in the dispensary, she who had organised and supported her election as dispensary mistress and, when she finally became abbess, allowed her to take over the infirmary as well, 'for it is written in the rule of St Benedict that it must be the abbess's greatest concern that the sick suffer no neglect'. Without Madonna Chiara there would be no treatment of the Bishop's ailments and therefore no flow of special outside supplies. Without Madonna Chiara there would be no distillery, a smaller herb garden, fewer shelves with fewer bottles to be broken, fewer notebooks of remedies to be destroyed. Without Madonna Chiara . . .

Zuana looks up to see two of her books on the table. In her chest there are others, lovingly cared for over all these years. Is she really willing to be instrumental in their destruction? For what? To alleviate the misery and starvation of one obstreperous novice? 'She is only a young woman who did not want to become a nun. The world is full of them.'

The truth is that Zuana herself does not understand why this girl has become so important to her. There have been times when she wonders if it is some affliction of the womb: she has seen it enough in others; how an older nun might seek out a novice or postulant or boarder of the age that her own child would have been should she have had one. Such rapports are often characterised by undue care and attention, for while everyone knows the creation of favourites is prohibited, it is also unstoppable.

Yet it has never been like that for her. As a child without brothers or sisters she had always been familiar with her aloneness, her self-sufficiency. And yet, and yet . . . this young woman with her sense of fury and injustice has somehow infiltrated her way into Zuana's life. That she likes her is undeniable. Despite her spirit and her truculence. Or perhaps because of them. No doubt she sees something of herself in her; the curiosity as well as the determination. And it is true that had she married, had she become a wife instead of a nun, then her own child might indeed now be Serafina's age. How would she feel about her then? It is a painful question. While Santa Caterina has been a good home to her, would she choose to give a daughter up to such a life? And if not, does that mean she is willing to risk bringing down the convent to help her?

The abbess is right. The world is full of them: daughters who are too young, too old, too ill, too ugly, too difficult, too stupid, too smart. Waste. Banishment. Burial alive. Custom. The way things are. What can she do about it? It is not as if there is so much out there to celebrate. Freedom? What freedom? To marry the man you are told to and no other? If she had been living outside the walls Serafina might still have found her singing composer half-dead on some river bank, only the knives would have been wielded by her father's family rather than the abbess's. Love is not a marketable commodity: you take what you are given, even if it is your husband's pleasure to bruise your skin and breed bastards out of prettier loins. It is simply how it is. What point is there in railing against it? And why, in God's name, single out one spoilt young girl from all the rest?

The sand is at the bottom of the glass. She stares at it, then turns it over again.

'*The voice of the Lord is powerful. I will praise the Lord, with my whole heart.*'

She closes her eyes and tries not to think.

'*The voice of the Lord is full of majesty.*'

She knows the words as well as any remedy.

'*For His mercy is everlasting and His truth endureth to all generations . . .*'

She prays until the words make no sense and when the sand comes to rest for a second – or is it a third? – time she gets up and makes her way to the dispensary. She takes down a bottle of eau de vie, then moves out into the cloister, where a half moon throws the well in the middle of the courtyard into grey relief, as it did all those months before when she first visited a howling, furious young entrant.

If she were to ask herself now why she is doing this, it is unlikely, even after all the meditation and prayers, that she would be able to answer. The truth is that there has been no great revelation between her and God. No transmission of grace, nothing with which she could protect herself in confession for the disobedience she is about to commit. There are words she might use. Words she believes in. Compassion. Caring. The need to address suffering, the offering of comfort. But they are more the language of the healer than of the nun.

She knows this – but it does not stop her. If anything, now, it spurs her on.

Outside the door, she uses the taper she has brought to light the candle concealed in her robe. As she enters, its glow illuminates the room enough to show that the bed is empty. For a second she feels panic, remembering Serafina's last absence, but then, soon enough, she sees her. She is sitting on the floor with her back to the wall, in the same place where Zuana had found her on that first night. Only now there is no rebellion, no fury, no noise at all, just a small figure swamped by her robe, hunched over, arms wrapped tightly round her knees, head bowed, rocking slightly to and fro.

Zuana crouches down beside her. If the girl is aware of her, she does nothing to show it. Zuana's sin of disobedience is already sealed by her presence there. Now, in the middle of the Great Silence, she must compound it further with speech. 'Benedictus.' She says the word gently under her breath, though she knows there can be no absolution of a reply. This time the words 'Deo gracias' remain unsaid. So be it.

She moves the candle closer. 'You sleep when you should be awake and you are awake when you should be sleeping.'

The huddled figure remains silent, still no sign she has heard or even noticed her.

'Come, let me put you to bed.'

'I am praying,' she says at last, her voice dull and flat.

'You are not on your knees.'

'If one is humble enough He hears you wherever you are.'

'What have you eaten today?' Under the bed the bundle of bread sits untouched. 'Serafina, look at me. What have you eaten?'

The girl lifts her head briefly: close to, the planes of her face are sharp angles, her eyes black in deeply scooped sockets, her wrists on her knees as thin as kindling wood. How much body is left inside the sack of clothes? How long before her skin starts bruising purple from lack of flesh? Zuana feels shock like a cold hand squeezing at her throat. Could Umiliana be so unaware of the damage that her search for God is causing?

'Leave me alone,' she says dully.

'No, I will not leave you alone. Your penance is over. You are ill. You need to eat.'

'I am fasting still.'

'No. You are starving.'

'Ha! What do you know about it?'

'I know that without food a person dies.'

The girl shakes her head. 'You don't know what it feels like. How can you? You have never seen Him.'

'No, you are right, I haven't.'

'Well, I have! I have seen Him.' And for the first time there is a spark of something. She jerks up her head. 'And I will again.' Then, as if the move has taken too much energy, she slumps back against the wall. 'Suora Umiliana says that He will come if I make myself pure for Him.'

'And what about the rest of the convent? Do we not have a place in your search for purity? What about using your voice to praise God? Suora Benedicta waits every day for you. Or your work in the dispensary. I . . . we, the sick, need your help.'

'Pure voices don't need an audience.' She shakes her head fiercely. 'And you care only for bodies, not souls.'

'Who am I speaking to now? Serafina or Umiliana?' Zuana is surprised by the anger in her own voice.

She shrugs. 'In a good convent there will be no need of medicines. For God will take care of us.'

'Oh! Is that how you want to live? Or maybe it is how you want to die.'

'Aaah . . . leave me alone.' She brings her hands up to her head to ward off the attack of Zuana's words.

'No. I won't. Where are you, Serafina? Where did all that fury and defiance go?'

'I told you,' she says, her voice dead and sullen again. 'I don't feel anything.'

'I don't believe that is true. I think you are trying not to feel anything, because it hurts so much. I think that is why you have stopped eating. But it will not help.'

But she is not listening any more. She sits rocking to and fro, head on her hands, staring dully into the dark. After a while she pulls herself up, slowly, wobbly almost, like a new-born calf not yet steady on its feet. She moves past Zuana as if she was not there and goes to the bed, where she lies down with her face to the wall, curling herself up and pulling the blanket over her.

The room is quiet. Outside, the convent sleeps. And beyond it, the city, too.

'No-one can live without sustenance, Serafina.'

She does not respond, or move a muscle. Yet she is not sleeping. Zuana is sure of that.

'So I have brought you some.'

She takes the letter out from under her robe and unfolds it.

FORTY-TWO

"'My dearest Isabetta,

'If this letter reaches your hands, I would understand if you did not want to read it. Yet please, for the sake of what once was between us, continue.'"

His handwriting is dense and elaborate, as if he has put his heart into every pen stroke, and in the candlelight the words dance and move on the page. Zuana keeps her voice low, for fear it might penetrate beyond the walls of the cell. Occasionally she stumbles over a phrase and has to stop and begin again. But none of this matters. Not once the first words have been uttered . . .

"'Should you have come through the locked doors on to the dock that night you will know that I was not there to meet you. I, who had promised on pain of death to be there, deserted you. But what you do not know is that it was only death – or the extreme closeness of it – that kept me from you. A few nights before our planned meeting I was set upon by a group of erstwhile friends, who attacked me with daggers and left me for dead on the river bank. There have been moments since then when I have wished I had indeed died. But God was with me and I have been saved.

"'I write this from the house of two good people who found me, took me in and cared for me. You spoke once about how you feared your incarceration was God's punishment for our love. At my worst I wondered if this was my punishment, too. I knew that if I lived I would never see you again. But now it comes to that moment, I cannot go without trying to communicate with you one last time. To tell you that I did not, nor ever would, knowingly desert you . . .'"

Zuana pauses. She is a stranger to the art of love letters. At the time when other young girls were sighing over sonnets and court madrigals she had been tending seedlings and memorising the names of the organs of the body. It is not something she mourns, for how can one miss what one has never had? And yet, and yet . . . how honestly and persuasively he writes, this young man. The abbess would no doubt say it is all lies, born out of lust like flies on a dung heap. But then how would she know, either? She returns to the page.

"'I am in desperate straits. I have no money (all that I owned and had gathered for our life together was about my person that night) and I am disfigured in ways that I fear will disqualify me from any kind of polite work. Nevertheless I shall try. I am leaving Ferrara to travel south, to Naples, where I hear there is a thriving musical culture and where I may find someone who is content to keep their eyes closed while I sing.

"'I will never speak to a living soul of our liaison. You told me once that men say such things easily. You were always wiser than your years. But you do not know everything. I will never love nor marry another. That is the promise I made to God if he would let me live and it will be my pleasure to keep it. I hear your voice each night before I go to sleep, its beauty seducing the very sweetness out of silence, and when I wake it is the first thing I remember. I ask for no more.

"'I hope the sister you spoke of, whose goodwill I now depend on to bring this letter, may help you to find a way to live. Forgive me for whatever pain I have caused you. Pray for me, my dear Isabetta.

"'I remain, for ever, your Jacopo.'"

The silence in the cell grows. The girl remains motionless, her face to the wall. Somewhere inside her, though, there is movement. It is as if she is rising slowly from some deep place on the ocean bed, pulled out of the dark by the promise of a world above the water . . .

As she breaks the surface she has an image of a young man walking towards her through hazy sunlight, long, dark hair and broad, open face.

'He did not desert me,' she says, so quietly that Zuana can barely hear her.

'No. He did not.'

'He loved me.'

'And, it seems, still does . . .'

Now, finally, she turns over. Zuana holds out the letter and her hand comes out from the blanket, pale fingers, snap-thin wrist. She pulls it towards her, then lets it fall on to the bed, as if it is somehow too heavy to hold.

Zuana takes a small bottle out from under her robe and uncorks it. The air picks up the tangy smell of eau de vie. She pours some out on to a wooden plate, picks up the lump of bread from under the bed and dips a small chunk into the liquid to soften it. 'So? Will you eat now?'

The girl looks at her, frowning, as if she is having trouble focusing.

Zuana's hand holds out the dripping bread.

'I . . . I can't . . .' She shakes her head. 'I can't . . .'

'What? Is Umiliana's voice become stronger than his?'

His . . . Him. But which him? The very idea seems to unsteady her. 'I told you, I can't. Leave me alone.' And her voice is suddenly hard, full of snake-spit and anger.

Zuana does not move. She has seen this once before, years ago, in a sad, mad young nun who starved herself almost to death: the way in which after a certain point the emptiness becomes its own force, like a whirlpool sucking and destroying anything or anyone who dares challenge its supremacy. If it was not to do with the yearning for purity one might almost fear that the devil had a hand in it, for there is something of his malicious pleasure in such self-destruction.

'Isabetta. Isabetta . . .'

She says this name, *her* name, twice, then again. And again. For every student of medicine knows that there are times when a word can be its own talisman and carry a certain power of healing.

'Isabetta, listen to me. I may not be a nun who sees visions but this I do know. God is as much in life as He is in death. And without a true vocation, starvation is no way to reach Him.'

The girl shakes her head again. 'Suora Umiliana says—'

'Suora Umiliana is not to be trusted. She is looking to take over the convent by mounting an attack on the authority of the abbess, and your starving purity is most helpful to her now. If you had eaten more, or had more of your wits about you, you of all people would see that.'

Such confidence. Such certainty! As she says this, Zuana thinks how much like the abbess she herself now sounds. Except that when she remembers the old novice mistress scooping up the fainting girl from under the cross, or catches again the look of triumph in her face when their paths met outside Madonna Chiara's chambers, she knows it to be true. The abbess was right. The world is full of young women who do not want to become nuns. But she was also wrong. For this young woman is no longer just another one of them. In the midst of this chess game of Church and convent politics, she has been unwittingly elevated to the role of a more powerful piece, greater than her worth but also vulnerable to being used and sacrificed.

And it is not just her. For, like it or not, by bringing the girl the letter Zuana herself has become one of the players. Now it is her turn to move.

'Yet meanwhile – are you listening to me, Isabetta? – meanwhile there is someone outside these walls who cares for you deeply. A young man who has risked a good deal to get in touch with you and who surely deserves an answer.'

The girl stares at her, then shakes her head as if to rid herself of the fog within. 'What do you mean, an answer? What are you talking about? It is over. I am in prison and he is half dead and gone.' And now she lets out a low wailing moan, the words awakening memory and the memory awakening despair.

'Hush. Hush . . . You will wake the whole convent. Yes, you are in prison. But some of it is of your own making. And from what I hear, though his wounds are grave he will not die of them, nor will he be on the road to Naples – not yet, at least. Perhaps you should look at the page again. Look in the bottom corner around the edge. Someone has written an address there.'

She had only seen it herself later, when studying again the content. The letters were small and not in the same hand. An apothecary's wife would surely know how to write, if only to help label her husband's bottles.

The girl pulls herself up and holds the page towards the candlelight. She locates the address, then her eyes go back to the letter. She runs her finger over the lines of ink, then brings the paper to her nose as if to drink in the scent of him.

Does a man's smell come through his handwriting? It is one of the many things Zuana will never know. She holds out the hand again with the soaked bread.

At last the girl takes it, moving it slowly towards her mouth. To her mouth but no further. The portcullis of her teeth remains clamped shut. The air is charged with the conflict: words from without and the will from within. How does this half-starved young woman know any more which is the true voice?

'Eat, Isabetta. It is the only way.'

Her teeth part and she starts to chew, slowly, stubbornly, a dribble of saliva trickling down from her mouth.

'Good. Good.'

She swallows, then takes another bite.

'Oh, you are doing fine. Well done.'

And now the tears come, running silently down her cheeks, as if eating must be the saddest thing on earth.

'Not too fast. Here, drink something. It is full of nourishment.' She hands her the vial. 'Just a little at first . . . Good. Now rest a bit.'

She leans her head back against the wall, her eyes closed, as the tears fall. The two women sit for a while in silence, the night curled around them.

Zuana puts another small soaked piece into her hands.

'I feel sick,' she says. 'I feel sick . . .'

'That is because your body has forgotten what to do with food. Make sure you chew slowly. Each mouthful.'

But she cannot chew anything, for suddenly now she is crying too much, strangled sobs, as if her heart is breaking all over again. Even when the body is drying up with starvation there are always more tears.

'I'm scared, I'm scared.' She crushes the bread within her fingers.

'There is nothing to be scared of.'

'Oh yes there is. You don't understand. Suora Umiliana will

damn me, the abbess will hate me and I will still die in here while he is out there.'

Zuana looks at her. What can she say? She cannot lie to her, for she is right: that will be her future. Just another young woman who did not want to become a nun. When she thinks about it later, she does not remember an actual decision. All she knows is the compulsion to bring a body back from death towards life.

Surely God would not damn her for such an action.

'Eat the bread while I read the letter again, Isabetta. It seems to me that you have missed the proposal of marriage it contains.'

The girl stares at her. 'What? What are you talking about?'

'Look, I know little enough about such things but a man who has promised God that he will not love nor marry any other woman must be sure enough about the one he wants to spend his life with. Is that not what you want, too?'

'Sweet Jesus, what are you saying? You are mad.'

'Well, if I am mad then you had better get healthy to help cure me.'

And she hands her another piece of soaked bread.

PART FOUR

FORTY-THREE

Zuana barely has time to reach her own cell before the bell for Matins starts to sound.

She and Serafina take their respective places in chapel without a glance or any sign between them. But even with her eyes to the floor, it is impossible for Zuana not to feel the abbess's gaze upon her. On them both. Does she know of her visit to the novice already? Well, if she does not, she will do soon enough, for the watch sister is a loyal soul and neither as deaf nor as stupid as some might like to believe.

Back in her cell again, Zuana kneels in darkness for a while then gets up and lies on her pallet. Prayer can do only so much. She needs a different kind of intervention now.

'Dear father, there is a disease inside the convent,' she says under her breath. 'A deep malignancy. A young woman needs to be released from here — but in a manner that saves the convent rather than taking it down with her. What remedy can there be for this?'

In the silence that follows — she no longer expects him to answer but there is quiet in the place left by his absence — she begins, slowly, to fashion a plan. As befits the complexity of the malady it will call for the combination of different ingredients: a number of 'simples' that must be compounded together not only in the right doses but also at the right moment. Despite her tiredness she feels an energy, almost an excitement, growing within her. When she finally closes her eyes her sleep is deep and dreamless.

Next morning she prepares the first ingredient. It is both straightforward and difficult: a young man in the house of an apothecary by the west gate must be prevented from leaving the city. Even if the girl had strength and wit enough now to write a letter, no convent censor would pass any communication from a novice unless approved by the abbess first. Zuana, however, is a choir nun of many years' standing and can write to whomever she chooses so long as the content is not inappropriate. In the morning hour of private prayer she takes a sheet of paper and writes a letter, already memorised in her head.

'Dear sister in healing,

'I write further to our conversation about the welfare of your patient who suffered such grievous wounds on his body and neck. Having studied my notes I can suggest that while case-wort and yarrow will help the skin to join, honey mixed with cobwebs and egg white can also be applied to minimise scarring. However, it is most important that the patient remains in your care and within your walls at present. In particular he must not undergo any journey, since friction on the torso will cause the wounds to re-open before proper healing has taken place. With regard to the great pain he feels in his chest, in the vicinity of his heart, I am hoping in due course to find a remedy and will forward it when I do so.

'I remain yours in the glory of God and the purity of the convent of Santa Caterina.'

She finds Suora Matilda in a small room behind the gatehouse.

The post of convent censor is a weighty one, as the nun who takes it on must possess not only authority and experience (those who deal with the outside world must be over forty years of age) but also excellent eyesight, and these qualities do not always go together. Though not directly of Madonna's Chiara's own family, until now Matilda has been a loyal servant to the abbess; although the recent revelations in chapter suggest that her loyalty may be wavering.

Luckily, Zuana's connection with her is more robust. When she was younger Matilda suffered from a chronic complaint of itching and stinging when passing water. It had taken her a while to confess such an intimate ailment (she is not the only one – it can drive many sisters mad in the heat of a Ferrarese summer) but the doses of vaccinium juice Zuana had given her had brought much relief, and she has held a fondness for her ever since.

'It is not often you have recourse to the outside world, Suora Zuana.'

'No. But I had a visitor recently.'

'Oh yes, I know. A daughter of one of your father's pupils, wasn't it?'

Zuana smiles. How could such an occasion ever have remained a secret?

'She is the wife of an apothecary now and came to ask advice on treatment for her husband. It was an urgent request and I must answer her with all possible speed.'

Thus prepared in advance for the substance of what she must pass, the sister opens the letter and starts to read, holding the paper almost at arm's length to do so. Zuana has already noticed how in chapel she screws up her eyes sometimes to follow the daily prayers in her breviary.

'Cobwebs and honey, eh?' Suora Matilda, evidently relieved to have managed the small print, closes the letter and brings her stamp down upon it. 'When I was a child my nonna used to say that spiders' silk was the thread of life. She would make the servants collect webs from the cellar. It always made me squirm.'

'She was a healer then, your grandmother?'

'Oh, I don't know about that. She was more of a termagant to me.' She pauses. 'Though these days I think she was the better for being so strict. It is important to live by strict rules, wouldn't you agree?'

'Oh, most certainly.' Zuana smiles, taking a small vial from under her robe and placing it on the desk next to her. 'You sacrifice your eyes selflessly for the good of the convent. A few drops of witch hazel will help to keep them sharp on our behalf.'

The sister hesitates for a second – rules are rules, after all – then closes her hand over the container. 'You are most kind. As you say the letter is urgent I will make sure it goes this afternoon.'

While the first day goes well, that night and the ones that follow it are not so smooth. After Compline, when the convent has finally fallen asleep, Zuana makes her way to the girl's cell again, bringing food saved from her own plate and extra supplies traded from the kitchen. She must stay with her now until everything is consumed. Eating. It is such a natural act until it is transformed into an ordeal. But then once a certain level of starvation has been reached it is not only the flesh that is affected but also the spirit.

'I can't. I've had enough.'

'You have eaten barely anything.'

'How can you say that?' she snarls. 'I am stuffed like a stuck goose.'

'That is because your stomach is shrunken. You must finish it.'

'I'll eat it later.'

'No – you will eat it now.'

'Aaagh!'

If it is hard for Zuana it is worse for the girl. Each night she finds herself seated in front of a mountain of congealed food – thick, foul, like the devil's vomit. Before she takes the first spoonful her body is in revolt, her stomach heaving, her throat closing up at the sight of it. Each mouthful is gross to the taste, like chewing raw flesh and swallowing poison. It is all she can do not to spit it back across the room.

'Eat, Isabetta.'

'Don't eat, Serafina.'

There are nights when she fears she is going mad, when she can hear Umiliana's voice drowning out Zuana's, rising up out of her as if it were her own; times when even the thought of Jacopo is not enough to prise her lips apart. Were it not for Zuana she would give up before she has begun. They are locked together in the struggle: the push-pull of hope and despair. In between the tears then there are eruptions of fiery rebellion, growlings of fury or blunt refusals. It is remarkable how the coiled snake of resistance continues to hiss and spit, as if halfway to heaven – or maybe it is to hell – she will not, *will not*, give up.

Eventually, however, the exhaustion beneath the hunger reduces her to a kind of docility, a numb surrender watered by tears.

'Dearest Isabetta, I did not, nor ever would, knowingly desert you.'

Zuana woos her mouth back open by reading extracts from the letter.

'Dearest Isabetta . . .'

How long is it since anyone called her that? Isabetta. Her own name is a stranger to her now. Who is this young woman who once answered to it? Who is this man who once loved her?

'I hear your voice each night before I go to sleep, its beauty seducing the very sweetness out of silence, and when I wake it is the first thing I remember. I ask for no more.'

She listens carefully, like a child hearing again a story that she once loved. And sometimes it seems she can almost remember, can almost go back there; a face, a touch, the echo of a voice. Except where and how did all these things happen between them?

'I will never love nor marry another. That is the promise I made to God if he would let me live and it will be my pleasure to keep it . . . Pray for me, my dear Isabetta.'

But will she ever really be Isabetta again? After a while it is too tiring to ask herself the questions. To imagine a future, she must let go of the comfort of feeling nothing. It seems it is not just her body that has shrunk but her whole world.

Afterwards, when the horror of the eating is over, she is given, and takes – for she is acquiescent by now – a dose of eau de vie to help the process of digestion. It does little to quieten the war of attrition that is starting to take place in her body. After the first few days her gut launches its own rebellion, sending out nausea and cramps so that at times it is all she can do to sit without doubling over with the pain. Where before she folded herself up against the cold, now she lays curled over her own throbbing entrails.

Meanwhile, if the physical re-feeding is a challenge then so is the extra level of dissembling that must now accompany it. Once outside her cell, whatever her exhaustion or confusion, Serafina needs to be clever. And deft. At every meal in the refectory, the convent must see her eat, though in a way that makes it clear to Umiliana that no food is actually passing into her mouth but is instead hidden away under her robe to ensure her continued fasting. And Umiliana, as always, is eagle-eyed over the journey of her most beloved novice.

As the food starts to give her back some strength so the constipation begins, her bowels filling up with stones that grow bigger and harder each day. It feels as if her whole body is bloated with the poison of waste. She remembers the Bishop and the way he leaked blood and bad temper everywhere he went. Is this how it will be for me? she wonders. Will I grow back into a body made decrepit by starvation? She looks at herself. Her skin inside her shift is grey, veins running like gnarled branches underneath. Hideous. She is hideous. How can any man ever love her?

Zuana tells her again that it takes time for a body to reacquaint itself with the normality of eating, that it will pass, it will get easier. But what if it doesn't? What if she simply swells up until she rips open or explodes? Zuana now supplements the eau de vie with senna: senna, the great healer of life, to clean the spleen and the liver and the heart and, in this dosage, strong enough to move the bowels of a horse. But not, it seems, those of a starved novice.

On the sixth morning at Lauds the pain and pressure is so bad that she almost passes out. Eugenia, as usual, is at her side in chapel, and supports her until she gets her breath back. She straightens up, the sweat of pain glistening on her skin, only to find herself staring into the faces of a dozen choir nuns and novices in the opposite stalls. They look almost disappointed to find her still on her feet. Plainly every move she makes has the convent enthralled. But then it is not nothing to watch a body forcing itself ever thinner in its search for God.

Suora Umiliana, meanwhile, is not distressed. On the contrary, she is excited. She, who knows the arc of starvation as well as she knows her psalms, understands that there are moments when one is hard pushed to tell pain from the arrival of transcendence. It is not the right time, anyway. The chapel is still empty, the figure of Christ still in the hands of workmen. If – no, when – this wondrous young soul is called, it should be when He is back to watch over her.

For Umiliana, too, has her plan; her own dream of well-being that warms and sustains her in the darkness. She has nurtured an army of novices in her time and there have been those, such as Perseveranza or Obedienza or Stefana, even the young Carità, who have emerged humble and dedicated brides of Christ. Just as she herself has always yearned to be. She has burned with the love of Jesus for so many years now; worked, fasted, prayed, given her life to Santa Caterina; and yet, and yet . . . she cannot help but feel that there is something lacking.

It is Umiliana's fate to have stood in this same convent chapel, an impressionable young nun barely nineteen years old, when a living saint, a small, stunted figure, humble and mysterious beyond words, opened her palms during Matins to reveal the bleeding stigmata of Christ himself. For the rest of the service, with the choir transfixed around her, this tiny but vast soul had sung her way through the office, tears streaming down her face, before limping back to her cell leaving a trail of bloody footprints in her wake.

As a child Umiliana had heard of such wonders – who had not? – and from the earliest moment they had affected her deeply. She had always dreamed of being pure enough . . . prayed that she might one day be made so humble. 'Living saints', they called them. In the years before the heretic madness spread there had seemed to be so many: Lucia of Narni, Angela of Foligno, Camilla of Brodi. Her mother had made sure she heard of every one, feeding their life stories like rich worms into her open fledgling mouth. If only all young girls were so instructed so young . . .

Even without her mother's piety, she would have yearned for the veil. As a child she'd continually had to be restrained for being too fierce with herself. And while the family was never one of the most powerful in the city, their name had certainly been good enough to find her a place at Santa Caterina. By the time she had entered at the age of twelve she had already had callouses on her knees and found most of her fellow novices vain and frivolous. Surely it was to be only a matter of time and self-abasement, before . . .

Except it had not happened. Despite all the praying and passion (one is so sure, so young) she had yet to feel the touch of ecstasy and had begun fearing that she would never be worthy enough. That night, as she had stood staring at the blood trickling from Suora Magdalena's hands, she had understood the truth: she herself would never be so blessed.

When you love someone so much, it can be unbearably painful to be passed over. But Christ gives different challenges to different souls and Umiliana had shouldered her own cross without complaint, sewing, copying, cooking, gardening, with as much humility as she could muster, until she had found a way to move into a position where her passion and dedication could help guide younger souls. No-one would doubt that she had been an honest and just novice mistress and that a number of her charges grew to love her as much as they once loathed her. But all the time, through all of them, she had been watching, waiting, in case such a moment might come again. And it had never been more important than now, when false truths were everywhere and the Church itself was bent on more discipline and less licence.

If she were truthful, she had not (though surely this was true no longer?) been entirely sure about Serafina. At the beginning she had seen only a spoilt, angry rebel, full of vanity and carnality. But then had come the changes. First the early encounter with Suora Magdalena, followed by the arrival of her voice, pure as angel's breath if only it could have been allowed to rise straight to God rather than trained to seduce through the public grille. Then her sudden showy display of piety – well, God had seen through that fast enough, sending her spinning into that terrible night of fitting and of illness, which had broken her body and brought her so close to death. And without Magdalena she would certainly have died. That was the moment when Umiliana had known for sure. There had been other nuns and novices, some worthy beyond measure, who had expired alone in agony. Yet Santa Caterina's living saint had come out of her cell for this girl, and had triggered in her such a hunger for repentance and fasting. Finally, as if there could be any doubt, Magdalena had died at the same moment as Christ had slid halfway from the cross while Serafina herself had been taking communion.

Yes, there was something of power in this young woman, something put there almost despite herself. She had sensed it inside her despair, had nurtured it, watched the spirit quickening as the body starved. She, Suora Umiliana, had prayed for a force like this to help her in her cleansing of the convent. And now it had been given to her.

That evening she comes, as she always does, in the hour between dinner and Compline to pray with Serafina. Eager for each nuance of feeling that her young protégée experiences, she questions her about what happened in chapel that morning when she had almost collapsed. Had she been in pain? What had she felt? Or heard? Was there any noise or rushing in her ears, the echo of a voice perhaps, or a disturbance of her vision?

Serafina tells her what she wants to hear.

Not all of it is pretence. In those long, starving nights before Zuana came to her, there were occasions when she could swear she saw things: strange, half-formed shapes growing out of shadows, sudden auras and flashes of light at the edges of her vision. If she stared for long enough into darkness it turned itself into colour, oranges and burning yellows like running veins of gold in black rock. Once, in the no man's land between sleeping and waking, she was sure she saw a face coming out of the gloom – His face, bearded, framed by night-black hair, eyes wet with tears of compassion – oh, please God, she thought, let those tears be for me. In contrast, her dreams were full of nothing, though when she woke sometimes she heard music – voices – in her cell, vibrating notes far too high and pure to be human, and they made her feel giddy and weightless, as if she could lift off the bed to join them.

When, haltingly, she recounts these things to Umiliana, the old nun seems almost beside herself with joy.

Such experiences do not come to the girl any more. With food as ballast she is weighted back down to earth now, her very solidity interrupting the quivering of air around her. If she is truthful, with such ordinariness comes, sometimes, a certain sadness, a wonder at what has been lost. But she does not let herself think of that. She is leaving this place, leaving both its visions and its horrors, and she will do whatever it takes to get herself out . . .

'Help me. I long for Him so. Help me, please.' She knows the lines well enough.

'Prayer, Serafina. Prayer and the denial of the flesh. It is the only way. When you are filled with emptiness it will happen. He will come. The pain you had today is surely a sign. The hour of Matins is the best time. He is so close then. All you have to do is welcome Him in. You are ready. The convent is ready. For Him.'

In some ways Umiliana is right. As the food starts to swell her wits as well as her gut, Serafina becomes aware of a sea change in the world around her. Many of the nuns are themselves fasting, with such enthusiasm that there are times when one can hear a descant of protesting stomachs as they gather in chapel. During the work hours, the choir struggles with *The Lamentations of Jeremiah*: the very architecture of this music is stricter than they are used to and Suora Benedicta's arrangement for their voices can do little to change or enrich it.

Jerusalem hath grievously sinned . . .

The words reverberate around the cloisters.

She hath wept in the night, and her tears are on her cheeks.

And there are some for whom the text feels like a commentary on Santa Caterina itself.

All that honoured her despise her,
Because they have seen her shame.

In the evenings hardly any nuns visit Apollonia's cell now; they are too busy on their knees in their own. A kind of stillness descends on the convent, heavy, cloying, like the stillness before a storm. A further chapter meeting passes without incident. Though the atmosphere remains charged, no-one seems to have the energy for further drama. It is announced that the great crucifix is repaired and will be returned to the convent and re-hung within the week. Even this news is received quietly. Umiliana, who is more of a politician than she herself knows, says nothing. Yet her soul remains taut as an overstretched lute string, and every evening she continues to pour her longing into the novice's ears. She is waiting. As are they all.

FORTY-FOUR

While it will take at least a month for there to be enough change in her body for anyone to notice, after nearly two weeks of re-feeding the girl's face is altering a little: the great hollows under her eyes are growing less dark and there is a touch of colour in her cheeks. It is time to add the next ingredient. The abbess must be brought into the plan.

Zuana is under no illusion as to how daunting a task this is. She knows how angry she will be. How angry she is already. Since their last meeting Madonna Chiara has spent an increasing amount of time in her chambers, seeing visitors or writing letters. Those with sharp eyes would say she looks tired. Zuana knows better. A woman who is used to being in control of the world around her is watching it fall out of her grip. No, she will not want to hear this plan. It is therefore all the more important that Zuana finds ways to convince her.

That night, along with the usual food Zuana brings two small pouches to the girl's cell. After they have eaten she hands her the first one.

'Be careful with it.'

Apollonia has been generous with her face powder. 'Take it as a thank you for what you did for my sister,' she had said. 'Though

I must say, I never expected to find you in need of such things. But many of us are changing our behaviour now. You should join us for a concert one evening. They may not continue much longer.'

Serafina – or rather Isabetta, for now that the food is working in her that is how she is beginning to think of herself again – opens the pouch and slips her finger in, then dusts the white powder across her cheeks.

'You must use it sparingly. Umiliana, in particular, can spot make-up from halfway across the choir stalls.'

Zuana takes the other pouch and puts it on the cot.

'As to this, I have measured the amount exactly. You remember the proportions for the water?'

She nods.

'Good. It is vital that you go ahead only if and when you have the sign. And that you do and say exactly what we have discussed. Do you understand?'

'I understand.'

'No more, no less. There will be no second chance.'

'Yes, yes, I understand.' She is jumpy tonight. They both are. 'You think it will come to this?'

'I don't know. But if it does, then she will need to see that you have the will and the stomach to carry it further.'

Zuana hands her the sharp little knife with which she had once cut and peeled the figwort root. Ah – how long ago was that?

'You are sure you can do this?' Zuana says.

'Oh yes, I am sure.' And along with the colour in her cheeks there is now a flash of brightness to her eye. 'It can hardly hurt more than my gut.'

The next morning Zuana goes to the abbess. There are no pleasantries between them on this visit: no offer of wine, nor a place by the fire.

'I have come to confess my disobedience, Madonna Chiara. Against your wishes I have been visiting the novice at night. And in doing so I have broken the Great Silence repeatedly.'

'Yes. Perhaps you might tell me something I do not know. How much she is putting into her stomach, for instance. She looked half dead at Lauds.'

'It was constipation, a necessary side effect of eating again. The fast is ended. And with it Umiliana's influence over her.'

'Well, I am glad to hear it.'

Zuana takes a breath. She is more nervous than she has ever been in her life. 'Madonna Chiara, I would give anything to protect this convent. I rejoice in the sustenance and comfort it brings me and many women like me . . .' She starts quietly, but the words ripen fast and fall over each other in their eagerness to get out. She stops and gathers herself.

'The novice is equally loyal to you. Though she is strong-spirited, there is no spite in her. She was brought into Umiliana's orbit by despair. But if we help her, she will reject her. And she will keep her silence until the grave: anything and everything that has gone on inside these walls, or outside them – she will forget as if it had never happened.'

She stops now. She can feel a fine sweat on her forehead. The abbess's gaze is cool, even cold now.

'What a passionate speech, Suora Zuana. Not like you at all. So tell me about this "help" we must give her to buy her silence. That is what you mean, isn't it? From what I see she has food, nursing and, it seems, the attention of half the convent. Pray, what more "help" could she require?'

Zuana does not flinch. 'That she be allowed to leave this place and start a life with that young man, somewhere a long way away from here.'

The abbess stares at her for a moment. 'My! Her wits have returned fast. Unless the idea did not come from her directly . . .'

'I have given it a great deal of thought, Madonna Chiara. And there is a way—'

'Oh, there are many ways,' she says, cutting across her. 'I could open the gates for her this evening. Or perhaps I should let her petition the Bishop so the shame can bring an inspection down upon us? Let me guess . . . You have had the arrogance to take it upon yourself to examine the body of Santa Caterina and you find – what? – some kind of "remedy" for its ills. I dare say your father has given you some help in this.' And her voice is cruel with sarcasm.

'My father does not speak to me any more,' Zuana says quietly. 'These thoughts are mine and mine alone.'

'In which case you are more at fault than I imagined. It seems that you are the one with greensickness, even if you are too old for it. Has she turned your head, too? Seduced you as she has all the others, so that now you are willing to ruin the convent for her sake?'

'No. That is not how it is.' Zuana's voice is clear, without quaver or fear now. 'I love this place as much as you do.'

'You will forgive me if I harbour some doubt of that.'

'I would—'

'Be quiet!' And there is real fury in her voice.

Zuana does as she is ordered. The abbess is silent for a moment, hands clasped tightly in her lap, as if she understands that she has overreached herself. Finally she raises her head.

'Our audience is finished. Your penance—'

'Madonna Chiara—'

'You will not interrupt me further!' For now she sees enemies all around and will have none of it. 'Your penance is that from this moment on you are confined to your cell until I have decided what to do with you.'

There is nothing more she can do. Zuana bows her head to denote her obedience.

'And the novice?' she says quietly.

'If she needs further assistance then I will give it.'

By the office of Compline it is clear that something has happened to Zuana. Her choir stall has been empty since Sext. If it was illness the abbess would surely have said something before the Great Silence so that she might be included in their prayers. Instead, she appears to be curiously oblivious to the absence.

As the assembled nuns settle themselves, Isabetta lifts her head towards the empty place. Her face is drawn and deathly pale in the twilight. Not all of its pallor is a result of powder.

Zuana's instructions had been very clear. 'If I am there, then just before the office begins I will bring my right hand to my forehead and hold it there, as if I am suffering some pain. That will be the signal for you to go ahead.'

'And if you are not there?'

'If I am not there . . . then you must take my absence as your sign.'

Benedicta sings the first notes and Isabetta follows her lead. When she was at her weakest it had been all she could do to hold on to the order of the office and her thoughts had often strayed into the shadows at the edges of the candlelight, where Umiliana's stories had been at their richest: angels moving in and out of the smoke, and a young nun pierced with the joy of the Lord, her tears and blood mingling in full sight of them all. There had been moments when she had felt her own palms prickling in longing, only to discover later that she had been digging her nails into herself, leaving pathetic red weals in the skin.

But now the chapel is just a place for nuns to pray and the office only more words. Now she knows the only way she will draw blood from her own hands is to use a knife. Across the pews she sees the abbess, standing tall and firm. Look at her: this is a woman who knows how to use knives to get what she most wants. How much does she hate her? It is not something she has let herself feel. But she tastes it now and it is so strong it makes her almost giddy.

Yes, she can do this.

Back in her cell, at the appointed time, she gets out the pouch and, using a dark corner of the floor as her palate, mixes water into the small heap of granules. Then she takes out the knife. If she hesitates it is only for a second, before she plunges the blade point into her flesh, letting out a hiss of pain as it penetrates the layers of skin. She shifts the knife to the damaged hand and does the same, though with more difficulty this time, to the other palm. In the candlelight the blood oozes, both bright and dark. She conceals the blade then moves over to the corner where the mixture is wet and presses her palms hard into the puddle. When they come up they are saturated with red.

She moves back to the outer bedchamber, blows out the candle and begins to scream.

The convent is dead asleep but three people are fast out of their cells. The watch sister is first but before she gets to the door the abbess is halfway across the cloisters, ahead of Suora Umiliana, who arrives as fast as her older, creakier limbs can carry her.

The watch sister waits by the cell door but does not open it, nor say anything. The Great Silence is more powerful than any noise.

'Benedictus.' It is Umiliana who offers the word, breathlessly, bowing her head quickly to the abbess.

'Deo gracias.'

'This need not disturb you, Madonna abbess. I will see to her.'

'No, Suora Umiliana.'

'She is a novice under instruction. It is my dut—'

'*I* will see to her.'

'But—'

'But nothing. You do not run this convent yet, Suora Umiliana. That is my privilege and burden.' The tone brooks no argument. 'You will go back to your cell.'

And because there is no other way, except by physically barging past her, Umiliana turns back and, as the watch sister steps aside, the abbess goes in.

Inside, the girl stands in the corner with her back to her, the howling now muted into a single, high note, vibrating on what feels like an endless breath.

Madonna Chiara lifts her candle into the darkness. 'So, Serafina. What is this nonsense that you break the Great Silence for?'

There is a small pause then Isabetta turns towards her, as she does so lifting up her hands and opening her palms to show the wounds. Dark red blood drips down on to the floor around her as quietly, without hysteria or malice, she says what it has been decided that she will say.

'Madonna Chiara, I was put into this convent against my will. And against my will I have been kept here. I mean you no harm. And if you let me go, then I swear I will keep silent until my dying day. But if I am forced to stay here then I promise I will bring chaos down upon all your heads.'

As she says these words, the abbess pushes the door closed behind her so there will be no chance of them being overheard.

FORTY-FIVE

'You are called to see the abbess.'

Letizia is fluttery with agitation. Zuana, who has not slept, has been ready, waiting for hours. As they cross the courtyard she deliberately does not look in the direction of the girl's cell, though she cannot help but notice the figure in the upper-floor window of the embroidery room. Suora Francesca, who is not able to impose silence when the chatter has nothing to say, will be presiding over a hum of gossip now. The starving novice had started screaming in the night and the abbess – the abbess herself – went to see her. Beside this news, how can they sit quietly embroidering yet another letter E on another pillowcase? But even pillowcases, humble though they are, have their place in the great scheme of things. And Zuana has made it her business to know that they are working on the last pieces of a trousseau for a young woman from a lesser branch of the d'Este family, which must be ready for delivery soon so that there can be time for fittings and further alterations before the wedding ten days after Easter. The ingredients are almost all gathered.

The head pops back from the upper window as Letizia moves past the door of the abbess's cell without stopping.

'Where are we going?'

'She told me to bring you to the chapel.'

Zuana has worked with this girl for as long as she has been in the convent. She would dearly like to ask her now what she knows. But Letizia is too anxious and as soon as they reach the chapel she scuttles away.

Zuana enters as quietly as the great door allows.

Once inside, the reason for the abbess's presence there becomes obvious. On the flagstones beneath the altar is the great, newly repaired crucifix, lying in all its glory, ready to be lifted back into place. In between the choir stalls a tower, hoist and pulley are waiting to start the process.

The abbess is on her knees to one side of the cross, prostrated upon the ground, her body reaching out towards His own. His sculpted flesh is so close that if she were to put out her hands any further she would surely touch it.

Zuana hesitates. She has seen her often enough in chapel, where she always makes the prettiest picture of a nun at prayer, but as she watches her here it appears that she is at a deeper, private devotion. She finds herself almost embarrassed to be watching.

After a while, as she turns towards the door, the voice says, 'Sit, Zuana. I will be with you soon.'

Perhaps not so private after all.

From her vantage point in the pews Zuana now studies the sculpture. On the ground, the Christ's figure seems larger than life-size. Along with making repairs to the crossbar and the hand, the workmen have cleaned and revarnished the body, removing a century of candle smoke and grime so that the surface of His skin seems to glow.

At last the abbess straightens up. She sits back on her heels for a moment, staring at the body, then leans over and kisses the wood of the cross before getting to her feet.

'You know when I first came here, as a child, the story was that the man who sculpted this had used the body of his own son, who had died in a brawl, as his model.'

Her voice is calm, conversational even. 'It was said that his grief was so overwhelming that it informed his hand when it came to his chisel on the wood. He'd been a handsome young man, by all accounts. A favourite with the young women. I used to wonder how it could be that his body had now become that of Christ. For there was never any doubt that this was who this was.'

She finds herself a place to sit near her dispensary mistress and spreads her skirts around her.

'Over the years I have come to learn that we nuns are wondrously adept at seeing what we believe . . . or believing what we see — or want to see — even when it is not there.'

Her manner is a long way from the rage with which they had parted company less than a day before. The rule of their order is clear on such things: a Benedictine nun must not give way to anger, nor foster a desire for revenge. She must love her enemy and make peace with an adversary before the setting of the sun. And she must never, never despair of God's mercy. It is an arduous list and the abbess must be seen to be a shining example to all around her.

Even when she has not agreed with her, Zuana has admired her more than any abbess before her. Would that she could feel that way again.

'It appears I have you to thank for the fact that she did not stab herself in the middle of Matins.'

'It was not simply me, Madonna Chiara. The girl herself has no wish to do you or the convent harm.'

'No, she did make that clear. Nevertheless she hates me. The eyes show more than the words.' She pauses. 'Well, in her place

I would hate me, too. I assume you supplied the extra blood to make the performance complete?'

Zuana hesitates, then nods.

'It was most impressive. I hope you left enough for Federica's blessed cakes. Though it is likely that there will be no Carnival feast by next year.'

'No,' Zuana says firmly. 'There will be a feast. You will still be abbess. And then, as now, you will be much loved and admired.'

'Oh, Zuana, please. Do me the courtesy of refraining from false praise. We are, I think, beyond that. We are here to negotiate, are we not? In which case let us get on with it.'

'Here?' Her eyes slip to the crucifix.

'Why not? We will never have a better witness. And I would not like it to be thought that we sought to hide anything from Him.'

And so Zuana speaks, first of the disease and then of the remedy. The words she uses are clear and simple, as befits a good physician or scholar who has studied something deeply and wishes to convince others of its efficacy. The abbess, for her part, listens well, never once taking her eyes off her face.

On the chapel floor, on the cross, Christ's face is turned away from the two nuns. The falling angle of his head suggests a man close to death rather than one still in agony. For Him the worst is passed and there is resurrection to come.

'Do you know the greatest fear women have when they enter a convent against their will?' the abbess says at last. 'It will surprise you, I think, for often they do not even know it themselves. It is not about children, nor the latest fashion nor even stories of the marriage bed. No. At root it is that if they do not find comfort in God, they will die of boredom. Boredom . . .' She shakes her head. 'I must say, in all the years I have been abbess of this convent that has never been my problem.'

'It is very clever, Zuana, your plan. You have always had the clearest mind when it comes to understanding problems and finding a solution. Still, it is not so much a remedy as blackmail.'

'Oh, it is not meant to be.'

'No? And if I still refuse? What then? I dare say there is enough dye left for her to disturb a good many offices. You have not seen her hands. She was most enthusiastic with the knife. If *she* were not in ecstasy, Suora Umiliana certainly would be. But then of course you know all that.' She gives a deep, almost theatrical sigh. 'So tell me, this "potion"? You have used it before?'

'I . . . well, no. It is not possible to try it with any certainty upon oneself.'

'No, I would think not.'

'But I have studied a number of sources.'

'From apothecaries or story tellers?'

'I . . . I don't see –'

'Ah, Zuana!' The smile lifts her lips, but does not reach her eyes. 'For someone who knows so much, you are sweetly ignorant. Mariotto and Giannozza . . . Giulietta e Romeo . . . they go by many names. You have not heard their tragic tale? Well, it is too late now. The good Fathers of Trent consigned Salernitano's stories to the flames, though I dare say that will only make them more popular.'

'You are right,' Zuana says quietly. 'I know nothing of such stories nor care less. The source I have for the remedy comes from a traveller from the East and from my father.'

'. . . whose own books we must do our best to protect.' The abbess slides her hand over her skirts; a gesture that denotes business as usual. 'So, you had better tell me the rest of it.

How, for instance, will her ailing young pup learn what he must do?'

'She will send him a letter.'

'What? You have an address for him?'

Zuana drops her eyes.

'And you are sure he will respond?'

'Yes. I am sure.'

'What if something goes wrong? If the draught does not work? Is too weak? Or too strong? What if she dies?'

'She will not die.' Zuana's voice is firm. 'Though . . .' She stops for a second. 'Though if that were to happen, then you need have no fear, for her secrets would die with her.'

'Well! You have indeed thought of it all. Except perhaps for one thing. It is clear what the convent will lose by your plan: an unwilling songbird novice and much of her considerable dowry. But as to what we might gain . . .?'

Zuana, though she may be ignorant in some things, has been expecting this question. This time when she finishes talking, the Abbess does not hesitate at all.

Now, at last, the ingredients can be mixed together.

Under Zuana's tutelage, the girl writes to a young man who has sworn to love and marry no-one but her. While the letter contains enough phrases of longing to leave no doubt of her feeling, its main purpose is to issue instructions, and in this the words are Zuana's, for there can be no mistakes here. When it is finished, instead of the censor, the abbess reads it herself and dispatches it privately.

If there is any doubt as to the young man's fidelity it is dispelled within hours. The messenger who takes the sealed papers is kept waiting so he can bring back an answer straight away. It is almost as if the recipient had been waiting for it. Which, of course, in some ways he had. The reply is delivered directly into the abbess's hands, so that she is the first to read the outpouring of passionate love from the young man who will be instrumental in the escape of one of her novices. The irony is not lost on any of them.

The next day the abbess makes an unexpected visit to the sewing room to make sure the novices and sisters there are chattering less and sewing a little harder, so that the trousseau will be ready and packed for dispatch within the week.

For her part, Zuana is busy with her books and her choir of cures. She is cross-referencing between two sources: her father's own notebooks and a volume by one Alessio Piemontese, who claimed to have travelled the world in search of nature's wonders and secrets. Though the ingredients in both are the same, there are discrepancies of measurements between the versions. In the end she errs in favour of her father's, though it comes along with his warning: 'This has not been tested by myself but comes from verbal sources of others', scrawled close to the edge of the page.

For these few days Isabetta, in contrast, does nothing, which is in some ways hardest of all. By now she does not even bother to properly conceal the food she is not eating at table, so that everyone can see how viciously she is starving herself. For the rest, she sings and prays ostentatiously, hands together or hidden in her robes, face chalk-white, body hunched and fragile as she trots like a new-born lamb in the footsteps of the novice mistress.

As promised, the crucifix is mounted in time for Palm Sunday. The nuns take part in a procession around the convent that ends in the chapel, where there is a public service and mass, all of which take place without further mishap.

Matins that night is a glorious affair. In celebration of the return of our Lord, the chapel sister lights an array of great candles to further illuminate His homecoming. Everyone is eager. Even those half asleep with fasting and prayer take their places on time tonight.

Umiliana is early into her seat. This, she is sure, will be an office to be remembered. Above her head Christ glows in the candlelight, His sweet, suffering body its own miracle of transformation, His flesh suddenly so real, the blood from His hands and feet a shocking red against the pale, varnished skin. When she was young and at her most febrile she would imagine the weight of that tortured body lying across her knees, imagine the wonder of holding Him in her arms. She has loved Him all her life, this perfect, gentle, powerful, beautiful man, beside whom any other bridegroom could only be found crassly wanting. She sits, her hands gathered in her lap, watching as the novices arrive and Serafina takes her huddled place among the rest of the night procession.

How frail and ghostly pale she looks, more spirit than body, surely. Except for the eyes. The eyes are so bright these last days: as if a great light is shining somewhere behind them. Oh, if only Umiliana had reached her cell more quickly the night she had started screaming. She had been amazed when, the next day, the girl described to her how a trio of spitting black devils had been in there with her, kicking and pushing her to the ground every time she tried to pray. Serafina had even shown her the ripening bruises to prove it. Oh, the wonder of it. Of course the girl had been frightened, fearful that such an attack proved that she was not worthy of God's mercy. But what Umiliana knows, and she does not, is that such a violent testing often comes with the final awakening of grace. The testaments of the humblest visionaries tell stories of wrestling physically with devils, of their violence and taunting. She, Umiliana, has been plagued by a few such tribulations in her time. But unlike the saints and now this young girl, the beatings never left a mark on her.

The opening chant begins. Umiliana raises her eyes to the body of Christ. He is above us now. He is here and will make His presence felt.

Except that He does not.

Matins passes with joyful song amid warm candlelight. The novice seems so tired she can barely open her mouth. While in her choir stall the office draws to a close Umiliana gives herself up to prayer, swallowing her disappointment and accepting His will humbly, almost numbly, as she has done for so long in her life.

It is only as the nuns leave, and she stands watching the novices file out, that she sees Serafina trip on the hem of her skirts and pull one hand from under her habit in order to steady herself on the edge of the pew. And as she does so, a spasm of sudden pain crosses her face in a way that makes Umiliana's heart beat faster.

FORTY-SIX

The chapter meeting the next day is so full of necessary business that it is verging on dull.

Easter is almost upon them, and with it the reliving of the terrible, wondrous story of Christ's persecution and death on the cross and His resurrection. While the novices and young choir nuns are visibly excited – Lent seems to have lasted for ever – a few of the elder ones are thinking how quickly this season is come around again. If it is true that years seem to move faster for the old, then it is also a marvel of convent life that what at first appears a desert of time is actually a dense calendar of all manner of liturgical feasts, city celebrations, special masses for benefactors and saints' days. The demands of Easter are among the most arduous and between questions about psalm settings and the Good Friday procession through cloisters behind the convent's great silver crucifix, there is ample room for disagreement. Maybe for that reason the meeting starts with everyone being exceedingly polite to one another, as if the slightest objection will unleash the storm waiting to break.

They are in the middle of a discussion about the Easter Sunday feast, which breaks the Lent fast, when Suora Zuana asks – and is given permission – to speak out of turn.

'Madonna abbess, as fasting is not compulsory for novices, may I ask if those who are doing so might be allowed to eat normally again before Easter Sunday? As dispensary mistress I am becoming fearful of the impact of the regime upon their health.'

The room stiffens. Or rather those nuns who support Umiliana stiffen, in readiness for her rejoinder. In the front row, Suora Benedicta nods animatedly; the choir is ragged without the inspiration of its finest voice. But it is the abbess who answers first.

'While I appreciate your concern, Suora Zuana, this is surely more the business of the novice mistress than it is your own.'

'I . . . um . . .' Umiliana is momentarily taken aback by this unexpected support. 'I am not sure what the dispensary sister is referring to. The only fasting done by a novice was in response to an imposed penance and has been over for some time.'

'With respect, Suora Umiliana, I do not think that is true. The novice in question has grown steadily thinner through the weeks and, while the food may go on to her plate, I believe she is not eating it at all, only hiding it away to dispose of later. It is not good for one so young to be so depleted of nourishment.'

Zuana is not the only one to be staring directly at the novices' bench. By now everyone has noticed how clumsy Serafina has become at mealtimes, with bits of food falling to the ground or being so obviously hidden that there is almost no pretence about it. Yet no-one has said a thing. When someone is wasting away so dramatically the fascination can, for a while, overwhelm the concern.

'I am grateful to you for the observation but if my novice's *true* health was in any danger, I assure you I would have noticed it by now.'

'Yes, indeed.' The abbess again confounds expectations. 'If there was anything to worry about, I am confident Suora

Umiliana would have seen it.' There is the briefest of pauses. A few are no doubt remembering the recent screaming. 'I know she disturbed the peace of the convent a few nights ago but I believe that was because she had bad dreams . . .'

The discussion has taken on a strange, almost surreal, quality, since Serafina herself, the person at the centre of it, is being totally ignored. She sits, huddled and gaunt, on the novice bench. For some time those around her have been aware that her breath is coming in fast little spurts with occasional quiet grunts, like a small animal trying to bury itself further into its lair.

'Meanwhile, we have many more things to discuss and must move on. Rest assured, Suora Umiliana, the convent has the greatest faith in your judgeme—'

But the abbess does not get any further.

The noise – for it is indeed a noise – coming out of the novice is grown suddenly louder. For a young woman with such a pure voice, the lack of harmony in this rising wail is immediately disturbing.

'Aaaaaaaah!'

Umiliana, who has kept her in her sight, sees it coming. Oh, sweet Jesus! She might have chosen a more devout setting but one does not argue with God's ways . . . She is half out of her seat but the chapter rows are packed and she cannot get there.

The novice, however, is now standing out from the front row, in the middle of the floor.

'Aaaaaahhhhh!' She lifts her hands out above her head, exposing two gory palms, blood streaking down her arms and dripping to the floor. Then, when there can be no mistaking what people are seeing, she grabs her skirts and lifts them high, a good deal higher than is necessary, to reveal, at the bottom of long, bare legs, feet dotted with blood, though nowhere near as much as the mess of her hands . . .

The room sits stunned.

She starts to jump and dance, as if trying to get her weight off her feet, and the wail turns into a howl as if she is being tortured, while her skirts reach up as far as her thighs. If this is a thing of wonder then it certainly does not appear to be that way for the girl herself. There is surely no ecstasy here. Only panic and terror – and hysteria.

The abbess gets to her first. 'What have you done? Novice Serafina, what is this?'

And Serafina turns on her, pushing her hands almost into the abbess's face and yelling, 'It's Him. It's Him. She told me He would come.'

'Who told you?'

Now she waves her hands in the direction of the novice mistress, spraying flecks of blood over the heads of the nuns. 'See,' she says. 'See, Suora Umiliana. I prayed and He came. Christ's wounds. But – oh, oh, loving Jesus, why does it hurt so much? Ooooaa! Oaagggh!'

Behind her a few of the other novices are moaning now, as much in fear as in wonder. Umiliana stands transfixed. Inside her, there is a great falling away. She has waited so long for this moment. Yet she is not tasting ecstasy either. Far from it. She has spent too long in the company of volatile young women not to recognise hysteria when she sees it. This is not God's work. The novice is suffering from some other ailment.

She is not so proud that she cannot admit it – but even as she is pushing her way towards the girl something else happens first. As she jitters and twirls, howling like a stuck pig, there is a loud clatter as an object drops from the inside of her habit and skitters across the stone floor.

The nuns closest to the girl see it immediately. But it takes the abbess picking it up and holding it aloft for its true significance to become apparent to all present: a small, shining knife, with what can only be streaks of blood on the blade.

'My herb knife!' Zuana's voice now rises above the throng. 'It is my herb knife. It disappeared weeks ago from the dispensary, when I was ill. Oh, oh, she must have taken it then.'

After this no-one can say or do anything, because the place is in such uproar. In the middle of it all the girl whirls and howls, shaking her hands in the face of anyone who comes near her so that the blood spatters around the room, until eventually she is restrained by the abbess and the watch sister and a few other of the braver nuns. She continues to spit and struggle as they pin her to the ground. Then, equally suddenly, she gives way, her body going totally limp and curling in upon itself until she looks more like a pile of rags than a person. 'Ooh, I am sorry, I am sorry,' she moans over and over again. 'Oh, oh, I am so hungry. Please, please can I eat now? Please, someone help me.'

On the orders of the abbess she is picked up by the watch sister and carried from the room under the supervision of the dispensary mistress. 'Take her to the infirmary and put restraints on her. Come back when you can.'

As Zuana leaves she sees Suora Umiliana dropping to her knees where she stands, her head in her hands.

FORTY-SEVEN

In the infirmary they pick the nearest bed by the door.

Clementia is beside herself with excitement. 'Oh, the angel has come! The angel has come! Welcome, poor thing. She is so small now. Oh no, no, don't put her in that bed. They all die there.'

No-one is listening to her, though. The girl puts up no fight as the restraints go on. It is as if she is utterly exhausted, almost unconscious. The watch sister stands staring down at her. 'I always knew she would come to no good,' she says grimly. 'Still, imagine Suora Umiliana being so fooled.'

'You can go now,' Zuana says. 'I will give her a draught to make sure she sleeps and join you when I can.'

The watch sister, who spends much of her life bored rigid while the convent sleeps, scuttles back to the drama in the chapter room.

Zuana waits until the door closes then leans over the cot. 'You did well,' she whispers.

The girl opens her eyes. 'Owww, my hands are burning so.'

'I know. But you must lie quietly now. I will bring you something for them later.'

The door opens. Augustina with her blunt face and blunt hands stands waiting. 'I am called for?'

'Yes, you are to sit with the novice. Let no-one come close to her and be careful. She is very ill indeed.'

But as she starts to rise, the girl pulls at her.

'Suora Zuana,' her voice is so small that Zuana has to bend her head to her lips to catch the words. 'I . . . I am scared.'

'I know,' she smiles. 'But it will be all right.'

By the time she straightens up, her face is grim again.

Back in chapter, the convent is on its knees.

'Bring us to safe harbour from the tempest we are travelling through. For while we are not worthy of your grace, we strive to be your true and humble servants.'

From the side of her eye the abbess spots Zuana in the door-way and brings the prayers to a close. She motions for them all to rise and sit again.

'Dear, dear sisters, we have indeed been subject to a dreadful storm – for which, as your abbess, I must hold myself responsi-ble. Ah – Suora Zuana. Tell us, please – how is the girl?'

'She is restrained.'

'Good. Did you have a chance to examine her?'

'Only enough to know that she has wounded herself severely. And is pitifully thin and undernourished.'

'Which may have contributed to her madness.' The abbess bows her head for a moment as if asking now for help outside herself. 'However,' she looks up again. 'It is perhaps worth us all remembering that this sad young woman was . . . well, most . . . erratic in her behaviour when she first entered.'

In the fourth row Suora Umiliana sits, pale, eyes on the floor. The room falls quiet. She starts to stand . . .

'Madonna abbess, I—'

'Suora Umiliana,' the abbess's voice cuts across her gently.
'You will, I know, be feeling this pain more acutely than any of us.
For you have given so much of your time and blessed instruction
on her behalf. How much more important is it then that we ask
for God's understanding on this before we offer up any blame.
And if there is blame, then it will fall on my shoulders, for I am
the abbess. Please, please, dear sister, sit and rest yourself.'

This kindness silences Umiliana faster than any rebuke. It also
leaves the floor to Chiara. She lifts herself up, resting her hands
on the lions' heads of the chair. It is a familiar, almost comforting gesture that they all know well. Which is all to the good,
because they are in great need of comfort now.

'You will know, I think, that even before the distressing events
of today I have been concerned about the welfare of the convent.
We are living in turbulent times. There is change and debate
everywhere, and it is not a surprise if some of this anxiety finds
its way inside the walls, with disagreements and confusions as to
how we should be conducting our lives as nuns. In many cities
others are asking the same questions – and some are being forced
to make changes under grave duress.' The abbess sighs. 'These
past few weeks I have spent many nights in prayer asking for
God's advice in this, my great task of caring for His flock. And
He has taken pity on my distress and come to my aid. He has
helped me to understand much. And perhaps the most important thing He has helped me to see is how some of the burden we
have been labouring under has come from the presence of this
young woman . . .'

She pauses. The room is utterly still, waiting on her words.

'Dear sisters, I would ask you to consider this now, as He
revealed it to me. How since the novice Serafina arrived with us
all those months ago, her fury, her disobedience, the fame and
glory that came with her voice, her tremendous sudden piety,

her illness, her secret confession with its dramatic penance, her exaggerated fasting nigh unto starvation and now this – this exhibition of fraud and madness . . . all this behaviour has taken its toll on the peace and comfort of Santa Caterina. While we have done our best to care for and contain her – in particular the work of Suora Zuana in the dispensary, Suora Benedicta in the choir, and the selfless care and discipline of Suora Umiliana – despite all our efforts, this young woman has grown more rather than less distressed. It is perhaps not a surprise.

'All these stages of behaviour, these phases of the moon that she has passed through – for there has been some correlation between her mood swings and the moon's cycles – have one thing in common: they have needed, no, demanded – and received – our attention. Such symptoms are consistent with a most virulent form of greensickness, which is something that can beset young girls of her age and at its worst bring full-blown lunacy. Until this point Santa Caterina has been mercifully free of it. I had some worry about this on that very first morning – Suora Zuana will no doubt remember that we discussed the possibility that the girl was sick rather than simply rebellious. I wrote then to her father to ask for further information. His reply was reassuring. And yet to no avail. Since then it has only grown worse rather than better. So much so that it is surely no surprise that we have all, in some way or other, been influenced by it. For what we have been living through is the presence of a mad young woman who has dedicated her life to performance rather than piety.'

All this the abbess says slowly and with quiet conviction, leaving pauses every now and then so that you would think the words were somehow precious, fragile things that must be handled with care; either that, or that they are so heavy one must hold them for a while in order to absorb them.

The message she offers is simple: a young woman has destroyed the equilibrium of the convent by dedicating herself to deceit rather than devotion. Very simple, in fact, yet it speaks to many of the nuns present.

Zuana looks out over the sea of faces. To the left of the room sit the novices, a group of young women overshadowed by Serafina for so long but who can now perhaps feel vindicated for their occasional flashes of envy or lack of charity towards her. Could it be that they have been pious enough to suspect that she was a fraud all along? Close by, Suora Eugenia is no doubt remembering how contented she had been as the convent song-bird before Serafina had opened her mouth at Vespers, and how lost and tortured she has become since.

On the converse' bench Letizia hears again the girl's sniping, angry tone, so different from her public piety, as they crossed the cloisters together to tend the chief conversa in her cell, while Candida thinks about all those evenings she spent brushing her hair, and how she can always tell the ones who yearn to be touched more, even when they seek to deny it.

In among the choir nuns, the twins, who have long since had to make do with being ignored, remember that once she tripped up one of them in her hurry to get to chapel and never apolo-gised. Suora Benedicta thinks that though she composes for God, the young girl often seemed more interested in singing for her own pleasure, while Suora Federica knows that she never really liked her, even though she felt compelled to pick her out for the first marzipan strawberry, and wishes now that she had put more wormwood into her penance food. Devout old Suora Agnesina reminds herself that she was never sure of her, even when Umiliana spoke so hotly about her emerging purity. Felicità, meanwhile, does not feel so bad about the resentment she has harboured towards Umiliana, whose time has been taken up with this shallow novice rather than other more deserving sisters such as herself.

And Suora Umiliana? Well, Suora Umiliana is thinking and remembering a great number of things.

'Performance rather than piety. The noisy seeking of attention over the gentler business of living humbly inside God's love. That has been a fear close to your heart, I know, Suora Umiliana. And one must say that in this you are right,' the abbess says, with a generosity that cannot help but draw attention to Umiliana's own gullibility and failed judgement in this whole sordid business.

'We need to come back to the true path: "*Not to love strife. Not to love pride. Not to be jealous or entertain envy. To hate one's own will. To love one's neighbour as oneself and—*"'

And here she does not need to add — because each nun knows the words of the rule of St Benedict backwards — '*And to obey the commands of the abbess in all things.*'

'In this way I am sure we will ride out the storm and return to our convent as it once was, a place of harmony and honest worship.'

The room is silent. It is a remarkable performance, and no-one is more impressed than Zuana.

The bones of the plan, the central ingredients, had been hers. But this . . . this elaboration . . . this decoration has come spinning out of the abbess's own head, and its skill and cleverness amaze her. Here is a woman who cares so much for the reputation of her convent that she was willing to allow a young man to be killed to prevent scandal coming upon them; but also a woman willing to forgo the chance of revenge on her most potent opponent in order to bring peace and reconciliation. For, as she well knows, only in that way can they hope to avoid interference from outside.

Zuana thinks back again to the rule of the order. *'The abbess is one to whom much hath been entrusted, from whom much will be required; the difficult and arduous task of governing souls and accommodating herself to a variety of characters, mingling gentleness with severity, so that she not only suffers no loss in the flock but may rejoice in the increase of a worthy fold.'*

Who else in this room could do it as well as her?

She lifts her hand gently.

'Yes, Suora Zuana? You have permission to speak.'

'I . . . well, I wonder what are we to do with the novice now?'

The abbess sighs. 'We must try our hardest to bring her back from her fasting madness into health and then address her spiritual state. The first, I think, falls to you.'

'I will do my best.' She bows her head. 'But I must say that examining her in the infirmary just now, I found her to be in a grave state. In her lunacy she has been using the knife to harm herself in all manner of ways.'

'My dear Suora Zuana, every sister in this convent knows that you will do whatever can be done. I shall ask Father Romero to come to her now. The rest is up to God. We shall pray for his guidance.'

The nuns of Santa Caterina retire to their cells for prayer and private contemplation with an unexpected sense of peace and harmony. And as they kneel praying, long into the dark, there are those who swear that they hear a voice coming out of the infirmary, the soaring notes of a young songbird, and though some fear it to be further madness, it is hard not to be seduced by its purity, and wonder perhaps whether their prayers have been answered and this disturbed young woman is at last made welcome by God.

At the darkest part of that same night, long after Suora Zuana has bid goodnight to her patients, Clementia wakes to see a figure in the room; a figure she swears is that of the Virgin herself, for she comes on quiet footfall with a white veil over her face and the smell of flowers around her. She stands by the girl's bed and immediately the novice sits up and prays with her as if she was not near to death at all. Then the Virgin seems to lean over and kiss her and offer her the communion cup, from which she drinks deeply. The girl lies down again and after the figure has prayed for a while by her side she leaves as quietly as she came in.

Clementia is known to be as mad as a field of spring lambs, yet when it is discovered, close on sunrise, that the girl has quietly died in the night, this account of hers moves like a soft breeze through the convent, bringing a sense of wonder and hope to all who hear it.

FORTY-EIGHT

In the midst of death, however, life must go on, and a convent leading up to Easter is a busy place.

Letizia and Suora Zuana, who had been the ones to find the girl without pulse or any sign of life, take the body to the small mortuary room behind the dispensary, where they wash and dress it for burial. In lieu of a public laying out prayers are said in chapel. While everyone is mad with curiosity to see the corpse, it is the abbess's duty to return the convent to normal life as soon as possible, and with her authority renewed she is obeyed without question.

That same day is also when the trousseau for the noble wedding must be completed and packed for collection next morning. Such is the importance of the commission that the abbess herself supervises the process as the chest is brought downstairs to a room close to the infirmary ready for transportation to the river storehouse that afternoon.

Zuana and Letizia place the girl in the rough wood coffin, covering her body with a length of white muslin (the gold cloth is used only for those who have taken their vows). Zuana then dismisses Letizia — who has been unexpectedly affected by the sight of the bone-thin young body, to the point where she is overcome by tears – and keeps vigil herself during the afternoon work hour.

Halfway through she is joined by the novice mistress, who has humbly gone to the abbess and asked if she might be allowed to say her own private farewell.

The two women kneel by the coffin together. The last time they tended a corpse was at the death of Suora Imbersaga, when Zuana had been so moved by the novice mistress's febrile joy. Now she cannot help but be aware of a dark turmoil within her fellow choir nun, as if however much she tries she cannot, will not, forgive herself for whatever her part was in this strange young woman's death.

Eventually, after what feels like hours of prayer, the older woman rises slowly to her feet, and makes her way silently to the door.

'Suora Umiliana?'

She stops and waits.

'You told me once that you wished you had been my novice mistress. Well, I share that feeling and, if you would let me, I would like to come to you sometimes, to talk more about how I might reach closer to the Holy Father.'

The old woman shivers. 'You should not come to me,' she says harshly. 'I am not worthy.'

'Oh, but I think you are. Please. I do believe that you might help me.'

And while there are some things in this room that are ripe with deceit, this is not one of them.

Umiliana stares at her, nodding slightly, her white hairs and pitted chin trembling as the tears start to flow.

'I will do my best.'

*

Just before Vespers the abbess calls the chief conversa to her chambers and asks her to wait until after supper before they move the chest to the storehouse, since she herself would like to make a last check on the contents.

When the nuns disperse to their cells for private prayer, Zuana and the abbess meet in the mortuary. Between them they easily lift the girl's body out of the coffin and carry it through a now unlocked door to the room where the trousseau chest is waiting. As they place her under layers of embroidered wedding silk, Zuana searches for a pulse. It is steady enough when she finds it, though faint, like that of someone heading towards death. The consensus of the two remedies says that a body can remain as if in a state close to death for up twenty-four hours and still emerge in health. But the first source is an observation from some heathen tribe found in the Levant and the second, her father's, relies on descriptions but no living proof. They will just have to hope. At rest the girl looks so fragile, more bone than body still, her hands carefully bandaged with salve beneath. Such a long way from the peach-ripe young beauty who first entered. But then, with the scars of having half his throat cut open, her prospective husband will surely be no prettier.

Before they close the lid, the abbess unwraps something from beneath her cloak and sets it under the young girl's bandaged hands. It is a jewelled crucifix, less precious than the one she uses for special feast days but rich enough to buy the beginnings of a new life for the person who possesses it. The instructions have already been made clear: on no account should she attempt to sell or pawn it within the city of Ferrara or its dominions. But once she – they – are far enough away, it is theirs to do with as they see fit. No-one will question where it came from and even if they did there will be no record of a precious cross missing from any convent in Ferrara, and certainly none of any escapee who might have stolen it. The novice Serafina will be long dead and buried by then, her obituary, largely indistinguishable from a hundred others, inscribed in the convent necrology by Suora Scholastica's careful hand, and her dowry passed on to the convent.

The girl had listened and understood. 'I don't deserve it,' she had said, staring at the crucifix.

'I don't know about that but I fear you will find it hard to live without it.'

Though as the two women now stand looking down at her, surely the same thought is going through both their heads . . .

'Because she is so weak I gave her too little rather than too much,' Zuana says quietly. 'I pray it will be the right amount.'

Her words put speed into their step and they close the chest (picked for its empty knots, through which a certain amount of air will flow) and return to the mortuary, where they face the problem of how to weight down the coffin enough not to arouse suspicion when it is carried to the chapel and burial plot next morning.

Zuana has the answer already. From the dispensary she brings an armful of books and lays them at the bottom.

The abbess stares at her. 'We are both sacrificing jewels, it seems.'

Zuana shakes her head. 'She is not so heavy – and like you I have greater ones. Many of the remedies in these I have tried and found wanting. The better ones I have already memorised.'

'Good.' She pauses. 'Perhaps it would be wise for you to memorise more.'

Zuana feels her hollowness open up inside her. 'When? When will it come?'

'I do not know for certain. Her leaving will steady us for a while. But it will happen, for in the end it does not depend on us. If it is not this Bishop then it will be the next, or the one after him.' She smiles. 'I am sorry.'

But of course Zuana has known it all along. How bad will it be? Though she can fill her mind with information, she will be able to do little with it if they see fit to destroy her choir of cures. She imagines the convent graveyard in the future, with two neatly dug new graves. Perhaps God will see fit to take them both by the time the worst happens.

'Come,' the abbess says briskly. 'We had better finish this.'

Together they fashion a softer shape made from the abbess's old shifts to lie on top of the books, then cover the whole thing with the thick muslin. The abbess has already agreed with Father Romero that by the time he comes at dawn to conduct the service the coffin will be nailed down. Until then either Zuana or she herself will keep the night vigil over the 'body'.

There is nothing more to do.

'God be with you, sister Zuana.'

'And with you, Madonna abbess.'

And so, leaving Zuana with the coffin full of books, Madonna Chiara calls for the chief conversa and supervises as four sturdy younger conversa hoist the trousseau chest on to the cart and pull it through the gardens in the fading light down to the store-house, where it is placed in the outer chamber, ready for the bargemen to find it there next morning.

FORTY-NINE

Her palms throb. Her palms throb and her throat hurts. Her throat hurts and she cannot breathe well. When she opens her eyes she is blind. In the few seconds it takes her to remember and make sense of where she is, she is gripped by a panic, which smothers as powerfully as the layers of heavy fabric that cover her face when she tries to move.

She relaxes her body and tries to breathe more calmly. There is air but it feels thick in her nostrils and she knows from a thousand stories of premature burial that it cannot last for ever.

But she is not buried. She is in the trousseau chest. In the storehouse. And somewhere out there, behind the door, on the river, is a boat even now perhaps pulling up and . . .

Yes, yes. That is surely what is happening. They have been through this, Zuana and she, a dozen times. How, as soon as the convent is asleep, Zuana will make her way across the gardens and, using the abbess's keys, will let herself through first one door and then the other. She will open the chest, the girl will get out, and together they will go out through the outer doors to wait on the dock until . . .

She must have woken too early. 'I cannot say for certain how long the draught will last. It would be better if you woke sooner rather than later, for it will be hard to move you if you are still under the drug.'

She had listened to every word, never taking her eyes off Zuana's face as she had explained it once, then once again. She trusts this woman absolutely and knows that she would never do anything to hurt her. But while Zuana does not say it to her directly, she also knows that this is the first time she has used this remedy, so that she cannot be certain one way or another how strong or how long . . .

What if she did not give her enough? What if she has woken halfway through? Perhaps she is not yet reached the storeroom. There may be converse in the room even now, ready to heave up the chest and move it down the stairs out into the grounds. Be quiet, Isabetta, she says to herself, be calm. You must not make any noise now. Nor waste any air.

She begins to pray: that she will make this man a good wife. That for all that they have been through, they will care for, as well as love, each other and be mindful of God's commandments. She asks God that He will look after all those she leaves behind. She begs to be forgiven for her many trespasses, as she now willingly forgives those that, in their way, trespassed against her. Suora Umiliana, who meant no harm even if she could not help but cause it. The abbess, who did what her duty demanded but without whom she would not be free at all. And Suora Zuana . . . oh, Suora Zuana . . . what can she ask of God on her behalf? But as she searches for the words she feels the calm slipping away as the weight of cloth sinks more heavily on her face. She feels the urge to sing – to hear her own voice as a companion – but she does not dare.

How long has she been awake? Too long now, surely. Her head aches. Yes, the draught must have been strong enough. In which case how can it be that Zuana is not come? What if . . .

What if? The two words release a wave of terror that seems to use up all the air around her so that she finds herself gasping.

What if someone is taken ill in the night and Zuana cannot get here?

What if in some way the plan has been found out?

What if there never was a plan?

Or what if this was the plan all along . . .?

Sweet Jesus, what if this is the abbess's final revenge to ensure her silence and she is not in the storehouse at all but in the mortuary? Or worse – what if it is done already and she is even now buried, deep under the earth in the graveyard, as punishment for having brought the convent so close to ruin? What if, after all, she is going to die?

Once thought, it cannot be un-thought. As the panic hits she forces her bandaged hands up through the layers of silk till her knuckles crash into the lid above. The holes in her hands burn and throb as she pushes. But the wood is too heavy. It is nailed down. Oh, dear God, it is nailed down. She fills her lungs with whatever air is left and starts to shout. It must end as it began – with terror and tears and useless hammering against wood in the night.

'Help – oh, help me, I—'

And now she hears it: a knocking and scraping above her, then the sound of a key clunking and shifting in the lock and a lid being lifted and pushed back.

'Hush, oh, hush. You must not make noise. I am here.'

The layers of cloth are pulled off and she takes a great gulp of air. In the darkness she makes out Zuana's broad, smiling face above her.

'I thought . . .'

'I know – but there is no time now. Come, come. The watch sister was a tiger tonight and it took me longer to get away.'

Zuana's voice wraps itself around her, encouraging, cajoling, as it has done for so long.

'Here, drink this. Eau de vie. Just a few sips. It will give you some strength. I have put some in a bag for you. Give me the crucifix. Where is it? Did you let go of it? No, I see it here. I will put that in the pouch, too. I have made up two vials of the liquid. One is for the apothecary. A good dispensary can never have enough and the other you may trade for some small monies to get you out of the city. Ah, quickly, quickly, Isabetta. Can you walk?'

As they move across the room they can both hear it now – something bumping against the wood of the dock outside.

Zuana fumbles with the lock on the door. It opens with a fearful creak – the wind and rain have swollen and twisted the wood since the last time they were both here.

The dock is longer than she remembers it. On one side it slides into black water. But at the other end, close to the convent's rowing boat, another small boat is docking, with a candle lantern at its prow. There are two figures aboard. Two? Zuana's heart jumps for a moment. But he would have to bring someone to help, of course. The loyal apothecary, perhaps.

The man in the prow climbs up and on to the deck. Zuana holds up her own lantern to meet him. There is light enough to see that he is tall, lanky, with a scarf tied high around his neck and down one side of his face a jagged dark line.

Isabetta sees him, too. She stands frozen to the spot. So frozen that in the end Zuana must give her a little push.

She moves slowly, half limping towards him. They stop when there is still space between them. One might think they would fling themselves into each other's arms. But instead it seems they are not sure they know each other any more. After a second's pause, he puts out a hand towards her and she gives him her bandaged one in return. He holds it most gently. The moment appears to last for ever.

'You must go. Go now.'

Zuana's voice pushes them on.

The girl turns and smiles quickly, and then they are gone; the two of them clambering into the boat, the ropes freed from the mooring, the second man manoeuvring the craft backwards, turning, then rowing quickly out into the water until they are eaten up by the darkness and all one can hear is the splash and chop of oars.

Zuana stands for a short time listening, then goes back inside and locks the door. She replaces the wedding shift and the top sheets, smoothing out their surfaces as best she can, and puts the lid back into place before moving into the inner storeroom and then from there out into the convent grounds, locking each door carefully behind her.

She makes her way quickly back across the orchard and gardens towards the second cloisters. As she passes the herb plot, it comes upon her to wonder whether or not the calendula will be sprouting yet, and she makes a note to check it first thing at work hour, for she has grown somewhat lax in the affairs of the dispensary of late and it will not be long until spring is fully upon them.

In her cell, she says a prayer that their new life together will be pure, and then prays for the souls of all those around her in the convent, for their benefactors and rulers of the city, both alive and dead, before lying down to sleep.

As she lets her mind slide away, she recites a few of the remedies from the books that will be buried in the graveyard tomorrow. From now on, every night, she will memorise a few more. Of course she will never be able to reproduce her library in her head. That would be impossible. Not even her father could do so much.

'The work of revealing God's secrets through nature is not meant to be easy, Faustina. You would do well to remember the words of Hippocrates: "Life is short, the art long, opportunities fleeting, experiment treacherous and judgement difficult." Ah, such humility in a man born so long before Christ. For all our knowledge now he is yet to be surpassed.'

Well, she will do the best she can. Though it would be better if she could find an assistant among the novices, a young soul with energy and aptitude, so that together they might form a chain to hand on to those who come after the fruits of that which she now knows.

Tomorrow she will talk to the abbess about it.

She closes her eyes and sleeps. And the convent sleeps silently around her.

AUTHOR'S NOTE

All the characters in this novel are imaginary, as is the convent of Santa Caterina, though its history and architecture draw heavily on those of Sant'Antonio in Polesine in Ferrara, which still exists today as an enclosed Benedictine community.

The history in which the novel is embedded, however, is all fact.

One of the final decrees of the Council of Trent before it disbanded in December 1563 was a rushed but detailed reform of nunneries, in response to the fierce challenges and criticisms thrown up by the Protestant Reformation. These changes, which were extensive, took time to be implemented, depending on the zeal of the local bishops, the order, the convent and the opposing influence of local families.

But eventually reform did come. In the city of Ferrara the power of the d'Este family protected the convents for a while but the failure of Duke Alfonso III to produce a legitimate heir, despite three wives, meant that in 1597, after his death, the city and its dominions were absorbed into the Papal States. By the turn of the sixteenth century, when rampant dowry inflation resulted in almost half of all noblewomen in

Italian cities becoming nuns, convent life had changed for ever.

Inspections, or 'visitations', as they were known, brought in the new rules. All contact with the outside world was brutally restricted; stray holes or windows bricked up, grilles put in place everywhere. Walls were made higher (sometimes with the last courses of bricks put up without mortar, in case anyone should try to lean a ladder against them, to climb in or out). Churches were redesigned so that the congregation saw nothing of the nuns within. Parlatori were similarly divided, with grilles and drawn curtains so that families could no longer freely mingle together. Performance and music suffered particularly. In some cities plays and all forms of polyphony were banned and convent orchestras – apart from a single organ – prohibited. Inspectors visited nuns' cells and confiscated furniture, books, and all kinds of 'luxuries' and private possessions.

This repression did not go unchallenged. Once the inspectors had gone and the gates were closed, in many convents a certain laxity returned, and the battle went on over a number of years. In some places the nuns refused such changes; in a few they even fought physically to retain their freedoms. They were, however, always subdued.

In terms of documentation, a few voices of protest have survived. In the early seventeenth century Archangela Tarabotti, the eldest of six daughters and lame from birth, wrote a polemic on the evils of enforced convent entry which was published some twenty years later. Perhaps as poignant and more succinct is the following fragment from a letter sent in 1586 by a nun from Santi Naborre e Felice Convent in Bologna to the Pope himself:

Many of us are shut up against our will and deprived of all contact with the outside world. Living with such strictness and abandoned by everyone, we have only hell, in this world and the next.

This novel is dedicated to those women, and to the legion of others who came before and after them.

BIBLIOGRAPHY

Anderson, Frank J., *An Illustrated History of Herbals* (Columbia University Press, 1977)

Baxandall, Michael, *Painting and Experience in 15th Century Italy* (Oxford University Press,1988)

Baernstein, Renee P., *A Convent Tale* (Routledge Press, 2002)

Bell, Rudolf M., *Holy Anorexia* (University of Chicago Press, 1985)

Bornstein, Daniel (ed.), *Women and Religion in Medieval and Renaissance Italy* (University of Chicago Press, 1996)

Broedel, Hans Peter, *The Malleus Maleficarum and the Construction of Witchcraft* (Manchester University Press, 2003)

Brown, Judith C., *Immodest Acts: The Life of a Lesbian Nun in Renaissance Italy* (Oxford University Press, 1986)

Burke, Peter, *Popular Culture in Early Modern Europe* (Scholar Press, 1994)

Butler Greenfield, Amy, *A Perfect Red* (Black Swan, 2006)

Bynum Walker, Carolyn, *Holy Feast and Holy Fast: the Religious Significance of Food to Medieval Women* (University of California Press, 1987)

—— *Jesus as Mother* (University of California Press, 1982)

Camporesi, Piero, *The Anatomy of the Senses* (Cambridge Polity Press, 1994)

—— *Bread of Dreams* (Cambridge Polity Press, 1989)

—— *The Incorruptible Flesh* (Cambridge University Press, 1988)

Cardono, Girolamo, *The Book of My Life* (New York Review of Books, 2002)

Clark, Stuart, *Thinking with Demons* (Clarendon Press, 1997)

Dear, Peter, *Revolutionising the Sciences: European Knowledge and its Ambitions 1500–1700* (Princeton Paperbacks, 2001)

Debus, A. G., *Man and Nature in the Renaissance* (Cambridge University Press, 1978)

Eamon, William, *Science and the Secrets of Nature* (Princeton University Press, 1994)

Eisenbichler, Konrad (ed.), *The Pre-Modern Teenager: Youth in Society 1150–1650* (University of Toronto, 2002)

Evangelisti, Silvia, *Nuns: A History of Convent Life* (Oxford University Press, 2007)

Fenlon, Iain, *Music and Culture in Late Renaissance Italy* (Oxford University Press, 2002)

Findlen, Paula, *Possessing Nature* (University of California Press, 1994)

Glucklich, Ariel, *Sacred Pain: Hurting the Body for the Sake of the Soul* (Oxford University Press, 2001)

Hills, Helen, *Invisible City: Architecture of Devotion in 17th Century Neapolitan Convents* (Oxford University Press, 2004)

Horne, P., 'Reformation and Counter Reformation at Ferrar' (Italian Studies, 1958)

Hufton, Olwen H. (ed.), *Women in Religious Life* (European University Institute, 1996)

Jacobson Schutte, Anne, *Aspiring Saints* (Johns Hopkins University Press, 2001)

Kendrick, Robert, *Celestial Sirens: Nuns and Their Music in Early Modern Milan* (Clarendon Press, 1996)

Laven, Mary, *Virgins of Venice* (Viking Press, 2002)

Le Goff, Jacques, *The Medieval Imagination* (University of Chicago Press, 1988)

Lowe, Kate, *Nuns' Chronicles and Convent Culture in Renaissance and Counter-Reformation Italy* (Cambridge University Press, 2003)

Maclean, Ian, *The Renaissance Notion of Women* (Cambridge University Press, 1980)

McNamara, Jo Ann Kay, *Sisters in Arms* (Harvard University Press, 1996)

Matter, Anne and Coakley, John (eds), *Creative Women in Medieval and Early Modern Italy* (University of Pennsylvania Press, 1992)

Monson, Craig A., *Disembodied Voices: Music and Culture in an Early Modern Italian Convent* (University of California Press, 1995)

Monson, Craig A. (ed.), *The Crannied Wall: Women, Religion and the Arts in Early Modern Europe* (University of Michigan Press, 1992)

Mooney, C. M. (ed.), *Gendered Voices* (University of Pennsylvania Press, 1992)

Nutton, Vivian, 'The Rise of Medical Humanism in Ferrara', Renaissance Studies, 1997)

Park, Katharine and Daston, Lorraine (eds), *Wonders and the Order of Nature 1150–1750* (Zone Books, 1998)

Porter, Roy, *The Greatest Benefit to Mankind: Medical History of Humanity* (HarperCollins, 1997)

Reardon, Colleen, *Holy Concord within Sacred Walls: Nuns and Music in Siena, 1575–1700* (Oxford University Press, 2001)

Rose, Mary Beth (ed.), *Women in the Middle Ages and the Renaissance* (Syracuse University Press, 1986)

Ruggiero, Guido, *The Boundaries of Eros* (Oxford University Press, 1996)

Siraisi, Nancy G., *Medieval and Early Renaissance Medicine* (University of Chicago Press, 1990)

Sobel, Dava, *To Father: the Letters of Sister Maria Celeste to Galileo* (Fourth Estate, 2001)

Sperling, Jutta Gisela, *Convents and the Body Politic in Late Renaissance Venice* (University of Chicago Press, 1999)

Trexler, Richard C., *Public Life in Renaissance Florence* (Academic Press, 1980)

—— *The Women of Renaissance Florence* (Pegasus, 1998)

Walker, D. P., *Spiritual and Demon Magic from Ficino to Campanella* (Sutton Press, 2000)

Ward, Benedicta (trans.), *The Desert Fathers: Sayings of Early Christian Monks* (Penguin Classics, 2003)

Wear, A., French, R. K. and Lonie, I. M. (eds), *The Medical Renaissance of the 16th Century* (Cambridge University Press, 1985)

Weaver, Elissa B., *Convent Theatre in Early Modern Italy: Spiritual Fun and Learning for Women* (Cambridge University Press, 2001)

Weinstein, Donald and Bell, Rudolf M. (eds), *Saints and Society* (University of Chicago Press, 1982)

Woolfson, Jonathan (ed.), *Renaissance Historiography* (Palgrave Macmillan, 2005)

Zarri, Gabriella and Scaraffia, Lucetta (eds), *Women and Faith* (Harvard University Press, 1999)

ACKNOWLEDGEMENTS

Thank you to the staff of the British Library who, with unfailing efficiency and good humour, delivered truckloads of books to Humanities Reading Room One, a place where – should one be able to find a seat – a writer comes close to heaven on earth in London.

Vivian Nutton, Professor of the History of Medicine, University College London, was kind enough to help me with the medicine and science of the time. Kate Lowe at Queen Mary's College, University of London, was boundlessly generous and knowledgeable about the world of Italian Renaissance nuns. Laurie Stras and Deborah Roberts of the innovative musical consort Musica Secreta opened my ears and my heart to the wonders and complexities of convent music. *Sacred Hearts* owes a great deal to all of them. Its mistakes, however, are entirely my own.

In Ferrara, Italy, visits to Corpus Domini and Sant'Antonio in Polesine provided emotional as well as physical geography; while the city itself is so welcoming and visually evocative of its past that I fail to understand why it isn't overwhelmed by tourists (though that is also one of its great pleasures).

As always, deepest thanks go to my agents Clare Alexander

and Sally Riley, my American editor Susanna Porter and, in London, Elise Dillsworth and the one and only Lennie Goodings, Publisher of Virago Press.

Writers are not the most even-keeled of human beings when working on a book. I'd like to apologise to my daughters, Zoe and Georgia, for the excessive number of conversations about nuns in our house, and, for their critical support, to thank Eileen Horne, Christopher Bollas, Gillian Slovo, Maria Maragonis, Don Guttenplan, Ian Grojnowski, Scarlett MccGwire, Joseph Calderone, Sue Woodman, Christina Shewall and Isabella Planner. But final thanks must go to Tez Bentley who, as well as giving my words the polish of his rigorous sub-editor's pen, suffered (and I do not use the word lightly) alongside me when the going got really rough. It is fitting, perhaps, that for a novel with no men in it there should have been one on the outside whose sanity and generosity kept me from madness.

London, 2009
www.sarahdunant.co.uk